THE REVELATIONS

THE
FALLEN RACE
TRILOGY

BOOK TWO: THE REVELATIONS
by COLIN PATRICK GARVEY

www.thefallenrace.com

PaddyPiper Books, LLC

ISBN: 978-0-9847675-3-3

Book Cover/Website Design by Jacob Matthew
Book Design by GKS Creative

Printed in the United States of America

To My Sisters Kerri, Jill (i.e. Sloan) and Meg, and
Brothers-in-Law Jon and Tim and
My Second Family, Beppie, Tom, Courtney and Matt

ONE

Port Sheldon, Michigan

The helicopter ferried Parker, Augie, and four men to a marina a mile or two from Eisley's home. At the marina, they commandeered a boat, Parker deciding it safer to approach the house by boat in order to make the least amount of noise possible. In the event Sergeant Kaley is lying low at his uncle's house, they do not want to scare him off by landing a chopper on the back lawn. Their party already managed to frighten the hell out of the marina owner, who doubted the legality of Parker and his men "borrowing" a boat from the marina. Parker quickly calmed the man with assurances that the boat would be returned unscathed, with the general providing as collateral the backing of the United States government. The man cracked a joke about the national deficit, but ultimately found that he probably did not have much of a choice as he faced the hardened stares of several armed men.

Augie gathered the four men to accompany him and General Parker immediately after receiving the approval of General Cozey. While the men were looking forward to a few solid hours of sack time, the thought of a little adventure certainly piqued their interest. They had been analyzing data and filling out assorted paperwork for the last eight plus hours and felt like they were running in circles. Some time out in the field would definitely be a welcome diversion, however brief. Besides, you could hardly say no to General Parker.

The men are not packing any serious weaponry, but they do have their sidearms just in case. In case of what, Lieutenant Colonel Hermann informed them, is strictly classified for now. They immediately understood that they are primarily muscle, a show of force in this situation, and they are present in order to protect the general in case the shit goes down. Not that the general needs a security detail, but they would certainly discourage a potential enemy from engaging the general and his trusted aide in a firefight, if indeed that is their enemy's intention.

All that Augie knows about Eisley's house is the address and that it sits on the water, and the reconnaissance ends there. They know Eisley is an ex-naval intelligence officer and had even boasted a clearance for top secret (TS) information at one time in the United States government. Parker had never met Eisley, but he knows the government does not hand out TS clearances to Joe Sixpack on the street. A TS clearance entails information that is nothing less than crucial to the nation's security and welfare. Eisley obviously must have been an important, highly regarded officer in the naval intelligence ranks to be afforded such a clearance. Furthermore, he must have been smart enough to stay alive and retire from the business in one piece, which not everyone who works in this particular occupation can claim. Little does Parker know that Eisley's luck expired only a short time ago.

Augie instructed the men to fan out around the house once the boat comes ashore, and Augie and General Parker would bring up the rear. He emphasized for them to be extremely cautious, to specifically watch where they step because you never know what kind of surprises, i.e. booby traps, a man like Eisley may have constructed around his home. Once the perimeter appears secure, Augie and Parker would enter the home, two of the men would quickly follow, and the other two would stand watch outside.

Parker does not typically carry a sidearm, but he is willing to make an exception in this case, which Augie is more than happy to provide.

When they are approximately 50 feet from shore, Augie softly calls out, "That's it, boys."

The boat is slowly tooling along when Augie indicates a house approaching on their right. The engine produces a minimal amount of noise, something they tested before selecting the appropriate boat from the marina. They also switched off the exterior lights of the boat, not wanting to alert anyone on shore to their presence.

One of the men steers the boat towards Eisley's home, swinging the wheel around to avoid hitting his pier. Augie instructs the man to steer the boat onto a sloping embankment next to the pier, letting it come to rest of its own accord. Within several seconds of hitting the shore, the men disembark, followed by General Parker and Augie. The four men encircle the house, scanning the trees, the bushes, and the exterior of the house for signs of movement. There is none.

Augie receives an "all clear" signal from each of the men, and he nods his head at Parker. They ascend a short flight of stairs that lead to the back door. Without much fanfare, Augie kicks the door open and both men quickly hug either side of the doorframe, ensuring that if any hostiles are waiting for them, their shots would hit nothing but empty air. Augie peeks inside and quickly pulls his head back in case the enemy is extremely patient and not the least bit trigger-happy. No sounds can be heard from inside.

Augie places the radio to his mouth and whispers, "Roth, Hudson, follow us in."

Augie moves through the doorway, his sidearm sweeping around what appears to be the kitchen, the only illumination emanating from a small light over the stove. General Parker follows and covers the other side of the room. They quickly separate from each other, knowing each other's movements so well that they could sense where the other is in the house with their eyes closed. They both call out nearly simultaneously, "All clear."

Roth and Hudson soon follow through the back door and Augie directs them where to search. The four men move throughout the house, turning on lights, checking under beds, and rummaging through every closet, searching for something useful.

After several minutes searching the house, they find nothing. Clearly disappointed, the four of them mill around, looking for anything that might make the trip worthwhile. They look through Eisley's mail, check around a desk with a computer on it, and look through his cabinets and drawers.

Parker looks around the kitchen, observing the orderliness of-

He looks in the sink and sees two plates, along with a couple sets of silverware and two glasses. A quizzical expression crosses his face.

"Augie," he asks, "Eisley lived alone, right?"

Augie arrives in the doorway of the kitchen and responds, "Yes, sir, he was widowed. Why?"

Parker points to the sink and Augie sees the dishes.

"Well, maybe he wasn't very clean," Augie suggests.

Parker looks skeptically at Augie, recognizing that he is trying to play devil's advocate.

"Augie," Parker mockingly scolds, "Eisley was a Navy man and ex-intelligence officer. That just screams 'neat freak.'

"Besides," the general motions around, "look at the rest of the house."

Augie has to admit the place is practically spotless except for the dishes in the sink.

"Eisley had company tonight," Parker says confidently.

The general continues to look around with his keen eye. He stops and bends down near the doorway they entered through. He moves his hand over something and calls back, "Come look at this, Augie."

Augie moves towards the general and peers over his shoulder. He sees what appears to be a mini-sensor along the floorboard, tucked inconspicuously beneath a cabinet. The sensor rests directly inside the back door, and would instantly alert Eisley if an intruder has entered his home.

"It's disabled," Parker says, matter-of-factly.

Parker continues to look around, muttering under his breath, "He did not have time to turn it on . . ."

Augie waits a moment, allowing the general time to reason it out, as he tends to do.

"He left in a hurry," Parker states, more to himself than to Augie.

The general stands up and exits the kitchen. Augie follows him, watching the general as he moves into the living room, still mulling something over as he paces back and forth. The general stops and stares at an end table. Parker moves toward it and picks up a cordless phone from the table. He glances back at Augie.

With a shrug, he says casually, "When all else fails."

Parker turns on the cordless phone and hits the "REDIAL" button, patiently waiting, as if he is calling for a pizza.

The phone rings once, twice, and before the third ring, a gruff voice on the other end answers.

"Yes?"

Parker's voice catches in his throat. He had not actually anticipated anyone answering, and when someone did, he realized he had not thought of what to say. At the same time, adding to his hesitancy, something clicked in his mind when the man on the other end answered, a recognition of sorts, something from a long time ago.

The voice . . . he had heard the voice before.

But where?

The voice says impatiently, "Hello?"

As authoritatively as he can muster, Parker responds, "Who is this?"

He hopes he can bully a quick answer from the man on the other end of the line.

It does not work. There is a sudden click, and then Parker hears a dial tone. The mystery guest hung up.

Augie looks at him expectantly when Parker suddenly realizes who the voice of the man on the other end of the line belongs to.

"Jesus Christ, Augie, it sounded like . . . Moriah," Parker says breathlessly.

Augie gives the general a bewildered look, and then inquires, "You mean Joshua Moriah's son?"

Parker nods, "The same."

"When is the last time you saw him, let alone spoke to him?" Augie asks.

Parker considers this for a moment before responding, "It must have been not long after his father passed away."

"That was ten, fifteen years ago. Are you sure, sir?" Augie asks skeptically.

"Augie," Parker says, "I never forget a face *or* a voice. It was him. I'm almost sure it was him."

"Almost sure, sir? I thought he dropped out of sight," Augie notes. "I mean, there were rumors and stories here and there, but nothing substantiated."

"I've heard all the rumors before, Augie. His father was a patriot. Too much of a patriot if you know what I mean," Parker adds.

That is the second time the general has said that in the last few hours, Augie thinks. *The first time was in reference to Colonel Fizer.*

Augie shakes his head, "No, sir, not particularly."

Parker glances at the men in the other room and says quietly, "Let's just say Joshua might have been grooming his son to take his place after he was gone."

Augie also glances at the other men, a look of confusion spreading across his face.

"I'll explain later," Parker says dismissively, immediately ending the discussion.

Instantly, all the mystery and intrigue disappear from his features and he springs into action.

He tosses the phone to Augie and asks, "Can you get Waltman to trace that number and find out where he's at?"

Waltman is a contact at the Department of Justice that Augie was kind enough to inform the general about. Occasionally, Waltman had been willing to perform the odd favor for Augie when called upon, and this would definitely be one of those situations.

Augie usually does not second-guess the general, *ever*, but it seems like the general is reaching a bit on this one, grasping at something that is not there.

"Sir, pardon for asking, but you want me to have Waltman try to trace the number for a person whose voice you heard for ten seconds? It just feels like we're jumping the gun here. I mean, it could be the number of Eisley's-"

"Augie," Parker interrupts, "we're wasting valuable time. He hung up on me, so he is obviously suspicious now. He could dump the phone and just like that, there goes what could be a vital lead.

"Listen, Augie," Parker continues, his eyes boring into Augie's, "we're at the home of a man who lives right down the street from the site of a terrorist attack, an ex-intelligence officer whose nephew was last seen on duty at Evans. Now I just heard the voice of a man who I have not seen or talked to in over a decade, whose father knew more secrets concerning our government than both of us could possibly fathom, and you think it might be a coincidence?"

The general's tone hardens and his eyes seem to grow dark, "There are no coincidences in this business, Lieutenant Colonel Hermann, you and I both know that. Now I am going to get to the bottom of this, but I need you to keep digging along with me.

"Make it happen," Parker says sternly, with a kind of finality in his voice.

Augie nods his head, a faint hint of regret creeping in as he realizes that he cannot recall an occasion when he openly questioned the general's orders, for whatever reason. The pressure to find those responsible and the scarcity of immediate leads has begun to gnaw at Augie, who is likely not alone.

He dials Waltman's number, knowing that he will likely be working late at a time like this. Waltman picks up on the first ring and Augie quickly explains the situation. After the usual "This-could-put-my-ass-in-a-sling" rhetoric from Waltman, he caves and says he will call back Augie within a few minutes.

Those minutes tick by like hours as they wait for Waltman's call. Finally, after an excruciatingly long three and a half minutes, Waltman calls back.

"Okay . . . yeah . . . got it. Perfect, thanks Walt. Yeah, I know I owe you a steak dinner," Augie says, as he hangs up the phone.

Parker looks at him expectantly, "Anything?"

"General," Augie answers, "they got a trace. He was moving westbound at an incredibly high velocity when-"

"Wait, high velocity?" Parker interrupts.

"He's in a plane, sir," Augie clarifies. "They captured a cell phone signal moving hundreds of miles an hour through the air for several seconds when suddenly, the signal disappeared."

"He probably recognized my voice and got rid of the phone, or just turned it off," Parker suggests.

Augie shakes his head, "No, sir. Walt said they still could have traced it even if it was turned off. He destroyed it."

"Did they get a lock on his location? What about the plane? Can they follow it somehow?" Parker fires off the questions without giving Augie a chance to answer.

"Sir," Augie says calmly, "they're working on it. What they do know is that the signal was traced high above the plains of . . get this . . central Montana."

"Montana? Could he have used a scrambler to throw us off the scent?" Parker inquires.

"They ran it, sir, it's a clear, crisp signal. They'll contact the airports on the plane's route to see if they can get more information on its final destination, where it took off from, and whatever else they can gather."

"Alright," Parker says, with a pleased look on his face, "he'll contact you when he knows something more?"

"Yes, sir," Augie responds, waiting for the general to tell him that he told him so. But the general surprises him.

"Good work, Augie," he commends. "You never cease to amaze."

"One of my many talents, sir," Augie gallantly replies.

The general moves towards the back door of the house and continues deftly delivering orders, "Call Anderson, tell him we're coming to pick him up in Tamawaca, and to have that disc with him. Call our pilot at the airfield and instruct him to have the plane fully fueled and that we'll be there within the hour."

The general turns to look at Augie and says, as if they are about to embark on a road trip, "We're heading west, Augie, pack your trunks and your shades."

"Yes, sir," Augie responds, smiling at the general's rather jocular comment in the midst of all the seriousness.

But then, just as quickly, the lighthearted moment disappears. As the general reaches the doorway, he turns around, squares his shoulders, and gives a rapid, crisp salute.

"Thanks, swabby, I pray you and your nephew are alright," he says wistfully, the tone of his voice betraying what he feels inside. With that, the general disappears out the door, Augie following closely behind.

* * *

After the brief exchange, Moriah contemplated whether the man on the other end of the line recognized his voice. However terse their conversation, Moriah managed to recognize his.

General Theodore Parker. The one and only, Moriah thinks.

Dammit, why did I fail to look at the number of the incoming caller before answering?

He would have seen Eisley's number and known it could not have possibly been him. Instead, in his haste and with all the surrounding distractions, he absent-mindedly answered the phone.

Parker had known his father, not intimately, and certainly not in a friendly manner, but rather they were acquaintances in the social circles of Washington politics. Of course, Parker has always been known to avoid dabbling in the political realm of the country's affairs, his animosity of special interests and lobbyists well-known and long-standing. Parker has never been a man prone to kowtow to these groups, as he tends to view most situations in black and white, right versus wrong. After all, he is a military man, and not one to put up with bull-shit or willing to follow anyone's secret agenda. Parker understood, however, that some of the most important and crucial decisions regarding the nation considered the *politics* involved, and he recognized this as both neces-sary and ever-present, and he learned to deal with it.

Moriah's father, on the other hand, worked the intri-cacies of Washington politics like a card shark at a penny ante poker game. He knew the right buttons to push and he became an expert at working the system. He also knew the Foundation was above all that, that the group did not have to answer to anybody or anything. He realized, however, that his agenda could be implemented more smoothly and with less problems when he had the right people in government on board. He guided the Foundation and the nation through difficult times with the assistance of these people because he understood what they wanted. It was actually quite simple: they wanted to look good for their constituents, they wanted to be re-elected, and they wanted their families financially secure. When these factors were met, the elder Moriah found that working the halls of Congress was fairly easy.

When Alex Moriah became older and less naïve, his father instructed him on the inner workings of the coun-try, the purpose and obligations of the Foundation, and how its plans are carried out by the many men and women who work on its behalf across the globe. The elder Moriah taught his son the leadership abilities he would use, and he explained the responsibilities his son would one day inherit after he had passed on. Joshua taught his son how to nurture and foster relationships with his inform-ers, how to tell them what they wanted and indeed, what they *needed*, to hear; he taught him how to make the tough decisions that needed to be made, and how a conscience is a component they could ill afford; he revealed to him that the fate of humanity could one day rest in his hands, and what he needed to do to ensure its survival; and most importantly, he taught him how to always cover his ass in case the shit hits the fan.

The younger Moriah knew his father and General Parker always had an adversarial relationship, but Alex never knew the root cause of the tension between them. He questioned his father about it on more than one occasion, but the elder Moriah always managed to brush off his son's queries. What Alex did know is that Parker held a bitter disdain for his father, obviously jealous of the man's power and envious of his father's various connections in Washington. Alex can still feel the bile rise in his throat when he recalls Parker expressing his insincere condolences after his father passed away. Shaking the man's hand, Moriah had wanted to punch his lights out, but he restrained himself.

Alex knew that his power would one day surpass the power held by Parker and other high-ranking military officers, intelligence directors, cabinet members, and the President himself. He knew that he would have the last laugh, and Parker would be nothing more than an insignificant pawn in the overall scheme of things.

How could I have been so careless though?

Moriah maintains an army of informants, contacts, spies, and snitches throughout the country who keep him abreast of every situation that needs monitoring, but more often than not, he scolds himself, he should be using intermediaries. His primary concern, however, with using intermediaries is that a crucial fact or vital piece of intelligence may become lost in the transmission. Moriah prefers to hear it, as the saying goes, from the horse's mouth, without a third party filtering the information to him. Of course, this lends itself to problems from time to time, as evidenced by his most recent phone call.

While Moriah debated for far too long, unaware that his indecisiveness was assisting the Department of Justice in their search, he weighed the options of severing communication lines with his various contacts, especially during this most crucial of times, or being located by Parker and his merry band of do-gooders. Finally, he makes his decision.

He places the phone on the floor of the cabin and uses the bottom of the plane's fire extinguisher to crush the phone into a multitude of pieces. Moriah grounds the pieces into the floor with his foot, not knowing that in this case, he was too late when it came to making a quick, *and the most prudent*, decision.

TWO

Tamawaca, Michigan

Private Anderson leans against the railing of the balcony on the third story of the *Easy Does It* and sharply inhales from a *Parliament* cigarette. He slowly exhales and leans his head back so he is staring into the heavens, thinking about Rushmore and whether the poor bastard is still alive.

He and Rushmore became quite close after both of them started working together at Evans at virtually the same time. They had worked many of the same shifts, and afterwards one of them could usually talk the other into blowing off some steam or unwinding at a local watering hole. Inevitably, after both of them were severely over-served, their life stories were exchanged, along with the many political arguments, philosophical discussions, and other frank talk enlisted men tend to share with someone of the same rank. Anderson and Rushmore became fast friends, had met each other's girlfriends, and generally hung out during their down time when they were not on duty at Evans.

The image of his friend being carried out of the bar in Chicago like a stumbling drunk is frozen in his mind, to be replayed over and over again, as if someone is constantly hitting the "rewind" button in his brain. Rushmore must have known he was being watched and decided that the best course of action to protect the evidence was to pass it off. Anderson admires how incredibly courageous his friend acted and now, he wonders whether Rushmore sacrificed his life in order to keep the disc's contents from falling into the wrong hands.

This last thought lingers in his mind as he closes his eyes, allowing a slight breeze from the lake to wash over him, taking a momentary pleasure in its coolness. Anderson leans his head back when suddenly, he hears a faint sound coming from the balcony of the cottage next to him. In Tamawaca, the cottages were built practically on top of each other, and the local joke is that if you need to borrow anything from your neighbor, just reach in through the window.

Anderson hears the sound again, like a burst of air escaping a tire. He stares across at the neighboring balcony, his eyes trying to penetrate the gloom of the cottage. He leans slightly over the railing, intent on determining the origins of the sound.

As he peers over, suddenly a face comes into view and whispers, "Over here."

Anderson is so startled by the sudden appearance of the face that he nearly topples over the railing. The man was cloaked in the shadows before deciding to reveal himself, scaring the bejesus out of Anderson. The man, startled himself by Anderson's reaction, returns to the shadows, with only a sliver of his face visible.

Anderson notes that the man's face is rather plain, and he is practically bald except for small patches of hair on either side of his head. He possesses a look of a man tense with anxiety, paranoia even, as his head darts around, looking for other signs of life.

"Who the hell are you?" Anderson calls out.

The man motions with a finger to his mouth and whispers, probably louder than he wants to, "Shhhhhh."

Anderson continues staring at the man, thinking what an unusual situation this seems to be. They appear to be the only two people around and yet the man is looking around as if there are demons huddled in the shadows around them, listening and watching.

Not wanting to spook the man any further, Anderson says very softly, "What are you doing up here?"

The man's eyes finally come to rest on Anderson. He motions for Anderson to come over to the balcony he is standing on.

Anderson looks at the roof as it slopes down from the balcony about six to seven feet, whereupon the adjoining cottage's balcony is a short jump across a void between the two houses. Although the gap is minimal, Anderson does not like entertaining the idea of leaping across no man's land and coming up short. He looks at the man, intending to express his displeasure with the situation when the man, sensing his reluctance, pleads with him.

"Please . . . there is no other way," the man says.

The man's statement is odd, but Anderson senses an urgency to his voice, a tone of desperation even. He looks at the man and nods his head, catching a glimmer of relief in the man's eyes.

He hoists a leg over the railing, gripping it with both hands, and pulls the other leg over. He maintains a hold of the railing as he looks over and measures the distance from where he is to the railing on the other balcony. He does a quick calculation in his head where his "launching point" will be, and briefly wonders why in the world he is doing this.

Anderson lets go of the railing and scampers down the roof. He jumps as far as he can, easily clearing the gap between the cottages. Unfortunately though, he lands with his midsection squarely on the railing of the neighboring balcony, his legs dangling over the sides. The blow nearly takes the wind out of him, and he loses his grip for a moment. Then, from out of the shadows, Anderson's new friend grips his arms and pulls him up. Anderson is surprised at how strong the man is despite such a slight frame. The man seems to lift Anderson like he is nothing more than a paperweight.

Anderson drags himself over the railing and onto the balcony. He brushes himself off and finally, he looks at the mystery man who has beckoned him over.

"My name is Nitchie, Dr. Warren Nitchie," extending his hand towards Anderson.

"Private James Anderson," Anderson replies, tentatively shaking the other man's hand.

Anderson continues to stare at Dr. Nitchie, waiting for an explanation. "Okay, Dr. Nitchie, what's with the cloak-and-dagger stuff?" he asks.

"Private Anderson-"

"You can call me Jimmy," Anderson interrupts.

As if he did not even hear him, Nitchie continues, "Private Anderson, there is something very bad going on here."

The statement is delivered with the gravest of tones, and it chills Anderson's blood to hear it.

"What do you mean?" Anderson asks.

"Well," Nitchie starts, "I do not know if you are aware, but I am a new member of the team in charge of the evidence-gathering at the scene and the investigation into what occurred here."

Dr. Nitchie stops and waits for Anderson to acknowledge this in some way, but the latter simply shakes his head no.

The doctor continues, "Well, so far, I have been assigned a number of what I would deem 'tedious' responsibilities to conduct. Mostly trivial tasks . . tasks that seemed to me, well, somewhat . . superfluous."

"Superfluous?"

"Yes, superfluous," Nitchie explains. "You know . . like unnecessary, redundant."

"Gotcha," Anderson nods.

Nitchie looks hesitant for a moment before continuing, "I suppose that might be expected given the fact I replaced a member who had fallen ill and was unable to join her other team members in the investigation. So I guess you could call me the new guy on the team, but, well . . um, I feel-"

"What is it, Doctor?" Anderson prods.

Anderson detects a note of embarrassment in the man's voice as he explains, "I feel I'm being underutilized. I mean, I have a PhD in forensic pathology, in addition to a PhD in-"

Anderson cannot restrain himself, "You're a modest fellow, huh?"

Dr. Nitchie sighs, not one to boast of his academic accolades, but he certainly can recognize sarcasm when he hears it.

"I'm sorry, Private Anderson, I don't mean to sound so conceited, but-"

"That's okay, Doc," Anderson interrupts, knowing the doctor was not trying to be boastful or arrogant. "I was just needling you a bit."

Nitchie emits a brief chortle, but it sounds more like a pig snort. "Yes, I know, Private Anderson, I'm just trying to explain myself."

Anderson continues to eye the doctor, but he says nothing. His suspicion of the doctor has lessened since being spooked by him in the shadows, but Anderson still does not know what to make of him.

Likewise, the doctor gazes at Anderson expectantly.

"May I ask who is in charge of the investigation at the site?" Nitchie inquires.

"Well, as far as I know," Anderson responds, "that would be General Cozey, on orders from the President himself."

The air seems to go out of Dr. Nitchie and once again, the paranoia begins to dance wildly in the doctor's eyes.

"That is what I thought," the doctor says in a rather resigned voice. "But . . you arrived here with General Parker, right? He is one of the highest-ranking military officers in the country, is he not?" he asks hopefully.

"He is," Anderson confirms, "and he is overseeing the investigation of the entire attack. General Cozey is in charge of the on-site investigation, and of course he answers to General Parker, but it is still General Cozey's show around here."

Again, the doctor's shoulders seem to slump forward and he appears extremely disheartened. Anderson finally grows tired of beating around the bushes.

"Dr. Nitchie," he says sternly, "I don't have a lot of time to keep playing twenty questions. Why don't you tell me what's on your mind?"

The doctor's voice lowers to a whisper, but the urgency in his tone cannot be mistaken. "General Cozey's assistants, I overheard them talking. It seems that Waterston, the head of our team, was supposed to debrief General Parker some time ago, but he's been . . indisposed. They mentioned delaying him from speaking with Parker as long as possible. Well, I think I might know why."

"And why's that, Doc?" Anderson plays along.

The doctor hesitates, and then continues, "Because nothing is what it appears to be here, Private Anderson."

Frustrated by the cryptic conversation and round-about question-and-answer with the doctor, Anderson loudly blurts out, "Give me something to work with here, Doc."

The doctor shushes him again, looks around warily, and then turns back towards Anderson.

"Since I arrived here," he explains, "I have been virtually ignored by the rest of the team, been told nothing, have not even spoken to Dr. Waterston, and been given responsibilities an intern could do.

"I have seen other members of the team working, but not really working. They analyze something, then they fail to record what they have observed. Pieces of evidence are scattered around, nothing seems to be labeled or catalogued properly, and I even witnessed one colleague drop an item from the site on the floor of the lab and leave it there. There is something very wrong here, Private Anderson, and I am not entirely sure what."

"Well," Anderson suggests, "maybe these guys are getting tired, even a little sloppy. Maybe they feel a little under the gun, like we all do, and are just trying to do their jobs as fast as they can. It does not mean there is anything wrong, Doc."

Nitchie looks at him skeptically and firmly states, "Every member of a CST or SRU team knows proper protocol and procedures when it comes to evidence-gathering and processing. What I witnessed was bungling and carelessness of the highest order.

"Now, I do not know for certain what is going on here, but I do know that General Cozey's aides-"

"Bason and Stringer," Anderson offers.

"Right, Bason and Stringer," Nitchie confirms. "They appear to be thick as thieves, and they are not allowing information to reach General Parker or anyone else for that matter. Not that the information would be all that accurate."

"What do you mean?" Anderson asks, his curiosity piqued.

Nitchie looks at Anderson before asking his own question, "Did you hear that an unusual type of radiation was found at the site?"

Anderson nods, "Yeah, I heard Augie, um, Lieutenant Colonel Hermann, talking to General Parker about it on the plane ride over here. Something about a form of unknown radiation not found on Earth."

Nitchie nods as the conversation veers into more familiar territory for him. "Something like that, Private Anderson. And they're even lucky they received that piece of information. I overheard Bason and Stringer saying that an administrative assistant inadvertently scanned this information to someone at the Pentagon, who passed it on to the President and some of his closest advisers, as well as General Parker and Lieutenant Colonel Hermann. Apparently, the admin acted on her own, without direct orders from her superior. In any case, I heard the phrase, 'damage control,' and how they could allow nothing else to get through."

"But the radiation thing is true?" Anderson asks.

"Yes and no. How familiar are you with extraterrestrial solar radiation?"

Anderson shoots the doctor a wry grin, "Doctor, my education stopped at the twelfth grade."

"Well," the doctor continues without missing a beat, "don't think about little green men or anything like that quite yet. Extraterrestrial solar radiation is simply the solar radiation outside of Earth's atmosphere."

"So this radiation never comes through our atmosphere?" Anderson asks.

Nitchie shakes his head, "No, it does. There are many different factors that affect the intensity of this radiation on a given day, particularly as it relates to the distance our planet is from the sun. This radiation is scattered throughout the atmosphere, but as I said, it depends on a variety of factors, including absorption by water vapor, ozone and carbon dioxide, as well as cloudiness, longitude and latitude, altitude, and-"

"Make a long story short, Doc," Anderson says impatiently.

"Right. Well, the amount that reaches the earth's surface tends to be very minimal, nothing that should cause severe harm to humans, and certainly not enough to cause radiation burns on a home."

"This extraterrestrial radiation was found on a cottage here?" Anderson asks, disbelief creeping into his voice.

"Well, first, Private Anderson," Nitchie clarifies, "this radiation has not been confirmed to be extraterrestrial, but it definitely possesses some of the same characteristics, and it does not appear to be from any type of man-made object. And second, *cottages*, Private Anderson. This radiation was discovered on several homes that sit on the beachfront."

"So what could have caused these burns?" Anderson inquires.

"I don't know the answer to that, but the intensity of the radiation burns lead me to believe it is something rarely found on this planet, if ever."

There are a few moments of silence as the two men contemplate the significance of Nitchie's statement.

Anderson breaks the silence with a question, "So this kind of radiation couldn't have been from the bombs that were detonated here?"

Without answering, Nitchie reaches down towards his feet, and Anderson notices a small pouch the doctor is carrying with him. The doctor puts on a pair of plastic, disposable gloves, and then reaches in the pouch and pulls out a shiny, silver object that seems to reflect the moonlight.

Anderson moves in closer for a better look at the object when Nitchie raises his hand and, for the first time, speaks above a whisper, "That's far enough, Private Anderson. I don't know what effect this may have on humans."

Doubly curious now, Anderson stays where he is but leans his head in as close to Nitchie as possible in order to study the object. There, cupped in the doctor's hands, is a small fish, a trout, approximately eight inches long and three inches wide. The eyes are milky and lifeless, showing Anderson what he already knows simply by looking at it: the fish is dead. Anderson also notices running along the top of the fish's body is a patchy, reddish mark. Once again, his curiosity gets the better of him and he reaches his hand out to feel the unusual mark.

"Please do not touch it, Private, I am not entirely sure what it is," Nitchie warns.

Anderson quickly pulls his hand back as if he has touched a hot stove.

"This little guy," Nitchie explains, "has the same radiation burns as the marks found on the cottages. But I don't think it was what killed him."

Anderson looks at the doctor, who seems to be enjoying the suspense of the moment.

Nitchie continues, "I did a rather cursory autopsy on it and found that it actually drowned. There appeared to be significant damage to the fish's gills and it appeared unable to take in oxygen through the water."

"So," Anderson wonders, "what happened?"

Nitchie ponders the question for a moment before responding, "Perhaps the radiation was responsible for damaging the gills. Or maybe the radiation caused a momentary paralyzing effect, rendering the fish unable to swim. It's possible the radiation caused a temporary blindness, or somehow the fish's equilibrium was disturbed when it came in contact with this radiation. Perhaps the radiation itself somehow depleted oxygen from the water-"

"Alright, Doc, my head's starting to spin," Anderson interrupts. "How did you get a hold of this thing?"

"I swiped it from the lab when no one was looking," Nitchie sheepishly admits.

Anderson gives the doctor a surprised look.

"I know I probably shouldn't have," Nitchie explains, "but, well, there was a whole bin full of them, and no one appeared really interested in analyzing them."

"A whole bin of them?" Anderson asks.

"Yes," Nitchie confirms, "apparently a large number of them were found washed up on shore. But again, no one appeared too interested in looking at them, so I didn't think anyone would notice."

"I don't get it, Doc," Anderson admits. "If there was a whole bunch of these dead fish, and they all contained the same radiation burns, the blast radius must have been huge to affect all these fish-"

Anderson notices Nitchie staring at him with an ace-up-his-sleeve look and he stops in mid-sentence. "What is it?" he asks the doctor.

"You're on the right track, Private Anderson," Nitchie indicates. "I've got something else I need to show you."

Nitchie leans down again and rummages inside the pouch for a moment before finding what he is looking for, bringing the object up for inspection under the moonlight. Anderson leans in closer, attempting to discern what Nitchie is holding, which appears to be wrapped in a solid, plastic container. Suddenly, Anderson realizes he is staring at a human arm, separated from the torso directly below the shoulder.

"Jesus Christ," Anderson breathes.

He instinctively steps back in disgust, while at the same time he cannot look away from it. He brings his hand up to the container and instantly feels a ripple of cold radiate from it. He glances at Nitchie, who explains, "I put it on ice, to preserve it."

"For what? You running away with it?" Anderson asks jokingly.

"I may have to," Nitchie deadpans.

"Why?"

Without missing a beat, Nitchie earnestly says, "This is evidence, Private Anderson. Evidence that whatever these people," he motions towards the lab constructed below, "have told General Parker or General Cozey or the press simply is not the truth. In fact, it's pure and utter bullshit."

It sounds funny to hear the straight-laced doctor cuss, but Anderson refrains from laughing.

"No radiation marks anywhere," Nitchie explains as he turns the container over and over. "You see? No burns similar to our fish. That's one thing. Second, look at the edges of the wound where supposedly the arm was ripped from the torso."

Anderson leans in for a closer look, "Yeah, so?"

"If this arm was part of a body that was involved in an explosion from several bombs that were detonated here, as they claim, then the edges would be much more ragged, much more uneven. Look at the edges here," the doctor notes, pointing with his index finger along the edges of the wound, "it's practically even all around, almost like a perfect separation, a perfect slice if you will."

"What are you getting at, Doc?" Anderson asks, the paranoia starting to take root in him, too.

"And third," the doctor continues, "the heat and pressure from a bomb instantly cauterizes the flesh, creating a solid-like coat across the surface of the wound."

Again, Nitchie points to the edges of the wound. "I see no evidence of cauterization here, and in fact, no marks whatsoever that would indicate this arm, and the body that was attached to it, met with a violent end, let alone that it came from a victim at this site."

"So where did it come from?" Anderson wonders.

Nitchie sighs, a hint of despair in his voice, "I don't know, Private Anderson, but if I had to guess, it looks like it came from a medical school cadaver."

At first, Anderson thinks Nitchie is trying his hand at some morbid humor, but when he looks at the man's face, he realizes he is serious as a heart attack.

"I stole a quick look in a few of the other bodybags they had stored in the morgue, and all the . . . 'parts' I saw were similar to this extremity: no radiation marks, no rough edges, no cauterization. They looked like they were all parts from bodies donated to . . science."

Nitchie says this last word with a touch of regret, like he is ashamed to be associated with the scientific community at a time like this. Or maybe he finally realizes the magnitude and scope of what he is saying.

Anderson motions to the arm, "So if this isn't from a victim of the attack, what happened to the real victims? Where are they?"

"Private Anderson, I don't know where they are," Nitchie acknowledges, "but I think the people I'm working with know something everybody else doesn't. What I do know is you need to question everything you've been told with respect to what occurred here. Everything is suspect, and the first question you should ask is whether there was even an attack here last night."

"Doc," Anderson asks incredulously, "are you telling me that this is some kind of a hoax? Why go to the trouble of using bogus body parts if no one is going to see them?"

"The bodybags, Private Anderson," Nitchie counters. "I'm sure 'they' did not plan on someone who is not even supposed to be here, someone like me, to start sifting through the bodybags looking for confirmation of what happened here. Those bodybags, though, regardless of what they contain, leave a powerful and lasting impression when those images are beamed around the world. Nobody questions what they contain because everybody knows what a bodybag is for. The nation only questions what is being done to find the people responsible."

While Anderson remains hesitant to believe Nitchie, he has to admit the man does not fail to examine all the angles. Nevertheless, Anderson may be skeptical of the doctor because of the startling implications he, along with the rest of the world, would be forced to face if the doctor is telling the truth. Indeed, it is the doctor's inferences that frighten Anderson the most. He shudders to think that the alleged attack was not an attack at all, but something else entirely, and he wonders what other things are not what they seem here.

Finally, Nitchie seems to realize he has been missing for too long and he urgently says, "Alright, Private, I need to get back before someone misses me, which is unlikely considering how much mind they've paid me so far, but no sense in setting off any alarms. I need you to explain to General Parker as soon as you can everything that I have told you. Tell him about the lackadaisical procedures, tell him about Bason and Stringer pulling the strings, tell him about the radiation, and for God's sake, have him examine the bodybags before they ship them out of here for good. And tell him that nothing-"

"-is what it seems," Anderson finishes. "Yeah, I know, I'll tell him."

The doctor appears to flash Anderson what would probably be called a smile, if it did not look so awkward on his face.

"Right," Nitchie confirms.

He replaces the extremity in the pouch and slings the pouch over his shoulder.

"Thank you, Private Anderson," Nitchie says, extending his hand.

Anderson hesitates for a moment, still wary of the doctor and looking rather shell-shocked.

"Thank you, Doc," Anderson replies, grasping his hand, "I think."

Nitchie turns and walks away when Anderson calls to him in a hushed whisper, "Hey, good luck, Doc. Come get me if you get caught in a jam."

The doctor turns around and looks at him with an appreciative eye. Anderson adds, "You know where to find me."

Nitchie nods and then disappears into the darkness of the cottage.

* * *

Sergeant Jon Kaley feels his body jostled around, but it seems to be a controlled jostle, like he is strapped in tightly to a moving car, with frequent and gradual turns. Still, he does not particularly enjoy the disconcerting and nausea-inducing feeling, and he attempts to open his eyes in order to rectify the situation.

He sees a flash of bright lights, but his eyes are too sensitive and they involuntarily close. The brief glance allowed him to see he is lying prone in what appears to be a hospital gurney, his arms and legs seemingly immobile. He feels a pair of warm tears escape his eyes and roll down the side of his face until they disappear into his hair. He tries to open his eyes once more, but again, they reflexively shut before he can focus on where he is and assess his surroundings.

Suddenly, he feels like he is on an angle, and indeed, he seems to be traveling up an incline. He hears an engine rumble to life and what he thinks is the sound of propeller blades batting at the air.

Am I being loaded onto a plane? A helicopter?

Then he hears a voice, one that sounds familiar to him. The voice is gruff, terse, someone he knows from the military. It is a voice that does not conjure pleasant memories. After this voice, he hears another distinct voice, one he definitely recognizes. Kaley is unable to comprehend what the voice is saying at first, but suddenly the man is right in his ear.

With a sinking feeling, he hears the voice of his commanding officer, Colonel Malcolm Fizer, whispering, "You should have listened to me in the beginning, Sergeant Kaley. Now you'll see."

A few moments later, Kaley hears several clicking noises, and his arms and legs suddenly do not feel restrained. It is only temporary, however, as his hands are clasped together in front of him and a set of handcuffs are placed on them. He is roughly tossed into a seat and feels a slight prick in his shoulder. Next, he hears the whine of the engines, and the plane suddenly accelerates and lifts into the air in a matter of seconds.

As the plane ascends, he begins to drift back into unconsciousness, but before he is fully immersed in it, his final thought is a melancholic one, full of despair and hopelessness: he feels like the loneliest person in the world, with no one who knows where he is and no one coming to help him. Little does he know there is someone on his side, and she remains determined, albeit slightly cramped, only a few feet below him.

THREE

"In the last days of June and first few days of July 1947," Sloan begins, "the country was in a 'flying saucer' frenzy. A man named Kenneth Arnold witnessed nine flying discs cruising through the Cascade Mountains on June twenty-fourth. Early on the morning of July ninth, in Chicago, two men, Tommy O'Brian and Tim Donegan, saw what they described as four or five dimly illuminated objects moving southwest. About 15 minutes later, a man named William Valetta reported five or six domed discs in flight, heading east over Lake Michigan. These men all reported hearing a strange swishing noise, a blue light that surrounded the objects, and a wisp of smoke in the discs' wake.

"Also on the same day, in Springfield, Illinois, Marvin Wright and John Alinger reported one single, shiny gray disc flying in the sky. In Idaho, a man named Dave Johnson was flying in his private plane when he reported seeing one flat disc briefly flash by him. He attempted to film the object, but when he developed the film, no image appeared.

"And of course," Sloan says, with a sly smile, "anyone who possesses even a cursory knowledge of UFOs knows about the mysterious 'weather balloon' that crashed on William Brazel's ranch outside Roswell, New Mexico, which he reported on July fifth."

"Is that funny, Ms. Sloan?" Sean asks. "You look like you know where the ace is hiding," he adds.

"I'll get to Roswell in a minute, Professor."

"You can just call me Sean-"

"There were a total of 800 sightings reported," Sloan continues, "some corroborated and some obviously not. By the middle of July, however, the sightings and reports had diminished, but that's when the paranoia set in.

"The newspapers and a vast number of people were convinced the government was up to something. Certain members of the press did their part to play up the sightings, and the government's unusually tight lips about the incidents further strengthened conspiracy theories and allegations of secret military projects involving these objects. Eventually, the stories lost their momentum.

"But a new branch of science was born from the phenomenon, ufology, and this created an entirely new culture of people. These people sincerely believed the objects were from another world, and because the government appeared so secretive about the sightings, it was suggested that they were working in collusion with extraterrestrial beings. An emerging ideology of distrusting the government and other authorities began to pervade society at every level."

"To be fair, Ms. Sloan, it also created a bunch of raving nutbags," Sean remarks.

"That's true, Mr. O'Connell," she acknowledges, "but once in a while even crazy people hit the nail on the head."

Sean hesitates a moment, then slowly says, "You mean . ."

Sloan slyly smiles.

" . . extraterrestrials?" Sean asks incredulously. He immediately thinks of Rosenstein and Abraham's treatise he read in the coffeehouse only hours before.

"Extraterrestrial biological entities to be exact, or EBEs. And not only that," Sloan indicates, "but contact."

Sean is too speechless to even respond. The last few years of his life have been immersed in discussions of conspiracies, theories, and speculation about a number of major events in history. Some of the arguments raised were rooted in fact, while others took a more scenic route around the facts. Regardless, since his dismissal from the military, his perspective, and indeed his life, has taken on more suspicious undertones. His distrust of the government and his wariness of its good intentions are deeply ingrained from experience. This distrust will likely never diminish, and his hatred continues to burn ever more fervently at the way he was treated by an institution he believed was entirely pure and just, one in which he placed his faith in wholeheartedly.

Actual alien contact, however, is on a completely different level. The amount of indisputable, concrete facts associated with extraterrestrials is minimal. Sean had, of course, included the subject in many of his conspiracy courses, given that it is one of the most widely recognized and popular topics linking the government and a potential cover-up of epic proportions. However, he never truly delved into the subject in his courses with as much enthusiasm as what he deemed more material topics. When he did, he usually presented any discussion of extraterrestrials with the proviso that the government was using "little green men" as a front for their own secret manipulations. His suspicion of the government on this topic never fully ripened because, frankly, he does not believe in the existence of aliens or the idea they have been visiting our planet for some time with the government's knowledge. Next to the JFK assassination, however, the notion of a government cover-up regarding the existence of extraterrestrials has to be the matriarch of all conspiracies.

"One of the discs Mr. Valetta saw heading east over Lake Michigan crashed, Mr. O'Connell," Sloan explains. "Of the three-member crew, two were uninjured, while the remaining being died from its wounds, proving once again that seatbelts do save lives."

"What happened to the other two?" Sean asks.

"They were captured," Sloan answers.

"By who?"

"Naval intelligence actually located the ship and captured the extraterrestrials," Sloan indicates, "but the EBEs quickly found themselves in the hands of a group known as the Foundation."

The name instantly registers with Sean, who whispers more to himself than to Sloan, "The Foundation."

Sloan looks at Sean and asks, "Have you heard of them?"

Sean casually replies, "A man I know mentioned that name to me once, a long time ago."

"Dr. Rosenstein?" Sloan asks, more a statement than a question.

Sean looks at her and once again, she has that sly smile on her face that indicates she knows something he does not, which is turning out to be an awful lot.

"How do you know that name?"

"I was a student once, too," Sloan notes.

The surprise is evident in his voice, "You were a student of Dr. Rosenstein's?"

She nods.

Sean leans forward eagerly, "Do you know where he is?"

She smiles at his question, which only frustrates Sean.

"For Christ's sake, tell me where he is, he knows things that-"

"I know things, Mr. O'Connell," Sloan interrupts, with a touch of indignation in her voice. "And I'm trying to help you understand," she adds.

Sean takes a deep breath, trying to calm himself down and keep his mind focused. It seems to be veering off in ten different directions, with a whole list of questions in each direction.

"Dr. Rosenstein sent me to find you," she states.

She pauses a moment, then continues, "He diverted me from my previous mission and when the people who hired me find out, assuming they haven't already, well . . ."

Sloan lets the words hang in the air, an unspoken premonition of dread judging by the tone of her voice, like a thundercloud threatening to douse the unfortunate people below it. Assuming she is not being melodramatic for its own sake, and Sean doubts that she is, he can presume Sloan has risked her life to find and help him, an act he will be eternally grateful for, if that is indeed the case. Despite Sloan having saved his life, however, Sean does not completely trust her, and before he would be willing to throw himself in front of a moving bus to repay her, he needs to gather more information.

"And what was your previous mission?" Sean asks, not expecting a straight answer.

Sloan surprises him, however, and responds matter-of-factly, "To kill your friend . . Jon Kaley."

"*What?*" Sean exclaims. "But why?"

"Because he knows things," Sloan cryptically replies.

"Like what things?" Sean presses.

"Like things that occurred on a beach in Michigan last night," she states.

"Jon knows what happened there last night?"

"Pieces of it," Sloan indicates.

"He's involved in this?"

"Not intentionally," Sloan answers.

"And what do you know?" Sean prods.

Once again, Sloan flashes that sly smile, but she does not say a word.

Quietly, Sean asks, "Do you know where my family is?"

Sloan's smile instantly disappears and is replaced by a look of anxiety. She bites her lower lip and says softly, "Sometimes . . things don't always go as planned, Professor."

She looks like she is going to continue, to explain further, but she remains silent, a tense look blanketing her face. When she said this, Sean thought he detected a note of sadness in her voice, as if she were speaking of her own family. Questions begin to buzz inside his head, too many for him to focus on asking only one. Sloan possesses some knowledge of his family, and Sean uses all of his willpower to hold back from shaking her to death and demanding that she tell him everything she knows.

"Can you at least tell me," Sean pleads, "*are they alive?*"

"Professor-"

"*ARE THEY ALIVE?*" Sean demands.

He feels like he is going to explode, emotionally exhausted from the thoughts racing through his head and from trying to find the elusive answers to the questions that plague him. Sean simply wants to know if they are alive, because if they are alive, then there is hope he can find them. And if there is hope, then he has at last been thrown a lifeline over the pit of despair and anguish hollowing out his insides. The despair grows each time he thinks he might never be able to find his family, let alone discover what has happened to them.

"I honestly don't know, Professor," Sloan says in a near whisper. "I wish I did, but I don't," she adds.

No lifeline here, Sean thinks.

A few moments pass, Sean attempting to control the anger and frustration welling up inside him while Sloan stares straight ahead at the road before them. She glances at him several times, waiting to see when she can continue.

Finally, Sean breaks the silence, "Are you an assassin, Ms. Sloan?"

"Yes," she confirms, "among other things."

"And who hired you to kill my friend?" he asks disdainfully.

Sloan responds with a question of her own, "What do you know about the Foundation?"

"We had way too much to drink one night," Sean recalls, "and Dr. Rosenstein blurted out something about the Foundation, and how they involved his wife in something they shouldn't have."

She waits for him to continue, but he says nothing more. She asks, "That's it?"

"Listen," Sean explains, "we were completely tossed that night and I hardly remember a thing. He never mentioned the name again and I did not feel right pressing him on it, so I didn't ask. I don't even know if he remembers telling me."

Sloan continues her story, which sounds almost like it has been rehearsed, "The Foundation, Mr. O'Connell, is a clandestine group of men and women that have been secretly manipulating this country's political, economic, and foreign policies and agendas for the better part of a century. Their power seems to have no limits, and their influence no boundaries. They are everywhere, Professor, and absolutely nowhere. They will stop at nothing and no one is safe if they become an obstacle to the group's plans."

She pauses a moment before continuing, "They are unbelievably ruthless and cunning, Professor, and it is this group the extraterrestrials found themselves in the company of shortly after being captured."

"And this group hired you to kill Kaley?" Sean asks.

"Not only that, Professor," she notes, "but recover an item from him concerning the attack. Some type of . . evidence he has on him, a disc."

"A disc? What's on the disc?" Sean asks.

"They did not disclose that information, but I suspect it is something absolutely damning to the group. Otherwise, I wouldn't have been called in."

"You're that good, Ms. Sloan?"

"I never miss," she deadpans.

Sean's question was asked more in jest, but he does not doubt the sincerity of Sloan's response.

"I suspect that the man gunning for you at the gas station was also hired by the group," she adds.

Sounding rather awkward, Sean stammers, "Thanks, by the way, for . . helping me out back there."

My guardian angel at least deserves a thank you, Sean thinks.

Sloan nods, but does not say a word.

A few moments pass before Sean finally asks, "So how did these extraterrestrials end up with the Foundation if it was Navy intelligence who found them?"

"That's how powerful the group is, Mr. O'Connell," she explains. "Whatever strings they need to pull are pulled. A majority of the members occupy positions in the highest echelons of the military, intelligence, and political branches, and they collectively decide whether the group should take an active and participatory role in certain areas, and areas where a more 'hands-off' approach will suffice.

"The bottom line, Professor," Sloan continues, "is that they do what they want, they direct and guide this country in whatever manner they choose, they maintain a vast army of people around the globe who do their bidding, and they are virtually untouchable. Their name does not appear anywhere except in several obscure conspiracy newsletters or on Internet message boards that ninety-nine percent of the population will never see."

"So what is it that the Foundation did with the EBEs?" Sean questions.

"The more appropriate question," Sloan replies, "is what they did *not* do to them."

Before allowing Sean to respond, Sloan explains, "Physically, the EBEs were put through the wringer. Every type of physiological test imaginable was conducted on them. They tested their endurance, their strength, their propensity for pain, and the list goes on and on.

"But what alarmed the Foundation was no matter the amount or intensity of the exertion placed on their bodies, the EBEs always managed to astound their captors by first, passing every physical challenge presented to them, and second, the recuperation period for their bodies after a unusually rigorous or strenuous test was minimal. They could run a marathon one day and the next day they would still be able to swim the length of the English Channel.

"They are horses, Mr. O'Connell," Sloan concludes, "thoroughbreds."

"Sounds like they were nearly flawless," Sean remarks.

Sloan turns toward Sean and glares at him. "You're exactly right, Professor," she says emphatically, "but not just were, *are.*"

For a moment, Sean waits for Sloan to explain what she means, but instead she continues with what seems like her linear narrative. Her indication of the present tense, however, suggests these beings are not a thing of the past, a chilling thought to be sure.

"Nearly flawless except for one thing," Sloan notes, turning back to face the road.

She waits a moment before explaining, "Extreme cold, Professor. While their bodies are remarkably unaffected by extreme heat, and they seem to actually thrive in warmer temperatures, their ability to withstand colder environments is, well . . the best way to put it . . absolute shit. It seems to be their only real weakness."

"They're unaffected by bullets, knives, run-of-the-mill human weapons?" Sean wonders.

"I would not say they are unaffected. Their skin type is similar to ours, but extremely elastic."

Sloan poses a question, "Tell me, Professor, have you heard of biotechnology?"

"Sure," Sean nods, "I've heard of it, vaguely. I don't really know the basic concepts-"

"Some scientists believe," she interrupts, "biotechnology will one day alter the essence of what a human being is, both physically and possibly cognitively. It could change the way people are 'built,' and it starts cell by cell. It is essentially evolution by choice, rather than by Darwin's theory of natural selection.

"A small minority even believe biotechnology has been happening for years, decades even, and those behind it are in the process of creating a superhuman, a person immune to all the diseases that plague mankind, a person who cannot be killed by conventional weapons, a person who requires little, if any, sleep. In short, a warrior of the future, a supersoldier."

"Yeah, I've heard and read about those stories for years, Ms. Sloan," Sean notes. "Secret military projects attempting to create the ultimate soldier, someone with the strength of a hundred men, who never needs to rest and can never be killed."

"Well, Mr. O'Connell," Sloan says pointedly, "our alien race may have mastered their own line of biotechnology."

There is a moment of silence between them as Sean stares at Sloan.

"They can't be killed?" Sean asks incredulously.

"Oh, they're not quite there yet," Sloan responds. "At least we don't think so."

That's comforting, Sean thinks.

"When the EBEs were captured," Sloan explains, "all sorts of medical tests were performed on them. Scans of their brains, x-rays, the whole lot. They discovered what could only be described as an extremely strong and extremely durable endoskeleton present inside their bodies. This skeleton is not like ours, with bones that are brittle and capable of being broken.

"When they performed an autopsy on the creature that died in the crash," she continues, "they found that this endoskeleton is tough, comprised of a substance they believed to be some type of liquid metal, but they were not certain because nothing like it had ever been seen on Earth. It has the consistency of a ball of putty, but the strength of something much greater than steel. They also discovered the skeleton is extraordinarily sinuous, that it can move in any direction without having the burden of joints to slow it down.

"In essence, Professor," Sloan summarizes, "it is a defense system, built from the inside."

"Are you telling me," Sean begins, "that if any kind of trauma or weapon is about to strike their bodies, this . . endoskeleton adjusts itself appropriately and braces the body for . . ?"

"Impact?" Sloan offers.

"Yes," Sean agrees.

Sloan nods, "Something to that effect."

"So why did one of the EBEs die in the crash and the other two survive?" Sean wonders.

"Like I said before," Sloan replies, "two of them had been secured at the time the craft went down, while the third being was not. The Foundation speculated that there was so much trauma to the body, and in so many different places, the endoskeleton could not protect the creature from all of it."

"Speculated?"

"Truth be told," Sloan clarifies, "the Foundation could not determine much simply from studying the dead EBE. Since the substance was something they had never seen before, they tried to extract information about it from the surviving EBEs, but needless to say, they were not forthcoming with anything useful."

"Language barrier?" Sean jokes.

"Not a bit, Professor," Sloan responds evenly.

Sean hesitates, then asks, "You're telling me they could . . speak our language?"

"Without even the hint of an accent," Sloan notes. "Occasionally the EBEs' grammar or phrasing sounded unusual or their pronunciation was incorrect, and they did not understand some slang words, but for the most part, it was like they had been speaking it since birth.

"In fact," Sloan continues, "they could speak hundreds of different human languages, including a dialect spoken only by a reclusive tribe in Africa that has virtually no human contact."

Before Sean can ask how this is possible, Sloan notes, "I'll explain in a minute."

She continues with her story, "While the EBEs were not forthcoming with certain information, they did encourage several rather unorthodox experiments to be conducted on them."

"Like?"

"They requested that their captors use a lethal object on them, such as a knife or gun."

"And did they?" Sean asks.

"Of course," Sloan confirms. "They found the EBEs' skin actually seems to conform around an object. For instance, when a bullet was fired into their body, their endoskeleton adjusts itself to the bullet's velocity and mass and gives it a soft, easy landing. It's like shooting a pillow and afterwards finding the bullet resting on top, having not even made a hole. It's radical stuff, Professor."

"What about hollow-point bullets, or bullets that disperse razor-like shrapnel upon impact?" Sean wonders.

Sloan looks amusingly at Sean, "Mr. O'Connell, that type of technology was not around over fifty years ago, but I would anticipate the same results."

"So," Sean begins, "the Foundation doesn't have them any-"

"Besides," Sloan interrupts, "the group has devised what they believe to be a much more efficient way to terminate these organisms."

Sloan turns and stares steely-eyed at Sean, "That way, I believe, is what continues to give you nightmares, Professor."

Jesus, how the hell does she know about that? Sean thinks. *There is only one person she could have received that information from.*

Sean had confided in Rosenstein about that day in the jungle years ago, and Sean begins to wonder who else Rosenstein told his story to. The information is highly classified, and if it is revealed Sean shared the events of that day with a civilian, he could find himself in some hot water with the government. The threat of prosecution, however, quickly takes a back seat to what he has just learned.

Sloan's remark suggests there is a connection between that horrible day in the jungle and these extraterrestrials. Sean immediately thinks of the unusual "weapons" the brass issued to his squad to use on the villagers. Suddenly, there are several pressing questions Sean now considers.

Who or what were the targets that day? Had my team been thrown to the wolves, ordered into a fight against an enemy we had little chance of defeating? If so, were our superiors fully aware of our slight chances? Were we deliberately placed in harm's way? Was my team and our new "weapons" the real test subjects?

Sean recalls the amount of ammunition his squad expended on the villagers, and how the enemy continued their relentless assault, as if the bullets had no effect on them. The bizarre sound of the bullets meeting their targets' bodies echoes in his mind, and suddenly, with the new information gleaned from Sloan, things become considerably clearer from that day.

"I see Al has been sharing some stories with you, Ms. Sloan," Sean says indignantly.

Sloan does not respond and continues to stare straight ahead.

After a few moments pass, Sean asks, "If these EBEs were so much stronger than us and had no reason to fear our conventional weapons, why didn't they simply overpower their captors and escape?"

"Who said they didn't?"

Sean is quiet for a moment. "So they did escape?"

Ignoring the question, Sloan asks, "Do you mind if I continue?"

Without waiting for Sean to reply, she continues, "Now, besides their incredible physical attributes, what really dusted the Foundation are their cognitive abilities. They are remarkable problem-solvers, and are able to learn new things at an alarming rate.

"The Foundation gave the pair several math problems only a handful of humans on the planet can solve, and they were able to produce the answers to them in less than four minutes; they can speak fluently any human language after hearing only a few words; they are so familiar with the names and parts of the human body, they would embarrass a veteran surgeon; they were able to land a crippled plane in a flight simulator on their first attempt; they can build anything as simple as a birdhouse or as complex as a television; they were able to read a dissertation on electrical engineering in a tenth of the time it would take the fastest speed reader to complete it, not to mention provide a complete and concise summary of it; they had perfect scores on the SATs, the bar exam, the CPA exam, and the list goes on and on.

"In short, Professor, they seem to possess an astute knowledge of everything concerning the human race and the planet we inhabit."

"But how is that possible?" Sean desperately asks. "How could they know things, human things, they have never come in contact with before? Unless . . "

"Yes?" Sloan asks patiently.

"Unless they have been watching us all along," Sean finishes his thought.

Sloan smirks and states, "You're starting to catch on, Professor."

Sean waits in anticipation, preparing for another one of Sloan's deft maneuvers away from the subject. Instead, she slows the car and steers it toward the shoulder of the highway. It is completely black outside the car except for the illumination supplied by their headlights. Nothing and no one appears to be in the immediate vicinity.

"What are you doing?" Sean asks, looking around in alarm, half-expecting to see an EBE directly outside his window.

Without answering, Sloan reaches beneath her seat and holds up what appears to be the smallest spray bottle ever invented. Sloan brings the car to a stop and remarks, "A present from the doctor."

She opens her window and instructs him, "Take a look outside, Professor."

Sloan pulls the handle on the spray bottle and a light mist is expelled. Sean's jaw nearly hits the floor of the car.

The mist possesses a greenish hue and is luminous, practically glowing in the darkness. The mist illuminates what appear to be hundreds of tiny bugs. However, unlike ordinary bugs, these have a silvery, metallic appearance.

"Do you see them, Professor?" Sloan asks.

Sean stares spellbound at them as the mist begins to dissipate.

"What are they?" he asks, transfixed by the miniscule creatures.

Before Sloan answers, she punches the gas pedal and moves back onto the two-lane highway, picking up speed and leaving the little critters in their wake.

"Are you familiar at all with nanoprobes?"

"You've got me there, Ms. Sloan," Sean concedes.

Sloan explains, "What you just saw were tiny robotic crafts, sent by our galactic neighbors, who most likely have been gathering information on us and our planet for a considerable length of time. These nanoprobes may explain how they know so much about us."

Sean stares at her dumbfounded, uncertain which question to ask first out of the dozens bouncing around inside his head.

"Just think about the absolute efficiency of it, Professor," she points out. "Miniaturized probes that require a minimum amount of energy, thrust across trillions of miles of interstellar space. For all we know, these things could have been observing the dinosaurs on Earth sixty-five million years ago."

"But how do they transmit information back to whoever or . . whatever sent them?"

Sloan shakes her head, "This we do not know."

We?

"Whenever they have been 'caught,' the probes seem to shut down and simply turn to dust, almost like a self-destruction process. It is unknown how they gather, store, or transmit their information. The only thing we know about them is now we can see them" – Sloan holds up the tiny spray bottle – "and that they're not ours.

"By that, I mean the human race's," she clarifies.

"I gathered," Sean responds.

There are a few moments of silence as Sean attempts to digest the utterly mind-boggling information Sloan has fed him. He turns the information over and over again, trying to process it, categorize it, or simply understand it. The ramifications this information could have on the annals of history are so vast and far-reaching, his knee-jerk reaction is to remain skeptical, to doubt the validity of Sloan's story. Sean will not allow himself to believe what she has told him as fact because it would change everything we ever thought we knew about ourselves and our history.

"Ms. Sloan," Sean says gravely, "you are telling me that these beings have been watching us, peeking over our shoulders for possibly the entirety of our history. Everything we have ever done as a race, good or bad, is suspect of having been studied and analyzed. Our strengths . . our weaknesses . ."

Sean trails off for a moment when another thought occurs to him.

"Who's to say they haven't been manipulating us from the very beginning?" Sean wonders. "Steering us to satisfy their own whims or maybe even guiding us to our own destruction. Our history books will have to be re-written because we forgot to include the small but vital fact that we are not alone, we are constantly being watched and potentially manipulated, and the watchers are a far more technologically-advanced race than we could ever possibly hope to become."

Sloan has remained silent during Sean's brief tirade, but now she gives him a shame-on-you look. As if scolding a child, she states, "Professor, you of all people should know the history books contain the simplest version of events, with a number of distortions, omissions, even blatant lies. Keeping it simple is easier for people to understand . . and accept for that matter."

Sean does not respond. He feels nauseous and lightheaded. Everything he has learned and everything he has taught his students is now tainted by doubt. Furthermore, there is the possible implication that throughout human history, we have been mere pawns in a game controlled by a vastly superior race.

In a way, Sean also feels betrayed and a slight anger towards Rosenstein. Sloan is obviously too young to have received this information firsthand, and Sean suspects Rosenstein must trust Sloan enough to have shared all these secrets with her.

But why not with me?

The information Sloan has shared with him puts every other conspiracy theory floating around in the ether to shame. Ultimately, this is the conspiracy that could change everything, and given that this has been an area of intense study for him the last few years, he feels like a fool for remaining completely oblivious to it.

Why was Rosenstein so willing to share his secrets with this Sloan character, but not me? Did he not trust me? For Christ's sake, I am the man's protégé, why would he not want me to know about this? And knowing Rosenstein and his penchant for agitation, why had he neglected to blow the lid off this conspiracy a long time ago?

In all of their discussions and friendly arguments, Sean could not recall Rosenstein ever mentioning anything about alien conspiracies, let alone any writings on the topic save the treatise Sean read only hours ago. Sean simply assumed that Rosenstein shared his own mindset: that there are plenty of conspiracies to explore here on Earth without needing to delve into outlandish rumors and stories surrounding alien visitors and their nefarious plans for our planet.

Sloan suddenly breaks into his reverie, "Are you okay, Professor? Not that I blame you, but you are looking a little pale."

Sean absently nods his head, betraying how he actually feels.

"I'd like to continue, if you don't mind," she says rather gently, sensing Sean is practically on information overload.

Sean manages to squeak out a word or two for her to continue.

Sloan takes a deep breath, "There is one final trait the EBEs possess, probably their most important strength and a characteristic that can make them virtually unstoppable."

Sloan glances at Sean and sees that he is once again listening intently to her.

"The Foundation discovered it on what would essentially be the final night of the EBEs' captivity . . when Jericho escaped," Sloan says, with a perceptible note of reverence in her voice.

"Jericho?" Sean asks.

"Don't forget, Professor," Sloan explains, "this was back in God-fearing times, when most people still went to church on Sundays. They named their captured EBEs Jericho and Gabriel, biblical names if ever there were any.

"Both performed nearly identical in terms of physical and cognitive abilities. Neither seemed to be smarter or more intelligent than the other. The EBEs were questioned regarding ranks, class systems, and social hierarchy in their culture, but their captors never received clear answers to these questions. Nevertheless, the researchers sensed Jericho was what we would call the 'alpha male' of the two, with more leadership-type qualities and a kind of assumed dominance and superiority over Gabriel. He always seemed to 'see all the angles,' as one researcher noted, while Gabriel was viewed as more innocent, trusting, even naïve in his tendencies.

"Jericho seemed the opposite of Gabriel: controlling, self-assured, and, according to another researcher's notes, 'inherently devious.' On the flip side though, Jericho also exuded a wealth of charm towards his human captors, even charisma. He seemed to naturally understand humans and their emotions, their strengths, and of course, their weaknesses.

"And one night, it seemed, he decided to exploit those weaknesses."

Sloan pauses a moment and glances at Sean, who seems utterly enthralled by her story.

"No questions, Professor?" she asks.

"I'm with you, Ms. Sloan," Sean encourages.

"As I mentioned before," she continues, "their skin is extremely pliable, adaptable even, because of their unique endoskeleton. Without getting entirely science fiction on you, Professor, it was discovered that night the EBEs can actually alter their bodies and faces to appear as anyone they have come in contact with."

"You're talking about . . . shapeshifters?" Sean asks, no longer surprised at what the EBEs are capable of.

"You're familiar with the term?"

"Of course I am," Sean replies. "Nearly every culture in the world has some kind of shapeshifting myth, Ms. Sloan, which usually involves a human being turning into an animal or vice versa. Vampires and werewolves are probably the most commonly known shapeshifters in our culture. And several Native American tribes believe the thunderbird can change into a human."

"Impressive, Professor," Sloan notes. "There are also the 'nagas,' or snake people, prevalent in India and Nepal, who legend has it can turn into a snake or a hybrid between the two. Or the Brazilian 'encantados,' which are creatures, usually dolphins, with the ability to change into human form."

"I thought shapeshifting is thought to be physically and scientifically impossible," Sean argues.

"Well, as you may have gathered, Mr. O'Connell," Sloan replies, "the EBEs have shattered many of our commonly-held beliefs regarding what a body is capable of, especially with the aid of advanced technology. It is thought that it has to do with their endoskeleton, but to be honest, no one has been able to determine how they do it."

"What did they look like when they were captured?" Sean wonders.

"Good question, Professor," Sloan indicates. "Gabriel and Jericho were initially found in the waters directly above where their ship crashed. Their features were so similar to a human's, it was hardly questioned whether they actually looked different from us. Their faces were very sharp, angular-like, and their skin was dark. They certainly looked strange to their captors, not entirely human, but not so different as to appear like the little green men or the aliens with the bulbous heads and huge eyes that we so often have depicted."

"That is something I want to ask you about, Ms. Sloan," Sean says.

After a moment of hesitation, he continues, "I am curious what they look like in their, um . . well, their . . "

"Natural state?" Sloan offers.

Sean nods.

A bemused look crosses her face, "Well, if you're picturing the creature from *Predator* or *Aliens* or something along those lines . . "

She pauses as Sean waits for her to continue.

". . well, keep wondering, Professor. No one has actually seen their natural form, at least no one we know about."

There's that "we" again, Sean thinks.

"You'll find, Professor," Sloan explains, "that throughout history, in reports given by witnesses who claim they have seen extraterrestrials, the descriptions they provide are similar to what I just mentioned: dark skin and pointy or angular faces. The Foundation simply assumed the EBEs looked similar to humans, if not exactly like them. A narrow-minded and anthropomorphic point of view to be sure. But who would have thought they could actually *shift* their complexions and *alter* their bodies to mimic a human being?

"That night – and I do have to mention that despite the longevity the EBEs remained captives of the Foundation, the group still maintained extremely stringent containment procedures – Jericho 'replicated' the head of the research team, killed six security personnel, and escaped into the night, never to be seen again."

"Jesus," Sean breathes. "What happened to the other EBE . . um, Gabriel, right?"

"That's right," Sloan confirms. "Like I said before, Gabriel was the more innocent and naïve of the two, but even he realized Jericho left him out to dry, and he offered to help the group find Jericho and bring him back. But . . "

"But what?"

"But," Sloan explains, "the head of the research team was so infuriated with Jericho, and so worried about another escapee, he had Gabriel promptly terminated."

Despite the finality of Sloan's statement, Sean thinks he might have misheard her.

"Terminated? As in executed?" Sean questions.

Sloan nods.

"Just like that?" Sean asks, clearly unsettled. "How did they do it? I mean, since they couldn't be killed by conventional weapons-"

"They froze him to death," Sloan responds deadpan, not a touch of sympathy or pity in her voice.

"I don't understand," Sean argues, "these creatures have managed to create a defense system that can essentially render our weapons ineffective, but their . . what was it again? Biotechnology? It can't fend off something as simple as a cold environment?"

"I think you're splitting hairs, Mr. O'Connell," Sloan counters. "To devise a defense system that can virtually blunt all trauma that threatens to harm them, I would consider that an utterly remarkable feat."

"I would agree, Ms. Sloan," Sean acknowledges, "but being susceptible to a cold environment seems to me like a pretty significant weakness, especially on a planet like ours."

Another thought occurs to Sean. "Out of curiosity, could this sophisticated endoskeleton be the root cause of their vulnerability to cold environments?"

"The Foundation had the exact same thought, Professor," Sloan smirks. "That somehow the endoskeleton is susceptible to cold and breaks down in such a climate. And, in essence, taking the EBE with it."

After a pause, Sean addresses another thought on his mind.

"How long were they in the Foundation's . . custody?"

"Nearly two years," Sloan answers.

"See, that bothers me, Ms. Sloan," Sean indicates. "Since you've clearly noted the fact that they are physically and mentally superior to us, as well as their ability to change their appearance, why did they wait so long before escaping? In fact, I have a hard time understanding how they were captured in the first place."

"Very good point, Professor," Sloan nods. "And believe me, that has been widely discussed and theorized from the beginning.

"The most common and accepted explanation why the EBEs were captured was because they wanted to be captured. Many believed this was done for two reasons. First, by being in close contact with human beings for such an extended period of time as the EBEs were, it afforded them an opportunity to understand us more deeply . . deeper than, say, a nanoprobe could get. So while the Foundation conducted their tests, they had no idea that at the same time, they were being closely studied and analyzed by the EBEs, test subjects themselves in a manner of speaking.

"It was suggested that the second reason for the EBEs' acquiescence to captivity was because they wanted to display their extraordinary abilities to their human captors. While several members of the Foundation argued that arrogance and pride are strictly human characteristics, and that it is foolish to believe the EBEs possessed such traits, the flip side to the argument is that it was a subtle method of intimidation used by the extraterrestrials on their captors."

"In other words," Sean states, "the EBEs were laying down the gauntlet, challenging us to try and match their technology. They were insinuating that if there is ever a war between us, we already know the end result."

"Exactly, Professor," Sloan affirms.

"Then, when Jericho decided he had learned enough," Sean concludes, "and they had adequately 'shown off' their unique abilities to their captors, he drops one final bombshell by shape-shifting into the head of the research team and splitting, leaving his partner holding the bag."

Sloan nods and they remain silent for a moment.

"But why leave Gabriel behind?" Sean asks. "What was the purpose of that? I mean, the way you describe these . . beings, there must have been a rationale behind it."

Sloan shifts in her seat and shrugs, "That was never very clear. Some believed that Gabriel, despite being treated like a lab rat with all the testing and experiments, began to like his human captors. He came to admire their curious and exploratory nature, something that seemingly angered Jericho.

"Others suggested that Gabriel and Jericho were not 'getting along' around the time Jericho escaped. Supposedly they had several heated exchanges in their native language just prior to the escape. Some even believed Jericho was simply acting out and would return soon, that he would be unable to handle the outside world and would come back with his tail between his legs. A ridiculous assertion considering the way these beings are able to adapt to their surroundings.

"The fact is, Professor, no one really knows why Jericho left Gabriel behind," Sloan says. "But there is no doubt this is what doomed Gabriel to his fate. And whether Jericho knew that would happen, well . . I certainly wouldn't put it past the son-of-a-bitch."

FOUR

General Parker and Lieutenant Colonel Hermann arrive back in Tamawaca and notice almost immediately the media throng has thinned considerably outside the makeshift gate constructed to keep the press corps at bay. A number of them have been dispatched to cover the explosion that occurred on Lake Michigan, not far from the site of the terrorist attack. Those who do not have access to a helicopter to reach the location where the explosion occurred, however, have become more vocal regarding the lack of information provided by General Cozey and his staff. What the remaining members of the media lack in sheer numbers, they compensate for in the escalated level of disruption and cries of censorship starting to be heard. They want answers, they plead that they *need answers* to their unending flow of questions:

Was the Sword of Allah responsible? How many victims were there? What type of bombs or incendiary devices were used? Are there clues to the whereabouts of the perpetrators? Was there any warning of the attack or any

information received by the American intelligence com-
munity that an attack was forthcoming? How could this
happen again on American soil? Was the explosion on the
lake only a couple hours before somehow related?

After their tireless rhetoric was exhausted regarding the people's right to know and that freedom of the press was being curtailed, they began to ardently appeal to whoever would listen that they are not being allowed to do their jobs. Every media outlet around the world obviously reported news of the attack, but what they need now are *details*. They need sound bites, interviews, the who-what-how-why of the attack, and most importantly, they need to fill in the blanks for their readers and viewers as to how something like this could happen again.

The media's earlier compliance with Cozey's gag order was perhaps a brief bout of fervent nationalism, a surge of patriotism that allowed for a short respite from attacking a story of this magnitude with their usual ferocity and ruthlessness. They had relented because they expected, in fact anticipated, periodic reports and updates of what had been discovered thus far. When they continued to receive little to no new information, they began to feel stonewalled, ignored, and disregarded, actions the American press has never been inclined to accept lying down. They are no longer the respectful, pacified group initially humbled by the shock of the attack, but have transformed into an unruly, cantankerous mob that demands information. Unfortunately for them, no information appears to be looming on the horizon.

As Parker's helicopter slowly descends behind the gate, neither General Cozey nor his staff are anywhere to be found. Seven or eight soldiers hold the media throng in check, but judging from the returning choppers that were out at sea, they soon will have more people to worry about.

More fuel for the fire, Parker thinks.

The scene is spiraling into chaos and it is becoming abundantly clear General Cozey is losing control of the situation. General Parker may need to have a word with him, but first he would like to view the footage on Private Rushmore's disc and speak with Dr. Waterston, whose constant avoidance of the general has become highly suspicious.

On the return trip to Tamawaca, Augie had received a call, the matter of which he has yet to explain to General Parker. After reading Augie's expression, however, it was obvious to Parker that whoever the caller was, they had a few interesting things to say. Augie indicated that he would explain to the general once they touched down, so he would not have to shout to be heard over the roar from the rotors.

When the helicopter is hovering only a few feet off the ground, Parker and Augie hop down from the chopper and walk quickly towards the beach.

Augie places his hand on Parker's elbow and leans in close, urgently delivering the new information he received only moments ago, "They just finished interrogating one of the fishermen who spotted our Arabic party up north. The man cracked, sir, and rather easily I should add."

"Were they gentle, Augie?" Parker asks with a wry grin.

"Just some minor threats, General," Augie responds, "and no physical harm."

Parker does not know if Augie is being serious or facetious and frankly, he does not want to know.

"The man admitted he was approached several days ago," Augie explains, "and told that in exchange for a large sum of cash, he needed to gather a few buddies and be at a certain location on the lake the morning of July fifth. They were to take note of what they saw and report it once they came in for the day."

"Jesus Christ," Parker says, shaking his head in disbelief, "what the hell is going on, Augie?"

"I don't know, sir," Augie replies, "but it's starting to unravel, isn't it?"

"So the Arabic men on the boat are actually . . . *real*?"

Augie nods, "Seem to be, sir."

"Then they were planted there by someone," Parker says, his frustration mounting.

Augie nods again in agreement.

"What about the other group of witnesses?" Parker asks. "Cozey mentioned a second group who corroborated what the first group saw."

"My guys are working on them, sir, but I suspect it's only a matter of finding out which one of the men in the group was approached and propositioned. I'm sure he'll have a similar story to tell though," Augie asserts.

Parker nods, not necessarily pleased with the new development, but satisfied progress is being made in debunking the witnesses' stories.

"Alright, let's see what's happening around here," Parker says warily, uncertain where the next surprise will come from. He would not have to wait very long.

As Parker and Augie walk towards Cozey's headquarters, they are suddenly intercepted by Private Anderson, who appears out of the darkness behind the cottage next to the *Easy Does It*, a tense look on his face.

He whispers in a low, conspiratorial tone, "There is something I need to tell you both, *immediately.*"

He leads them away from the spotlight of the television cameras and phalanx of reporters and into the shadows of the cottages. They follow without protest, knowing the look on Anderson's face. He holds invaluable information, simply waiting to burst forth.

Anderson leads them to a walkway behind a cottage, briefly looks around, and relays what the mysterious Dr. Nitchie disclosed to him. He tells them about the lackadaisical procedures on the part of the forensic team; Dr. Nitchie's own trivial role and the feeling he is being ignored by the rest of the team; Bason and Stringer preventing Dr. Waterston from speaking with General Parker and the duo performing "damage control" on the inadvertent scan to the Pentagon regarding the unusual radiation discovered at the site; the extraterrestrial-like radiation found on the fish, similar to the radiation identified on several of the beachfront cottages; the arm with no radiation marks or cauterization and which Dr. Nitchie speculated was taken from a medical school cadaver, and other bodybags filled with similar extremities; and Nitchie's repeated assertion that nothing here is what it seems.

By the end, General Parker is steaming mad and appears to be on the verge of an eruption. Anderson's mention of the medical school cadavers instantly explains something that had been nagging at Parker. He had previously pondered what type of bombs completely eradicate a human being, bombs that simply destroy every fiber of a person's being without leaving a trace of them behind, regardless of the distance from the center of the blast. A nuclear bomb could be capable of this, but it was obvious a nuclear bomb had not been detonated in Tamawaca. The bombs were conventional, and even the most deadly conventional bomb should leave people on the outer edge of the blast radius somewhat intact, albeit charred.

When they arrived, however, they were informed there were only *pieces* and *fragments* of people remaining, which would be used to match with a relative's DNA to determine their identities. There are *no actual bodies*, relatively intact ones at least, and *no faces* to identify. This was something that had bothered Parker from the beginning, and now he is starting to understand why.

"You said that this . . Dr. Nitchie informed you that he looked in other bodybags and found the same thing? Just . . . pieces?"

"Yes, sir," Anderson confirms, "that's what he said."

Thinking aloud, Parker continues, "So . . . the 'parts' were taken from medical school cadavers and used to fill up the bodybags for the TV cameras, but the victims' loved ones would be given no chance to identify the remains."

A few seconds pass with no one saying a word. Finally, Parker asks the obvious question, "So where are the people of Tamawaca?"

He looks at Augie and then at Anderson, neither of whom attempts to offer an explanation. Too many times lately he has been asking questions that do not seem to have answers, and he is tired of feeling like they are constantly running around in circles. It is finally time to obtain some answers.

"We need to talk to Dr. Waterston," Parker says, "and maybe our pal Dr. Nitchie."

Parker turns and begins walking with purpose towards the forensic lab constructed next to the *Easy Does It*, with Augie and Private Anderson following at his heels.

"Um, sir," Anderson says hesitantly, glancing at Augie, "I don't want to get Dr. Nitchie into any hot water for what he told me. He seems to have risked a-"

General Parker cuts him off, "I'll use my utmost discretion, Private, but if we need him to speak up and point out the bad guys, we're going to have him do it."

"Uh . . yes, sir," Anderson says, not looking or feeling the least bit relieved by General Parker's comment.

They walk past the *Easy Does It*, which looks quiet at the moment compared to the scene a few hundred yards away at the gate. They notice the floodlights that were erected on the beach have been taken down, and there does not appear to be anyone from the forensic team present. They also notice the various markers that were planted in the sand have all been removed. Much of the debris from the explosions has been cleared away, and the only signs of disturbance to the beach are the massive amounts of displaced sand and the numerous blackened craters throughout. The sound of the waves crashing onto the shore seems louder now, like it is reverberating to the horizon and returning ten-fold.

"Looks like they've closed up shop," Parker remarks. "And rather quickly."

"Sir," Augie asks, "what exactly are you going to say?"

Parker responds over his shoulder, "I don't know, I'll think of that when I get there."

A moment later, they arrive there: a sealed door that can only be opened from the inside of the lab. There is a small, rectangular, transparent window located in the middle of the door. Parker peers in and for a moment, he looks confused. His confusion quickly turns to anger and he starts pounding on the door with his fist.

A few seconds later, there is a sharp buzzing sound and the door unlocks. Parker yanks the door open and moves inside, with Augie and Anderson following behind. When all three of them are inside the lab, they look around in disbelief.

The lab is completely empty and utterly spotless. It is as if no one had been working here for the previous 18 hours. A strong smell of disinfectant hangs in the air and, amidst this sterile environment, stands Bason and Stringer.

Stringer is the first to speak, "Is there something you're looking for, General Parker?"

She attempts to sound casual, as if the surroundings are completely normal, but Parker and company can see the cat just ate the tweety bird. Parker does not play the diplomacy game and he has no time to beat around the bush.

"For one thing," he begins, "you can wipe that fucking smirk off your face. Where the hell is Dr. Waterston? What happened to the lab?"

"Sir, the forensic team packed up and headed back to D.C.," Bason responds placatingly. "They said they had gathered everything they could at the scene and were returning home for additional research and analysis. They indicated that they have more tests to conduct at their base of operations."

"I'll bet they do. Who authorized the shutdown?" Parker demands.

"General Cozey, sir," Bason responds. "He was initially going to wait for you to return before allowing them to leave, but he was not sure when or if you were coming back," Bason says, his tone somewhat accusatory.

"Dr. Waterston," Stringer adds, "said he urgently needed to return, sir. It really could not wait."

"Where are the bodybags?" Parker asks. "Where's all the evidence that was gathered here?"

"It has all been packaged and shipped ahead of the team, sir," Stringer answers. "The bodybags have been transferred to the state coroner's office, where they will conduct the DNA matching with relatives in order to identify the remains."

"Son-of-a-bitch," Parker hisses.

"Something the matter, sir?" Bason asks, attempting to mollify the general, but still managing to sound smug at the same time.

Ignoring Bason's question, Parker casually asks, "Where is Dr. Nitchie?"

Anderson winces at the mention of the doctor's name.

"Who?" Stringer asks, appearing confused.

"Dr. Warren Nitchie," Parker replies. "He is part of the forensic team . . a recent addition I believe."

Bason and Stringer glance at each other.

"Uh, sir," Bason says, "I don't believe there is a Dr. Nitchie on the forensic team."

"I've never heard of him," Stringer adds, shaking her head.

Anderson speaks for the first time, more to vindicate himself than anything. He does not want General Parker and Lieutenant Colonel Hermann thinking he fabricated the whole story.

"He replaced a sick member of the team," he offers. "He just found out about the assignment this morning."

Parker and Augie momentarily stare at Anderson, and he immediately recognizes by their look that he does not have a speaking part in this play. He clamps up and focuses on the floor, while a sinking feeling in the pit of his stomach suddenly forms.

They know who Nitchie is, he thinks, *but they're playing dumb and acting like they've never heard of him. They must have found out what he revealed to me and silenced him.*

"There was no one," Stringer asserts, "who reported ill from the forensic team. As far as we know, everyone was present and accounted for, sir."

Parker looks for some kind of "tell" that would suggest she is lying, but he does not see one. Of course, searching for a tell typically only works if a person is unaccustomed to lying on a consistent basis. With Bason and Stringer, stretching the truth could be a full-time occupation.

"Is there anything else we can help you with, General?" Bason condescendingly asks, as if they have been extremely helpful up to this point.

Parker eyes each of them for a couple of moments, letting them wonder what he is thinking.

Finally, primarily to elicit a reaction, Parker calmly states, "Let's start with something simple. You're both under arrest for crimes against the United States of America."

Parker turns to Augie and orders, "Lieutenant Colonel Hermann, place them both under arrest and read them their rights under military law."

"Yes, sir," Augie responds, as he starts moving towards them.

Both Bason and Stringer feign utter surprise, but when they realize Parker and Augie are serious about placing them under arrest, their masks drop. Without even trying to protest or argue, they instead draw their sidearms and point them at Parker and Augie.

Bingo, thinks Parker. *Guilty as can be. Now will it be worth it?*

"That's as far as you go, Lieutenant Colonel Hermann," Stringer warns.

Augie stops in his tracks and looks at the general, who does not even bat an eyelash.

"You both just made the biggest mistake of your lives," Parker says menacingly. Knowing where it will hurt, Parker continues, "You have committed career suicide, and your general is going down with you."

Despite Parker's threat, they do not seem the least bit concerned, the arrogance clearly evident on their faces.

"I doubt that, General," Bason remarks.

"If anything," Stringer adds, "we will gain something here tonight."

"With a five-star general out of the way, it looks like there will be room to move up the ladder for *our* general," Bason predicts.

"You know how powerful the group is, General," Stringer states. "They can do anything they want, and they've assured us that, along with General Cozey, we'll be moving up in the world as a reward for our . . substantial risk."

Augie casts a questioning glance in Parker's direction, but the latter remains focused on Bason and Stringer, the anger burning fervently in his eyes.

"You don't think anyone will miss a five-star general or his assistant?" Parker asks incredulously.

Parker motions behind him towards Private Anderson, who stands there dumbfounded, thinking of ways he can save them all. Hero scenarios dance around inside his head as he briefly and prematurely envisions himself at the medal ceremony.

"They might not miss a lowly private," Parker says, "but I'm fairly certain the Pentagon will make some inquiries related to our . ." - Parker motions towards himself and Augie - "disappearance."

Stringer and Bason look at one another and they exchange a sly, creepy grin. Parker does not like that look.

"There will be no disappearance, General," Stringer states, "for any of you."

"There will be nothing left of your bodies," Bason indicates matter-of-factly, "amid the wreckage of your private jet due to take off from Windmill Airfield in a little less than an hour. The National Transportation Safety Board will blame the cause of the crash on mechanical errors, which is being taken care of as we speak."

"Nothing suspicious about that," Stringer adds.

"And no need to bring anything to read," Bason cracks, "you'll be dead by the time we throw you on board."

"And the pilot?" Augie asks, not entirely interested in the answer, but the longer they stall, the greater the chance of something happening far more favorable than death.

"Yours has been replaced," Stringer answers, "with one of ours. He is a skilled skydiver, so he'll be bailing out after he transmits a distress signal."

Parker has to admit that for disposing of a five-star general and his assistant, the plan has a rather simple elegance, an element he would appreciate more if he was not the intended recipient of said plan. Still, he has been in plenty of tight situations before, along with Augie, and they had managed to emerge from all of them intact, albeit with the occasional battle scar or two. He begins to weigh their options, which are severely limited.

Augie has his sidearm, Anderson is not packing, and Parker has the gun he was loaned on their trip to Eisley's house tucked in his back waistband. There is nothing useful around the lab because it has been completely cleaned out. Nevertheless, Parker does not intend to go out without a fight, and he knows Augie will not take this lying down either, especially from a couple of fuckers like Bason and Stringer.

Back in the jungles of Vietnam, Laos, and Cambodia, Augie and Parker often used the word *danh tu*, a Vietnamese word that essentially means "fight." They both liked the sound of the word, and when either of them embarked on a mission without the other, their parting last word usually was an exclamatory *danh tu*. While totally unnecessary, for neither of them needed a motivational ploy to become energized for a mission, they had succeeded and returned back safely after each one, designating the word as a kind of "good luck" handle.

Parker is about to exclaim this very word as a signal for Augie to make a move, but before he can do so, two things happen nearly simultaneously that make it unnecessary.

First, Wagner's *Ride of the Valkyries* explodes on Augie's cell phone, his personalized ringtone causing everyone in the room to jump. And second, the lights in the makeshift lab go out, pitching the room into total darkness with the exception of a small sliver of light sneaking in through the small, rectangular window in the lab door.

The next thing that can be heard in the lab is a screeching noise that sounds like a wild animal, and then a figure suddenly barrels out from the shadows, moving with astonishing speed towards Bason and Stringer. A moment later, high-pitched screams pierce the air, screams that have no business coming from the throat of a human being.

FIVE

Lieutenant Julianna Dawson can no longer take it. She is hot, cramped, and she feels like she is running out of air, although she is nearly certain that she has tricked her brain into believing there is a limited air supply in her tiny hideaway.

The plane ride has seemed like an utter eternity, and she has begun to wonder if they are attempting to fly around the world. The plane started traveling what seemed like north, perhaps even northeast, but after less than an hour, the plane landed. When they resumed their flight, the plane appeared to be heading due west or possibly northwest, and she figures that the real estate below might soon become scarce.

During their descent and subsequent approach prior to landing, Dawson was absolutely terrified as the wind whipped violently around her and she felt herself being tugged out into the night sky, a metal beam above her providing the only thing to cling to. Coupled with this terror, however, was also a strange exhilaration as they made their approach, basking in the adventure of the experience and knowing that she was starting to shatter her inherent fear of flying. The landing was actually smooth and, besides the rather discomfiting smell of burnt rubber and a momentary puff of smoke when they touched down, uneventful.

As soon as the plane landed, she desperately wanted to take a look around in order to determine where they were, but she feared being spotted and decided to remain in her cubbyhole. She had to make do with listening rather than observing.

Dawson knew the airport was not heavily trafficked because she did not hear the sound of another plane departing or arriving the entire time they were on the ground. There also seemed to be a surprising lack of illumination around the airfield, with only a few floodlights at intervals along the runway. She had not noticed any lights in the distance on their approach either, which also seemed strange. Similar to the airfield they initially departed from, it was like the runway was located in the middle of nowhere.

After they taxied to a stop, as the engines gradually whined down, she thought she heard Colonel Fizer's voice, but her eardrums had yet to "pop" from the air pressure and everything she heard had a kind of hollow, muffled quality to it. She also heard another voice: a terse, gruff voice similar to Fizer's, but it sounded much angrier, more on edge.

Moments later, she heard a fuel hose connected to the tank of the Cessna, and she tensed as she saw a shadow pass below her compartment. Then a booted foot kicked the tire below her, apparently checking the pressure, and her breath caught in her throat. She instinctively moved as far back into the compartment as she could, balling her frame up until she was barely larger than a classroom globe. The shadow moved on and she resumed her breathing and her heart continued its steady pounding.

It was then that she noticed on the opposite side of the wheel well a dull, silver latch. She had not noticed it before because it is directly above where the wheels sit upon being retracted into the plane. She immediately recognized the logic in having a removable panel above the plane's wheels in case the pilot has a mechanical malfunction with the landing gear and needs to examine it mid-flight. She scolded herself for not using any common sense.

As soon as she began wondering if she could reach the latch once the wheels were retracted, she heard what sounded like something being loaded onto the plane, followed by several heavy footfalls above her in the cabin. No more than five minutes later, the fuel hose was disconnected from the Cessna's tank, the cabin door was shut, and they started taxiing down the runway. After about a minute or two, the Cessna turned completely around, rapidly accelerated down the runway, and lifted into the air. Once again, she was facing her fear of flying head on, both literally and figuratively, as the tiny plane left the comfort of solid ground for the skies above.

After the pilot retracts the landing gear, she finds herself back at square one, confined again in her tiny compartment and immersed in total darkness. She deliberates whether she can contort her body over the wheels to access the latch and sneak a peek into the cabin above her. She has used her penlight sparingly, fully aware of its limited battery life and hoping to conserve a little juice in case she needs it down the road. There is approximately two or three feet between the retracted wheels and the latch, and since the compartment is not large enough for her to stand up in, she considers the angles she has to negotiate and how best to maneuver her body in the limited space in order for her to reach the latch.

Dawson turns on the penlight, places it in her mouth, and eases herself into the narrow space between the wheels and the top of the compartment. She moves slowly, not wanting to become permanently lodged in the tight quarters because of sudden movements. Several times she stops and listens intently, trying to discern any sounds above that would indicate the location of the first class passengers. All she hears, however, is the steady drone of the engines and her own labored breathing. Sweat is pouring in rivulets down her face and her back is drenched in both perspiration and grease, with her previously white tank top now the color of charcoal. Her uniform pants feel like they have been stitched into her legs and her feet are submerged in a sweaty broth of her own making.

At last, she arrives within arm's reach of the latch and grabs a hold of it. Disregarding her previously cautious nature, she attempts to pull herself the rest of the way using the latch as leverage, quickly paying for her hurried movement. The back of her tank top snags on something and she hears a tearing sound, followed by a shooting pain in the middle of her back.

She grimaces and grits her teeth, ignoring the pain. She can feel the blood starting to ooze from the cut, and she would reach for the area to assess the damage if she could maneuver her arms behind her, but this is a physical impossibility. She moves slowly a few more inches and her perspiration mixes with the grease, seeping into the wound and causing a burning sensation she does not care to think about at the present time.

Now comes the moment of truth. If the latch does not turn, she might be on the verge of busting through the compartment door and demanding that the pilot land the plane at the nearest airfield, simply to avoid a possible duel with her sanity in the confined space she occupies. Of course, her only weapon is a rather ordinary-looking pocketknife, so her persuasive powers are severely limited. If the latch does turn, well . . .

I'll just have to improvise, she thinks.

First things first as she takes a large breath and exhales. She turns the latch without resistance and eases the panel outward, slowly, while simultaneously sliding out from her hiding spot. Something sharp digs into her back, into the cut, and more pain ensues. Once again, she grits her teeth and bears it. She finally pulls her body clear out of the compartment below.

Dawson looks around her, only to discover she has moved from one confined space to another, albeit slightly larger than the previous one. She then realizes she is still several feet below the main cabin and a sinking feeling starts to envelop her, a fear she may be stuck here forever. She sweeps the penlight around the area and her feeling of despair quickly disappears when she sees another latch a few feet away, connected to a panel that appears to be directly under the cabin. She replaces the panel door on the compartment she has just exited and crawls toward the second latch, the ceiling above her no more than three feet high.

THE FALLEN RACE TRILOGY

She arrives at the second latch and notices there is a small step directly below it. She places her knees on the step while the rest of her body is hunched below the panel, and she grasps the latch. Once again, she takes a deep breath, trying to slow her heavy breathing and get her heart rate under control. She is a pool of sweat, blood, and grease, and she fleetingly wonders if this could be construed as "combat" experience. Dawson will be sure to pose this question to her superiors if she comes out of this alive.

She turns the latch easily and she hears a slight click. Unlike the other panel, she slowly slides this one horizontally on a track, the panel no more than two and a half feet wide and about three feet long. She cautiously peers above it and sees a very narrow aisle, with several rows of leather seats on either side. The main cabin is dimly lit, the only illumination coming from several miniature bulbs that line the aisle at three-foot intervals, resembling the aisle lights in a movie theatre.

Her gaze continues down the aisle as it leads to the cockpit, which appears to be occupied by two people. One of them is Colonel Fizer, seated in the co-pilot's seat, a headset wrapped around his head. The other man, the pilot, is wearing a mesh baseball cap and a similar headset. Neither of the men speak as they both stare into the blackness of the night sky. There is another person in the first row of seats on the left side behind the pilot, the person's legs outstretched into the aisle. Dawson cannot see who the figure is or what he or she might be doing, but she notices the person has camouflage pants on.

Someone else from the military? she thinks. *Is he or she armed?*

Dawson takes out her pocketknife, which still reeks of gasoline from puncturing the tank on her jeep, and she starts to hoist herself out of the compartment when she does a double take to her left. She pauses, her arms straddling the panel opening, and she immediately lowers herself back into the compartment, with only her head protruding above the opening.

In the last row of seats, only a few yards from her position, she spies a pair of feet.

Dawson debates what she should do, with her first inclination to crawl back into the recesses of the plane to her original hideaway. But then she thinks about the hell of being stuck below and her curious nature gets the better of her. She looks toward the cockpit and sees Fizer and the pilot still wordlessly staring ahead, and the person in the first row of seats remains motionless.

Dawson leans out of the panel opening, steals one more glance towards the front of the plane, and then slowly moves her head around the back of the seat.

She gasps.

A man sits in the seat slumped over, apparently unconscious, his hands cuffed in front of him. He wears a sand-colored shirt that appears to be a size too small and camouflage pants, like the person sitting in the first row of seats. The man's head occasionally lolls erratically from side to side, as if he is having a seizure. Dawson notices a large bruise on the side of his neck that seems to run underneath his shirt. The bruise is a nasty shade of crimson and purple and looks to have occurred recently. She also notices what appears to be an extremely dirty bandage wrapped around his hand.

Despite the fact the man must be dangerous on

account of the handcuffs, she feels an immediate sympathy towards him. Besides, the man cannot be all that bad if he is at odds with Colonel Fizer.

The enemy of my enemy is my friend, Dawson recalls the old saying.

Still, she debates what to do next. She glances towards the cockpit once again, but sees no movement. Dawson looks back at the unconscious man, whose head once again jerks awkwardly to the side. In spite of her reservations, she feels she at least owes it to the man to determine if he is stable and breathing normally. She does possess basic medical training, and she cannot in good conscience scramble back to her lair without checking on him first.

Dawson slowly rises out of the compartment, all the while staring towards the front of the plane, keeping an eye out for any movement that would indicate she has been spotted. She grips her pocketknife tightly, thinking that the gasoline-soaked blade is enough to defend herself in case they try to capture her. Deep down, she is not quite sure she believes that.

Her legs clear the compartment, and she crawls the few remaining feet into the row with the unconscious man. She slowly glances out from behind the row of seats in front of her and sees that Fizer and the pilot remain undisturbed, while the person in the first row still has not moved. Dawson reaches into the aisle and gently slides the panel door back into place.

She turns around to face the man and moves closer to him, not entirely certain what she can do for him. She first checks the pulse on his wrist and while not entirely strong, it is constant. His breathing is fairly ragged, but it too possesses a rhythmic quality, indicating that he is not struggling to pull oxygen into his lungs. She notes that his wrist is icy, and she puts her hand to his forehead and on his cheek to find his face cold and clammy. She sees goose bumps on his arms and suddenly realizes why his head appears so spasmodic: he is shivering because he is freezing, causing his whole body to quake involuntarily.

Not knowing what else to do, Dawson rubs her hands up and down his arms, attempting to generate some heat and force his circulatory system to pump the blood around his body. The man's face possesses an unhealthy pallor except for the large bruise on the side of his neck. Dawson stops and takes a closer look at the bruise, gingerly lifting his shirt, trying to be as gentle as possible.

Suddenly, the man shifts slightly in his seat and he emits a guttural groan, followed by a hoarse whisper, "Mike . . ."

Dawson is so startled that she nearly falls backwards into the aisle. She regains her balance and places her index finger over her mouth, indicating for him to be quiet even though his eyes remain closed.

The man groans again, and this time it lasts for several seconds. Dawson is certain that it is loud enough to be heard by Fizer and company, and she immediately ducks down in the row of seats, desperately looking around for somewhere to hide.

"What the hell was that?" someone asks.

"Sounds like our prisoner is starting to stir," Fizer responds. "Go check on him, Sergeant Major," he orders.

"Yes, sir," another person replies.

The sound of approaching footsteps can be heard and moments later, Dawson is staring at a pair of black, shiny boots a few inches from her face. She has managed to cram herself underneath the prisoner's seat, her feet pressed up against a wall that abuts the last row of seats on either side. She holds her breath for fear the slightest noise will give her away. She feels a sharp pain in her ribs, which have taken exception to being jostled into such a tight and awkward angle underneath the seat. Sweat covers her face and she notices blood on her hand-

Her heart flutters as she realizes she is not cut on her hand. Dawson did not notice any blood on the unconscious man, so it has to be from the cut on her back. While moving around, blood from the wound must have dripped somewhere and then she unwittingly placed her hand in it.

Shit, did I leave a trail of it from the compartment door?

Then, without having time to worry about the possible repercussions, an overhead light is switched on in the row.

"Are we awake yet, Sergeant Kaley?" the man asks eagerly.

The prisoner, Kaley, mutters something indiscernible.

The man looming over Kaley leans down and places his hands on his knees. "I'm having trouble understanding you, Sergeant, what did you say?" he asks, clearly enjoying the unfavorable position Sergeant Kaley finds himself in.

There is a pause that seems to last forever as Dawson continues to hold her breath. Suddenly, she hears a dull *thud*, and the man hovering over Kaley is rocked backward into the row of seats in front of them, the man's feet nearly coming out from under him.

Dawson sees several drops of blood fall to the ground and she briefly thinks how perfectly serendipitous this is for her situation. If she has to guess, she thinks the man's face met Sergeant Kaley's head fairly flush.

"I said 'I'm awake,' Ruethorn," Kaley grumbles.

With a roar, Ruethorn launches himself at Kaley. An instant later, Dawson hears what appears to be the sound of Kaley on the receiving end of several sharp blows, one roundhouse after another, as the seat above her wobbles back and forth like a heavy bag. She grimaces as she hears the helpless grunting of Kaley after each punch.

How brave this Ruethorn must be to conduct target practice on a man who cannot fight back, she sarcastically thinks. *Well, at least not with his arms.*

Dawson's first instinct is to help the defenseless Kaley and before her mind can rationalize the dire consequences for both of them if she is captured too, she reaches out with her knife towards Ruethorn. Ironically, it is Colonel Fizer who stops her from committing a grave mistake.

"Sergeant Ruethorn!" Fizer shouts, causing Dawson to suddenly jerk the knife back.

Fizer charges down the aisle towards them, but not before Ruethorn lands one more punch.

"That's enough, Sergeant," Fizer chides, although he sounds almost amused, like a parent gently disapproving of their child grabbing one last cookie from the jar.

Ruethorn straightens up and smoothes out his uniform, breathing heavily from his retaliatory outburst at the prisoner.

"Good to see you're awake, Sergeant Kaley," Fizer says somberly. "You could become a very valuable bargaining chip in case your professor friend tries to be a hero. Otherwise, I would have put a bullet in your head and you'd be getting packaged at the fertilizer factory. But for now, we're going to at least need you to be . . . alive."

Fizer and Ruethorn both smirk at the comment. "You obviously remember Sergeant Major Ruethorn," Fizer adds.

There is silence, and then Dawson hears Kaley mumble, as if he has marbles in his mouth, "Not fondly."

A moment later, Kaley spits a mouthful of blood at their feet.

"No, I wouldn't expect so," Fizer concurs.

"I'm really sorry about your uncle, Kaley," Ruethorn says, dripping in fake sincerity, "but you have to admit, he did go out like a *pussy*."

There are a few moments of silence before Kaley finally responds, "At least he sent your whole squad to hell, Sergeant, and . ."

Kaley chuckles ". . it looks like *that* is going to leave a nasty scar."

Dawson cannot see what Kaley is referring to, but a moment later the seat jolts backward, causing her to nearly cry out. The seat rocks back and forth several times, with Kaley once again on the receiving end of another blow.

Dawson grits her teeth, this time not in pain but in anger, wanting to leap out and at least *attempt* to make it a fair fight. But whatever element of surprise she may have on her side, her position is precarious at best. With Fizer and Ruethorn owning the higher ground, the odds are firmly stacked against her. She does not like it, but she remains in place for the time being.

Fizer appears to lean down, similar to the dangerous position Ruethorn placed himself in moments earlier. She wonders if Kaley will have the same response.

"If you would have followed orders, Sergeant Kaley," Fizer says coldly, "your uncle would still be alive, and you . ."

Fizer trails off, pauses, and then continues, his tone one of disappointment, "You'd be back at Evans rehabilitating your . . reputation, becoming a good soldier again."

Fizer shakes his head in exasperation and orders Ruethorn, "Cuff him to the armrest, I don't want him roaming around in flight."

Ruethorn bends down and unlocks one of Kaley's handcuffs and attaches it to the armrest. While doing this, he whispers matter-of-factly to Kaley, "I just want you to know it's going to be me who does it. You might see it coming, you might not, but I'm punching your ticket, do you understand?"

Dawson does not hear Kaley respond. Ruethorn shuts off the overhead light while Fizer tosses a handkerchief to Kaley and tells him to clean up. Fizer and Ruethorn walk back towards the front of the plane. Ruethorn snidely remarks over his shoulder, "Stay sharp, Sergeant."

Dawson hears a muffled conversation at the front of the plane, followed by several minutes of silence. After waiting a couple more minutes to pass, Dawson taps on one of Kaley's feet, trying not to startle him. A moment later, Kaley leans down in his seat and looks upside down at her, his face a bloody mess from Ruethorn's beating.

"I didn't think I imagined you," he whispers, a slight smile crossing his face. "When's the drink cart coming around?"

Despite the situation, Dawson allows herself to return the smile, but only briefly. She pulls herself out from under the seat and leans in close to whisper.

"Are you okay?" she asks, concerned. "You look like . ."

"A pile of horseshit?" he offers.

"Not the exact words I'd use, but close," she replies. "I'm Second Lieutenant Julianna Dawson," she adds.

"Well, hello Second Lieutenant Julianna Dawson, it's nice to meet you. I'm Sergeant-"

"Kaley," she finishes. "Yeah, I know, I got that."

"Good. Now you want to tell me why the hell you're on this plane?" he asks, gently dabbing the handkerchief on his nose and mouth, which look like they have recently been placed in a meat grinder.

"It's a long story," she explains. "I was assigned by General Theodore Parker to be a liaison between him and Colonel Fizer at Evans. Well, Fizer decided to skip town and I caught the redeye with him," she says, motioning around. "You?"

"It's an even longer story," Kaley responds, wincing at a particularly tender spot on his face. "I was on duty at Evans last night and-"

He pauses, then asks, "It's still July fifth, right?"

She nods and adds, "Soon to be the sixth."

"Yeah, well, I was at Evans last night," Kaley explains, "and witnessed something I wasn't supposed to, managed to obtain evidence of what I saw and then soon lost it, survived an assassination squad's attempt on my life, and I'm directly responsible for getting two people killed within the last twenty-four hours."

He stares at her, challenging her to top his list. "What have you got?"

"I can't compete with that," Dawson concedes.

"I didn't think so," Kaley replies.

"Listen, I'm real sorry about your uncle," she says.

Kaley grimaces, noticeably distressed.

"What was it that you saw last night?" she probes.

"Story for another time, Dawson," Kaley says evasively. "Let's just say there seems to be a big gap between perception of the attack and what is reality."

"Yeah, I've gathered that," she remarks.

Kaley glances towards the front of the plane, "You mentioned General Parker, the five-star general, I assume?"

She nods.

"Do you have any way to contact him?" Kaley asks.

"I haven't been able to get a signal on my cell phone the last few hours, but I can try again. I need to head back below the cabin though, so they don't hear me."

"So that's where your seat is?" Kaley smirks.

"Yeah, first class cabin," Dawson sarcastically remarks.

"I'd see if your fare is refundable," he jokes.

"I'll talk to customer service after we land," Dawson shoots back.

"Okay, if you reach Parker," Kaley notes, "tell him Colonel Fizer is involved-"

"He already knows that," Dawson interrupts.

"He does?"

"Well, I assume he suspects Fizer of something," she says. "Why else would they assign a liaison to essentially shadow him at Evans?"

"Good point," he notes. "Alright, tell him that a Sergeant Major Ruethorn is also involved. He is the commander, or was the commander, of a rogue Special Forces squad based out of Georgia. Parker will know who you're talking about. They've been looking for this prick for a while, him and his goons," he says bitterly, a spark of utter hatred in his voice.

"Can you tell which direction we've been going?" Kaley asks.

"Well, we started out going what seemed like north, or slightly northeast," Dawson indicates, "but after we picked you up, I think we've been heading almost due west, maybe northwest a bit."

Kaley nods, "Okay, either way, they can probably trace our location from your cell phone. Besides, we can't just fly anywhere without a control tower or radar picking us up. Have them check if anyone has reported receiving any radio transmissions from us or, I suspect in their case-" he nods towards the front - "avoidance of radio contact."

"Got it," she replies.

"One last thing," he notes. "Can you find me something I can use to try and jimmy these cuffs?"

Dawson holds up her pocketknife and offers it, "Will this work?"

Kaley takes the knife and remarks in mock alarm, "Were you saving this for a rainy day or just waiting until *after* they beat me to a bloody pulp?"

"I thought about using it if I could count on you for taking at least one of them out," she retorts, "but you were too busy imitating a heavy bag."

Kaley smirks and admits, "Touché."

"I'll be back," Dawson promises.

She crouches down behind the row of seats in front of them and glances toward the cockpit.

"Hey . ."

"Yeah?" she asks, looking back.

"Thanks, Florence," Kaley says, referring to a slightly famous nurse.

"One more reference like that, Kaley, and I'll beat these assholes to the punch," she responds icily.

He tries to suppress a grin, but to no avail.

She scrambles to the panel door, opens it, and crawls back down. As she closes the panel door behind her, Kaley whispers, "Don't forget my drink."

What an asshole, she thinks. *Typical macho bozo cannot accept the fact he is being helped by a woman.*

Dawson takes out her cell phone, which she had turned off earlier to save the battery, and switches it on. The phone buzzes to life and she immediately punches in Lieutenant Colonel Hermann's number.

Seconds pass as it searches for a signal, and then, after an interminable wait, the call goes through. On the other end, Augie would probably say he has never received a call at so fortuitous a time. Dawson anxiously waits for an answer.

SIX

"There is something you said before," Sean says, "that I've been thinking about, about the EBEs' intolerance for cold."

"Yes?" Sloan patiently asks.

Sean recalls his encounter at Rosenstein's home with the . . .

Was it a man? Or something else?

The mist discharged from the vents at Rosenstein's home was extremely cold, so cold that tiny ice crystals formed on his arm after only a matter of seconds.

"Well, how cold is cold?" Sean wonders. "I mean, can they stand it for a certain period of time? Are they susceptible to the slightest cold environment?"

"Actually," Sloan explains, "the Foundation determined the EBEs' vulnerability to cold more by accident. One day, not long before Jericho escaped, the research team decided to place the EBEs in two extreme environments. In the first environment, they exposed the EBEs to sub-arctic winds and below-freezing temperatures.

Barely two minutes into the experiment, both Gabriel and Jericho collapsed. The researchers were secretly ecstatic: they had finally discovered a weakness in the EBEs after all signs had indicated these creatures were practically indestructible.

"Despite this discovery, the researchers never again tested the EBEs' tolerance for extreme cold. Primarily because they did not want to lose their only *living* extra-terrestrial biological 'samples,' but several researchers claimed it was unnecessarily cruel and inhumane. When these individuals suddenly obtained a conscience along the way is anybody's guess.

"Nevertheless, the group duly noted this weakness and began studying a more efficient way to exterminate them in the event . . . hostilities arose between the two sides."

"So, is there a certain temperature threshold they cannot cross?" Sean questions.

"The EBEs indicated they were familiar with our scales for measuring temperature in degrees Fahrenheit and Celsius. Curiously enough, after the experiment, they informed the researchers their bodies cannot withstand temperatures below the freezing point of water: thirty-two degrees Fahrenheit. If they are exposed to temperatures below this for a substantial amount of time, they claimed that they would 'expire.'

"Conversely," Sloan continues, "the research team found the EBEs' physical and mental performance was off-the-charts when they were in the exact opposite environment: extreme heat. They thrived in this type of setting, and several members of the team hypothesized that the EBEs must live on a planet in close proximity to a sun like ours. And with the durable nature of their skin, they are able to survive and in fact, flourish."

"Wait," Sean interjects, "in two years, they were never able to determine where the EBEs came from?"

"The EBEs, Professor," Sloan sighs, "were extremely forthcoming with certain information, but downright secretive with other details, specifically anything involving their technology or their place of origin.

"We talked earlier about their motives for being 'captured' so easily. Navy intelligence discovered Gabriel and Jericho patiently bobbing on the surface of the water at the location where their craft went down, with one witness describing the pair as seemingly 'waiting' for them to arrive. Shortly after, Jericho gave his captors the 'keys' to his ship and described how they could access the craft and other vital details regarding it, as well as the fact one of their comrades 'expired' in the crash.

"If Jericho," Sloan continues, "did not instruct his captors how to access the craft, it is likely they would still be studying it from the outside."

"It's that complicated?" Sean asks.

"Not really," Sloan shakes her head, "but I'm not sure they would have eventually figured it out."

Sloan pauses a moment, then continues, "I already mentioned a possible theory why the EBEs were so acquiescent to capture: to 'show off' their unique abilities. They gave the Foundation access to their craft for a similar reason – so we could marvel at their technology without knowing exactly how it works.

"Essentially, this was the approach they took with all of the pertinent information related to their race and their technology. The EBEs displayed their biotechnology-altered bodies and incredible endoskeletons, but they did not inform their captors how it worked or what it consisted of. They provided access to their ship, but they did not explain their propulsion system or how they could have reached our planet. They did not supply this information to the Foundation because they did not want the human race replicating it, and potentially surpassing their own advanced technology. And like any smart adversary, they did not inform their captors about their primary weakness, deciding instead at the risk of their own lives to let the researchers find out for themselves.

"What's more, they would not divulge where their home is for the purpose of protecting it, although they were fully aware humanity did not have the means to reach it anytime in the foreseeable future. But better safe than sorry, I suppose."

Sloan flashes another one of her sly smiles, which Sean catches in his periphery.

"What's that for?"

"Well, Professor," Sloan casually remarks, "the EBEs did reveal why they had come to our planet."

"Really?" Sean asks, clearly surprised.

"They claimed that their planet was dying," Sloan explains. "Within a century, possibly a half-century, the planet would be inhospitable for their society. So the flying saucer frenzy in 1947 we witnessed here on Earth was their attempt to determine whether our planet would be a suitable place to take up residence in the near future."

Sloan glances at Sean and can see he is attempting to process the implications of what she has just told him.

"Scouts," Sloan clarifies, "a reconnaissance force sent here to determine if it is safe for the rest of them, analyze our current defense systems, and assess their chances of assuming control of the planet."

"A scout team," Sean notes, and suddenly he snaps his fingers. "Of course, standard military procedure for any potential invasion."

"But not just scouts, Mr. O'Connell," Sloan cautions. "*The start of the invasion.* In the meantime, until the rest of their comrades arrive, they would develop a strategy based on our vulnerabilities. They would study our strengths and evaluate how to exploit our weaknesses. Essentially, they would coordinate the invasion, and they would do it from the inside."

"From the inside?" Sean repeats.

"They would walk among us, Professor," Sloan explains. "Throughout our world, they would adapt to the customs and mores specific to the culture and they would blend in. They would become a part of society, human society, and they would study us on a grand scale."

"But they must have been limited to certain areas of the planet," Sean argues, "places where the temperature never reached the freezing point."

"Not true, Professor," Sloan counters. "It was discovered during Gabriel's autopsy an object they did not find during the first EBE's autopsy: a device implanted in the endoskeleton which apparently maintains their core temperature at a regulated level, a level that would prevent them from freezing to death in a colder climate. Obviously, the device is not completely flawless, which was evident in the sub-arctic wind experiment, but for the most part the device functions properly.

"And more importantly," Sloan adds, "it allows them to live and work most anywhere in the world. They obviously do not settle near the poles or places with a median temperature at or below thirty-two degrees, but they pervade society today, Professor, and they are waiting for the invasion to begin."

This instantly sends chills down Sean's spine as he contemplates the idea that for the past half-century, extraterrestrials have been walking among our society, unbeknownst to everyone except for a small minority. Neighbors, colleagues, friends . . . they could have come from another world, a world they are seeking to replace.

With our own, Sean thinks.

"But when does this invasion start?" Sean asks, knowing a direct answer is highly unlikely.

This is quickly confirmed when Sloan turns her head and smirks.

The woman is fucking maddening!

"Has it already started, Ms. Sloan?" Sean persists. "Did it start last night in Tamawaca?"

Sloan considers this and then responds matter-of-factly, "In a manner of speaking, maybe it did."

"Jesus . ." Sean whispers.

Sloan waits a few moments before asking, "Can I continue, Professor?"

Sean absently nods his head, but he is not sure he wants to hear more.

"Around two years after Jericho escaped," Sloan continues, "and after the Foundation turned the whole world upside down trying to find him, they decided to seek another perspective on the situation, a view outside the box. The group had their own researchers and analysts, of course, mulling over all the information and data obtained from the EBEs, and they continued to study the craft in the depths of Lake Michigan-"

"They never tried to salvage it from the lake?" Sean interrupts.

"They certainly thought about it," Sloan replies, "but the location of the craft in the middle of the lake and the extreme depth made it extremely difficult. The most significant drawback, though, was the immense size of the craft. Various engineers were brought in and consulted, but none of them could devise a realistic way to retrieve it from the bottom."

"So they studied it underwater?"

"Yes," Sloan confirms. "They essentially built a self-sustaining underwater environment around the craft dedicated to studying it around the clock, with a rotating group of scientists every four to six months."

"Unbelievable," Sean states in wonderment.

"Everything was studied and analyzed a thousand times over," Sloan continues, "the ship, trying to determine Jericho's location, the strengths and weaknesses of the alien race, their propulsion system, whether we could ever replicate their technology, and probably most importantly, our chances for survival in the event of a war."

Sean comes to a sudden realization, "Rosenstein's paper."

"Exactly," Sloan nods. "In the spring of 1951, what were considered two of the finest and brightest minds in America were graduating from their respective universities: Albert Rosenstein from the University of Chicago and Jonas Abraham from Yale University.

"Shortly after graduation, these two men were simultaneously approached by employees from the Department of Defense. They were informed that they were part of an elite, an exception rather than the rule, that they were the cream of the crop and so unbelievably talented that the DOD was approaching them about prospective employment rather than the other way around.

"They offered them both a job, top secret work, with access to documents and research only a handful of people had ever laid eyes on. They informed them that they would be involved with cutting-edge technology, they would possess the very highest security clearance, that money would never be a problem for the rest of their lives. They would be at the forefront of a new war, and of course, not unreasonably, these two young men believed the DOD was referring to the escalating Cold War."

Sloan turns towards Sean, "Little could they know, Professor."

Sean moves forward in his seat, enthusiasm soaking his voice, "So that's what led to Rosenstein and Abraham's paper. The DOD asked them to assess the alien race's technology, compare it to our own, and draw a conclusion as to whether we could survive an invasion?"

"Correct, except for one thing," Sloan notes. "It was not the DOD, Professor, but the Foundation behind it all. The DOD was just a front, a cover, something Rosenstein and Abraham could hang their hats on, a respected name they could tell their families. It might have been justified had they simply been trying to protect these two men, but what they were really doing was protecting themselves."

"Covering their asses," Sean mutters.

"One of the prevailing qualities of human nature," Sloan says sardonically.

Sean is about to ask a question, but he hesitates, anxious to hear the answer. He forges ahead.

"Tell me, Ms. Sloan," he asks, "was their assessment correct? Is it hopeless or do we stand a chance?"

With hardened eyes that suddenly turn soft, Sloan replies, "Yes . . and no."

Always a mystery with her, Sean thinks.

"Toward the end of 1951," Sloan continues, "with their superiors growing impatient, Rosenstein and Abraham issued their report, and the conclusions, as you already know, were dire. They foresaw little chance for humanity to defend itself in the event of an invasion, and they believed that most of the human race would perish in the attack."

"I know, I read the report," Sean says rather defensively.

"I know you did," Sloan states evenly, "but even men as smart as Rosenstein and Abraham cannot accurately predict the advances the human race would make in fifty years time. Let alone what advances our galactic neighbors may make, or not make for that matter."

Sean does not fail to notice Sloan's tone as she said this, a faint glimmer of hope perhaps.

"Something I noticed while reading it," Sean notes, "was the report cited absolutely no sources and gave no indication where Rosenstein and Abraham received their information, or from whom. I was curious about that – was that done intentionally?"

"Of course," Sloan confirms. "They were explicitly instructed by their superiors to make no mention of the source of their data or how it was acquired. They were simply informed that their reading audience would know exactly what they were referring to. It was entirely unnecessary to cite specific locations, important dates, anything that could compromise highly classified information should the report fall into the wrong hands."

"But it never did?" Sean inquires.

Sloan shrugs her shoulders, "No one can say with complete certainty whether it did. We do know the report never made it into the press. But there was speculation, and this was only speculation, that it did fall into the hands of none other than their escapee."

"Jericho?" Sean exclaims.

Sloan nods and explains, "In mid-July 1952, a copy of the report mysteriously went missing. A few days later, on July twentieth, a round, disc-like object buzzed right by the White House. And for the next few nights there were 'blips' on the radar screens at Washington National Airport's control tower. The Air Defense Command sent fighter jets to the scene to intercept the objects, but the pilots did not find anything in the vicinity once they arrived. But multiple witnesses on the ground reported seeing unusual lights in the sky.

"At the end of July, the missing report found its way back to its rightful place, with an added touch by whoever checked it out: a rough sketch of the White House engulfed in flames."

An audible gasp escapes Sean's lips.

"They obviously could not prove Jericho was responsible," Sloan indicates, "but many in the Foundation believed only Jericho would have the audacity to pull such a stunt. They suspected he was showing them up, confirming what the report predicted: that he could destroy them whenever he chooses, and when the time comes, the invasion will be unstoppable."

"Jesus," Sean breathes.

"It gets better," Sloan notes. "Around the same time the White House was being paid a visit, the U.S. intelligence community received strange reports from Moscow that several unusual objects had been spotted near the Kremlin. The objects were described as roundish, disc-like, and shiny, with strange incandescent lights surrounding them. The descriptions of the objects were nearly identical to reports of UFOs seen around the United States.

"To the Foundation, this was nearly irrefutable proof that it was Jericho behind it all, he and his comrades conducting fly-bys over the most recognizable symbols of the two great superpowers. Jericho was very much aware who the big dogs on the block were, so to speak, and by brazenly toying with each country, he was out to show a bigger and meaner dog had arrived. Simply put, Jericho was taunting them, daring them to try and do something about him. And to a certain extent, they did.

"Through covert channels," Sloan explains, "the Foundation was able to use their influence to 'persuade' the American government to contact the Russian government with a proposition. They essentially brokered a deal between the two nations whereby a pact was secured. Setting aside and ignoring each other's constant attempts at spying on one another in regards to the dealings of this world, they decided to become partners in combating visitors with hostile intentions from an outside world."

"They signed a pact?" Sean asks. "What did it say?"

Again, Sloan gives him a disapproving look as if he is the most naïve person in the world.

"These people are not apt to leave a paper trail, Mr. O'Connell. Nothing formal was written and no names were involved. It was more of a . . . handshake agreement, with several key components."

"Like?" Sean prods.

"Like information regarding extraterrestrials, UFOs, or anything having to do with unexplained phenomena is to be openly shared with and disseminated to one another. It was intended to be a mutual exchange of information, ideas, and defenses against possible attack. No more than a handful of people from each country would have access to these reports and documents, but both sides felt it was a step in the right direction as far as defending their respective spheres of the planet."

"Wait a minute, Ms. Sloan," Sean begins, "you're telling me that a group as American as apple pie approached the reds about collaborating together, and they readily agreed? Just like that?"

"Obviously, Professor," Sloan counters, "there was suspicion and downright paranoia in both camps from the start. And without a doubt, we neglected to share *all* the information we had on the subject, just as we suspected they did the same. But let me tell you something."

Sloan turns to Sean and locks eyes with him. "The Foundation does not fear anybody or anything. They have *concerns*, but they do not get scared.

"The Foundation was scared of this alien race and they still are, with good reason. They reached out to the Soviets at the time because they knew they would need all the information and help they could get, even if it came from their most hated enemy."

"Two superpowers are better than one, right Ms. Sloan?" Sean smirks.

"I suppose," she responds, ignoring his sarcasm. "But the Soviets most likely agreed for the same reason the Foundation approached them: they were absolutely terrified of these beings."

"Did we ever determine what spooked them so bad?" Sean wonders.

"I was getting to that, Professor," Sloan indicates. "The Soviets also maintained a large cache of files on UFOs and possible extraterrestrial encounters within their borders, and it was suspected they may have once had their own biological samples to study, although they never confirmed this to us."

"Biological samples?" Sean echoes. "You mean actual EBEs, like Jericho?"

"Yes," Sloan nods, "but like I said, this was never verified."

"Did we ever tell them about Gabriel and Jericho?" Sean questions.

"Absolutely not," Sloan replies. "That was information we 'forgot' to share with them. But it was obvious from the wording in several of their reports that they knew more than what they were telling us, too."

"What do you mean?"

"For instance," Sloan explains, "they made several subtle references to the suspicion that these beings are not susceptible to conventional weapons such as guns and knives. They also noted that a majority of their 'sightings' occurred in the southern part of the country, speculating that these beings might be averse to cooler climates."

"Acute observation," Sean remarks.

"The Foundation thought so, too," Sloan indicates.

Sean shakes his head and, not bothering to mask the disbelief in his voice, states, "I still can't believe that these two countries that despised each other so deeply were willing to open up their most classified files to one another."

"A lack of knowledge and understanding leads to fear," Sloan notes, "and fear leads to unconventional solutions, such as forming an alliance with your primary enemy."

"The two superpowers of the world coming together to ward off the evil space creatures," Sean says sarcastically. "It's hard to swallow, Ms. Sloan."

Sloan does not appear offended or the least bit annoyed by Sean's skepticism. "Like everything else I've told you tonight, right Professor?" she counters.

There is a momentary pause, and then she continues.

"Nevertheless, a pact was reached, and the cornerstone of that pact left the ultimate decision in the other nation's bloody hands."

She has suddenly grabbed Sean's rapt attention again, and he asks, "What does that mean?"

Sloan smiles mischievously and asks, "Are we ready to start believing again?"

The smile disappears and she explains, "Well, the final part of the pact was that any living EBE discovered within either country's respective borders is to be immediately terminated without exception."

"And how would this be monitored?" Sean inquires.

"It couldn't," Sloan answers. "The whole pact was as vague as possible. But this final stipulation left little wiggle room: it was termination of the entity without mercy and without prejudice. It was not to be studied except during an autopsy. It was an agreement based on each other's word, something neither side would ever trust, but for this-" she pauses, "they would have to."

"Just like that?" Sean asks.

"Just like that," Sloan nods.

"So what did they share with us? Anything good?"

"Well, in the beginning," Sloan responds, "reports of sightings, eyewitness testimony, locations where the greatest amount of UFO activity occurred, nothing extraordinarily mind-blowing. And to be honest, we reciprocated the same type of information. Like I said, we did not mention Jericho or Gabriel or any captured wreckage, although both sides suspected that the other was not being entirely candid.

"But the Soviets did open the Foundation's eyes to an element that, surprisingly, they had never really considered."

"What was that?" Sean asks.

"Well," Sloan begins, "the Soviet government decided to conduct an experiment in an isolated town a couple hundred miles northeast of Moscow. For several months, stealth aircraft fitted with strange, blinking lights circled the night sky above the town. At the start, these sightings were fairly irregular and infrequent. But then the flyovers started occurring two or three times a week, and finally, they were occurring almost on a daily basis. Along with these bizarre UFOs, the townspeople began seeing unusual-looking creatures walking through the woods that surround the town. The creatures looked like nothing they had ever seen, and nearly every witness said the creatures did not appear human.

"Soon, the Soviets began amping up the terror. The town's animals started disappearing, and the people would find them outside the woods, gutted like a fish, if they found them at all. The villagers would awake in the morning to discover weird astrological symbols smeared on their front doors. The lights in the sky overhead became more frenetic, almost urgent in a way. Screams and explosions were heard throughout the night, seemingly getting closer as the days passed.

"The people prayed night and day, pleading with God to rescue them from what they believed to be the coming Armageddon. Non-believers suddenly became devout. Most of the people locked their doors and barricaded themselves inside their homes, even during the day.

"Finally, one moonless night, with the village quiet as a tomb, explosions ripped through the silence, shaking the villagers' homes and terrifying them from their beds. Fires raged outside, but the men were too frightened to leave their homes to put them out. Dead animal carcasses appeared in the village square and bloodcurdling screams echoed throughout the night.

"When the people looked outside their windows, what they saw frightened them beyond belief."

"What was it?" Sean asks in a near whisper.

"They saw nearly thirty creatures, the same beings they had witnessed walking through the woods the last few months. There was practically one creature for each home, standing only several feet away from the front door. A strange glow radiated from each one and an odd, expressionless face stared back at the villagers. The creatures did not move or do anything except stand and wait, daring the villagers to take action. And the villagers did, but not what they were expecting.

"Several families attempted to flee towards the nearest town, about twenty-five miles away, but they all froze to death in the brutal, Russian winter. A handful of families decided to remain inside their homes, waiting for whatever had come for them to knock on their doors. But the rest of the families, over half the village-"

For a brief moment, Sloan's voice catches. Sean looks at her intently, wondering if she is pausing for dramatic effect or is truly empathetic towards the villagers. Sean is about to say something, but the moment quickly passes and she continues her narrative.

"The patriarchs of over half these families decided they were not going to allow these 'things' to harm their wives or their children, and they . . . ended it themselves, believing the afterlife was a better option."

"Jesus Christ," Sean exhales.

"If only," Sloan responds. "It quickly became apparent the villagers were not resisting or fighting back because they were absolutely petrified with fear. After gunshots began ringing out across the town, the creatures fled into the night and were never seen again. Suffice it to say, there were no more reports of blinking lights, horrifying screams, and butchered animals.

"No more than a dozen villagers remained, and when they attempted to tell their stories to the local provincial government, or anyone else who would listen, they were dismissed as lunatics and crackpots."

"And the creatures?" Sean asks.

"Soviet Special Forces, disguised by the finest make-up artists in Russian cinema and theatre."

"Motherfuckers," Sean hisses.

"My sentiments too, Mr. O'Connell," Sloan agrees.

"What was the fucking purpose of this whole 'experiment'? What was it intended for?" Sean asks, his voice rising.

"The Soviets," Sloan explains, "were attempting to determine the typical civilian reaction from an encounter with an extraterrestrial."

"They needed a bunch of innocent people to die to tell them that people would flip out if they came face-to-face with an alien?" Sean asks incredulously.

"To be fair," Sloan responds, "and I'm by no means defending their actions, they did not know these people would kill themselves. In fact, they did not really know what the villagers would do. Perhaps naively and hopelessly optimistic, they believed the villagers would fight back and repel the attack. The Special Forces soldiers were even covered from head to toe in body armor in case the villagers began blasting away."

"Looks like they didn't need it," Sean bitterly remarks.

"No, they didn't, Professor. But nevertheless, it was an attempt to gauge the stress reactions of a random, uncontrolled population in their own environment. If anything, the Soviets believed that defending their homes was a principle the people would cling to and dictate their actions on this night."

"And they were wrong," Sean says sternly.

Sloan turns towards him and emphasizes, "I am not trying to justify the Soviets' actions, Professor. I am simply trying to explain their reasoning behind it. They figured it was a necessary sociological experiment. Unfortunately, it backfired."

"Definition of an understatement, Ms. Sloan," Sean remarks.

A few moments of silence pass between them.

"I'm surprised the Soviets even shared this information with us," Sean says.

"We were too," Sloan confirms. "Despite their misgivings and embarrassment over the episode though, the Soviets felt it was important enough to share with us. Maybe the guilt from it caused them to confide in us, but who really knows."

"And what was the Foundation's reaction?"

"Well, once the Foundation overlooked the disastrous results of it, they too saw it as something that might have been necessary and even beneficial."

"Unbelievable," Sean shakes his head in disbelief.

Sloan continues, "They even respected the Soviets a little more for their willingness to ignore the morality of it all, and that their intentions were on behalf of the greater good.

"A virtue, I've explained," Sloan points out, "the Foundation has always held in high regard."

"What the hell is this world coming to?" Sean asks in exasperation.

"We'll soon find out," Sloan mutters under her breath.

"What impact did this information have on the Foundation?" Sean asks. "Did this . . 'experiment' affect how our government conducted extraterrestrial-"

"Have you ever heard of the Robertson Panel?" Sloan interrupts.

"Um . ."

Without waiting for an answer, she explains, "In January 1953, the CIA, with obvious prodding by the Foundation, convened a board of scientists chaired by Dr. H.P. Robertson. The group met in the Pentagon for five days and supposedly reviewed the most credible UFO cases the U.S. government had in its possession.

"The panel dismissed each and every one of them. Not only that, their recommendations urged the government to go to extreme lengths to stifle any and all UFO reports. They even suggested an anti-UFO education campaign and they believed the mass media could help disseminate the information. They went as far as proposing the use of psychologists familiar with mass psychology to help design the program.

"Their last recommendation was that all UFO enthusiast groups be placed under surveillance, as a precaution of course."

"And the government listened?" Sean asks.

"The recommendations were not tacked on a bulletin board in the lobby of the Capitol, Professor. A few of the highest-ranking military officers, along with several top intelligence officials, reviewed the report and most likely duly noted it."

"I'm guessing," Sean speculates, "the Foundation influenced the panel's recommendations?"

"They didn't really have to," Sloan replies. "They knew from the start these so-called 'credible' reports they submitted to the panel were some of the most outlandish and far-fetched of all the UFO eyewitness accounts in the government's files. They suspected the panel would easily see holes in all of the reports and dismiss their legitimacy. The Foundation accurately predicted that the panel would conclude that these accounts are not only ridiculous, but could be dangerous as well, which is likely what led to the group's final recommendations."

Sighing, Sean asks, "So . . what happened next? I don't know if anything could surprise me now."

"Oh, I might have a few more in store for you, Professor," Sloan indicates. "But actually, things were quiet for a few years, until at least the late 1950s. During what UFO enthusiasts dubbed the 'quiet years,' few sightings were reported throughout the world. What the Foundation began to notice, however, was an increasing number of people who claimed to be abducted by extraterrestrials.

"These stories ranged from the simple, such as the victims describing very benign aliens who asked them several questions and then suddenly released them unharmed, to the more complex, with the victims recounting invasive and oftentimes excruciatingly painful procedures performed upon their bodies.

"Several victims displayed scars where the alleged surgeries occurred, while others claimed the wounds miraculously healed when the aliens touched them. Some asserted that the aliens implanted a tracking device in them in order to monitor them at all times. Others maintained they had been abducted hundreds of times, dating back to when they were small children. Still others alleged the aliens maintained detailed files on each and every person on the planet, and sooner or later, everybody would eventually get a visit, so to speak."

"Shit, how the hell did they know what or even who to believe?" Sean wonders.

"Well, the short answer is that they didn't," Sloan responds. "But at one point, the Foundation had almost as many people working for them on the 'extraterrestrial issue' as they did devoted to the Cold War. These agents scoured the globe tracking down stories and victims, friends and families of victims, and witnesses. They examined alleged abduction sites and purported operation scars, attempting to validate these stories and whether it appeared to be a legitimate extraterrestrial or UFO encounter, or it was simply some nut looking for attention."

"And what did they find?"

"Most of the stories were dismissed because the 'victims' had a history of being mentally unstable, paranoid, delusional, even schizophrenic, while some were clearly just looking for publicity. But . . ."

Sean waits expectantly as Sloan stares into the distance.

"A select few seemed to be telling the truth," she continues. "These people were genuinely fearful and paranoid of something. Most of them were unable to articulate what or who abducted them, but they all possessed radiation burns on their bodies, *extraterrestrial* radiation burns."

"Extraterrestrial?"

"And not only that," Sloan indicates, "but all of the victims were found to have a scar from an incision located here." Sloan points to the back of her head, a few inches below the top.

"The Foundation interviewed all of the victims who were willing to talk to them and several who needed . . coercing," Sloan says diplomatically.

"They discovered that a majority of the victims' recollections were the same: they were alone, oftentimes in an isolated location, walking, driving, riding a bike, whatever.

They recalled a sudden impact, like someone walked up to them and punched them square in the stomach, knocking the wind out of them."

Sean immediately thinks about the way he was tossed from his porch in Tamawaca by a sudden and mysterious force.

"But the way the victims described it," Sloan explains, "it was like the wind was knocked out of their entire bodies. And the next thing they knew, they awoke in the same place they had been taken from, feeling sore, drained, and completely exhausted. Some recalled patches of images here and there, figures hovering over them, bright lights in their eyes, being poked and prodded. Others recalled waking up and feeling a strange sensation on the top of their heads. Several victims even remembered seeing images from childhood they had not thought about in years."

Sloan pauses a moment.

"But the one glaring characteristic all of the victims seemed to share was a sudden, newfound timidity. Obviously, the Foundation initially attributed this to the traumatic experience they had, or at least believed they had. But the victims were subsequently monitored and observed in their work environments and in certain social situations, and the Foundation noticed a clear loss of rebelliousness and resistance to authority. Whatever they were instructed to do, they did. They followed rules to a fault and never questioned otherwise. In short, they were pushovers, easily suggestible, like hypnosis victims, but with no way to snap them out of it. It was as if something was taken from them . . . permanently."

"From their alleged operation?" Sean guesses.

"That was the common perception, Professor," Sloan concurs. "Another interesting characteristic these victims all seemed to share was an aversion to extreme cold and a strange, sudden tolerance of heat."

"Just like Gabriel and Jericho," Sean murmurs.

"Exactly," Sloan affirms.

"What happened to these people?" Sean asks. "I mean, could they, or did they still lead normal lives? Despite their . . problems."

"A minority were able to adapt, yes," Sloan reports. "But most of them became very withdrawn from society, distrustful of others, and downright paranoid. Obviously, with good reason," she adds.

"The Foundation tried to keep tabs on most of them, tracking their progress or lack thereof. A curious thing they found with all of the victims they interviewed: there were no multiple abductions of any of them."

Sloan pauses a moment before stating, "Except one."

SEVEN

The screams are over almost as quickly as they began. The only sounds that remain are Wagner's *Ride of the Valkyries* emanating from Augie's cell phone and several shallow, gasping sounds, as if someone is struggling for breath. There follows a dripping sound, a couple of low grunts, and lastly, several dull thuds that coincide with a strange, slurping sound. Augie does not answer his phone, but finally the ringtone abruptly stops. There is a brief silence in the lab.

At last, General Parker calls out, "Augie? Anderson? Give me a sign."

"Here, sir," Augie answers.

"Okay, sir," Anderson chimes in.

The lab remains pitched in darkness except for the thin rectangle of light filtering in through the window in the door, which hardly provides any illumination beyond mere shadows. Despite this, everyone in the lab can practically *feel* and *sense* another presence in the room.

Striking an authoritative tone, Parker demands, "Identify yourself, we are armed and we will shoot without hesitation."

Suddenly, a figure emerges on the other side of the lab and meekly calls out, "Private Anderson?"

Anderson instantly recognizes the voice. "Dr. Nitchie?"

"Yes," Nitchie confirms, "it's me."

The three men move hesitantly towards Dr. Nitchie.

"Dr. Nitchie?" Parker inquires.

Nitchie turns towards the three men, but his face remains bathed in shadow. They do clearly see, however, in Nitchie's left hand a blood-soaked knife that gleams in the darkness.

"Yes, sir," Nitchie responds.

"What did you-" Parker begins, but he stops when he sees the two figures on the ground, not moving.

"My God," Augie gasps, as he leans down next to the bodies of Bason and Stringer, neither of whom appear to be breathing.

Anderson takes a few hard swallows while even Parker is left speechless. Though the room is nearly engulfed in shadows, their eyes have adjusted enough to the dark to be able to see more clearly.

The bodies of Bason and Stringer have been completely ravaged in the midsections, with their torsos appearing like they have been hollowed out. Intestines, entrails, and blood spill from their wounds. Both bodies rest at awkward angles and their eyes remain open, while their mouths are frozen in a kind of permanent, silent scream. The only sounds now are the *drip-drip-drip* of blood on the floor and the breathing of the four men. The bodies continue to twitch involuntarily, several last spasms of the death throes.

"I, I, I didn't want to kill them," Nitchie stutters, "but, but you were in trouble, and you looked like you needed help . ."

Nitchie sounds like he is addressing all of them, but he looks only at Private Anderson. Anderson, not knowing what else to do, nods his head, as if to reassure Nitchie. Or maybe he is trying to reassure himself.

Parker, Augie, and Anderson all seem to be thinking the same thing – how did this seemingly mild-mannered doctor get the drop on *two armed soldiers* and completely gut both of them in a matter of seconds? And what the hell was that primordial scream heard just prior to the attack?

"Dr. Nitchie," Parker says, visibly shaken, "let me express our gratitude to you for saving our lives, but you understand there will be a military inquiry into these soldiers' deaths?"

Parker continues, hesitantly, "You will have to be detained for some initial questioning."

Nitchie nods his head in understanding and quietly says, "Of course, I'll fully cooperate with any investigation."

Warily eyeing the knife in Nitchie's hand, Parker calmly asks, "Why don't we lay down the knife, Doctor?"

Nitchie looks at the knife in his hand and, as if seeing it for the first time, his face contorts into a mixture of horror and surprise. It appears he has no idea how it arrived in his hand.

"Oh, yes, of course," he says, gently placing the knife on the ground.

His head bowed, Nitchie stands up and there is an awkward pause as the other three men look back and forth between him and the bodies.

Parker is relieved once the knife is on the ground and he appears in control of the situation.

"Good," he says. "Now Augie, grab those MPs we saw near the gate, brief them on the situation, and have them escort Dr. Nitchie to wherever they need to question him. Also, have them get a forensic team down here immediately."

"Yes, sir," Augie complies.

Augie starts to exit and then stops. He looks at Dr. Nitchie and nods, as if in thanks. Augie hits the switch that opens the lab door and he hurries outside to find the MPs.

"Anderson," Parker says, never taking his eyes off of Dr. Nitchie, "pack up everything we need. We're taking a trip. Make sure you have the disc – we'll view it on the way."

"Yes, sir," Anderson replies. "But what about our plane? It might not be-"

"Call the local sheriff and have him arrest anyone within spitting distance of our plane, and see if they can find our pilot. I think we're going to need to commandeer a new plane," Parker notes.

"And maybe find a new pilot, sir," Anderson adds.

"True enough," Parker agrees.

Once again, there is an awkward silence as the three men stand there.

"Well, double-quick, Private," Parker orders.

Anderson nods and starts to exit when he also stops before Dr. Nitchie. Anderson pats the man on the shoulder and says gratefully, "Glad it wasn't us, Doc."

Dr. Nitchie nods appreciatively, pleased to at least receive Anderson's pardon for what he has done.

Nitchie continues to stare a hole into the floor, however, avoiding further eye contact with either of them, and in particular he avoids even glancing at the bodies of Bason and Stringer.

Anderson seems to want to say something more to Dr. Nitchie, but instead he exits the lab without another word.

This leaves only General Parker and the doctor in the lab, a silence enveloping the air, hanging there like a rain cloud about to burst forth. Neither man, however, disturbs the silence, as Nitchie continues to hang his head while General Parker looks between the doctor and the corpses. Besides the obvious fact that there are two dead bodies on the floor, something does not feel right to Parker, something that does not add up.

At last, Parker breaks the silence, which sounds like a gunshot in a library. "Dr. Nitchie," he starts, "if you don't mind me asking . . were you ever in the military? Special Forces or anything like that?"

There is a long pause as Nitchie slowly looks up, his head turned in Parker's direction, but he continues to avoid eye contact with the general.

"Um . . . Green Berets, sir," Nitchie says haltingly.

Then, with a little more confidence, he adds, "Served from '86 to '90, sir."

Parker considers this for a moment, trying to remember names and dates.

"'86 to '90," Parker repeats, carefully eyeing Nitchie. "So you were under . . Bud Franklin's command?"

For the first time, Nitchie looks Parker directly in the eyes. "No, sir," he responds. "Franklin retired before I got there."

Parker cannot be certain because of the shadows in the lab, but he thinks he spotted a brief smirk on Nitchie's face, as if Nitchie knows the general is trying to test him.

"Oh, that's right," Parker says casually.

Nitchie does not offer any other details about his time in the Green Berets, so Parker decides to press him on the issue.

"So who did you serve-"

"It is the Foundation," Nitchie interrupts.

"Excuse me?"

"It is the Foundation, sir," Nitchie repeats. "The Foundation is behind this."

"How do you know that?" Parker asks.

Nitchie smiles and says cryptically, "I know a lot of things about them, a lot of things you can, too."

"What do you mean?"

"Storage locker 5-0-3-5, 1200 Arlington Road, Washington, D.C. Honest Abe has the key in his lap."

"Dr. Nitchie-"

"Sir," Augie interrupts, entering the lab with two MPs in tow.

Damn. Bad timing, Augie, maybe the first time ever, Parker thinks.

Parker continues to eye Nitchie, but the doctor has turned his attention to the newly arrived MPs, and he suddenly looks very anxious. Parker has to remind himself that the doctor did save their lives, no matter how unusual the situation seems or how gruesome the killings were.

Parker looks at the MPs and motions towards the back of the lab, "Bodies are over there. Now I want you to cordon off the area around the lab and keep it as quiet as possible. We don't want the press getting wind of this. When the forensic team arrives, do not escort them through the gate – find another way. And take Dr. Nitchie here into custody."

"Yes, sir," the MPs simultaneously respond.

As the MPs move to take the doctor into custody, Parker addresses them, "Now I want to make it clear Dr. Nitchie is only being held for questioning. The act he committed was in self-defense, believing that we were in mortal danger, which, it seems, we were.

"While his use of force might have been-" Parker pauses, looking over at the bodies- "excessive, it was entirely justified considering the threats the deceased made to us just prior to the . . to their murders," he concludes.

The MPs acknowledge Parker with another round of "Yes, sirs."

"We'll inform the investigators once they arrive on scene," one of them adds.

"Good," Parker responds.

The MPs flank Dr. Nitchie and each man takes one of his arms. One of them steals a glance at the bodies and gasps under his breath, "My God."

This causes the other MP to look, too, and he grimaces when he sees the bodies.

The MPs lead Nitchie, who continues to stare at the floor, from the lab. A moment before he exits, however, Nitchie quickly glances back at Parker, and that smirk Parker thought he saw earlier is present. Parker is about to say something, but he hesitates, and then Nitchie is gone.

Within a few seconds, the lights in the lab flicker on, momentarily blinding Augie and Parker. Both men immediately rub at their eyes, trying to chase away the black spots clouding their vision.

"Who the hell turned those on?" Parker wonders.

"I don't know, sir," Augie replies.

Once their eyes adjust to the light, their attention is instantly drawn to the bodies, which appear so much more stark and unsettling under the harsh lights of the lab. The vividness of the blood is in such sharp contrast to the surrounding sterilized room. The bodies of Bason and Stringer look even more ravaged than the men initially thought. The depth at which Nitchie plunged the knife into their bodies nearly cut them in half. The total and complete ferocity of the act appears in fine detail, in every muscle that has been shredded and in every organ that has been ripped open. The eyes of Bason and Stringer have glazed over, rendering a vacant appearance to their faces, which is counterbalanced by the look of absolute terror their open mouths evoke.

Neither man speaks, awed by the scene before them despite having laid eyes on their share of disturbing acts of human violence throughout the years. Suddenly, they are interrupted by the voice of a man at the entrance of the lab.

"General Theodore Parker?" the man asks, looking at both men.

Parker and Augie turn around to see a man dressed in fatigues standing there, holding a manila envelope in his hand.

"That's me," Parker acknowledges.

The man briskly approaches, salutes, and holds out the envelope. "From Captain Darby, sir," the man says.

Parker accepts the envelope and nods, "Thank you, son, you're dismissed."

The man hesitates a moment, then says, "Pardon, sir, but Captain Darby wanted me to return the item to her after you had a chance to look at it, so . ."

"I understand," Parker nods. "Would you mind waiting outside until we're done in here?" Parker asks, although it sounds more like an order.

"Not at all, sir," the man responds. He salutes and then quickly heads outside.

"Captain Darby?" Augie asks.

Parker opens up the envelope and explains, "My friend in charge of the search-and-rescue for that explosion out on the lake. She must have something for me," he adds.

Inside, there is a note and a small plastic bag. Parker reads the note and then hands it to Augie. The note reads:

> *Teddy-*
> *We found debris from multiple vessels at the scene, but no bodies yet. We noted bullet holes in several pieces of debris, as well as spent casings floating all over the place. We also discovered what appears to be a machine-gun mounting that is fairly intact. It looks like a gun battle on the high seas, but where is everybody? This was also found at the scene and I figured you might be interested. What the hell went on out here? If you've got any ideas, let me know. I'm stumped.*
>
> *-Melissa*

Parker unfurls the plastic bag, reaches his hand in, and pulls out some type of patch. He turns it over and when he realizes what it is, he gasps.

The patch contains a skeleton brandishing a knife, a Special Forces symbol. Impaled on the knife is a peach, which represents the state of Georgia. In the background there is a lightning bolt, signifying speed and striking power. Across the top of the patch read the words, "To the Attack, Never Retreat," representing the motto of the group. At the bottom of the patch is the unit's nickname, "Death Stalkers."

After a few moments studying the patch, Augie asks in a near whisper, "Could it be?"

"It sure as shit could," Parker concedes.

Parker turns the patch over in his hands, the material heavy and damp.

He turns to Augie, "Go get Anderson. We're leaving in five minutes, right after I speak to General Cozey. We're following Moriah, Augie, it all starts with that little prick."

"Yes, sir," Augie says.

As they exit the lab, Augie suddenly remembers that he checked who called him when he was fetching the MPs.

"Oh, sir, I almost forgot," Augie states. "That was Dawson who called me."

"Who?" Parker asks.

"Lieutenant Dawson, sir," Augie reminds him, "our liaison at Evans who skipped off after Fizer."

"Oh, right," Parker recalls. "Did you talk to her?"

"Not yet, sir," Augie responds.

"Well, call her on the way to the airfield and find out what the hell Fizer is up to. And Augie?"

"Sir?"

"Let's put a spring in our step, huh?" Parker says, his eyes twinkling with excitement.

EIGHT

"Just one?" Sean questions.

Sloan nods her head in affirmation, "A man named Sebastian from Sonoma, California, claimed he had been abducted on multiple occasions by these extraterrestrials. He indicated that each time he was abducted, the extraterrestrials revealed more details about their plan for our world.

"Sebastian alleged that during a typical abduction, the extraterrestrials remove those portions of a human brain that regulate rebelliousness and defiance. These 'procedures' function as a kind of precursor to enslaving humanity once the alien race assumes control over the planet. Ultimately, their purpose is to ensure that we can be controlled and manipulated in whatever manner they choose after the invasion starts and we have subsequently been vanquished.

"He asserted that the alien race is planning on using human slaves to dig to the core of the earth. Massive domes would be constructed to trap heat from the earth's core and sunlight from space in these domes, thereby creating an atmosphere very similar to their own home planet."

"Are you kidding me?" Sean asks incredulously.

"It gets better," Sloan informs him. "Sebastian explained that they informed him that their numbers are rapidly increasing on Earth. They are prevalent in all sectors of society, learning about and studying all facets of human behavior, and they are closely monitoring our technological progress in relation to their own and whether this technology is in any way a threat to them."

"Is it?" Sean asks, a touch of both hope and desperation in his voice.

"No," Sloan responds bluntly.

Sean waits to see if she expands on her answer, but she does not.

He poses another question, "Was there any way of proving these extraterrestrials had infiltrated our society? I mean, in mass numbers as Sebastian claimed."

"Glad you asked, Professor," Sloan replies, "because the Foundation asked the same question of Sebastian."

"And?"

"And," Sloan states, "over the next several months Sebastian claimed to have been abducted nearly once a week, sometimes twice, and provided proof of the extraterrestrials' infiltration."

"Which was?"

"Documents," Sloan responds. "Typically classified, highly confidential documents."

"From government files?"

"Yes," Sloan confirms, "but also from defense contractors and weapons manufacturers that conducted business with the government. The documents included contracts, summary memos, new technology assessments, and other confidential information. These were documents only a handful of people could have access to, and yet here is this alleged abductee materializing every few days with stacks of classified documents, purportedly proving to the Foundation the existence of extraterrestrials in the highest echelons of government and the defense industry."

"Hold on a minute, Ms. Sloan," Sean interjects. "If these documents were highly confidential and only a few people had access to them, wouldn't it have been easy for the Foundation to weed out those responsible for providing them?"

"Oh, they did try, Mr. O'Connell," Sloan notes. "Mole hunt after mole hunt was conducted, and if you can believe it, not one EBE was discovered."

"Not one?" Sean asks skeptically.

"Not a single one," Sloan confirms.

"How is that possible?"

"The Foundation was baffled, too," Sloan notes, "at least at the time."

"What do you mean?" Sean asks.

"I'll get back to that," Sloan indicates. "But you surprise me, Professor – a suspicious guy by nature and yet you fail to question the source?"

Sean considers this for a moment and then hesitantly asks, "You mean . . Sebastian?"

Sloan nods, "Here was a man who did not fit the prototype of what the Foundation knew about a typical abductee – that you only get one free ride. Yet this man claimed to be abducted multiple times, nearly a hundred, and appeared out of thin air with these confidential documents every few days, proclaiming that extraterrestrials were infiltrating our society and studying us on a massive scale in preparation for an invasion."

"So . ." Sean begins, trying not to appear completely dense, ". . . if he was being abducted so often, the Foundation should have been shadowing him like a hawk, waiting to see the next time he got nabbed."

"You're on the right track, Professor," Sloan indicates. "They did shadow him like a hawk, but they never witnessed an abduction. He would disappear for days and then reappear with documents in hand, but they were unable to determine where he went during these 'absences' or catch up with his alleged captors."

"Sebastian was full of shit, wasn't he?" Sean asks.

"Yes and no, Professor," Sloan cryptically answers.

It's always a mystery with her, never a straight answer, Sean thinks.

"One day," Sloan continues, "Sebastian was gone for good. He stopped showing up at work, and a couple of his coworkers became concerned and went to his house. All of his belongings were still there, including his car, but the police found no evidence of foul play. The man more or less disappeared off the face of the earth, and after a few weeks everyone forgot about Sebastian – he did not have any real family or friends. The Foundation kept an eye on his house for a few months afterwards in case he reappeared, but he never did.

"Around six months after Sebastian's disappearance, the head of the research team that studied Gabriel and Jericho starts receiving phone calls at his home. Strange calls: somebody whispering on the other end, a weird language being spoken, sinister laughter, frequent hang-ups.

"So, finally," Sloan continues, "the man answers the phone in the middle of the night and just starts tearing into the caller on the other end of the line. After he stops to take a breath, the voice on the other end answers, very calmly and very slowly, 'Hello, Joshua.' It is a voice the man knows and recognizes, and it nearly gives him a heart attack to hear it."

"Joshua?" Sean inquires.

"Joshua Moriah," Sloan clarifies. "The man not only in charge of the research team, but also the head of our mysterious cabal."

"The Foundation?"

Sloan nods.

"Let me guess – Jericho was the caller," Sean states confidently.

"You're getting good, Professor," Sloan remarks.

"What did he say?"

"Well, disregarding any formal pleasantries, Jericho asked Joshua whether it was clear how utterly superior their race is compared to the human race. He boasted about their ability to subjugate humanity to their will while still allowing us to live in a timid, frightened state. He asserted that we would never be able to keep pace with their technological progress. And he confirmed their infiltration of our society and that once the invasion began, there would be nothing we could do to stop it."

"How did Moriah react to all of this?" Sean asks.

"Well, he tried to put on an admirable front," Sloan replies, "claiming that humanity's technology was advancing far more rapidly than Jericho could know, and that we would not simply roll over in a war. Moriah was fully aware of our slim chances against Jericho's race in the event of an invasion, but he was not inclined to acknowledge this. Jericho, however, had been around humans long enough to recognize false bravado on Moriah's part."

"And Jericho called him out on it?"

"He did not have to, Professor," Sloan states somberly. "Moriah was firmly grounded in reality, and Jericho knew Moriah was not one to ignore the stark facts of the situation: Jericho's race is simply superior, in their technology, in their physical and mental capacities, and most importantly, their ability to become any human being on the planet."

"So Moriah caved?" Sean questions.

"In a manner of speaking," Sloan confirms. "Moriah tried placating him with questions about what his group could do to save humanity, and he gave Jericho assurances that he would do whatever is necessary to avoid a war."

"I take it Jericho wasn't buying?" Sean speculates.

"He said the first thing the group could do was release Gabriel, which completely stunned Moriah into silence. Then Jericho proceeded to inform Moriah that he knew about Gabriel's . . termination, about their talks with the Soviets, how the Foundation was scouring the globe searching for abduction victims, and practically everything else the Foundation had been doing that Jericho would seemingly have no way of knowing about."

"He was simply toying with him," Sean remarks.

"To a certain extent, yes," Sloan concedes. "But Jericho also needed the Foundation's help. He made it clear if the Foundation were to assist him and his race, then after the invasion, their lives would be spared and no harm would come to them or their families. Not only that, but they would be the lone human liaisons between the alien race and the human race, living a life of luxury compared with the rest of the planet."

"Smells like bullshit to me," Sean comments.

"Jericho," Sloan continues, "informed Moriah that he would contact him again in a few days and expect an answer. Moriah immediately called an emergency meeting of the group, and they were all assembled within eight hours.

"The meeting was heated, to say the least, with essentially two sides. One side claimed it was un-American and cowardice to relent so easily to these beings, and they needed to fight them regardless if the outcome was already decided. The other side insisted they were not kowtowing to the extraterrestrials, but rather it was a way to stall for time until a better option could be found and then implemented."

"And what if they could not come up with a better option?" Sean asks.

"That's what the other side asked, too," Sloan acknowledges. "In the end, it was decided to help Jericho, for the sake of their families and in case an alternative could not be found in time."

"And I suppose they'd be in Jericho's good graces if they helped him," Sean points out.

"To be fair," Sloan notes, "Moriah never believed anything Jericho had to say, and he did not believe they would be spared if an invasion began."

"But he agreed anyway?"

"Yes," Sloan confirms. "A few days later, Jericho contacted him and Moriah threw the Foundation's lot in with the extraterrestrials."

"Such steely resolve," Sean says sarcastically.

Sloan ignores the comment and continues, "Twenty-four hours later, Moriah received diagrams and schematics for something the Foundation was to build."

"I thought you said these beings are master craftsmen," Sean argues, "that they can build things they have never even seen. Why would-"

"Let me finish, Professor," Sloan snaps. "They provided Moriah blueprints for what could be considered the first modern satellite, along with the rockets to propel them into space. They wanted the Foundation to build six of them to be launched from six different points on Earth, and they would follow what is called a geosynchronous orbit, which means-"

"They move at the same rate as Earth," Sean finishes.

Sloan nods, "That's right, Professor. A satellite in a GEO orbit always stays directly over the same spot on Earth. It is not constantly on the move like a satellite in elliptical or low orbit."

Now she is just showing off, Sean thinks.

"So where were these satellites supposed to be launched from?" Sean asks.

"Most of them were to be launched in what would be called geographically-sensitive areas," Sloan explains. "Places like South Africa, Russia, Columbia, South Korea, Turkey and, of course, one in North America, specifically Nova Scotia.

"Jericho knew that only with the Foundation's influence could these satellites be launched from these specific points on Earth."

"You're talking about political influence, Ms. Sloan, diplomatic influence," Sean states matter-of-factly.

"Exactly. Jericho was fully aware he could not simply construct a secret launching installation in each of these countries, along with the rockets and satellites to boot. It required too much of everything: materials, manpower, funding and yes, political influence. Even a being as clever and resourceful as Jericho could not *steal* all the materials he needed for such an undertaking."

"So," Sean concludes, "Jericho called in his own political favors?"

"Yes," Sloan affirms. "He decided instead to let the Foundation worry about it. They could quell the inevitable skepticism they'd receive from the leaders of these countries, use their diplomatic ties to smooth over the rough water that such a request would no doubt bring. The Foundation provided the manpower, the money, and the materials, and all they were asking in return was salvation from eternal slavery and colonization."

"And all these countries went for it?"

"Well, the Canadians were fairly easy to convince, and so was South Korea, considering we had recently lost over 50,000 troops in a war against their communist neighbors to the north. Columbia, South Africa, and Turkey were paid off, with the Foundation concocting a story about an international science experiment involving weather patterns, but I suppose they could have told them anything after the cash was presented. Money talks, you know."

"And Mother Russia?" Sean asks expectantly.

She sighs, "And the Soviets . . ."

She pauses for a moment and then a slight smirk crosses her face.

"The Soviets were different," Sloan continues. "They did not want money from us. That would have been the American way, the capitalist way of doing business. They wanted to know the real purpose behind this endeavor, the truth of what we were doing.

"When the Foundation showed the Soviets the blueprints they had 'anonymously' received, it quickly became clear what could buy them off. They wanted the technology, the know-how of reaching space, and the adulation from the world over for reaching it before the Americans did."

Sloan allows this last sentence to hang in the air for a moment, waiting for Sean as he slowly processes this veiled tidbit. A sudden realization hits him.

"The American public," Sloan explains, "might have been surprised and alarmed when *Sputnik* was launched on October 4, 1957, by the Soviets, but the Foundation sure as hell wasn't."

"They knew?" Sean asks breathlessly.

"Of course they knew," Sloan confirms. "They knew too when *Sputnik II* was launched a month later with a dog named Laika on board. It was not until nearly three months later, after the Soviets basked in the glow of admiration and the Americans' humiliation was complete, that we were able to launch our own first artificial satellite. It was all part of the deal, Professor."

"So we allowed the Soviets to use the technology we received from Jericho to beat us into space?" Sean questions.

Sloan shrugs indifferently, "At least we didn't cut a deal on the moon."

"And correct me if I'm wrong," Sean begins, "but you're also telling me that the birth of our space program and its catalyst for success was the direct result of the technology we received from . . an alien?"

"You know as well as anyone, Professor, that rewriting history can be a bitch." She pauses a moment before adding, "I would guess Jericho moved the space race ahead by about four or five years, possibly even a decade."

"So what was the purpose of these satellites, Ms. Sloan? What were they to be used for? To spy on us or something?"

"Come on, Professor, I thought you were getting good at this," Sloan teases. "They have the nanoprobes to spy on us.

"With EBEs scattered throughout the world," Sloan explains, "subtly embedding themselves into human society, they needed a way to communicate with one another. These satellites served that exact purpose, acting like a global telephone connecting the EBEs dispersed around the planet. On their end, they possess a device not unlike a cell phone that connects all of them with one another. Except their device never needs to be recharged, it contains a battery power greater than the half-life of uranium, and we are fairly certain they never get harassed to use their upgrade."

"I was waiting for that first joke, Ms. Sloan," Sean smiles.

"Don't hold your breath for the next one, Professor," she responds.

"So they were essentially communication satellites, allowing the EBEs to bounce messages off of them in one part of the world to be relayed to another part of the world."

Sloan nods and explains, "An area a satellite can 'see' is called its footprint. Because a GEO satellite is so high above the atmosphere, typically around 20,000 to 25,000 miles above the surface of the earth, these six footprints cover nearly the entire planet, with the exception of Antarctica and parts of the North Pole, places these creatures would never inhabit anyway."

"I'm curious," Sean notes. "Couldn't these satellites have been detected on radar?"

"Most countries back then," Sloan responds, "did not possess radar equipment sophisticated enough to detect an object thousands of miles up in space. But conceivably the satellites could have been captured on radar in the few minutes after launch, if it were not for one thing," Sloan adds.

"Do tell," Sean states.

"They were cloaked," Sloan says straight-faced.

Sean tilts his head, as if trying to wrap his mind around the science fiction term. He studies Sloan's face for any indication she is not serious.

"Come on, are you shitting me, Ms. Sloan?"

"Not at all, Professor. After the launch facilities and satellites were assembled in each of these countries according to the instructions provided, Jericho ordered the Foundation to abandon the sites. Presumably, Jericho and his cohorts inspected the sites to ensure us stupid humans got it right, and it is assumed they applied some type of cloaking device at that time."

"What kind of clo-"

"That has not been determined or how," Sloan interrupts, anticipating his question. "But we do know the satellites reached the area in space they were supposed to, they are in the exact same location they settled in over a half-century ago, and our tracking antennas on

Earth continue to pick up communications from their transmitters."

"The satellites are still intact?" Sean asks skeptically.

"Yes, as far as we know," Sloan responds. "Do not ask how because that is a question nobody has been able to answer," she adds.

"Aren't they concerned about us eavesdropping on their conversations?"

"No," Sloan answers bluntly. "Allegedly, it is impossible for a human being to decipher, let alone understand their language."

"I'm sure we've tried though, right Ms. Sloan?"

"Yes, we have," Sloan acknowledges, and she leaves it at that for now.

Without missing a beat, Sloan continues, "Not long after Moriah agreed to help Jericho, it was decided Rosenstein and Abraham were needed more than ever. They had been placed on an 'educational sabbatical' after they issued their report, and then followed the so-called quiet years."

"What the hell is an 'educational sabbatical'?" Sean asks.

"Do you know what kind of doctor Rosenstein is?" Sloan replies with her own question.

"Well, I think he is . . . um . . . a Doctor of Philosophy I assumed," Sean says, uncertainty seeping through his voice.

"Actually, Professor, he is a doctor of many sciences and disciplines. Both he and Abraham," she adds.

"Really?"

"Rosenstein and Abraham," Sloan explains, "received a crash course through medical school during their sabbatical. In addition to the traditional curriculum administered there, they also studied branches of science that most of the general public had never even heard of yet.

"They were schooled in biomedicine, studying the ability of organisms to withstand environmental stress, such as space travel; cytology, the microscopic study of individual cells; aerospace travel, focusing specifically on medical problems related to flying and space travel; evolutionary medicine, a perspective much despised at the time, which is the practice of medicine by applying evolutionary theory; and a half-dozen other disciplines including radiation therapy, bacteriology, biochemistry, immunology, microbiology, and toxicology."

"So . . Rosenstein and Abraham return and they essentially know a little something about everything," Sean remarks.

"I did not intend to make it sound like these subjects were quickly breezed over and then it was on to the next one," Sloan indicates. "Both men received an extremely intense and highly stressful introduction to these various disciplines, followed by a more thorough examination of the subject administered by the most accomplished men and women in these fields of study.

"They were relentlessly grilled and tested on this material as if the future of the human race was dependent on these two men, which is exactly how the Foundation saw it," Sloan states.

"Okay, so they were brought back for . . what exactly?" Sean wonders. "To give the group more bad news?"

"First," Sloan says, holding up a finger, "let me tell you about Roswell."

"Area 51?" Sean offers.

Sloan mockingly laughs. "It amazes me, Professor, that people can believe the government does such an awfully poor job of keeping an alien hotbed of activity, such as Roswell and Area 51, under wraps, away from the public eye."

"What do you mean?"

"Did no one think to ask whether it has been the government's intention – and by that I mean the Foundation's intention – to create this myth surrounding Roswell all along?" Sloan asks rhetorically.

She pauses, allowing Sean time to work it out for himself.

"So . . . it was a weather balloon that crashed on the rancher's property that day," Sean says hesitantly, "and the government just kind of . . ran with it."

"It was, in fact," Sloan corrects, "not a weather balloon as the military claimed. This was the cover-up to what they initially reported, which indicated they had recovered a 'flying disc.' It was not a weather balloon, nor was it extraterrestrial in origin.

"It was true the recovered material had not been viewed by many people on Earth, but it was very much man-made. The almost tinfoil-like material was being developed by the military as a kind of shroud for American spy planes and remote-operated spy balloons.

"You see, Professor, radar tracking of objects directs a pulse of microwaves towards an object, and the reflected echo of these waves identifies both the object's direction and distance. The military believed that by neutralizing this echo, by absorbing the microwaves instead of reflecting them, they could send their spy planes and balloons a couple miles above the Kremlin and the Soviets would never know they were there."

"I take it the experiment failed?" Sean speculates.

"Miserably," Sloan confirms. "The material was too lightweight and flimsy to withstand the rigors of being several thousand feet in the air, let alone a couple miles. Even if the material could absorb the microwaves instead of reflecting them, one thing it could not avoid reflecting was the Sun, giving its position away to every passing plane or anyone who might be monitoring the skies from the ground.

"The weather balloon story," Sloan continues, "was concocted primarily to throw off the reds. The U.S. military did not want the Soviets to know they were working on a secret project involving spy planes or spy balloons.

"But then a funny thing began to happen. People around the country, and around the world for that matter, started to believe the American government was secretly housing not only an extraterrestrial craft, but also several *extraterrestrial beings* at this military base in Roswell, New Mexico.

"Where the brass saw a p.r. nightmare, the Foundation saw a golden opportunity. They would feed the beast, leaking rumors themselves to members of the press, fabricating stories of alien experiments and other nonsense occurring at Roswell. You've heard of the Air Force's Project Blue Book files?"

A look of recognition flashes across Sean's face. "Yeah, I've heard of it. The Blue Book recorded all UFO reports that supposedly crossed an Air Force desk."

"Yes, well," Sloan says, "the Foundation decided to give Roswell even more prominence by not mentioning it in the Blue Book files at all. Their omission of it made it all the more suspicious, exactly what they were hoping for."

Sloan continues, "Soon after, and not coincidentally, the government launched a covert program based out of Roswell. Planes and spy balloons of odd dimensions that maneuvered at impossible angles were spotted by on-the-ground witnesses. And to enhance the effect, they attached blinking, multicolored lights to the crafts, not unlike what the Russians did in their disastrous experiment."

"So why the bullshit campaign? A diversion?" Sean asks.

"Exactly," Sloan says. "By this time, the Foundation had captured Gabriel and Jericho and, as I mentioned before, they continued to study and monitor their ship in Lake Michigan because, frankly, they did not know how to transport it. But they needed a place to study the EBEs and they figured Washington D.C. was too high-profile. So they decided on an obscure government installation on the opposite side of the country from Roswell: Spokane, Washington."

Sean's heart leaps with excitement at the mention of Spokane as he thinks about the clue Rosenstein left for him.

"There is a base located there," Sloan explains, "that previously housed nuclear warheads intended for the Soviet Union's eastern flank, had we ever launched them. Instead, the base became the new epicenter of extra-terrestrial study and research, starting with the main attraction: two recently captured EBEs."

"Is this obscure government installation Fairchild Air Force Base?" Sean wonders, recalling the name of the base located directly to the west of Spokane.

"That's right," Sloan confirms. "The decision was made even easier because of the large amount of UFOs reported around the Pacific Northwest during the 1947 blitz. The Foundation figured they might as well bring the EBEs to an area where their comrades seemed prevalent."

"And so that's where Rosenstein and Abraham were brought after their . . .'educational sabbatical'?" Sean asks.

"Yes," Sloan nods. "Rosenstein and Abraham were provided everything they needed in order to form a complete picture of the extraterrestrials that wanted our planet. Every piece of research and every test conducted on the EBEs, their strengths and weaknesses, eyewitness accounts, details and descriptions of their ship, theories regarding the ship's propulsion system, and anything else potentially useful to Rosenstein and Abraham's research.

"They also interviewed abduction victims and conducted experiments on them, concluding that their brain chemistry had been altered in some way by the alien race.

"In addition to the branches of science I already mentioned, the Foundation placed a strong emphasis on teaching Rosenstein and Abraham about neuroscience, which concerns the study of the nervous system, but the main focus is on the biology and physiology of the human brain. The Foundation wanted them to know everything there is to know about the human brain because obviously this is what the EBEs targeted in their abduction victims.

"After conducting their experiments on a number of abduction victims," Sloan explains, "Rosenstein and Abraham speculated that the alien race had altered the amygdala in the human brain, which is widely believed to be responsible for mediating aggression."

"Which might explain why so many abduction victims displayed a sudden fearfulness and apprehensiveness," Sean concludes.

"Right," Sloan nods. "Immediately, they began to develop a serum to counteract this sudden loss of aggressiveness, using rats as their first test subjects. A few results were positive, but the majority were not. In many cases, the serum did more harm than good, with some subjects becoming hyper-aggressive and violent towards each other, while others became so docile they wouldn't even move to get water or food, sitting as still as statues even when the violent ones began to attack them.

"The Foundation grew impatient though, calling for more tests and on more sophisticated animals. They believed, incorrectly as it was, that perhaps the results of these tests were negative because a rat's brain is so primitive compared to a human brain. They wanted tests conducted on animals closer to us on the evolutionary ladder: apes, monkeys, chimpanzees. Rosenstein strongly objected, citing the fact the serum samples had not registered enough positive results on the rats to warrant moving to the next group of test subjects. Needless to say he was overruled, and they began to test various serums on these poor creatures as well.

"The results," Sloan indicates, "were even worse. Similar to the rats, many of the subjects became hyper-aggressive, prone to violent outbursts that lasted anywhere from a few minutes to several hours. Oftentimes the subjects beat each other into bloody pulps, their energy level and stamina never seeming to wane during these long, brutal stretches.

"The tipping point for Rosenstein came when he arrived in the lab one morning to find a five-year-old chimp named Molly, who had been relatively docile after being tested with a certain serum, had literally torn her two younger brothers to pieces. She sat in a pool of blood, cradling her head and shaking back and forth, tears streaming down her face, like she could not have stopped what she did. This was the last straw for Rosenstein. He declared they needed to shut the project down and construct a different strategy.

"At this rather inopportune and illogical time, Abraham suggested that they needed to test the various serums on *human* subjects to at least determine if they were on the right track. He argued that although it caused certain subjects to react violently, it did, in fact, have the desired effect of raising their level of aggressiveness.

"Rosenstein erupted. He laid into Abraham, telling him they were not trying to create a bunch of savage predators, that their ethical responsibilities to their research and to these animals needed a higher ground. He threatened to quit if Abraham ever again mentioned the term 'human subjects.'"

"What was Abraham's reaction?"

"Well, at the time," Sloan responds, "he agreed that they needed to shut down and start over. But that was Abraham simply telling Rosenstein what he wanted to hear.

"The Foundation thought his idea of human subjects was intriguing and they decided this was the next logical step in the project. But they knew they had to be careful, especially with Rosenstein and some of the other research scientists, unsure who might suddenly develop a conscience. They obviously did not want to risk having someone from the project expose the experiments to the public or to the press."

"Sounds like they were just looking out for people's feelings," Sean remarks sarcastically.

"The leadership of the Foundation has always been rather impatient, expecting instant results and specifically ones favorable to them. When that does not happen, their decisions can be rash and ill-conceived. In this case, most members of the project believed that they were shutting it down and starting over from square one.

"In reality, the Foundation began placing subtle ads in local newspapers asking for anyone interested in making a buck to come be a part of 'new, groundbreaking scientific research.' The majority who answered these ads were homeless, penniless drifters or people on the fringes of society. They also coaxed a number of abduction victims into becoming subjects in the new experiments, assuring them that they could finally have their old lives back. The experiments were conducted in a converted barn in an isolated rural county fifty miles outside of town. Abraham oversaw the project while Rosenstein was kept in the dark about the new human element in their research."

Sloan pauses a moment while Sean thinks of asking a question, but hesitates, not certain he wants to know the answer.

"What did the various serums do to the subjects?"

"In many cases," she replies, "it completely ravaged their brains."

Sean shakes his head in disgust.

"If he or she wasn't an abduction victim," Sloan explains, "they only chose subjects who already possessed the same qualities the abductees had exhibited: nervousness, anxiety, paranoia, fear of others, and a general passiveness. With the animals, they actually tried to replicate the extraterrestrials' 'procedure' by removing certain parts of their brains thought to control behavior, and then administering the serum. They didn't crack open any humans just yet, so I applaud them for their restraint in that area."

"Yeah, real humanitarians they are," Sean comments.

"But many of the serums resulted in the same consequences as with the other test subjects," Sloan notes. "Violent, erratic behavior. Eventually, they were forced to construct cages for each subject because they were becoming too dangerous around one another.

"Another disturbing side effect the researchers discovered in some of the subjects was when they were not exhibiting this ultra-aggressive behavior, they sat calmly, vegetative-like, staring straight ahead, seemingly waiting for the next outburst to arrive. They became almost primitive, not showing any signs of rational human thought, but more along the lines of an emotionless predator.

"And then one day, Rosenstein stumbled onto what was happening. He found a stack of documents initialed by Abraham showing steadily increasing dosages, along with observation notes, dated only in the last few weeks, *after* the project was supposedly shut down. He initially believed they simply continued the project using animal subjects, but in the following week, he began making subtle inquiries, snooped around Abraham's files, and discovered, in his mind at least, the unthinkable.

"In the next few days, he confronted the people he suspected were still involved in the project – research assistants and fellow colleagues, some of whom were his close friends. He appealed to their consciences and to their ethics as doctors, and questioned how they could ever be a part of such a project. Most of the people he talked to were contrite, others less so, but nearly all of them were afraid what would happen to their careers if they backed out or blew the whistle on the project."

"Did these people know about the Foundation?" Sean wonders.

"Well, most of them believed some type of government agency was overseeing the project, albeit one that was unregulated and whose powers appeared limitless. They soon realized that this 'agency' could do seemingly whatever it wanted without having to answer to any bureaucratic body or commission. This kind of unbounded power pervaded the entire project and many of these men and women's ethical standards were completely destroyed in the process. But at the same time, they also grew afraid of their superiors and what they were capable of doing . . not only to the test subjects, but to their own families and careers."

"A culture of discipline rooted in fear," Sean notes. "Everyone falls in line based on intimidation and the threat of retribution."

"Yes, to a wide extent," Sloan responds. "The Foundation got wind of Rosenstein's inquiries and they debated what to do about it. Some were of the mind that he needed to be eliminated immediately before any harm could come to the project or to the group itself. Others thought Rosenstein had too many friends involved in the project, and they did not want to run the risk of alienating these people if Rosenstein suddenly disappeared without explanation. Still others thought a staged 'car accident' was the best way to go.

"But in the end it was decided Rosenstein needed to disappear, and that a quick and quiet assassination was the most practical way to solve the problem."

"Just like that, huh?"

"Yes, just like that," Sloan nods. "But Rosenstein did have an ally, one he did not even know of at the time. A person with a conflicted conscience who actually decided to do the right thing, no matter the repercussions. The man's name was Parker . . Franklin Parker."

NINE

Once again, Parker, Augie, and Private Anderson are cutting a path through the stratosphere at hundreds of miles an hour, their commandeered jet providing an adequate substitute for their original plane, which is currently grounded. Their original plane is now being held as evidence in what will likely be attempted murder charges against two men found by the local sheriff's department to be tampering with the hydraulic system. The two men will also face battery and unlawful imprisonment charges for their detainment of the plane's pilot. Due to the fact the attempted murders involved several American soldiers, there appeared to be some jurisdictional wrangling over whether a federal prosecutor should handle the case or the state's attorney of Michigan would be in charge.

Parker, however, did not concern himself with the trivial pissing match. His number one priority was to find a new plane and a pilot who could fly it. After presenting his credentials, namely his fully decorated uniform, Parker was able to coax a company with several corporate jets at the airfield to escort them where they needed to go. At the moment, this is simply westbound, towards Montana, but this could change at any moment. They only hope Augie's friend at the Department of Justice, Waltman, will provide them with more definitive coordinates as soon as possible.

Prior to their departure from Tamawaca, Parker broke the disconcerting news to General Cozey about Bason and Stringer. Suffice it to say, the man did not take the news well. When Parker informed Cozey that Bason and Stringer were plotting to kill him, along with Lieutenant Colonel Hermann and Private Anderson, he nearly toppled over. He appeared simultaneously stunned and nauseous, and he kept repeating that he could not believe it. After several assurances from Parker that it was true, Cozey started profusely apologizing, pledging he had no idea what his subordinates were involved in or the motives behind their actions.

Parker was nearly certain Cozey was being sincere and forthright with him, but despite this, it was Cozey's inability to recognize something was wrong directly under his nose that forced Parker to relieve him of his command. Added to which, Cozey simply did not seem to be in the right state of mind to continue leading the investigation. Parker briefly discussed the decision with the President, who concurred with the general's assessment of the situation.

Ironically, Parker was able to speak with the President of the United States, but Augie was still unable to reach Lieutenant Dawson. He had called several times on the way to the airfield, but each time the call went instantly to the lieutenant's voicemail, suggesting that the phone had been turned off or the battery had died.

After boarding the jet, Anderson cued up Rushmore's disc on a laptop he bogarted from the command center in Tamawaca. Now, after viewing the disc twice in its entirety, the three of them sit in stunned silence, helicopters and bombs replaying over and over in their heads. The disc proved that their collective suspicion of Colonel Fizer was fully justified. What the colonel presented to Parker and Augie at Evans was a fabrication, a reconstruction that never happened.

"I'm going to fucking kill him," Parker hisses through clenched teeth.

"I'm happy to help, sir," Augie volunteers.

"So what exactly does this mean?" Anderson asks hesitantly. "I know it shows Fizer is full of shit, which we kind of already knew, but what exactly does it *prove*?"

Parker and Augie glance at one another, recognizing that the private has a valid point.

What does it prove?

"Well," Augie begins, "for one thing, it does *disprove* the story of a 'terrorist attack' that has been disseminated to the entire world. And this disc is obviously one of the primary pieces in a puzzle that has all the makings of a conspiracy of the highest order."

The men say nothing for a few moments, lost in their own unanswered questions. *Where did the choppers come from? Why did they bomb what appeared to be an empty beach? Where are the people of Tamawaca? Are they still alive somewhere?*

The silence is punctuated by Augie's cell phone playing Wagner's *Ride of the Valkyries*. Annoyed at first, he sees the caller ID and quickly answers it.

"Dawson," he says excitedly.

"Where is she?" Parker immediately asks.

"Why are you whispering, Lieutenant?" Augie asks.

After a moment, Augie says gently but forcefully, "Alright, Dawson, calm down and just start from the beginning."

"Did she catch up to Fizer?" Parker loudly demands, clearly annoyed he is not hearing the answers directly. "Where are they?"

Augie gets up from his seat and moves a few feet away to avoid the general's barrage of questions, but also to clearly hear Dawson. Parker and Anderson stare at Augie, anxious for any news. Augie maintains a poker face, but then he utters, "Jesus Christ, that's unbelievable," which nearly pushes Parker over the edge.

"What is?" Parker presses.

After a few moments, Augie instructs her to keep him informed, be careful, and to let him know when they "touch down."

"Wait, let me talk to her," Parker implores.

Augie says "good luck" and disconnects.

He looks at Parker apologetically, "Sorry, sir, she did not have a lot of time to chitchat."

Augie relates Dawson's story of following the fleeing Colonel Fizer from Evans to the hidden runway in the woods, where she became an unexpected and unknown passenger on Fizer's ride, a twin-engine Cessna. He notes that Dawson believes they are also heading west, same as Moriah, and she informed Augie they stopped and picked up a couple of passengers.

"Ready for this?" Augie asks, keeping them both in tortuous suspense.

"Out with it, Hermann," Parker demands.

"Our missing staff sergeant, Jon Kaley, and our A.W.O.L. sergeant major, Victor Ruethorn," Augie says excitedly, looking directly at General Parker.

"Sergeant Kaley is okay?" Anderson asks.

Augie nods and continues staring at Parker, waiting for the old man to connect the dots.

"Holy shit, Augie, the patch," Parker says breathlessly. "No way that's a coincidence."

"Not a chance," Augie agrees.

"What patch?" Anderson asks.

"She found Ruethorn," Augie says incredulously.

"Stumbled onto him is more like it," Parker corrects him, "but yeah, she found him."

"Who?" Anderson asks.

"And Sergeant Kaley?" Parker inquires. "He's alright?"

"Yeah," Augie responds. "Well, I guess Ruethorn worked him over pretty good, but he's breathing and apparently trying to spring the cuffs they've got him in."

"Will someone tell me what the hell is going on?" Anderson pleads, causing both Parker and Augie to fall silent and immediately stare at him.

When he realizes the tone and choice of words he used to address two superior officers, his face reddens and he stammers, "Uh . . I mean . . I didn't mean-"

Parker smirks and concedes, "Sorry, Private, we are keeping you out of the loop a little bit, aren't we?"

Anderson shrugs and meekly responds, "Just a bit, sir, no big deal."

"Well, Private, suffice it to say," Parker states, "this is classified information, and my ass will be in a sling if anyone discovers that I disclosed this information to you."

"Understood, sir," Anderson replies, clearly thrilled at being privy to some juicy information.

Parker explains, "Sergeant Major Victor Ruethorn commands a Special Forces squad based out of Fort McPherson, Georgia, or at least used to. About a month and a half ago, the squad was preparing to conduct a set of training exercises down in Florida, but they never showed up. The squad reports to the United States Army Special Operations Command, or SOCOM, but neither they nor anyone else in the chain of command has heard from the group since. They are all considered A.W.O.L. and extremely dangerous."

"A rogue Special Forces squad?" Anderson utters. "Unbelievable."

"A patch worn by members of the squad was found near the wreckage of that explosion out on Lake Michigan," Augie notes.

"The group is one of the best in the business," Parker states, "but there's always been . . well, how do I put this? A shroud of mystery surrounding the group, I guess. Rumor has it that some of their missions are so secret, not even SOCOM knows the full details."

"There's also been questions regarding their handling of prisoners and their propensity for disregarding or ignoring civilian casualties," Augie indicates.

"They're a bunch of cowboys," Parker states succinctly, "plain and simple, with Ruethorn as the ranch boss. They follow their own rules, and there have even been whispers about who they actually report to."

"What do you mean, sir?" Anderson asks.

"Yeah, actually, sir," Augie pipes in, "I'm curious about that, too."

Parker sighs heavily, seemingly weighing something in his mind. He looks at both Anderson and Augie slowly and explains, "Augie, what I mentioned at Eisley's house, about the Moriahs and the elder being too much of a patriot . ."

"Yes, sir?"

"Well," Parker begins, "I need to tell a story, some of which is not rooted in indisputable fact, but is simply based on speculation and informed guesses. The story is about a group, an organization that has allegedly been in existence for nearly a century, possibly even longer.

"What may be said with any certainty is that the group is comprised of Americans," he continues, "Americans whose idea of patriotism goes beyond simply serving your country in times of war. This is serving your country for an entire lifetime, without question and without reservations, and it is considered one of the highest honors to do so. It is a secret society, not unlike the Freemasons or the Knights Templar, but the boundaries of the group's power are seemingly limitless."

Parker pauses a moment and continues, "The organization supposedly consists of some of the highest-ranking members of the military and intelligence communities, as well as defense contractors, cabinet members, and others in positions of power within the government and outside of it. If even half the rumors are true, then this group has secretly been manipulating our nation's domestic and international affairs for the better part of the last century."

Augie and Anderson sit in awed silence, completely stunned at the implications of Parker's words.

After a few moments, Augie says quietly, "I always heard rumors around Washington about a covert group, but never thought . . . well, I guess I didn't want to believe something like that could be true."

Augie looks deeply at the general, puzzled at first, and then he silently pleads for the general to discredit the rumors, to tell them it is all a bunch of horseshit.

Parker, however, has no reassurances for his protégé.

"The organization is known as the 'Foundation,' and this story begins a long time ago. But for me, it begins with my father, one of the bravest men I barely even knew."

Parker begins his story and all Anderson and Augie can do is listen, enraptured by the tale that unfolds before them.

TEN

Suddenly, Sloan veers off the highway and onto an exit ramp that is not even labeled or marked.

"Where are we going?" Sean asks, looking around in alarm at the darkness of the surrounding trees and not much else.

"You'll see when we get there," Sloan cryptically responds, a twinkle in her eyes Sean fails to notice.

"Have you heard the name before, Professor?" Sloan questions.

Sean continues to peer anxiously out his window, ignoring Sloan for the moment.

"Mr. O'Connell? You still with me?"

"Yeah," Sean nods, "I'd just like to know where you're taking me."

"It's a shortcut," she replies, turning onto another unmarked road off the exit ramp.

She turns her head and asks again, "Ever heard of him?"

"Who?" Sean asks distractedly.

"Franklin Parker," she says, exasperated. "His son is General Teddy Parker, a special advisor to the President and in charge of the investigation into the Tamawaca attack."

"No, I've never heard of Franklin Parker," Sean acknowledges, "but yes, I know who General Parker is. So what happened? This Franklin Parker helped out Rosenstein somehow?"

"'Helped out' is a bit of an understatement, Professor," Sloan indicates. "Frank Parker was a research scientist who worked closely on the serum project with Rosenstein and Abraham. He was a very intelligent man who enjoyed the work he was doing, but he, too, was starting to have moral and ethical objections with the direction of the project, although he never voiced them openly. He worked with Abraham behind Rosenstein's back after the new 'human' element was introduced in their research, but he soon felt the pull of a nagging conscience when he realized Abraham was ultimately doing more harm than good.

"Soon after, Frank Parker began compiling documents concerning intricate details of the project and their research. He was periodically asked by a friend who was part of the inner circle of the Foundation to provide certain members of the group a status update on their progress, or lack thereof, and Parker secretly recorded these discussions, as well as conversations with Abraham concerning the project. He even smuggled a novelty spy camera he bought at some cheap dime store into the 'Barn,' as it was known, and took hundreds upon hundreds of pictures. Damning evidence to the group, particularly of human 'subjects' locked in cages, if it were to come to light.

"Then Rosenstein discovered what was going on and one of the people he confronted was Frank Parker, who told him in so many words he was not interested in helping him."

"Why wouldn't he help him?" Sean asks, clearly surprised.

"You have to understand," Sloan explains, "Rosenstein was viewed as a maverick, a troublemaker, and people on the project soon realized the danger he faced with his talk of exposing the group and their research. No one wanted any part of that, and even those who agreed with Rosenstein, like Frank Parker, believed that if they colluded with Rosenstein as a whistleblower, their careers would be ruined or some harm would come to their families.

"Essentially, Rosenstein was on his own. Then, not long after Rosenstein's inquiries, Parker's friend in the Foundation informed him that several important documents were discovered missing, the same documents Parker himself had stolen, and Rosenstein was considered the prime suspect. Parker's friend also hinted that soon Rosenstein would no longer be a problem.

"The night Rosenstein was supposed to be murdered, Frank Parker decided he could not let it happen. Maybe he was ashamed for not initially helping Rosenstein, or maybe his conscience told him he owed it to those poor test subjects to make amends for his sins. Whatever the reason, Parker resolved that he could not allow any harm to come to Rosenstein."

Sloan sharply banks left onto a gravely road that snakes through the trees, and she slows the car to a crawl, the headlights illuminating little but darkness ahead.

She continues, "Parker arrived at Rosenstein's home a few hours before the assassination was to occur and informed him he was in danger. He told him he had a plan and asked Rosenstein to come with him. Rosenstein was, of course, skeptical at first given Parker's earlier reaction to his appeal for help, thinking it might be a trap. But Rosenstein trusted his instincts and believed the sincerity in Parker's voice and decided to go with him. He felt the alternative of waiting around to be killed was not much better anyway.

"Parker and Rosenstein immediately left the country on a chartered plane, with three huge briefcases in tow. They subsequently flew to several cities around the world: first London, then Paris, followed by Rome, Bangkok, Hong Kong, Bogotá and lastly, Mexico City.

"After each stop, the briefcases became a little lighter. Prior to departing the U.S., Parker had identified the banks in each city with the strongest reputation for security and privacy, institutions that were virtually impenetrable, both structurally and from a legal standpoint, in case the Foundation tried to go down that route.

"Parker placed a portion of the evidence he gathered on the project into the banks' safe-deposit boxes and burned all documentation related to the 'deposit.' One of Parker's provisions with respect to the contents is that if anything were to happen to Rosenstein, such as an untimely death, these documents and recordings would be sent to every major news organization around the world, placing the group in a very dangerous and uncomfortable position."

"Rosenstein must have thought he was fucking nuts," Sean remarks in disbelief.

"Rosenstein would later tell me," Sloan indicates, "that he thought Parker considered turning over his evidence anonymously to the authorities while still continuing to work for the group, in order to avoid suspicion, but no one really knew what Parker was thinking."

The car pulls into a clearing and a faint light suddenly appears ahead. Sean notices they are at the end of a long, winding driveway. Instantly, the familiar odors of a farm hit Sean directly in the face: the overpowering aroma of manure and compost, mixed with the scent of freshly plowed land. At the top of the driveway, he spots a farmhouse with a light on by the door and a front window illuminated by the glow of a television. A large silo sits behind the farmhouse and to the right of the house, he sees a sty occupied by several lounging pigs.

Sloan steers the car up the driveway, continuing past the farmhouse on the right until she abruptly stops the car, the headlights revealing an old, decrepit barn two hundred feet behind the house. The air looks heavy outside the car windows, leaden, packed with humidity.

Sloan gives the car a little gas and they slowly creep along until she stops directly outside the barn. She beeps the horn and almost immediately the doors to the barn are flung outward, revealing several stalls occupied by cows aimlessly lying there, not paying much mind to the newly arrived guests. A couple of them poke their heads over the stall doors for a brief peek, but they are more or less uninterested after a few moments.

Sean is not paying much attention to them either as he focuses on a large, covered object sitting idle in the middle of the barn. He audibly groans when he notices the unmistakable outline of helicopter blades at the top of the canopy.

He catches a shadow out of the corner of his eye as a figure wearing a slicker approaches the car, the hood covering the person's entire face. Sean did not even notice that it is drizzling outside when he suddenly becomes aware of something odd.

"Sean . . . "

Sean slowly turns his head towards Sloan and notices that for the first time, she is addressing him by his first name. And apparently, she has been doing it for some time.

"Sean . . . "

"Huh?"

She nods towards the figure, "It's time for him to take it from here."

Sean looks back as the approaching figure lowers the hood.

Sean gasps, "Rosenstein!"

ELEVEN

Sean is practically in a state of shock after finally coming face-to-face with Rosenstein, unable to fully comprehend that it is actually him. Maybe because Sean has learned so much about Rosenstein in the previous twenty-four hours that he has suddenly been cast in a different light. His collaborative treatise with Abraham and Sloan's own revelations have provided Sean a new perspective on the man. Perhaps Sean is merely content that Rosenstein is alive and well, as he expected Sloan to conclude her narrative with the news that Rosenstein had disappeared or he had gone into hiding indefinitely. Or maybe it is simply because Rosenstein's physical appearance has changed so dramatically from the last time Sean saw him.

The man's paunchiness is no longer evident, as he appears to have lost nearly sixty or seventy pounds from his frame. He is not exactly gaunt, but he is not suddenly toned either. His body and complexion have acquired a borderline unhealthy appearance, with the jowls of his face sinking beyond anything Sean has ever seen. His eyes remain kind and compassionate, but bloodshot, and his hair is a rumpled and greasy tangle of graying curls. In short, he looks like he has not slept in a few weeks. Knowing Rosenstein, this is probably only a slight exaggeration.

The helicopter flies low, skirting the treetops as a slight drizzle persists, but it does not seem to affect Sloan's visibility as she pilots the chopper, another hidden talent. They had abruptly taken off, Rosenstein not bothering to offer an explanation or to exchange even the most rudimentary pleasantries beyond a hearty handshake. Sloan sits up front in the pilot's seat while Rosenstein and Sean occupy the back seats.

There are so many questions Sean wants to ask Rosenstein, he does not even know where to start. Unfortunately, Rosenstein makes it abundantly clear there is no time to answer Sean's questions, but rather he must complete Sloan's narrative before they arrive at their destination, which seems to be known to everybody but Sean.

"Ah, yes, Frank Parker," Rosenstein nods solemnly, after having asked Sloan how much of the story she had completed.

"Parker got us out of the country," Rosenstein explains, "and took me practically around the world in a dizzying blur of cities and people. To be honest, I thought I was never coming back, but this man . ."

Sean thinks Rosenstein's voice catches for a moment, but he continues, "Our final stop was Mexico City. By that time, the Foundation found out what was going on and they seemed to be only a couple of cities behind us, but they were closing in fast. As I'm sure Ms. Sloan explained to you, Sean, the amount of contacts, informers, and associates the group maintains throughout the world is incalculable."

Sean nods, "Yeah, she mentioned it."

"So Parker rented a small fishing boat around dusk and we drove out to the middle of the sea. As we went further and further out, I kept asking him what the hell we were doing and where we were going, but he would not answer me. He just had this blank stare on his face."

"Did you think he might try to . . "

"Kill me?" Rosenstein finishes Sean's sentence. "Of course, the thought passed through my head once or twice, but I figured if he wanted me dead, he would have done it sooner.

"So," Rosenstein continues, "the sun had just set and almost immediately he cuts the engine. We're in the middle of nowhere and there is no other boat in sight, let alone another human being. I look around and when I look back at him-" Rosenstein points his index finger and raises his thumb – "he's holding a gun.

"I'm scared shitless at this point, thinking maybe I was wrong about him not having any intention to kill me. But he had this weird look on his face, peaceful even, which was amazing considering the circumstances. He told me the Foundation would eventually determine that I didn't steal the documents in his briefcases, and when they realize who did, they will never stop looking for him, *ever.* He needed the group to keep searching for him, to believe he is alive and well somewhere and could one day appear and expose the group and all his evidence.

"So he said that because he is a Christian man, he could not do it himself. He . . uh . . "

This time, Sean hears a definite hitch in Rosenstein's voice. Sean is certain that, like his own horrific day in the jungle so many years ago, it is a memory that continues to haunt the man each and every day of his life.

Rosenstein exhales the weight of the world and Sean can clearly see how painful it is for him to recollect that day.

" . . I told him I could not do it. He grabbed my hand, placed the gun in it, and attached several weights to his ankles. He looked me in the eye and said that I would be disrespecting him if I did not do it, because he had guaranteed my own and his family's safety forever.

"He told me that he had made certain the group was aware of the rules in a letter he left behind. If anything unnatural or suspicious happened to me or to Parker's family, the evidence would be made public, and he would come forward as a corroborating witness and expose everything he knew about the Foundation to the world. Obviously, this latter part was an empty threat. But even if they managed to obtain the evidence from each of the banks, something he did not put past them, as long as they feared he was still alive, they knew they were at risk and that he might be in possession of other damning evidence against them."

Rosenstein pauses, a distant look on his face, as if he is peering into the past, back to that day. Sean glances at Sloan, who remains stone-faced, emotionless.

"I put two bullets in his head and dumped him over the side of the boat," Rosenstein says quietly. "I have never forgiven myself for it, nor will I ever. I am in eternal debt to the man and not a day goes by that I do not say thank you to him, wherever he is."

The helicopter falls silent, or at least as silent as a helicopter can become with the muffled thumping of the blades. Sean stares at Rosenstein, the man's face a mix of sorrow and pain, and the only thing Sean can think to do is place a reassuring hand on his shoulder. Rosenstein slowly looks at him and nods his appreciation. He takes Sean's hand in both of his and gives it a brief pat before letting go.

"Al," Sean wonders, "why didn't Parker just blow the group out of the water in the first place? He could have exposed his evidence so that if anything suspicious did happen to him, everyone would know who the prime suspects were."

"I'm sure he thought about that," Rosenstein acknowledges, "but he was so afraid the group might someday retaliate against his family – his wife and son – for what he had done, he thought they would be safer if the evidence remained hidden. I think he reasoned that the group would not risk harming his family to determine what evidence he had on them."

"And he died to ensure their safety," Sean says in awe.

Rosenstein nods solemnly and states, "In his mind, it was the only way to truly keep them safe forever. If he was alive, the Foundation could use his family against him – they could torture them until he turned over the evidence. But by *pretending* he was alive, only in hiding, he knew the group would search to the ends of the earth for him. He bravely and selflessly, however, removed himself from the equation, forcing the group into a dead end with nowhere to turn."

"Except to you," Sean points out.

Rosenstein nods knowingly and continues, "I arrived back in the States several hours later and I was immediately detained by federal agents. I was taken to an isolated hangar and questioned continuously for two days by several Foundation men. They asked the same questions over and over again: the whereabouts of Parker, the documents and evidence he was carrying, the significance of the cities we visited and what we had been doing there.

"When I did not answer them," Rosenstein indicates, "they started threatening me. They said my life wasn't worth shit and nobody would miss me if I disappeared. They claimed they would find Parker soon enough and get their answers, and then we'd both receive a bullet to the head. It was crazy, desperate ravings, and I knew they were scared.

"What really got their balls in a bunch was that they did not know how damaging the evidence Parker had on them was. They might have had a general idea of what evidence he had, but they did not know the extent of it, and that was what drove them batshit loony. They did not have a 'playbook' for this situation because frankly, they never had one like it before. They also knew they could not physically harm me, so all of their threats were just bluster, and they knew that I knew that.

"Finally, they decided to turn me loose. And right before I left, they said something I will never forget, never in a million years. I knew I'd always remember it because it gave me the chills to hear it, and it was the first time since they started questioning me that they sounded smug and insolent, like they still had something on me.

"And, as it turns out," he adds dreadfully, "they did."

There is a long pause before Sean finally asks, "What did they say?"

There is a flash of fire in Rosenstein's eyes as he stares at Sean. "They said, 'Better check on your Peaches when you get home.'"

"Peaches?" Sean repeats, a blank look on his face.

"I looked at them, saw the arrogant smirks on their faces, and my heart almost jumped out of my chest. Peaches was a girl I'd met in Spokane, the prettiest girl in town, and the future Mrs. Rosenstein."

"Oh my God . . ."

"I called her Peaches," Rosenstein explains, "because I used to say her hair smelled like peaches all the time. It was something nobody else could have known besides us. So when they said my pet name for her, I flipped out.

"I raced back to Spokane, to an apartment she had off-campus – she was a graduate student of Gonzaga at the time. Her neighbors told me they had not seen her for a few days, but the last time they did see her, she had been worried sick because she couldn't find me anywhere.

"I waited in her apartment all day and night for her to come home. I drifted off to sleep and then, in the middle of the night, I woke up to this loud bang at the front door. I opened it to find . . ."

Rosenstein's voice again catches for a moment, but he continues, ". . . my love crumpled in a heap at the door. She was barely conscious and could not even speak. She was extremely dehydrated and her pulse was weak."

Sean feels his own blood beginning to boil, as over the years he had become as close with Mrs. Rosenstein as he had with her husband. She was the sweetest woman in the world and he had always felt an instant bond with her from the moment they met.

"I rushed her to the hospital, but the doctors could not figure out what was wrong with her. She slipped in and out of consciousness for several days, all the while I'm asking her what happened and where she had been. She kept muttering that she couldn't remember. This one time though, right before she drifted off again, she thought she recalled hearing a voice she knew. And I pressed her for whose voice it was . . ."

Rosenstein stares into the distance, a fire flashing in his eyes again as his voice rises in anger, ". . . and she whispered, 'Jonas,' before she fell unconscious again."

"The son-of-a-bitch," Sean hisses.

"My sentiments, too," Rosenstein nods. "I stormed back to where we worked to kill the bastard and found the place locked up. It was completely deserted with not a soul to be found anywhere. The barn where their 'test subjects' were held was destroyed, torched to the ground. They had closed up shop and moved on.

"The message was loud and clear: I may be untouchable, but my Peaches is fair game if I ever think about opening my mouth. You see, Parker did not know I had been dating her, and the stipulations for the release of his evidence only included anything unnatural happening to *me*, not to Pattie, and the Foundation knew that and used it to their advantage."

Rosenstein lets out a sigh of exhaustion and resignation.

"A few days later," he continues, "Pattie woke up, this time for good, and said she had to tell me something."

A crooked smile crosses Rosenstein's face, bittersweet in a way, and he states, "She told me she was several months pregnant, and she wanted to know if the baby was okay."

He shrugs, tears welling up in his eyes, "Well . . I didn't know what to tell her, the doctor hadn't said anything to me. Back in those days, it was a very delicate matter when a woman had a child out of wedlock, and the doctor was apparently trying to be discreet. I assumed he didn't tell me because he did not know if Pattie even knew.

"But she did," Rosenstein adds, practically beaming, "she knew."

"And the baby?" Sean asks tentatively.

"Was fine," Rosenstein replies, smiling.

Suddenly, Rosenstein's voice turns deadly serious, "But when we found out the baby was okay, I became terrified. I was afraid the Foundation would find out, if they didn't know already, and take the baby away or do God knows what else to it.

"So barely a day after Pattie woke up, I told her that she had to trust me and we fled from the hospital in the middle of the night. I told her everything I knew about the Foundation and everything I thought they were capable of. At first, she had trouble believing that a lone organization could wield so much power and so much influence, especially one so secretive."

He pauses, and then painfully continues, "I told her about Frank Parker and what I had done, and how I did not think I could ever live with myself for doing it. I lost it . . . I completely broke down. Everything just came to a head: the constant paranoia, the anxiety, the nervousness now of becoming a father, the crippling guilt from killing a man. I literally thought I was going to crumble into a million pieces right then and there. And then . .”

Rosenstein wryly smiles, a twinkle in his eye, and he continues, ". . Peaches picked me up. She said I did what I had to do to survive, and now we would do what *we* needed to do to survive. She brought me back from the depths of hell, I'll tell you.”

He pauses and says the next words very slowly, the pride and awe clearly evident in his voice, "She-was-a-fucking-rock.”

He continues, "For the next several months, we moved from town to town, city to city, got married along the way, and talked about the baby – what would we do, what could we do really. We were so scared what the Foundation might do that we . . .”

His voice wavers and trails off.

Sean's heart is thumping in his chest as he imagines himself in Rosenstein's shoes, trying to decide what *he* would do in such a situation.

Finding a reservoir of resolve, Rosenstein continues, "After many arguments and even more tears, we decided we needed to give the child up, for safety's sake. We simply could not live with the idea that every time the kid went to school, or every time he went out with friends, we might never see him again. The thought that he might be snatched from us at any moment by this ruthless and vengeful organization was too much for us to bear. We could not live like that, and no child should have to go through life under a cloud of imminent danger.

"We were absolutely heartbroken,” Rosenstein bemoans.

Sean stares at the man before him and his own heart flutters, breaking in half for his mentor and his friend.

Sean glances at Sloan, who did not appear to be listening to their conversation, but apparently she is judging by the saddened look on her face and a tear in her eye she is unwilling to let go.

The only sound once again is the rhythmic beating of the helicopter blades against the night sky. Sean returns his gaze to Rosenstein, who seems doubled over in pain. Sean doubts he can even continue, but Rosenstein raises his head and does just that.

"I delivered the baby myself – we could not risk having the child at a hospital where there would be all sorts of records, a birth certificate. I had one forged instead."

Grimacing, he explains, "It was an extremely painful delivery for Pattie, who lost a ton of blood. There was no one there with us, and I thought I might lose her. But . . she pulled through, as she always did."

"You mentioned a 'he' earlier," Sean notes. "The child was a boy?"

"Yes," Rosenstein confirms, beaming like a proud father for a moment before again lowering his head, his body hunched over as if he has been sucker-punched.

Sean places his hand on Rosenstein's shoulder to comfort him, "Al? You okay?"

Rosenstein slowly raises his head and now his eyes are welling with tears.

"Al?" Sean repeats. He has never seen Rosenstein so utterly distraught.

Rosenstein wipes his face. "You have to know, Sean, we did not have any other options. *We did not think we had any other choice*," he says forcefully.

Sean nods, "Okay, Al, I understand, you had no other choice. It was a . ."

Sean searches for the right words, but feels silly when he finally spits them out.

" . . terrible situation for you both. There wasn't much you could have done," he adds.

Rosenstein shakes his head back and forth and furiously wrings his hands.

He speaks in little more than a whisper, "You don't understand, kid. It was not a coincidence you ran into me at school or that we became so close. I've been following you since the beginning, during your childhood, through the military years . . I know what happened in that jungle more than you could ever imagine."

Rosenstein, his eyes puffy and red, finally looks Sean directly in the eyes, seemingly pleading for Sean to understand. And suddenly, Sean does.

There are moments in life, rare moments to be sure, but moments nonetheless where certain realizations strike unexpectedly and with brute force. They may arrive in the form of Cupid's arrow, the self-awareness of one's own mortality, or the panic that might ensue when first learning that you are about to become a parent. In Sean's case, however, his is a realization that everything he thinks he knows about his life and where he comes from is suddenly not true. Elements of his past he steadfastly believed in and things he rightfully assumed about himself have instantly been turned on their head. In the blink of an eye, he feels his life has become a lie, an untruth, a fabrication.

What else in my life is not mere coincidence? What other secrets are lurking below the surface?

He feels nauseous and his head is swimming. Millions of thoughts and questions seem to race across his brain in a millisecond, and for a moment he thinks he might simply spontaneously combust and disappear in a plume of smoke. But he does not.

Rosenstein's voice, calm and gentle as can be, is roping him back in. The man is only stating what *is*, a truth, a fact that will alter his life forever and everything he knows or seems to know in it. It is a simple statement, as plain and straightforward as can be, but at the same time bringing with it so much confusion and complexity. Rosenstein delivers it with a mix of both pride and shame.

"Sean . . ."

He knows what Rosenstein's next words are, but this fact does not make it any easier for him to hear them.

". . . I'm your father."

TWELVE

General Parker began his story by telling Augie and Anderson about a group, a clandestine group that has managed to guard its secrecy so effectively, no one outside the organization has any idea when the group formed, their structure, the leadership hierarchy, how many members the group contains, how much power the group possesses, or to what extent their influence stretches around the globe. There does not appear to be, nor has an enterprising journalist unearthed, any former or disillusioned members of the mysterious cabal.

While it has been rumored that the group is connected with everything from the JFK assassination to the Iran-Contra affair, from the Gulf of Tonkin incident to the assassination of Archduke Ferdinand and his wife that triggered the start of World War I, no one knows with any certainty which historical events the group has played a role in or what future endeavors they may be planning.

What the general does know about the group is what he has observed in the powerful halls of Washington and from an anonymous letter reduced to nothing more than ash a long time ago.

Initially, Parker did not believe in the idea of a covert group operating behind the curtain pulling the levers of power at their own will and discretion, manipulating events with a national and sometimes global impact. For one to believe in a group that inconspicuously steered this country in any direction it desired was to believe democracy was not flourishing in the nation that championed its values the most. It was to believe in an oligarchy and a secret one at that. It was to believe that *by the people, for the people*, and *of the people* was a farce, a sham, all-encompassing words penned by the Founding Fathers that no longer contained any meaning save their fancy definition for "democracy." It was to believe that men and women had died under false pretenses, for an ideology they were willing to commit the ultimate sacrifice for in a reality that did not support it. This was something Parker could not stomach, let alone start to believe.

However, he began to notice strange things in Washington that did not have an explicable meaning. Presidents, senators, cabinet members, military officers, intelligence directors – he had seen it with all of them. Sudden reversals of policy and opinion that virtually happened overnight, as if that individual went to sleep one night and woke up the following morning a completely different person. People that Parker sided with on an issue had mysterious changes of heart and suddenly became advocates for the opposing side. At first, he chalked it up to a simple lack of resolve on their part or for those who could be bought for the right price, bribery. These explanations, however, failed to justify in Parker's mind such a radical and dramatic departure from a strongly held belief to swiftly migrating to the other side of the fence.

While backtracking in politics occurs on a daily basis and is nothing new, coinciding with this behavior were the rumors Parker heard of a group whose influence and power behind the scenes in Washington was the deciding force in determining the course of the nation. The group directed policy decisions and pieces of legislation, defense spending, which contractors conducted business with the government, where American interests lie overseas, and they even allegedly had a hand in several landmark Supreme Court rulings. Speculation was intense and constant regarding who was part of the group and who were simply pawns used by the group to wield influence. One did not know whom to believe or trust, and the group simply added a new wrinkle, albeit a significant one, to the game.

Then, in the early 1980s, having lived and worked in the District for the past several years and nearly fed up with all the smoke and mirrors that defined the city, Parker received an anonymous letter. It arrived around a week after Parker's mother passed away and over twenty years since Parker's father disappeared, which was the term always associated with his father's death.

Disappeared.

As if he might *reappear* one day and reunite with his family in a tearful celebration full of hugs and reminiscing. Parker knew, however, this day would never come. His mother explained to him what she knew about the disappearance of his father, and the anonymous letter provided the closure necessary for Parker to finally move on with his life. The letter would also set Parker on a mission that he would embrace for decades to come.

At the time of his father's disappearance, Parker was stationed at a base in South Carolina when he was summoned by his mother to his parents' home outside Spokane, where they had moved only a year prior. Immediately upon his arrival, he was met outside the front door by his mother, who hurried him into a thicket of nearby woods, saying something about the house "not being safe" for their conversation.

She explained that over a week ago, his father arrived home from work distraught, completely shaken, and on the verge of a nervous breakdown. The elder Parker never told his wife the work he was involved in, other than it had to do with the government and it was top secret. They lived a comfortable life and always had plenty of money, so she did not complain or pry into his affairs.

Now, however, her husband appeared on the brink of a collapse, and she knew with certainty that it was work-related. She tried to extract any information from him that she could, but for several days he casually dismissed her concerns, claiming nothing was wrong. She knew better, however, by simply looking at him and seeing a zombie where her husband used to be.

Finally, he came clean . . . somewhat. He told her he had been involved in some "unconscionable" things at work and he could not believe he had repeatedly looked the other way. He said that he had sacrificed his own ethics and morals because he did not want to be the one to speak out. He told her there was one man who did have the courage to voice his outrage, but Parker had learned that this man would soon be silenced.

Parker told his wife he could not allow any harm to come to this man, that this would be his "atonement." He claimed he had a plan to make things right and that he could ensure his family's safety forever. She did not have the faintest clue what he was talking about or why they would be in danger, but not once did she doubt the sincerity in her husband's voice.

Parker retrieved his revolver from the closet, took three bulging briefcases, and kissed his wife goodbye. He told her not to worry and that "Teddy-boy" would take of her. She begged and pleaded for him to stay, that they could work things out, whatever they were, but Parker simply shook his head sadly and insisted that this was the only way.

Several hours after he left, a pair of non-descript men visited the house and asked his wife a number of questions about his whereabouts. They remained within sight of the house for the next few days. They tailed Mrs. Parker everywhere she went, believing that she might try to contact her husband. Finally, she snapped and confronted them, screaming at them to let her know if they find her husband so she can beat the snot out of him herself.

The men hung around another day until the younger Parker arrived from South Carolina, causing them to melt into the shadows. When her son arrived, Mrs. Parker told him everything that had happened. Deciding he needed to stay home to comfort his mother and possibly make some inquiries around town, Parker received a temporary leave from his base.

Almost immediately, he began to understand his mother's concern. Although "they" were not visible, Parker unnervingly felt he was being followed whenever he left the house. When they were home, he was certain the house was under constant surveillance.

The phone rang late one night around a week after Parker arrived home and confirmed his hunch. He answered it to hear a menacing voice telling him that his father was a coward who abandoned his family. The man claimed that his father was running scared and no matter where he went, "they" would hunt him down and kill him. The voice vowed that Parker and his mother would always be watched, that they would never have any peace in their lives. Parker never forgot the sound of that voice, and he would subsequently come face-to-face with the man behind it at the direction of the anonymous letter over two decades later.

After another week, the search for Frank Parker officially ended and he was presumed dead. Parker's mother eventually sold the house and moved closer to her son's base in South Carolina. She always believed until her own death that her husband made the ultimate sacrifice for something good and pure, but her son knew how frustrating and agonizing it was for her to never have that belief validated. Parker also knew that his mother probably never forgave his father for leaving them so suddenly and without so much as an explanation.

The anonymous letter confirmed what Frank Parker did was commit the ultimate sacrifice, for his family and for the mysterious writer. Frank Parker died for something he believed he needed to make amends for, and the writer deemed it the most heroic and courageous thing he had ever witnessed. The person wrote that he owed a debt to Frank Parker he could never repay. The writer also acknowledged that although he was behind his father's death, he was not the one "responsible." That burden lies with a man whom Parker would meet, or technically *hear,* at a dinner party in Washington several weeks later.

The writer identified the man, Joshua Moriah, as the head of a secret organization known as the Foundation, the same mysterious cabal Parker had heard rumors swirling around for years. The writer encouraged Parker to use his standing as a fully decorated war hero to continue to climb up the chain of command, to fight the good fight against the group, and to never compromise his values for anything or anybody. The writer advised Parker that he did not have to do this for his father, but rather he should do it on behalf of his father's ideals, the ones he valued so highly that he was willing to die for them.

"The writer closed by offering his condolences regarding my mother and noted that for safety's sake," Parker indicates, "torch the letter."

Parker shakes his head back and forth, "It's amazing, really, the timing of it. I was at the height of my despair with politics and all the bullshit that went with it, and was thinking about retiring and living the civilian life. And then this letter arrives and it encourages me to stay in the game, be an instigator, stir up trouble for the group whenever possible. And you know what?"

He pauses for a moment and looks at both of them.

"That's what I did and I still do today," Parker says with a satisfied grin.

"I went to that dinner party and I heard that voice on the phone a quarter-century ago, and *I just knew*. I knew the voice because I had never forgotten it. And I know his son's voice, too," Parker wryly adds, flashing Augie an "I-told-you-so" look.

Augie holds up his hands and remarks, "I'll never doubt you again, sir."

Parker nods and smiles.

"Sir," Anderson says, "if you don't mind me asking, didn't you want to kick this guy Moriah's freaking teeth in?"

"More than you could ever imagine, Private," Parker confirms. "But despite my certainty that he was the one who called me after my dad's disappearance, I didn't have any proof he was behind it save a letter that was a pile of dust.

"No, the most effective way for me to get my payback is to never go away and to constantly be a thorn in the group's side. It wasn't hard after a while to figure out who was in the group's pocket and who wasn't. I even discovered that a good friend of mine, someone I knew during the Vietnam War, Warren Marshfield-"

Parker looks at Augie and nods before Augie can ask the question, "Yes, that Marshfield."

"-is a member of the Foundation, along with one of his protégés, Malcolm Fizer."

"Holy shit," Anderson mutters.

"So that's why you and Fizer have never . . seen eye to eye, so to speak?" Augie questions.

"Partially," Parker replies, "but there is more to it than that."

"Like?" Augie presses.

"There have been rumors among certain members of the brass," Parker explains, "that Marshfield and Fizer were involved in a lot of CIA 'black bag'-type stuff, totally unauthorized shit that was overseen by one of the most notorious men of the Cold War era."

"Who?" Anderson asks, beating Augie to the punch.

With a sly smile, Parker responds, "Jonas Abraham."

"*The* Jonas Abraham?" Augie asks.

"The same," Parker nods.

"Who's Jonas Abraham?" Anderson asks.

Parker dismisses the question with a wave of his hand, "Whole different jar of bees, Private. But getting back to the Foundation . . when the elder Moriah kicked the bucket and passed the mantle of leadership to his son Alex, I made sure at his father's funeral he knew I was healthy as an ox and would be around for a while yet."

With a twinkle in his eye, Parker mischievously says, "And so far, I've kept my word."

*   *   *

The first thing Sean feels is he has been tricked, like he is in the midst of an elaborate joke that only he is not in on. In all honesty though, he is feeling so many different emotions at once, each one seems to represent a car arriving at an intersection in his mind at the same time. The result is a massive collision of conflicting emotions, and Sean's desire is to sift through the wreckage and tap into the one overriding feeling, which seems to be complete and utter rage.

Sean's initial impulse is to reach out and shake Rosenstein to pieces, to mercilessly grill him why he did not tell him sooner. It angered Sean to know that through all those late-night bull sessions, office visits, and happy hours, this man, *his father*, held a secret of such magnitude, yet chose not to divulge it to him.

But why? He did not trust me? Or was Rosenstein that afraid for my safety?

Sean immediately realizes why Sloan and Rosenstein told their narrative the way they did. Besides the obvious logic in reciting the story in a linear fashion, Rosenstein wanted Sean to understand the full context behind their decision to give him up. Rosenstein wanted him to know how painful and heart-wrenching of a choice it was for them, but also how absolutely necessary. The story was related in this manner to fully explain the extent of the Foundation's power and to show that Rosenstein and his wife's fear of the group was so great, they believed they would be placing their only child's life in mortal danger if they kept him. Sean wants his anger at Rosenstein to be total and absolute, but in the back of his mind, he keeps asking himself what he and Isabella would have done in such a situation.

Suddenly, he thinks about the disappearance of his family, *Rosenstein's family*, and a thought pops into his head.

"Are you responsible-" Sean starts to ask before faltering. He breathes deeply, attempting to control the fury building inside him, and he tries again, "Is my family missing because of you?"

Rosenstein sighs, pauses, and finally responds, "Sean, I-"

"It's a yes or no question, Al," Sean barks. More calmly now, he states, "Give me a yes or no answer."

"Sean, they're not missing," Rosenstein says quickly. "I know where they are and I'm taking you to them."

For the first time since Isabella and Conor's disappearance, Sean at last receives a glimmer of hope.

They're alive!

A sudden wellspring of relief washes over him and he momentarily basks in the sublime feeling this fact brings him.

There are a few moments of silence between them before Rosenstein breaks the silence.

"Your dad Marty is an old buddy from my hometown," Rosenstein explains. "He and your mom were having trouble conceiving and were planning on adopting. We met with them and I laid out the inherent dangers that this child, *you*, might possess. It was not an easy decision for them either, but they called us the next day and agreed to take you into their home.

"Your parents are . . good people, Sean," Rosenstein adds.

"I know that," Sean replies defensively.

"And I made them promise me they could never tell you who your real parents are, *ever*. That's how much I feared for your safety. So if you're looking to blame someone, it's all on me."

"It's squarely on your shoulders, Al," Sean agrees coldly. "Always will be."

A pained look crosses Rosenstein's face and Sean can clearly see he has hurt the old man, which was his intention. Despite the justifiable explanation he and Pattie had for giving him up, Sean feels a deep sense of betrayal upon hearing Rosenstein's secret. He simply cannot ignore the fact that during all their years of friendship, Rosenstein hid this shocking truth from him. Yet, his feelings of anger and betrayal battle a part of him that knows it was all done for his own safety and well-being.

Staring down at his feet, Rosenstein softly continues, "I told your parents that one day we might be able to tell you the truth, but not until I know you are out of harm's way. I've come to realize you may never be completely safe, but I thought you should know the truth . . at last."

Sean is lost in thought as he recalls fleeting childhood memories in an attempt to identify any clues that might have caused him to question his true origins. Growing up, he never really noticed he looked different from his parents because children, particularly boys, tend not to notice details like that. Being an only child, Sean did not have any siblings to compare himself to either. Now, however, thinking about Rosenstein's revelation, he remembers an episode when he was around 13-years-old that suddenly has meaning.

It occurred at a dinner party his parents held at their home. At the end of the night, his father was walking one of his friends to the front door, along with Sean, when his father's buddy said something to Sean that caused his father to fly into a rage. Marty nearly decked the man before the two of them were quickly separated.

Sean did not understand until this day why his father was so upset with his friend, but now the reason seems crystal clear. His father's friend had looked at Sean, squinted at him in an alcohol-induced haze, looked at Marty, then back to Sean and cracked, "You the mail-man's kid, Sean-boy?"

Sean can recall the man's laughter like a thunder-clap, and when the man glanced at Marty to see if he was laughing along with him, he saw instead a man red-faced with anger and ready to explode. Sean never understood the joke until this day and apparently, his father did not care for it either. His father never once mentioned the incident again and Sean did not care to ask.

As he recalls this nearly forgotten childhood memory, another realization suddenly comes into sharp focus for Sean. Whenever he spent time with the Rosensteins, be it a dinner or staying overnight at their house after a late-nighter with Al, he always had this unshakable feeling that reminded him of . . . *home*. It reminded him of being around his own family or his parents – the feeling you receive when you are in the presence of people you love and who love you back in equal measure. It is a feeling of warmth that has nothing to do with the temperature and a feeling of affection that has everything to do with being around the people you care about.

Sean feels he should be preparing himself for a breakdown of epic proportions given the intense and contradictory emotions swirling inside him. Surprisingly though, he is maintaining an even keel, all things considered. When taking a step back and attempting to comprehend them all, he realizes it is a Herculean task in and of itself.

In addition to the disappearance of his family and possibly his best friend, along with surviving an assassination attempt on his life, Sean could compile a laundry list of items that have occurred in the last few hours that would have cracked a lesser man. He had read a report written around sixty years ago regarding the possible colonization efforts of Earth by an alien race; received specific details of this alien race and their plans for world domination by an assassin, who also suggested that the alien race is working in collaboration with an organization that has been allegedly pulling the strings of power in the country and beyond its borders for around a century; and lastly, the bombshell from his former mentor and friend that he is, in fact, *his father*. To say it is a lot to digest would be an understatement.

While Sean would feel like a complete sap for readily accepting this information without a few reservations, he searches in vain to identify a motive for Sloan and Rosenstein to lie to him. The story seems so fantastic and so utterly far-fetched with all of its elaborate details and characters that its absolute unbelievability makes it all the more believable. Perhaps Sean is willing to accept it more readily than the average person because in his daily profession, he is constantly reading, studying, and researching similar extraordinary stories that stretch the imagination and test the boundaries of comprehension. This constant exposure to off-the-wall conspiracy theories and Big-Brother-is-watching paranoia allows him to grasp the tale that has unfolded before him, albeit reluctantly. Furthermore, it has enabled him to understand the nuances of truth and the oftentimes painful consequences it brings are entirely necessary if it eliminates the uncertainty and falsehoods surrounding a particular conspiracy.

"The truth . ." Sean repeats, as if hearing the word for the first time.

Rosenstein silently nods.

"And you've been following me all along?" Sean asks. "Since you . . . gave me up?"

"Yes," Rosenstein confirms. "Your dad and I established a quasi-cloak-and-dagger system where we could receive periodic updates on you and how you were doing. We did not want to risk meeting in public, conversations over the telephone, or letters through the post office, but Pattie and I always wanted to hear about what was going on in your life, I'm sure to the annoyance of your parents."

Rosenstein sighs heavily before continuing, "It was so hard for us to hear about how fast you were growing up and all the little things that went with it. Your first steps, your first words, the first time you went to school. We desperately wanted to be there with you for all of it, but . . well . . you know . ."

Rosenstein's voice trails off, leaving Sean to wonder if he is still searching for the right words or if it is simply too painful for him to continue. For the first time since Rosenstein's revelation, Sean actually feels sympathy for the man and his wife, for the hellish ordeal they went through, rather than looking at it through his own narrow viewpoint. Sean briefly contemplated what he and Isabella would have done when confronted with such a difficult decision, but he never actually *thought* about the pain and heartache such a decision would entail. Sean could not begin to comprehend the Rosensteins' pain because he could not actually *feel* it himself.

Now, the man before him – head bowed, hands clasped tightly together, a skeleton of himself – elicits nothing but sympathy. To give up your child not by choice, but out of necessity for fear of his life, and to know other people were raising *your child* despite being physically, mentally, and economically capable of doing so, Sean cannot fathom anything quite so wrenching and painful. He wants to reach out to Rosenstein and console him, but he knows he is not yet ready to cross that bridge.

Instead, Sean asks, "Did you and Pattie ever think about having another child?"

Rosenstein raises his head and quietly responds, "Of course we thought about it, all the time in fact. We never tried to have one, you know, on purpose, but there were times . ."

He continues, choking on the words, "Several times Pattie became pregnant and each time . . we considered what we should do and wondered whether 'they' were still watching us. But ultimately . . each and every time, and maybe even thankfully, we did not have to make that awful decision. Fate decided each time to take the child away from us before it came to that – Pattie miscarried every one, never making it past four months."

"I'm sorry," Sean says softly.

Rosenstein nods and his tone darkens, "I suspected, but obviously could never prove it, that whatever Jonas and the rest of them did to her back in Spokane, they had taken away her ability to bring a child into this world.

"That's why I always thought you were an absolute miracle," he says beaming, his eyes shimmering with tears. "Our miracle baby that we had to give up."

Now Sean's heart is crumbling into pieces, and he feels so ashamed for initially and perhaps selfishly being angry with Rosenstein.

"After she delivered you," Rosenstein explains, "I thought that even if we did have you at a hospital, it wouldn't have changed anything. The delivery was so painful for her, and there was so much . . so much blood . . I thought if she tried to have another baby, it could kill her."

Rosenstein pauses a moment before adding, "I think she knew that, too, and I soon realized that my pain was probably nothing compared to the pain a mother feels in giving up the only child she would ever conceive."

Sean feels a stinging sensation behind his eyes and, desperately wanting to change the subject, asks, "You mentioned that day in the jungle, and-"

Sean motions towards Sloan.

"-Ms. Sloan seemed to know about it, too. You told her?"

Rosenstein nods.

"You knew before I even told you all those years ago, didn't you?" Sean asks.

Sean sees the familiar wry smile spread across Rosenstein's face.

"I've got my sources, too," he coyly remarks.

"So you knew the purpose of the mission?"

"And I think you know now, too," Rosenstein points out.

"It wasn't about guerillas or cocaine smugglers that day," Sean says angrily, "was it? Those villagers . . . they were . . extraterrestrials?"

"Yes," Rosenstein confirms. "Extraterrestrials who became test subjects for this particular mission. They were the unwitting participants in a trial run for a device that could destroy them. And, judging from the results, destroy them it did."

"Excruciating pain and suffering included," Sean adds.

"What you used that day," Rosenstein explains, "was simply a prototype, a precursor of a more refined weapon to come."

"It seemed what we used that day worked pretty effectively," Sean notes bitterly.

"Effectively, but not efficiently," Rosenstein counters. "They've since developed similar weapons that cause instantaneous death and do not need to be used in such close proximity."

"The brass was monitoring us the whole time, weren't they?" Sean asks, his voice rising. "We were supposed to hoof it out with any captured guerillas and meet at a rendezvous point for extraction. They couldn't have been very far away because those helicopters came out of nowhere. They knew we were getting our asses handed to us and they did fucking *nothing,*" he says furiously.

"Yeah," Rosenstein nods, "they were only a few clicks away, but they weren't going to lift a finger until you and your men tested the devices to see what would happen. They wanted *results,* and in their eyes, your team was entirely expendable."

"My God," Sean laments, "my fucking men were completely annihilated by those . ."

Sean's voice trails off as a sudden realization hits him.

"Sean . ."

"That thing they carried," Sean recalls, "the weapon with the green glow . . it was in the jungle . . . and I saw that same green glow at your house. There was a picture of it sketched in your treatise."

Rosenstein simply nods his head.

"What the hell is it?" Sean asks.

"We're not entirely sure," Rosenstein concedes. "Some in the Foundation have dubbed it 'the baton.' It has been theorized that the device uses extreme heat or electricity that causes the cells in our body to expand at an accelerated rate and then essentially, explode. It's almost like a bomb being detonated inside our bodies."

Sean recalls his men being completely obliterated by the weapon, leaving nothing behind except a smattering of blood.

"The technology is extremely radical," Rosenstein states, "and as far as I know, it has yet to be deciphered."

Sean recalls the aftermath of the incident, "The brass wanted the two of us to go along with their 'official' version of events, which was a crock of shit. There was no mention of the testing of a new weapon, the device the enemy had used against us, or why there were no bodies to bring home to the families of the men killed in action. They blamed their deaths on us because we failed to use the new weapons immediately upon encountering the hostiles. We argued how a man could be on the receiving end of the amount of ammunition we fired and still keep coming, and our superiors informed us that this information would not be disclosed, either.

"Grant and I threatened to go to the press, to the men's families to tell them the truth, but we were warned that disclosing classified information is a violation of federal law and would entail a court martial and carry a possible sentence of thirty years in prison. They strong-armed us and we backed down, and it is something I will never forgive myself for. Grant signed off on the official report of the incident, but I refused to sign and they dishonorably discharged me, just like that."

With a mix of sadness and anger in his words, Sean says softly, "Grant committed suicide a couple years later. Apparently, it was too much for him to live with."

Rosenstein nods sympathetically, "I know it all, Sean."

There are a few moments of silence between them as Sean considers the loss of his men and the horrible aftermath of that day.

"So what was it they developed to kill these creatures?" Sean wonders. "Something having to do with extreme cold?"

"You're on the right track," Rosenstein confirms. "They created a kind of supercharged molecule comprised of several cooling agents that, when injected into the EBE, simply overloaded their monitoring system and killed them.

"As much as I despise the way they used you and your men as pawns to test the device, its success got the human race back in the game. Not to sound melodramatic or trite, but it was a game we had been losing for a long time, let alone seemed to be playing."

Sean once again recalls the encounter in Rosenstein's home.

"So the mist blown from the vents in your-"

"Oh, no," Rosenstein interrupts, shaking his head, "not what the Foundation developed by any means. I installed a unique vent system in case I ever received unexpected visitors – the otherworldly kind – and maintained a vacuum flask of liquid nitrogen on hand to scare them off."

"But how did you know-" Sean begins.

"I knew as soon as they entered my house," Rosenstein cuts him off. "A silent alarm was immediately tripped and although I was a couple hundred miles away, I can remotely access surveillance cameras in and around my house from anywhere in the world. I was watching them the whole time. I was hoping you wouldn't show, but . . well . . you know the story from there."

"But why would-"

Sean stops in mid-sentence as another realization suddenly dawns on him.

"That wasn't a man in your house, was it?" Sean asks.

Rosenstein shakes his head.

"It was an . . extraterrestrial?"

Rosenstein nods, a bemused expression on his face.

"An extraterrestrial that's been mentioned to me tonight?" Sean asks.

Rosenstein nods again.

"*Jericho*," Sean breathlessly utters, not even bothering to phrase it as a question because he already knows the answer.

"You're getting good, kid," Rosenstein says, a twinkle in his eye.

THIRTEEN

Waltman, Augie's contact at the Justice Department, was preoccupied with so many other things, he nearly forgot about the cell phone signal he traced and the plane his friend asked him to keep an eye on. When he got around to investigating it, Waltman determined that at several airports along the plane's western route, various air traffic controllers reported that the plane appeared to be having radio transmission problems, and they could not discern the plane's final destination or any other information regarding their flight plan. Each attempt at contacting the plane resulted in a garble of static intermixed with what they assumed was the pilot's voice, but this could obviously not be confirmed.

One air traffic controller speculated that the pilot is intentionally tuned to the wrong frequency to give the impression the plane is having communication problems in an effort to disguise where it is ultimately headed. While this was mere speculation and the air traffic controller admitted as much, Waltman immediately became suspicious of the mysterious plane.

Reinforcing these suspicions is that no one appears to know which airport the plane departed from, or why the pilot failed to file a flight plan or list a final destination, which is required by federal law. Given that Augie only calls in favors when he *really* needs something, the mysterious nature of the plane has certainly piqued Waltman's interest.

He had traced a rough estimate of the plane's route based on its current heading to determine if there are any airports or airfields that seem to be a logical destination, but this did not offer much. The nearest major airport on the plane's route is Spokane International in Washington, so Waltman contacted their air traffic control tower regarding the plane. He asked them to contact him in case they heard from the pilot or determined the plane's final destination. They promised to call if they found out any information, and only a few minutes prior, they delivered on that promise.

The control tower noted that the plane is not within their flight pattern, but it is located directly on the edge of it. It does not appear the plane intends to land at Spokane International, and the tower log and tracking system shows no planes matching its description scheduled to arrive there. However, the air traffic controllers noticed that the plane is gradually descending in altitude and therefore, they concluded that it is preparing to land *somewhere* around them.

Despite repeated efforts to contact the pilot, there was no response from the plane except a few scattered bursts of static. The control tower speculated that the plane could possibly land at Fairchild Air Force Base, located several miles west of Spokane. They indicated, however, that this seems unlikely given that Fairchild is a military installation and none of the controllers could ever recall a private plane landing at the base. Nevertheless, unless there is a hidden airstrip or secret airfield located around Spokane they are unaware of, there is nowhere else for the plane to land. Waltman thanked them and immediately contacted Fairchild to determine if they know anything about the phantom plane.

When at last Waltman is able to reach someone at Fairchild, the cool, detached voice on the other end of the line informs him that he knows nothing about a plane approaching the base. The man manages to sound downright menacing when he warns that even if there is a private plane approaching, it would not be allowed to land there. The man at Fairchild abruptly ends the call when Waltman points out he never mentioned that it is a private plane, as he suddenly hears a click followed by the dial tone. Waltman attempts to contact the base several more times, but no one answers his repeated calls, as if everyone at the base simply left for the night.

If Waltman was suspicious before, he is downright paranoid now. Something strange is definitely going on and he is certain the man he spoke with at Fairchild was lying through his teeth. He would bet that steak dinner Augie promised him on it. After a few minutes pondering the situation, Waltman decides he has followed the scent this far, but now it is time to inform Lieutenant Colonel Hermann where he thinks the trail ends.

*　　*　　*

Kaley has struggled mightily in his attempt to spring himself free of the handcuffs with the knife loaned to him by Dawson. His hand aches from the self-inflicted wound he suffered back in Chicago, but unfortunately this is the free hand he has to work with. He is having trouble steadying both hands since he awoke on the plane, shivers of cold rippling through him every few minutes, a cold sweat enveloping his body. This is a direct result of wearing a frigid wet suit for an extended period of time before being transferred to the relatively chilly conditions of air travel. Contributing to his frustration is the fact that he has very little light to work with and he must keep a constant eye on Fizer and Ruethorn at the front of the plane to ensure they do not suddenly get up to check on him.

Now, exacerbating his stress level, he feels the plane slowly descending in altitude. He has not seen or heard from Dawson since their "introduction" and he contemplates the possibility that he is on his own, a prospect that he is starting to accept. He cannot say he really blames her. She displayed tremendous courage and risked her own neck to emerge from her relatively safe hiding spot below the cabin to check on him. Not only that, Dawson provided him with a weapon, albeit one that does not appear capable of causing much damage, but a weapon nonetheless. If he is unable to pick the lock on the cuffs before they land, he has the reassurance of a weapon he can use to strike at Fizer and Ruethorn if the opportunity arises.

Kaley is also fully aware that he may simply be excess baggage at this point. His body aches from the last twenty-four hours and he is uncertain he can walk, let alone run, without assistance. His legs are heavy and sluggish, he has the chills, and he feels the onset of a raging fever starting to take shape. Kaley would not want to be saddled with someone in the shape he is in either.

Nearing a breaking point, he continues to struggle with the cuffs when suddenly he hears a *pssst* from the aisle. He cranes his neck around the seat, causing a shooting pain down his spine and back up through his brain. He sees the small panel door where Dawson emerged from earlier slightly open, but her face is not visible.

Whispering, she asks urgently, "You out of them, Houdini?"

Kaley checks the front of the plane to ensure they did not hear her, then he leans over and whispers, "I can't get them . . my hand . . it's fucking killing me . ."

Dawson can see, even from her angle, Kaley can barely keep his hands from trembling. She curses under her breath, debating whether to once again risk scrambling from her hiding spot and helping, or leaving Kaley to fend for himself. She is unsure what help she can offer, having never been in handcuffs before and possessing absolutely zero experience in trying to "pick" any type of lock. Still, as the plane continues its gradual descent, she watches Kaley struggle with the lock and feels a pang of sympathy for him, and knows there is only one choice she will make.

Dawson slides the panel door open and glances towards the front of the plane for movement, but does not see any. She pulls herself out of the hiding spot and quickly crawls into Kaley's row.

"You know we're landing soon," she states the obvious.

"Yeah, I noticed," Kaley responds sarcastically, glancing out the window.

The plane was in the midst of cloud cover for nearly the entire duration Kaley has been conscious, but now the plane has cleared the clouds and the few, scattered lights on the ground are plainly visible. Unfortunately for them, these lights are becoming larger by the second.

Dawson snatches the knife from him and crouches over the cuffs, gingerly inserting the tip into the keyhole.

"I've never been in handcuffs before," she notes. "I don't know how much help I'm going to be."

"You've never been in cuffs before? Weren't you ever a teenager?"

"Yeah," Dawson nods, "and I was a good teenager."

"There's no such thing, Dawson," Kaley flatly responds.

"Kaley," she says urgently, "are you going to help me here? What am I looking for?"

"I've never sprung myself from cuffs before," he concedes, "but I think there is a small 'catch' inside that, when it is turned or pressed, should unlock them."

"Thanks, that's incredibly helpful," she says, as she takes her turn at sarcasm.

Squinting, Dawson continues to work the cuffs with the meager light she has, moving the tip of the knife around in circles, but nothing happens.

Kaley tries to remain calm for both of them because he can clearly see Dawson is starting to panic. Her face is covered in sweat and her short hair is matted down, completely drenched in perspiration. She keeps stealing peeks out the window to monitor the progress of their descent, which certainly does not help matters. Kaley is starting to feel the pressure, too, but he knows if he shows any fear, it could be curtains for both of them. As Dawson leans down in front of him, he notices a rip in the back of her shirt and an accompanying patch of red around the tear.

"That's a pretty bad cut there, Dawson," Kaley remarks nonchalantly.

"Yeah, it is," she acknowledges, intensely studying the keyhole.

"You should have a doctor look at it," Kaley wryly says, attempting to keep her as calm as possible.

She distractedly glances at him and responds, "Maybe he can look at your mangled face, too."

Her tone is serious but not malicious in any way, but she clearly is not in the mood to engage in any jocular back-and-forth with him.

Kaley smirks and starts to reply when suddenly, the plane dips sharply, causing butterflies to swarm their stomachs.

"Shit," Dawson mutters, again glancing out the window.

Kaley does the same and he can see they have no more than two or three minutes before they land. Dawson grinds the knife inside the keyhole, desperately trying to locate the "catch." Kaley quickly realizes there is simply not enough time to continue, and he knows she can still crawl below the cabin to safety before the goons up front notice.

"Dawson, it's too big," he despairingly says. "The tip of the blade is just too big for the lock."

She ignores him and continues to wrangle with it.

"Dawson," he says urgently, getting right in her face, "it's not going to happen. Get below the cabin . . . *now*."

He is red-faced and seemingly the one on the verge of panic, more concerned with what could happen if

Fizer and Ruethorn discover her attempting to help him. Kaley cannot fathom having to live with being responsible for another person's death, especially with Eisley's fresh blood still on his hands. Dawson, however, continues to ignore him, as she is completely dialed in to the task at hand.

"Are you listening-"

Suddenly, they hear a *click* and Kaley's hand is free. He looks at her in amazement and she responds, grinning, "Okay, so maybe I was arrested once, but I've never picked a lock before tonight."

They both glance towards the front and then simultaneously out the window, the landing fast approaching. Dawson helps him out of his seat as a pained expression crosses his face. They crouch behind the row of seats in front of them.

She looks at him with concern, "Can you walk alright?"

"I think so," Kaley nods, though his expression tells a different story.

As Dawson looks at him skeptically, the plane suddenly hits some turbulence and it tilts slightly, causing her to lose her balance. She starts to fall sideways into the aisle and reaches her hand out for something to grab onto. Just when she thinks she is swiping at nothing but air and about to sound the alarm on their escape with a noisy crash to the floor, Kaley's hand, the bad one, shoots out, grabbing hers. He grimaces in pain, his face contorted in agony, but he manages to pull her back into the row with him.

Dawson can tell Kaley is weak, as this small feat of strength seemed to be a major expenditure of energy for him.

"Shit, thanks," she breathes.

"I figure I owe you one," he replies.

"More than one, Kaley," Dawson corrects.

They hear the landing gear being deployed and realize their time is nearly up.

Dawson whispers in his ear, "I'll go first. There's a small step right below the panel door, just follow me."

Kaley nods.

Dawson hastily moves towards the opening, sits down, places her feet on the step and is about to slide down when suddenly, they hear a voice behind them.

"Prepare for landing, Sergeant Kaley," Ruethorn smirks.

They both freeze, thinking that the great escape has abruptly come to an end. They look behind them and see that Ruethorn is still facing forward, realizing that it was simply a smartass comment said over his shoulder.

They look at each other and both breathe a momentary sigh of relief.

Dawson urgently motions Kaley to follow her and she slithers down the opening and out of view within seconds. Kaley hurries in after her, ignoring the pain that screams at him from every joint and muscle. He moves down the opening, contorting his body in a way that it does not seem to agree with. Jolts of shooting pain course throughout his body.

Kaley emerges below the cabin and sees nothing but darkness in front of him. Suddenly, a faint light illuminates Dawson's face as she instructs him, "Close the panel."

Kaley turns around, reaches out and slides the panel door along its track, closing it behind them. He turns back towards Dawson and notices she is holding a small penlight, their only source of illumination in this darkened space.

Dawson moves towards a small door set in the floor, with Kaley closely following behind. The moment she grips the handle, they hear the eerie silence that seems to envelope a plane just prior to landing. They both brace for the wheels to touch down.

A moment later, they feel the wheels kiss the runway and then a couple of bumps as the plane decreases speed. The plane shudders as the pilot applies the brakes.

"Go!" Kaley shouts at Dawson.

Dawson practically rips the small door off and they are instantly hit with a blast of air coursing through the opening. The sound of the wheel directly below them screeching against the ground is both deafening and disconcerting, but they have no time for their nerves to be rattled by a loud noise.

Dawson straddles the opening where the wheel has unfolded onto the runway, her hands clinging to the sides of the opening. The plane is slowing considerably and they both know it is now or never.

Although his body will completely disagree with their next course of action, he leans down and exclaims, "Do it, Dawson!"

She glances up at him and shouts back, "Close the door behind you!"

In the next instant she drops down behind the wheel, covering her head as she falls.

Kaley closes the door above him and scurries over to the opening. The plane is now slowly taxiing down the runway. He tries not to think about the pain the impact will cause to his tender body. He drapes his arms around his head and falls. He hits the ground awkwardly with a painful grunt and rolls for several feet.

Within seconds, Dawson is at his side urgently tugging him up and urging him on. They are both breathing heavily, but for the moment thankful to be free from their imprisonment, whether forced in Kaley's case or self-imposed in Dawson's case.

"Come on, we've got to find some cover," she indicates.

They look around, but do not see another living soul. They notice a fence topped with barbed wire a few hundred yards away, several airplane hangars adjacent to the runway, and in the distance what appear to be barracks.

"It looks like a military base, doesn't it?" Dawson asks, pulling him along with her.

"Sure does," Kaley agrees, "but where is everybody?"

"Yeah," Dawson replies, "it's too quiet."

They stumble off the runway, hurry towards the nearest hangar and duck behind it. They both peek around the corner of the hangar to see the plane slowly come to a stop at the end of the runway.

"Shit, now what?" Kaley asks.

"We've followed Fizer this far, let's see where else he takes us," Dawson suggests.

Kaley looks at her and nods, "It's been a blast so far."

They continue to peer at the plane, a very small cushion of darkness and shadows between it and them, but a cushion nonetheless.

* * *

Time to rouse Sergeant Kaley, Ruethorn thinks, a gleeful prospect to be sure.

Ruethorn unbuckles his seatbelt and says to Colonel Fizer, "I'll get our prisoner, sir."

"Alright," Fizer nods, "but keep him in one piece, Sergeant Major."

"Yes, sir," Ruethorn replies, a sly grin on his face.

He walks swiftly towards the back of the plane and gently says, "Sergeant Kaley . . this is your wakeup-"

Fizer stands up and notices Ruethorn stop dead in his tracks in the aisle, staring slack-jawed.

"What is it?" Fizer demands.

"Sir . . ."

"Well, is he awake?" Fizer asks, irritated, starting down the aisle.

When Fizer sees Ruethorn unholster his weapon, he knows there is something undeniably wrong.

"Sergeant Major, what is-"

Fizer is unable to finish his sentence once he arrives next to Ruethorn. Now it is Colonel Fizer's turn to stare in awe at the vacant seat Kaley previously occupied, with one cuff still attached to the armrest and the other cuff dangling open, practically taunting them.

Fizer immediately takes out his own sidearm and looks around wildly, "Where could he have gone?"

Ruethorn answers the question as he kneels down over a panel in the middle of the aisle and slides it to the side.

"Got a flashlight?" Ruethorn asks, peering into the dark compartment below.

Fizer turns towards the front and orders the pilot, "Turn all interior lights on."

The pilot complies and the compartment below is instantly illuminated. Ruethorn, with his gun pointed out in front of him, cautiously crawls through the opening.

"What the hell did he use to pick the lock?" Ruethorn asks over his shoulder.

Something catches Fizer's eye and he suddenly has an idea how Kaley escaped.

"He's not alone," Fizer murmurs, leaning down over the panel opening, studying it.

"There's a couple patches of fresh blood down here," Ruethorn calls up to him.

This is followed by the sound of a door opening, and then Ruethorn exclaims, "He must have bailed when we landed . . he has to be close cause he's not getting far in the shape he's in."

"He had help . . . ." Fizer begins, more to himself than to Ruethorn.

"I'm checking the runway," Ruethorn informs Fizer, and presumably he uses the same route Kaley did.

Fizer continues studying the side of the panel opening and mutters, "Help . . from a woman."

Fizer arrives at this conclusion because on the side of the panel opening is a bloody handprint. It is only a partial, but he is nearly certain that the long, elongated fingers are that of a woman's.

The jeep was simply a diversion, Fizer realizes, cursing himself for underestimating her and her for sneaking a ride right underneath his nose.

With a mix of rage and embarrassment, Fizer hisses through clenched teeth, "Dawson."

FOURTEEN

Three Months Ago – Rosenstein Home

At the front door, the two men embrace for what seems like the hundredth time in the last few days, holding each other tightly, the younger man patting the older man several times on the back and whispering reassurances in his ear. The older man's embrace is more akin to a clutch, leaning heavily on the younger man, both literally and figuratively. The younger man knows this and tries to be strong for both of them, biting his lip and holding back the tears for the pain and heartache the older man is going through. Conversely, the older man has no reason to hold back the tears, and although he feels he should have exhausted his supply by now, fresh ones begin to form as he wearily closes his eyes. He is sick and tired of crying like a baby, but he cannot help it.

Both of the men wear black suits and somber ties, and with a quick glance at their faces, one would probably guess that they are either going to or returning from a funeral. The late afternoon sun suggests that the latter is the case.

The men break from their embrace.

"You're sure you don't want us to stay with you? At least for a couple days?" Sean offers.

Shaking his head, Rosenstein responds in a voice gravelly and soft, "No, that's okay. I need to . . go through some of her things and . ."

"Really, Al, it's no problem for us to stay," Isabella says, standing next to Sean, "and we can help you do that stuff."

She shrugs and says gently, "It might be . . easier."

"Thanks, sweetheart," Rosenstein smiles weakly, "but I really feel I should be . . . alone for a while. I feel like she's still here, and I think I've got a few more things to say to her."

Isabella, holding tightly to Sean, briefly sobs and her eyes fill with tears. She reaches out to Rosenstein and cradles his face in her long, delicate hands. She kisses him on the cheek and rubs the other side of his face with her hand.

"Are you sure?" Isabella whispers.

He nods, and then takes her hands in his and kisses her forehead, "I'm sure."

Rosenstein motions towards Conor, who is in the front yard attempting to persuade a squirrel to play with him, to no avail. "Now go get that pistol some dinner, he must be starving."

Isabella nods her head and calls to her son, "Conor, come say bye to Al."

Conor abandons the squirrel and bounds up the front walkway as Rosenstein bends down to scoop him up in his arms.

"Bye, Al," Conor says.

Rosenstein gathers him up in his arms and hugs him tightly. "Bye, kid. You be good for your parents, huh?"

"I will," Conor replies.

"I know you will," Rosenstein nods.

Conor looks like he wants to say something, pauses, then his curiosity gets the better of him.

"Al . . do you think Pattie will send me any more of her peanut butter cookies?"

Rosenstein chuckles in spite of what would undoubtedly be a melancholic answer to Conor's question, marveling at the child's innocence and envious of his obliviousness to the meaning of life and death.

"Someday, kid, I hope so," Rosenstein chokes out.

This seems to satisfy Conor as Rosenstein puts him down, and the boy grabs his mom's outstretched hand.

"Will you call if you need anything?" Isabella asks. "Please."

"I will," he assures her.

Isabella's gaze lingers on Rosenstein one last time, and then she and Conor begin walking down the front path.

Sean looks at Rosenstein the same way his wife did, hesitant to leave him alone, wishing the old man would ask them to stay with him for a little while. But he doesn't.

Sean places his hand on Rosenstein's arm, the concern evident in his voice, "You know where to find us."

"Yeah," he replies. "I'll be . . fine. I just need to . . sleep, for days I think."

"Yeah," Sean agrees, "that sounds like a good idea."

Sean looks towards the car as Isabella and Conor climb in. He feels terrible, wanting to say something more, something profound, to give Rosenstein additional words of comfort, but he realizes he has probably said all he can for now. He feels bad for leaving him, but he knows Rosenstein wants to be alone right now, alone with his thoughts and alone with her.

"Okay," Sean finally says, "I'll give you a call tomorrow."

"Sure," Rosenstein responds, nodding his appreciation.

Sean pats him once more on the arm and then moves down the walkway towards the car.

"Sean?"

Sean turns around and eagerly asks, "Yeah, Al?"

Rosenstein stares at Sean for a moment, opens his mouth, but then hesitates.

"It's nothing," he says dismissively.

"You sure?" Sean asks, unconvinced.

"Yeah," Rosenstein responds. "Drive safe, okay?"

"Sure, Al," Sean assures him.

Sean waves goodbye, turns, and walks toward his waiting family.

Rosenstein quietly closes the front door and rests his head against it, his breathing heavy and labored, his heart racing with the prospect of revealing a decades-long secret. He was unable to muster the courage to do so.

"I should have told him, don't you think?" he asks the empty house. "We should have told him a long time ago."

After a few moments of silence as he waits for a response that he knows will never come, another wave of melancholy washes over him. He must accept the fact his questions to her will hang in the air unanswered now, although this would never stop him from talking to her. Hopefully, with each deafening silence to his questions, his heart will break less and less. Deep down though, he knows the hurt will never cease, and the most he can hope for is that it may gradually ease with each passing day.

Rosenstein slowly walks around the house recalling the memories they shared in each room, remembering all the laughter and all the happiness. He remembers conversations they had here and there, some serious and others lighthearted, and thinks how desperately he misses her already. As he stands in the master bedroom, peering into their closet, he hears a knock at the front door that breaks him out of his reverie.

Must be Sean, he thinks.

He hurries downstairs and opens the door. It is not Sean.

The person before him was a child he once knew. Now he has blossomed into a man with the same physical characteristics as his father, and he possesses the same air of invincibility and self-confidence his father always carried. One striking difference Rosenstein notes between the man and his father is the compassion in the son's eyes, a look of sympathy Rosenstein cannot determine is sincere or the work of a good actor.

Knowing the family, Rosenstein decides to err on the side of caution.

"You come to my house today?" he asks, his voice rising in anger. "On the day I bury my wife?"

"Dr. Rosenstein, I want to offer my condol-"

"Save that," Rosenstein interrupts, waving him away. "I'd like to be left alone, if you don't mind," he says, and he starts to shut the door.

Moriah places his hand on the door and says emphatically, "Please, Doctor, I need a moment of your time. It's extremely urgent."

Rosenstein warily eyes Moriah, then looks past him to a black Lincoln Town Car parked in the driveway. There are several men seated in the car, sunglasses covering their eyes, undoubtedly staring in their direction.

"Who are the goons?" Rosenstein asks, motioning towards them.

"They are no one," Moriah replies in the cryptic language that has likely been part of his life since day one.

"What's to stop me from killing you right here, right now?" Rosenstein challenges.

His eyes probing Rosenstein's, Moriah replies, "What if I were to tell you humanity's fate may rest in your hands, and that by killing me, you would essentially be sealing that fate to its ultimate destruction?"

Rosenstein again casts a suspicious eye on Moriah, trying to decide whether he is being straight with him or his obvious theatrics are a well-conceived ruse.

"Besides, we know you're not a killer," Moriah remarks, "are you?"

"And how do I know you're not here to *kill me*, Alex?"

"What possible-"

"Because to be blunt, I just lost my wife of forty years and I have no problem with seeing her sooner rather than later," Rosenstein asserts, fully believing the words he says.

"I do not doubt that, Dr. Rosenstein," Moriah acknowledges.

"But just so you know, I might take you with me," Rosenstein menacingly says.

"I assure you, my intention here today is not to harm you," Moriah responds diplomatically. "There is no possible reason to kill you, Dr. Rosenstein, especially after all this time."

"How about to finish off your father's business?" Rosenstein speculates.

"It was never my father's business to kill you, Dr. Rosenstein," Moriah responds calmly.

A few moments pass between them as an internal debate rages inside Rosenstein whether to trust this man or not. While he knows trust is a bond they will likely never share, Rosenstein relents and allows Moriah to enter in order to hear him out. Soon, they are seated in the living room across from each other.

Moriah begins, "First, let me set the record straight by saying what happened to your wife in Spokane all those years ago had nothing to do with my father, but was strictly Abraham acting rashly and without authority from either my father or from the group in general. My father always regretted the situation that occurred with you and Frank Parker, and he never wanted to see any harm come to either of you."

Despite what appears to be Moriah's sincere display, Rosenstein instantly discerns two motives behind his prepared speech. First, Moriah attempts to eliminate or at least mitigate the acrimony Rosenstein still holds against his father and the group by placing the blame solely on Abraham. Moriah knows there is no possible way for Rosenstein to confirm this, but by re-focusing the residual feelings of hostility Rosenstein has away from the group, Moriah reasons that it might be more difficult for Rosenstein to refuse to assist them, if that is indeed the motive behind his visit.

The second and more subtle reason was the mention of Frank Parker and "any harm" that may have come to him. Rosenstein believes Moriah was trying to elicit a quick, almost involuntary reaction at the mention of the man's name. It was not lost on Rosenstein when Moriah asked him if he was a killer only moments before. While one of them knows for certain Parker's fate and the other man is fairly certain of it given that the elder Parker would be nearly a century old if he were alive today, Rosenstein does not flinch, taking a small amount of joy in the fact that Moriah and his father will never know what happened to the man.

"Or to your families," Moriah adds.

"Alex," Rosenstein responds irritably, "you can drop the platitudes and any other bullshit that comes out of your mouth. You are not to utter the word 'Abraham' in this house again. Everything you say I assume is a lie until proven to be truthful. Given that much of what I'm sure you're about to say cannot be substantiated, this could be a real brief conversation."

Moriah nods and consents, "Okay, Doctor, then let's get to the heart of the matter."

"Yes," Rosenstein agrees, "tell me how the whole world is suddenly in my hands."

"You are aware of their satellites, Dr. Rosenstein?" he asks. "The six satellites that continue to remain in Earth's orbit even after all these years?"

"Yes," Rosenstein confirms.

"Well, you are also probably aware that we constantly monitor their communications, even though our cryptologists have yet to decipher their language or crack their codes."

"Still can't do it, huh?" Rosenstein smirks, garnering a small amount of pleasure from this as well. "I've always said they're smarter than us."

"It's hard to argue that," Moriah concedes. "Anyway, we've recently noticed a massive amount of communication between the satellites. It's a constant stream of information, unlike anything we have ever seen before."

He pauses, and then says pointedly, "We think something big is on the horizon."

"What do you mean 'big'?" Rosenstein asks.

Moriah briefly hesitates, "We don't know that."

Rosenstein catches Moriah's hesitancy, but he lets it slide. For now.

Moriah stares directly at him, "Doctor, we are at our wit's end and our cryptologists are at their breaking point. We've got some of the finest minds working on this, but we seem no closer to a breakthrough than we did on day one. We *need* to know what they are saying to each other, especially now."

The desperation is clearly evident in Moriah's voice, a cardinal sin according to his father. Desperation, his father once said, instantly provides the other side an advantage, an advantage you absolutely cannot allow when bargaining, negotiating, or simply requesting a favor. In this case, however, time is of the essence, and Moriah *is* truly desperate for Rosenstein's help. Moriah knows Rosenstein is probably one of the smartest men on the planet, and if he cannot unlock the extraterrestrials' language and codes, then most likely no one can.

The two men continue to stare at one another. Rosenstein does not utter a word, dragging it out as long as possible.

Finally, Rosenstein questions incredulously, "And now you want my help? Is that what you're asking?"

"I'd like you to look at the data," Moriah indicates, "see if you can-"

Rosenstein interrupts with fire in his voice, "After everything your group has put me through and put my wife through, you ask for my help? On the day I put her in the ground, no less. I don't even think your father would have the balls to do this."

Moriah starts to respond when Rosenstein cuts him off again. "What's on the horizon, Alex?"

"What?"

"Don't play dumb," Rosenstein spits. "I know you guys have an idea or pet theory of what this might mean."

"Dr. Rosenstein, really, we don't know-"

"Alright, I've heard enough," Rosenstein responds, rising to his feet.

"Dr. Rosenstein, please-"

"Get out of my house!" Rosenstein exclaims.

"Okay, Doctor, you win," Moriah concedes, motioning with his hands for Rosenstein to calm down.

Rosenstein stares daggers at him as he waits for an answer, simply looking for a justifiable reason to throw Moriah out on his ass. Rosenstein does not possess a temper and rarely raises his voice, but he could be excused for flying into a rage on this particular day.

"The deception never stops," Rosenstein notes, "does it, Alex?"

"I did not tell you, Doctor," Moriah explains, "because I do not want you to feel I am coercing you to help us."

"I can handle it," Rosenstein counters.

Moriah sighs and looks defeated. Again, though, Rosenstein cannot discern if he is watching a professional actor at work.

"I received a call yesterday," Moriah says somberly.

Moriah looks up and with his eyes firmly fixed on Rosenstein's, adds dreadfully, "From Jericho."

The name hangs in the air like a cloud of noxious smoke. Neither man says a word for a few moments, the house as silent as a tomb except for the monotonous tick of the second hand on a nearby clock. Rosenstein slowly sits down on the couch with a look that is distant, shocked to the core.

Nearly everything Rosenstein knows about Jericho was from researchers' detailed reports outlining his captivity and those who were in close contact with him on a daily basis. Rosenstein recalled how they wrote about him in near-reverent tones, in awe of the creature's physical and mental prowess. They admired the amazing characteristics Jericho possessed and marveled at how a being could evolve into such a perfect storm of genius-level intelligence and physical indestructibility. To them, Jericho was a once-in-a-lifetime subject, and it was their immense privilege to be given the opportunity to study him.

"What did he say?" Rosenstein asks in a whisper.

"It's what we always feared, Doctor," Moriah replies.

Rosenstein waits for Moriah to continue as his heart pounds against his chest. He knows exactly what Moriah is about to say, but he does not want to hear the words spoken aloud.

"You mean . ."

Moriah nods gravely, "That's right, Doctor . . . *an invasion.*"

A few moments of silence pass between them as Rosenstein contemplates the truly terrifying implications Moriah's confirmation brings to mind.

"An invasion?" Rosenstein asks anxiously. "He told you this?"

Moriah nods and explains, "In less than three months time. He informed me that if the members of the Foundation wish to be spared, along with their families, we are to meet with him prior to the launch of the attack."

"When and where?"

"In the early morning hours of July sixth, outside Spokane, near Fairchild," Moriah reveals, the date and location not lost on Rosenstein.

"Not without a sense of irony, is he?"

"The son-of-a-bitch chooses the anniversary of Roswell," Moriah notes, "and the place where all of our research was conducted, not to mention where we held him captive for nearly two years."

"I would use the term 'captive' very loosely in his case," Rosenstein remarks.

Moriah concedes this, nodding slightly.

"It makes sense though," Rosenstein indicates. "The Pacific Northwest has always maintained a higher rate of sightings and bizarre UFO occurrences than the rest of the country, except for maybe California. He is starting where I would guess a large number of his comrades already reside."

"He said," Moriah explains, "that this will be the launching point from which he will coordinate the attack. The Foundation members who wish to be spared are to meet with him and will assist in the aftermath of the invasion, as liaisons between the extraterrestrials and the remaining members of the human race who do not perish in the initial . . onslaught."

"And you believe him?"

"Of course not," Moriah responds. "But we have little choice in the matter and not much time to consider our options. He has given us three days to decide, and if we don't go along with him . . ."

Moriah allows the words to hang in the air, an unspoken premonition of dread. "He, at least, gives us a chance," he adds.

Rosenstein instantly recognizes how foolish and utterly naïve Moriah's way of thinking is, not to mention dangerous. Rosenstein wholeheartedly believes that casting your lot with Jericho would be akin to digging your own grave, and while he would be disinclined to tell Moriah this, Rosenstein is instinctively suspicious Moriah does not realize this for himself. Rosenstein knows Moriah did not assume the position he is in by acting rashly, and it would be downright reckless of him not to examine the repercussions of such a course of action. Along with a host of other questions, Rosenstein begins to contemplate whether the Foundation is being set up by Jericho, and whether he himself is being set up by Moriah.

Why would Jericho need a liaison, let alone a multitude of them? What if the extraterrestrials' intention is to leave no members of the human race alive? What if it is all one big Venus flytrap set by Jericho? Does Moriah believe any of them would be spared?

"Did Jericho say anything else about the attack? How it would be coordinated?" Rosenstein probes.

Moriah shakes his head, "No, no specifics. We believe military bases and installations and large cities will be the obvious first targets. Perhaps even places that hold special significance, like the White House, the Capitol, the

Kremlin, the Eiffel Tower, the London Bridge, or the Great Wall of China, could also be destroyed. The destruction of these landmarks have the potential to demoralize people and completely sweep the public into a mass panic, causing a breakdown in the functioning of society or thwart an attempt at mounting a defense or counterattack with the small pockets of people still alive.

"This leads me to why I'm here today, Dr. Rosenstein. We need your help in trying to decipher their communications. If it is indeed an invasion, we need to determine any strategic information they are sharing with one another and exactly how they will carry this out."

"So what are you planning to do about it?" Rosenstein challenges.

"For nearly the last decade," Moriah explains, "we have been gathering data on individuals in the developed world who have absolutely no past to speak of: no birth certificate, no school attendance records, and essentially no history whatsoever. Individuals who, in our minds, appear virtually out of thin air, enter the workforce, and go about their business as any other person would.

"As you can imagine, it has been a massive undertaking, with files that could fill a hundred Pentagons. And it has not been without its problems. You would not believe how many people in this world prefer, or are forced, to erase their past and live quietly under a fictitious name. We've come across gangsters turned informants, battered wives, abused or orphaned children, people who've had sex changes, disgraced priests, traumatized veterans, corporate whistleblowers, the whole spectrum. Not to mention drifters, con artists, criminals, and all the other undesirables living on the fringes of society."

"Wouldn't it be easier if everyone just lived in mainstream society and paid their taxes?" Rosenstein asks wryly.

"Yes, it would," Moriah replies stonily, ignoring Rosenstein's sarcasm.

"So," Moriah continues, "once these people were eliminated, we examined the remaining individuals we could not dismiss, which was still quite a substantial number. Aside from knocking on every one of their doors and asking them questions, which was obviously impractical, or simply killing them indiscriminately, which seemed a bit extreme, we debated how we could determine whether or not the particular individual is, in fact, an extraterrestrial living among us.

"We also had the additional problem of people in the developing world. There is no record trail for over fifty percent of this population, and so the majority of them could be considered potential 'suspects' in our eyes."

Moriah's tone suddenly darkens and his voice seems to shift an octave lower.

"And then there is a subset of extraterrestrials we have only recently discovered, just in the last few years, and are the most difficult to detect. They are also, in our eyes, the most dangerous."

Rosenstein does not fail to notice the anxiety in Moriah's voice.

"We have dubbed them, 'The Devourers,'" Moriah indicates, "and this group does not fit neatly in the bucket I mentioned earlier: those that suddenly appear out of the ether and become a cog in society, with apparently no past of their own.

"The Devourers inherit an actual human being's life. They assume the person's identity and have all the documentation they need to prove it. They first study the person, adopting their habits, their routines, their quirks. They learn everything about the person, from the name of their first dog, to their favorite cereal, to how they did on a seventh-grade biology exam, to their neighbor's favorite drink. Absolutely everything that could come up in the most casual of conversations. When they have determined everything they need to know about the person, he or she is eliminated and immediately 'replaced.' We believe in most cases, the same fate befalls the victim's immediate family, which is probably done for two reasons.

"First, they do not want to arouse suspicion among any human members of the family. Second, and more importantly, it is simply more practical to have the entire 'family' working in concert for the protection of what we call the 'primary EBE.'

"These are extraterrestrials in occupations that likely require the highest and most rigid security clearance, so they cannot risk the lack of a background or some history on this planet. They are virtually impossible to detect unless they stumble on an element of the person's past they forgot or overlooked. In the past couple years, we have covertly tried to unearth thousands of suspected EBEs, with very little success. We only know 'The Devourers' exist because of a handful of small victories."

"Hold on a minute, Alex," Rosenstein says. "How do you know that every one of the extraterrestrials who have infiltrated our society are not one of these . . . 'devourers'?"

Moriah returns Rosenstein's gaze and acknowledges, "We don't. For all I know, you could be an EBE."

"And apparently so could you," Rosenstein retorts. "So what's your solution?"

"Well," Moriah answers, "it was suggested that perhaps our satellites could potentially identify extraterrestrials."

"How?"

"An individual in our organization with a scientific background put forward the idea that an extraterrestrial may release a different type of body heat when compared to a human being," Moriah explains. "She suggested that by using thermal imaging, we may be able to pinpoint the location of EBEs around the world."

"And?" Rosenstein asks hopefully.

Moriah shakes his head, "Nothing, but while we were researching this, we think we discovered another way to identify them."

Moriah pauses a moment before continuing.

"Although we cannot break their code, we believe that when they transmit information to each other throughout the world, the communication devices they use discharge a brief but noticeable signal in the infrared portion of the electromagnetic spectrum. We have been charting these communications and where they originate from with the help of our satellites.

"These signals are extremely fast, with bursts occurring in less than one millisecond, so they have been difficult to detect. But over the course of the last two years, we think we have formed an accurate picture of how many EBEs there are and where they reside."

"So what the hell are you waiting for?" Rosenstein asks expectantly. "Why not take them out?"

"We cannot run the risk of alerting Jericho that we know where his 'friends' are. And," Moriah adds, "there are more EBEs than we initially thought, making it impossible to eliminate a substantial number without alerting the others."

"How many more?" Rosenstein cautiously asks.

Rosenstein can tell by Moriah's body language that he is trying to downplay his response, but his grave tone betrays him.

"Our initial estimates suggest . . . approximately thirty thousand in the continental United States, maybe more, maybe less."

"Holy shit," Rosenstein gasps.

"Possibly in the neighborhood of two to three hundred thousand throughout the rest of the world," Moriah speculates.

"All the armies of the world collaborating together would not stand a chance against them, Alex," Rosenstein warns, "not with their technology."

"We've been making our own technological strides the last few years, Doctor," he states confidently.

"To compete with them?" Rosenstein asks, unconvinced.

"Well, we think we can let them know a war will not be a one-sided affair," Moriah indicates.

"And how would you do that?"

"We believe," Moriah explains, "the extraterrestrials scattered throughout the world will gather at several pre-determined locations prior to the attack. A consolidation of forces, so to speak. While they may think there is strength in numbers, we see it as a perfect opportunity to showcase our latest weapon."

"Which is?" Rosenstein asks.

Moriah smiles mischievously, which instantly reminds Rosenstein of the man's father. The look sends tingles up Rosenstein's spine and an unsettling feeling suddenly inhabits his entire body.

"A space-based laser system constructed specifically with their lone weakness in mind," Moriah states.

"Extreme cold?"

"Exactly," Moriah confirms.

"What about refraction and optical scattering from traveling through the atmosphere?" Rosenstein posits. "How will the laser stay on target?"

"By using an x-ray laser that is not affected by the atmosphere," Moriah replies.

"I thought preliminary tests of this were a disaster," Rosenstein notes.

"They weren't," Moriah bluntly responds.

"Another white lie to the public, Alex?"

Moriah smirks, but does not respond.

"So how will you employ your new toy?" Rosenstein questions.

"If you are able to decipher their code," Moriah indicates, "we can potentially determine their gathering locations prior to the attack. If we can identify these, we will target and eliminate if not all, a significant number of EBEs assembled at these locations, landing a crippling blow to their manpower."

"What about reinforcements?" Rosenstein proposes. "Have you considered if the attack is not restricted to their . . earth-based personnel?"

Moriah hesitates, but then states, "Of course we've thought about it, but there is no way of planning for such a contingency given that we do not know how many of them there are or where they come from."

"Not very preventative," Rosenstein notes suspiciously. "It's unlike the Foundation to neglect to examine all the angles."

Moriah shrugs indifferently, as if it is only a minor annoyance. "At this point, we've got to plan for what we know, Doctor."

The elder Moriah would never be so dismissive about such an integral factor when the group formulated their plan, and Rosenstein doubts the younger Moriah's flippant attitude is genuine. Rosenstein would guess that the group has absolutely no solution if this particular situation arises.

"When are you planning on launching your attack, assuming the code is deciphered?"

"The best case scenario is that," Moriah answers, "assuming you are able to break the code, we have the locations designated and targeted prior to meeting with Jericho. His true intentions will determine how we proceed."

"True intentions?"

"We have considered that the mere threat of attacking his 'army' may cause him to reconsider his plans for an invasion at our meeting. If, however, it is obvious that a war is what he wants, then that is what he will get, and we will launch the attack."

"A preemptive strike?" Rosenstein asks.

"In a manner of speaking," Moriah nods.

Throughout the course of their conversation, Moriah's explanations have failed to instill any confidence in Rosenstein that the Foundation's plan can be successfully executed. There are simply too many uncertainties and variables. In Rosenstein's opinion, their plan is at the mercy and subject to the whims of that cruel and unpredictable element of *chance*, a component the elder Moriah always eliminated from any equation.

Rosenstein wonders why the Foundation is relying on *him* given his troubled history with the group, not to mention the fact that they seem to be overly dependent on his ability to crack an impenetrable code no one has been able to decipher in fifty years of study. It is entirely uncharacteristic for the group to inadequately plan and prepare for every possible scenario, including if he is unable to accomplish what they are asking. Perhaps the group is losing its edge and avoided looking at the situation until it was too late, ignoring the problem because they could not devise an effective solution.

"Alex, what if this doesn't pan out-"

"Like we're expecting?" Moriah finishes.

He offers a melancholic smile and shrugs, "We have looked at this from several different angles and simply put, this is our best option. We cannot marshal the forces of the world in three months time behind the idea we are about to be invaded by an alien race and prepare them for what is coming. Besides, we don't have the technology to beat them in a straight war, you know that as well as anyone."

Suddenly, Moriah's voice crackles with menace, "But we can show them we're not rolling over either, that they're not taking *this country* and *this world* without a fight. I'll be damned to hell if Jericho thinks he can get the better of us so easily. I'm going to make sure he does not walk out of our meeting alive."

Moriah sounds so certain of this, not for one second does Rosenstein doubt the sincerity in his voice. The threat does not appear to be pure bluster or a prideful boast, and its inevitability to Moriah seems without question. A few moments of silence pass between them, the only sound once again the ticking of the clock.

"Tough talk, Alex," Rosenstein remarks.

"Yeah, well," he responds, "that's my halftime speech."

Moriah abruptly stands up from the couch.

"Now here's my other pitch," Moriah indicates. "I realize this is not the best of times for you, Doctor, but unfortunately Jericho is working according to his own timetable. We need your answer in twenty-four hours. We can provide you what little we have gathered so far on the code, but whether it helps or not, who can say."

Moriah fishes an item out of his pocket and then places a small card on the table between them. "Call this number when you've made your decision."

Moriah starts to exit while Rosenstein remains motionless on the couch, not bothering to escort him out.

Moriah turns around. "My only request, Dr. Rosenstein, is that you disregard your past with us in weighing your decision, because it has no bearing on why I've come here today. Every being on the planet will suffer the burden of a full-scale invasion: families, children, the innocent. I ask that you consider your answer for humanity's sake, for the continued existence of the human race could very well be on the line."

On that final dramatic note, Moriah turns and strides out of Rosenstein's home, leaving the latter to contemplate his decision. Playing the "innocent" card seemed utterly transparent and underhanded, but Rosenstein has to admit, it was smart. Moriah knows Rosenstein could possibly choose to spurn the group's overture simply out of spite. In order to counteract this possible knee-jerk reaction, Moriah appealed to Rosenstein's conscience to consider all the families and children that would suffer in the event of an invasion.

To refuse to help the Foundation as they prepare what may be the only chance for humankind to thwart an invasion is the same as turning your back on your country and in this case, *your world*, when you are needed most. Rosenstein understood what Moriah was implying: by ignoring the group's pleas for assistance, he would in essence be contributing to the deaths of the "innocent." He despises the man even more for employing such a cheap and unfair tactic to persuade him to help the group, and though Rosenstein is not one to fall for such an obvious ploy, the thought of children being slaughtered in a wholesale invasion is enough to give him pause.

After several minutes of replaying the conversation over and over in his mind, Rosenstein recalls what Moriah said regarding their belief that the invasion would likely commence in large cities. Immediately, he springs up from the couch.

Sean and his family live in a suburb bordering the Chicago city limits, a fact that shoots a wave of panic through him. He grabs the phone and places a couple of calls. After accepting condolences for his loss, he comes right to the point. Within minutes, he has the answers he is seeking and a solution that will bring him peace of mind.

Next he dials Sean, who picks up on the second ring. After assurances he is fine and it is unnecessary for him to come over, Rosenstein asks, "How would you feel about teaching a class at Hope College in Holland this summer?"

Several Hours Later

Rosenstein awakes with a start. Despite the coolness of the night air blowing through his open window, his face is blanketed in sweat, his bed sheets damp with perspiration. He instinctively reaches over to the other side of the bed to find it empty, the sheets on her side cool and unwrinkled. For the briefest of moments, he thought it was all a terrible dream: her long, agonizing death, the funeral, rummaging through her belongings. Now, upon feeling the vacant half of the bed, he realizes again that she really is gone, and the hurt and heartache return with as much ferocity as before.

He wipes the sweat from his brow and swings his legs onto the floor, sighing heavily. He sits there for several minutes, taking large, deep breaths. He glances at a picture of them on his nightstand, snapped several years ago while they were vacationing in Florida, a gorgeous sunset in the background and their happy, smiling faces in the foreground. He looks away sadly, rises from the bed, and trudges towards their bathroom.

After splashing several handfuls of water on his face, he gently pats his face dry with a towel, studying himself in the mirror. He has to admit he really does look like shit. His eyes are red and strained, his face is creased with lines of anxiety and drooping wrinkles, and even after several hours of sleep, he still looks like he has not slept in days.

"Falling apart here, Peaches," he mutters as he shuts off the bathroom light.

Rosenstein returns to their bedroom and pulls the covers down to get back into bed. Suddenly, a strange, tingly sensation causes the hairs on the back of his neck to stand up.

Someone is in the room with me, he thinks.

He whirls around and instantly sees a silhouetted figure in the corner of the room, sitting in a chair Pattie bought years ago at a swap meet. The figure rises quickly from the chair and moves toward him.

Rosenstein fumbles with the handle on his nightstand drawer as he calls out in a panic, "Who are you?"

The figure lifts his hands up to reassure Rosenstein.

"It's alright, Doctor," the figure responds, "it's me."

At the familiar sound of the figure's voice, Rosenstein pauses. Instead of reaching into the drawer, he turns on the bedside lamp, illuminating the figure before him.

Rosenstein exhales sharply.

"Sebastian!"

Sebastian smiles uncomfortably, which quickly disappears and is replaced by a look of sadness.

"I am-" Sebastian starts.

He pauses a moment.

"I am so very sorry for your loss, Dr. Rosenstein."

He looks as if he wants to say something more, but hesitates, his eyes barely meeting Rosenstein's.

Rosenstein nods, "I appreciate that, Sebastian, but what the hell are you doing in my bedroom in the middle of the night?"

"Please forgive me for the late hour," he responds shyly, "but this could not wait. I understand you've . . learned some things in the last few hours."

"I've been told something about an invasion," Rosenstein notes.

"Yes," Sebastian confirms. "And they have asked for your help?"

"Yeah," Rosenstein acknowledges. "They think I can decipher your code."

"You can't," Sebastian bluntly responds. "No human

being can, it is impossible. Besides . . . they are not even looking in the right place."

Rosenstein gives him a quizzical look, but Sebastian does not offer any further explanation. Instead, he asks, "Have you decided your answer?"

"I've been praying to God and asking my wife for guidance, but unfortunately," Rosenstein notes sadly, "neither of them have answered yet."

Sebastian smiles sympathetically, but Rosenstein knows Sebastian is probably incapable of understanding.

A few moments of silence pass between them, and then Sebastian states matter-of-factly, "Moriah is not telling you the whole story, Doctor."

"I figured as much," Rosenstein sighs, clearly not surprised.

"They've got other plans, other contingencies they're working on," he indicates.

"Like?" Rosenstein presses.

Sebastian looks at him intently and responds, "The serum."

The word instantly ignites something in Rosenstein, something he had long ago buried in the past. It is a long-dormant feeling he was desperately hoping to never encounter again. The word triggers many painful memories, of both animals and people manipulated, used, and then simply discarded when they were no longer useful. He will always regret failing to immediately recognize the slippery ethical path they walked at the beginning of the project, and his conscience reminds him every day that he should have discovered sooner the human element introduced in their research.

"The serum," he murmurs, his face hardening.

"They think they have perfected it," Sebastian notes.

"And they have been testing it again?" Rosenstein asks, trepidation creeping into his voice.

"Mostly on rats and other rodents," Sebastian reports, "but you know they will not stop there, Doctor. Soon they will be forced to move up the evolutionary ladder, and inevitably they will begin testing it on people."

Rosenstein closes his eyes and shakes his head, unable to comprehend how this could be happening all over again. A sick, twisted déjà vu none of them apparently learned anything from the first time around.

A word Sebastian used a moment ago suddenly registers with Rosenstein and he asks, "Forced? What do you mean they'll be *forced*?"

"Jericho has learned of the serum," Sebastian explains. "He has made a rather unusual demand for his meeting with the group."

"What's the demand?"

"Jericho wants the Foundation to bring him a sample of abductees who have been administered a dose of the latest version of the serum."

"*What?*" Rosenstein exclaims.

Sebastian shrugs, "Apparently, he wants to see for himself the direct results of the serum on the abductees. He wants to determine firsthand its effectiveness."

"But what would it matter by that time-"

"If Jericho is planning on destroying the majority of the human race in an invasion?" Sebastian finishes Rosenstein's thought.

Rosenstein nods.

Again, Sebastian shrugs, "A good question, Doctor, and one that only Jericho can answer."

"Is the group going to meet his demand?" Rosenstein inquires.

"That's hard to say," Sebastian responds. "Many of these people have dropped out of sight, and it will be difficult, even for the Foundation, to find them and compel them to cooperate."

"I don't think they will have a choice in the matter, Sebastian," Rosenstein says darkly.

Sebastian nods solemnly.

"What happens if the serum . . has the desired effect they're looking for?" Rosenstein wonders.

"If the serum," Sebastian states, "has what they judge to be a 'success' rate in the seventy to eighty percent range, they will consider distributing it to military personnel and then to the general public."

"How the hell do they plan on getting the public to take it?" Rosenstein asks angrily. "Putting it in the water supply?"

"No, Doctor," Sebastian explains, "they plan on fabricating a mysterious threat that requires an immediate vaccination. The threat, something like SARS or avian bird flu, will emerge overseas, and the government and news agencies will sound the alarm, urging people that they need the vaccination to protect against it, and they need it *immediately*."

"My God, they'll cause a panic," Rosenstein cries. "People will start rioting and tearing hospitals and clinics apart looking for it. How will they manage to get it past all the various health agencies? It would be impossible. The Foundation cannot possibly convince the whole world they are in mortal danger."

"You surprise me, Dr. Rosenstein," Sebastian

remarks. "You are well aware of the Foundation's influence and when necessary, their ability to manipulate the media machine to do their bidding. They've done it before to incite wars, overthrow regimes, and to create general chaos. Would it be so difficult for them to convince the world of an impending global health crisis?"

"Maybe not," Rosenstein concedes, "but even if the serum proves effective and people are supposedly 'vaccinated,' how much would it really help us in a full-scale war against your race?"

"Like I said before, Doctor," Sebastian notes, "this is only a preliminary option they have been considering. I am certain everyone in the group holds their own doubts about the practicality of it all, not to mention the vast number of people in the medical community who would cause an uproar over the lack of studies and evidence conducted on this mysterious threat. But they have to entertain all options at this point because frankly, the group has failed to confront the possibility that this day would ever come."

I knew it, Rosenstein thinks, taking little pleasure in being right about his earlier assumption.

"Sebastian," Rosenstein says, "you mentioned before other *contingencies* they're working on . . what else are they considering?"

"Their final option is, granted, probably the most unrealistic one," Sebastian indicates, "but if achieved, it could change everything."

"Yes?"

"The war would no longer be a one-sided affair."

It instantly dawns on Rosenstein that virtually the same statement was uttered by Moriah to him only hours before.

Rosenstein leans in closer, staring intently at Sebastian. "What has happened?" he asks expectantly.

"Several months ago," Sebastian reports, "the Russians had a major breakthrough."

Rosenstein appears confused at first, knowing there are any number of unexplained aspects of the extraterrestrials' technology which have yet to be unraveled by the human race. As Rosenstein studies Sebastian's face, a look of surprise crosses his own when he realizes Sebastian is referring to the most important aspect of them all, one that would have lasting and far-reaching implications for humanity and its future progress.

"It's your propulsion system, isn't it?" Rosenstein asks. "*They did it?*"

Sebastian shakes his head slightly and notes, "Well, not entirely, but they've been able to almost completely mimic our gravity amplifiers and wave tubes."

"My God," Rosenstein breathes, clearly taken aback, "fucking Russians. I always thought we'd beat them to it."

"So did I," Sebastian admits. "The Americans have more money, more people working on it, and better resources. I even thought the Chinese or Japanese would replicate the technology before the Russians, and they don't even have a model to work from. But in the end, all it took was one person: a man named Anton Chenkov, a brilliant, young physicist who only started working on the project less than a year ago."

The "project" has been ongoing for over half a century, since the time the Russians received their own "model" spacecraft, a supposedly unmanned ship that crashed in the countryside two hundred miles outside of Moscow. The considerably smaller size of the craft in

Russia compared to the one that crashed in the United States and the fact it was not several hundred feet underwater allowed them to transport it to a research facility for further study, an added advantage over the Americans, who were forced to study their ship at the bottom of a lake. This advantage, however, seemed irrelevant, until now at least.

Soon after both crafts allegedly crash-landed on Earth in their respective territories, the Americans and Russians attempted to reverse-engineer the technology of the propulsion system. For many years to no avail. Recently, however, the theory of "zero point energy" began to gain traction and acceptance in numerous scientific circles, and researchers in both countries considered the theory as a possible explanation for the extraterrestrials' propulsion system.

The concept of zero point energy is based in quantum theory, and many believe it has the potential to be *the* major breakthrough in space vehicle propulsion. The theory is predicated on the fact that so-called empty space, what is commonly referred to scientifically as the "quantum vacuum," is actually teeming with activity. In this apparent empty space, there are minuscule electromagnetic fields that continuously fluctuate, even if the temperature drops to absolute zero. A number of physicists accept it as real energy which we cannot directly sense since it is the same everywhere, even within our own bodies.

The Department of Defense has been studying the theory for over two decades, and it is believed that if these fluctuations can somehow be tapped, the amount of energy produced would be enormous. This would allow not only deep-space voyages impossible by today's propulsion methods, but would also enable high-altitude surveillance aircraft to travel anywhere in the world within a short amount of time to observe a potential enemy, a prospect that has intrigued the Defense Department, along with the Foundation.

It is thought that in order for spacecraft capable of interstellar travel to approach the speed of light, energy must somehow be harnessed from this empty space. It has been speculated the amount of energy in the quantum vacuum is comparable to that of nuclear energy, and possibly even greater. Obviously, its potential as a viable energy source could be limitless.

Unfortunately, the primary obstacle to validating the zero point theory is that no human being has been able to devise a catalyst or engineering process that can extract this energy. Doubly unfortunate is the fact that the extraterrestrials had, discovering a way to travel through space without the aid of rocket propellant. It also enabled them to travel to Earth decades ago for the purpose of scouting it as a possible future home, and it likely allowed their nanoprobes to arrive on Earth to study the human race longer than anyone could have imagined.

"This . . . Chenkov proved the zero point energy theory is correct?"

"In a manner of speaking," Sebastian confirms.

"And the Russians shared their breakthrough with us?" Rosenstein asks skeptically.

Sebastian shakes his head, "No, not at first. They knew how important this knowledge could be and its potential to shift the balance of power back to the days after World War II.

"But they, too," Sebastian continues, "monitor our communications, and they got spooked when they noticed the overflow of data coming through, which I'm sure Moriah mentioned to you earlier. A meeting was promptly called with the Americans. When several Foundation members present at the meeting subtly mentioned a possible invasion, the Russians decided they would need the resources and manpower of the Americans working alongside their own if there is to be any chance of resistance.

"The Russians shared their breakthrough and the Americans promptly replicated the technology. Soon enough, they will catch up to their counterparts in attempting to harness this energy. After that, I figure it will be only a matter of time before experiments are conducted by both nations to determine if they have matched our technology."

"Do you think the experiments will be a success?" Rosenstein asks hopefully.

"It is possible," Sebastian replies evenly.

There is a pause as Rosenstein considers this. "What exactly are we, uh . . I mean the Foundation plan on doing with this new technology?"

"Shortly after receiving this information from the Russians," Sebastian explains, "the Foundation commissioned several defense contractors to begin building replicas of our ships, albeit on a smaller scale, at various top secret military installations around the country. They have set a deadline of eight weeks for approximately five hundred ships to be constructed, a gargantuan task by any standard and one that will be impossible to achieve. By my estimation, they will be fortunate to build two hundred, possibly two hundred and fifty, in eight weeks time, even with work commencing around the clock.

"The final four weeks leading up to the group's meeting with Jericho will be used to outfit the ships with what they hope to be a perfected and fully functioning propulsion system. *Our* propulsion system."

"The Foundation seems overly optimistic for a theory they have yet to see in action," Rosenstein notes. "Tell me, Sebastian, are they also trying to replicate your weapons system for these ships?"

Sebastian flashes a proud, if not completely arrogant look. "They have yet to determine how our weapons system functions, technology I do not anticipate them deciphering in the near future."

The "armament" found on the extraterrestrials' ship has been a source of constant frustration for the researchers who have studied it since the craft was discovered. With the acquisition of the weapon Sean O'Connell and his men encountered in the jungle all those years ago, what some members of the Foundation have deemed "the baton," it is thought the same factors at work in this small device are also present in the weapons system on the extraterrestrials' craft. Of course, this theory did not bring the researchers any closer in their pursuit to crack the technology, which has been studied thoroughly and extensively for some time. The elusiveness of the technology continues to baffle researchers, who have yet to determine how the system works.

"I would assume that for now," Sebastian continues, "they plan on outfitting the ships with the standard armament found on your fighter planes, which-"

Sebastian gives Rosenstein a look of sympathy, "-unfortunately will not be enough to challenge us."

Rosenstein shakes his head in exasperation. "All of these options – the serum, the space-based laser system, the mass building of ships based on the zero point theory – are heavily reliant on the incredibly unstable element of chance. It's like they are throwing everything they can at the wall to see what will stick. But not one of them seems to have the slightest likelihood of succeeding, let alone providing us an opportunity to win in a full-scale war," he concludes.

"To be fair," Sebastian indicates, "the ability to operate a craft on zero point energy allows maneuverability unlike anything you have ever seen, and this would at least give the human race a chance to compete in a battle of the skies with our ships. But will they have time to train enough pilots in the handling of a ship powered by zero point energy? Probably not. It requires an extremely talented pilot to acquire a skill that is not easily taught.

"In regards to the serum," he continues, "the Foundation views it more as a preventative measure against the loss of aggression that alleged abductees have displayed. While the Foundation does not know exactly how or why this is done, they do not see a drawback to raising the aggression level of American soldiers and the general public at large in fighting a superior foe."

"But," Rosenstein points out, "you already told the Foundation *why* it is done: as a prelude to the future enslavement of the human race."

"Perhaps," Sebastian replies cryptically. "Perhaps not."

Rosenstein searches for more answers in Sebastian's inscrutable face.

"Here's what I propose, Doctor," Sebastian offers. "You will agree to help them in their attempt to break our code. Within two months, you will inform them that you have deciphered the code."

"I will?" Rosenstein asks, clearly surprised.

"Yes," Sebastian indicates, "with my help. You will inform Moriah that an invasion is, indeed, imminent. You will also tell him that it is a full-scale assault, with specific instructions that *no* prisoners are to be taken. This will contradict what Jericho suggested regarding the Foundation acting as liaisons, and confirm their meeting with him is a trap. You will provide him coordinates for nearly a dozen locations around the world where my comrades will gather-"

"Moriah was right about that?" Rosenstein interjects.

"Yes," Sebastian confirms, "standard marshaling of forces at strategic points around the globe. Once Moriah has the coordinates and knows the meeting with Jericho is a trap, he will believe he has the upper hand. He wants Jericho dead, does he not?"

"He claimed Jericho would not walk out of their meeting alive," Rosenstein recalls.

"Then he probably won't," Sebastian states. "Both sides will assemble an army for the meeting as a show of force, and while it may start with the pretense of discussion and possible negotiations, these will not last long. A vicious battle will ensue, and we will both get what we want."

"And what is that?" Rosenstein asks warily.

"You want the members of the Foundation dead for what they did to your wife and all those innocent people years ago, and I want Jericho dead for . . other reasons," he indicates.

At the mention of his wife, Rosenstein's eyes grow misty and he turns his face away from Sebastian, gazing at the picture of the two of them on the nightstand.

"There is more than that, though, isn't there Dr. Rosenstein?" Sebastian asks gently.

Rosenstein closes his eyes.

Sebastian lowers his voice to a whisper, "You want them dead for forcing you to kill Frank Parker. You want them dead because they made you give up your son, your only child."

Rosenstein suddenly erupts, "How the hell do you know all of this? How is it possible, Sebastian?"

Sebastian does not respond, but simply stares back at Rosenstein, a look of compassion on his face.

Rosenstein lowers himself onto the bed and wearily cradles his head in his hands. After several moments, he finally looks up at Sebastian.

"I do want them dead," Rosenstein acknowledges. "I've wanted them dead for so long, sometimes I can think of nothing else. I hate myself for feeling that way, but I do. They are pure, unadulterated evil with no thought or empathy for any obstacle standing in the way of their 'agenda.' They have ruined more lives and done more harm than good throughout their existence than anyone could possibly imagine. I think all of them should be wiped from the face of the earth."

Sebastian nods, "Then that is what you will get, Doctor."

Again, Rosenstein glances at the picture of him and Pattie on the nightstand, her smiling face beaming at him.

"What about Abraham?" Rosenstein abruptly asks.

"His health is failing," Sebastian reports, "and he is too sick to be involved in anything the Foundation is doing."

Sebastian pauses and then adds, "He will be dead soon."

Rosenstein shakes his head, "Nothing is for sure, Sebastian, especially with that tough son-of-a-bitch. I'll tell Moriah I will hand over the gathering locations on one condition."

"What is that?"

"When they test the serum, which we know they eventually will," Rosenstein says confidently, still staring at the picture of Pattie, "I want Abraham to be one of the subjects."

"Doctor . . . it's supposed to be only abductees."

"I want him to know how it feels," Rosenstein menacingly says. "I want him to be on the other side of the cage."

Rosenstein turns and faces Sebastian, his eyes ablaze with fury. Sebastian studies Rosenstein for several moments before he nods.

"Alright, Doctor," he relents. "Inform Moriah that Abraham is to be one of the subjects or else you will not help them."

Rosenstein nods his appreciation and again glimpses at the picture of Pattie, giving her a slight wink.

"Moriah will wonder how you know about the serum," Sebastian notes.

"I'm confident that you can continue to avoid detection," Rosenstein states. "After all, you've been doing it for years."

"We will be in touch, Doctor," Sebastian replies, and he turns to leave.

"Sebastian?"

Sebastian stops and turns around.

"Why do you want Jericho dead?" Rosenstein asks.

Sebastian considers the question for a moment before responding, "Understand this, Doctor, we are typically a very benign species. We do what we need to do for survival. We do not kill each other, as it is known here, in 'cold blood,' nor do we do it to rob, for sport, or simply because we can. Life is more sacred to us than it is to your race.

"Jericho, however, has absorbed some of the most wicked and evil characteristics of your race. He is a disgrace, and his time has come," Sebastian concludes.

Rosenstein nods and waits for Sebastian to exit, but instead the latter removes an object from his pocket and places it on the dresser.

"You asked how I could possibly know all those things about you? Well, this might give you an idea."

Rosenstein looks at the object, which appears to be a miniature spray bottle.

"Give it a tug with the lights out," Sebastian suggests, and he turns to exit.

Once more, Rosenstein catches him at the threshold of the doorway.

"Sebastian?"

He turns his head around towards Rosenstein.

For a moment, a look of anxiety and fear blanket Rosenstein's face, as if he is afraid to ask his next question, or perhaps hear the answer to it.

"Can we survive it?" he hesitantly asks. "Can we survive the invasion?"

There is a long pause as Sebastian stares at him, seemingly teasing out the suspense of the moment.

"Who said there is even going to be an invasion?" Sebastian smirks.

A look of shock registers on Rosenstein's face, but before he can ask another question, Sebastian disappears from the doorway and melts into the night.

FIFTEEN

Moriah, Bellini, and several other members of the Foundation hurry from their plane, which only moments before landed at Fairchild Air Force Base, several miles west of Spokane, Washington. They walk briskly, all of them staring straight ahead, thinking about the business at hand. They do not speak, nor do they look around at their surroundings or at one another. Despite their focus and their purposeful strides, worry is etched on their faces and fear lurks behind their eyes.

Fear is not an emotion that these men and women typically display, let alone seem to possess. It is an anomaly, an aberration, a "statistical irregularity" on the scale of emotions. Fear is a feeling that, contrary to the general public, seems to lie dormant in these individuals, emerging only when humanity has at last come face-to-face with its greatest threat. The group's confidence in its ability to produce all the answers and devise the most effective solutions has, in this case, been severely tested. Indeed, they have never been more uncertain of the path they have chosen, of their plans to stop what could be humanity's ultimate destruction.

The plan has not unfolded without its hitches, but they prepared and anticipated obstacles along the way. Moriah remains confident, if not internally then at least in appearance, for the sake of the other members of the group, who look to him for guidance, leadership, and most importantly, assurances. Though he cannot deliver any guarantees or promises tonight, he is resolute in his belief that they can win this battle and essentially, this war.

Moriah would certainly agree, however, that the plan began rather inauspiciously, and they have encountered a steady stream of "issues" throughout. The problems started early, with Sean O'Connell killing one of their men and escaping from the beach, a fact wholly inexplicable to Moriah given that the man's family had been taken, along with the rest of the residents of Tamawaca. Now O'Connell remains at large and on the run, no doubt searching for his family and likely being helped by his dear old dad, Rosenstein, a man whose ability to learn confidential, inside information only members of the Foundation are privy to continues to baffle Moriah and the rest of the group.

Next, the group discovered that *documented footage* of the aftermath of what occurred in Tamawaca now exists, courtesy of Colonel Fizer's ineptitude. The colonel had assured Moriah that he would handle satellite coverage of the area, and it is abundantly clear that he had failed miserably to deliver on his promise. While Moriah is convinced Sergeant Kaley's copy of the footage was destroyed or is at the bottom of Lake Michigan by now, a search of

Private Rushmore revealed that he had not retained his copy, an unsettling fact to be sure.

Moriah partially blames himself, for he has always been reluctant to place any significant amount of responsibility in Fizer's hands, and his suspicions, unfortunately, appear warranted. Fizer's utter incompetence could have disastrous implications for the group. If the mysterious footage is located and exposed to the bright glare of the media spotlight, a barrage of questions will eventually come showering down upon the colonel. If Fizer cracks, Moriah wholeheartedly believes that the colonel would not hesitate to give up other members of the Foundation or the group itself in order to save his own skin.

In addition to all the various snags thus far, Moriah will eventually have to address the decimation of the group's Special Forces squad out of Fort McPherson, over half of whom perished in the battle against Kaley and Eisley. It is simple enough to explain away the death of one or two soldiers to their families, pinning the culprit on the standard and generic "training exercise accident." At some point, however, Moriah will be forced to "create" a plausible scenario for why the group went rogue and formulate a reasonable and justifiable account explaining how over half the squad was killed.

And the bodies continue to drop.

Moriah recently received word that two of the group's most loyal associates, Bason and Stringer, aides to General Cozey, were brutally murdered in Tamawaca. Equally maddening is the fact that he is still unable to determine exactly who was behind it and why.

The most recent piece of bad news was received moments prior to landing at Fairchild. A pair of the

Foundation's specialists were arrested by local police at the airfield where a "malfunction" was being arranged on General Parker's plane. Instead, the specialists are in the custody of the authorities, and Parker and Lieutenant Colonel Hermann continue their irritating roles as the Hardy Boys trying to unravel this mystery.

Despite encountering an inordinate amount of setbacks and obstacles that the group is typically unaccustomed to, these problems can be placed on the back burner at this point. After tonight, they may all be a moot point. After tonight, there may not be a mass media to report some of the "irregularities" in the attack at Tamawaca and there may not be an outraged public to answer to. All of these problems seem insignificant when compared with what is to occur tonight.

In fact, Moriah's primary concern is the possibility Jericho was present in Tamawaca and is aware of what occurred there. Moriah's ultimate fear is that Jericho has made "adjustments" in his game plan, that he has altered the sequence in which Moriah believes the events of tonight will unfold. Any radical changes at this point in the mission could well prove catastrophic. The point of no return passed long ago, and now is no longer the time to worry about things that are past, but rather focus on the present and attempt to ensure for humanity a future.

The men, with Moriah leading the way, stride towards a gigantic airplane hangar located within an isolated part of the base. This area of the base is bathed in darkness, as requested, with intermittent shadows the result of several dull lights scattered around the hangar. The large hangar door is closed, but Moriah and his entourage walk towards a smaller door on the side of the building.

Moriah dramatically flings the door open and calmly moves inside. He hears the low whispering of voices as he enters, his men following closely behind. With each footfall on the shiny, spotless floor, their echoes are gradually the only sound that remains as all conversation suddenly comes to a halt and every face in the hangar turns to look at him.

They stare at him and Moriah in turn looks around the hangar at each of them, noting a mixed assortment of emotions on their faces – apprehension, anxiety, desperation, fear – and he knows they are waiting to be told everything will unfold as they have envisioned. They want to be comforted in the knowledge that they, along with their families, will be safe after tonight, that they can all be assured of living a rich, full life. They want and indeed *crave* the reinforcement that their group will survive, that they will continue to make decisions on behalf of people who do not seek their counsel and nations that do not know they exist. They want to be informed that their actions tonight will not only save their country, but their world as well. Finally, they want to be reassured that the appropriate course of action has been chosen on behalf of the human race, and only by seeing the plan through to the end can they guarantee their race's continued existence.

Moriah continues to scan the hangar, knowing each and every face in this room, but he is unable to recall ever seeing the kind of emotions occupying each one. Despite Jericho's directive that the members' families should also be present if they wish to be spared, no one brought their family once they determined the meeting to be a trap. Each of them knows how dangerous Jericho is, and none of them want their families even remotely close to him for fear of what might happen to them. The members of the group have stashed their families at secluded and hopefully secure locations around the country. Moriah is well aware that in the worst case scenario, it is possible a significant number of them will never see their families again, a prospect Moriah will choose not to dwell on.

In this atmosphere of extreme trepidation, the group looks to their leader for any assurances that can soothe their troubled minds. Moriah knows a solid and dependable leader always monitors the pulse of his followers and always maintains a handle on their emotional state. Moriah is fully aware of the group's fragile mindset, and he realizes how easily, with his own words, he can push them to one extreme or another: total confidence or sheer panic. He also knows a good leader is honest with his troops and does not pull any punches when appropriate. Tonight, however, honesty may have no place in this hangar.

As the group waits expectantly, waiting for that first word to be uttered, Moriah continues his survey of the hangar. At that moment he realizes the magnitude of it all, the absolute uncertainty of what is to come, and he knows it is his job, his *obligation*, to quell the fear infiltrating the room.

Moriah opens his mouth and he proceeds to tell the assembled mass what they want to hear: the Foundation is strong, the Foundation is right, and most importantly, the Foundation will survive this night, at the expense of their enemies tonight and for generations to come.

*   *   *

General Parker, Lieutenant Colonel Hermann, and Private Anderson now have a specific destination thanks to Augie's contact at the Justice Department: Fairchild Air Force Base, outside of Spokane, Washington.

The men feel a combination of curious anticipation and nervous excitement, unsure what to expect when they arrive. Parker attempted to personally contact the base several times to speak with the commanding officer, but was rebuffed each time, the phone ringing incessantly into an uninhabited void. For no one to answer at a United States military installation once is unusual, but for it to occur repeatedly is a travesty and a severe breach of duty. When they arrive, Parker vowed to "set the assholes straight."

Compounding the general's already highly agitated state is the additional intelligence that arrived from one of Augie's contacts a short time ago. Augie's contact learned that approximately two months prior, a request for some unusual "equipment" for training exercises in Florida was placed by a Lieutenant Luis de Santo, second-in-command of a Special Forces squad based out of Fort McPherson, Georgia. Lieutenant de Santo is, essentially, the right-hand man to Sergeant Major Victor Ruethorn, and the equipment requested included a half-dozen Apache helicopters, a Navy *Spruance*-class destroyer, and several hundred pounds of explosives. The request was approved, but the authorizing party failed to sign the request form or even provide their seal. There was simply a rubber-stamp mark that read, "APPROVED." Such a request would have certainly raised eyebrows and assuredly generated a host of questions, making the rubber-stamp approval all the more disturbing and suspicious.

Augie's contact tracked where the request was submitted and ran straight into a dead end. After scouring the records at numerous bases in the Southeast, he could not find any such request or approval of said request by the commanding officers at these installations. Augie's contact instead decided to follow the trail of the equipment, and what he subsequently discovered stunned General Parker and Lieutenant Colonel Hermann.

The equipment was "released" by a military base located in Youngstown, Ohio, with the commanding officer none other than General Warren Marshfield, Parker's old friend, suspected member of the Foundation, and a man with close ties to Malcolm Fizer. For such a request to even arrive at the desk of General Marshfield, located in Ohio, from a squad based in Georgia and allegedly conducting exercises in Florida, was extremely strange, if not downright suspicious. The more important question may be how Marshfield had several Apache helicopters in his possession and a *Spruance*-class destroyer under his command in the first place.

Parker immediately attempted to contact General Marshfield to ask this very question, but the secretary at his base informed Parker the general had unexpectantly left to attend to family business and is currently unreachable. The timing seems uncanny – first Fizer goes A.W.O.L. and now Marshfield disappears under the guise of "family business."

"What's happening here, General?" Augie frustratingly asks.

"I don't know, Augie," Parker replies, "but the coincidences seem to be piling up. The answers must lie at Fairchild . . . something is happening there . . ."

They are approximately an hour flight time from their destination, yet to all of them it is an hour too long. Things are starting to unravel now, and Fairchild seems to be the hand that might pull the final string.

The sound of Augie's phone erupts yet again, jolting all of them from their own private thoughts. Parker and Anderson immediately stare at him, knowing the potential for more information and more clues is usually only a call away.

"Yes?" Augie answers.

He listens a moment before saying, "Give me the bad news first."

After a few seconds, Augie replies, "Yeah, a knife. There was blood on it, yeah."

There is a long pause as Augie listens intently.

"What? How can that be?" he disbelievingly asks.

After a few moments, Augie states, "Alright, now give me the worse news."

Parker sighs in exasperation, silently chiding himself for hoping the person on the other end of the line had a portion of good news in store for them.

Augie's jaw drops after listening for several seconds, and then he finally asks, "What did the MPs say?"

Another few moments pass before he sharply exclaims, "*What?*"

There is another long pause.

"Ask them again. Yeah . . okay, thanks Doctor."

Before Augie has even disconnected the call, Parker smothers him with questions. "What happened? What's going on with the MPs? Who was that?"

"You want the bad news or the worse news first?"

"I'll take it in your order," Parker responds, anticipating the worst regardless.

"That was the medical examiner who is conducting the autopsies on Bason and Stringer," Augie explains, "and he said that based *strictly* on a preliminary examination of their wounds, they are *not* consistent with that of a knife or dagger."

Parker waits expectantly. "Okay, so . . what did he think caused the wounds?"

Augie is reluctant to even say it, but he nonetheless relays the information from the ME, "He thinks the wounds were caused by the claws of some kind of an animal, but the wounds are unlike anything he has ever seen."

Augie pauses and then adds, "The savageness and the strength required to create those kinds of wounds . . . he could think of no animal capable of producing them, let alone a man."

"That's ridiculous," Parker states. "Did you tell him we discovered a knife in Nitchie's *hand*?"

Augie nods, "I told him, sir, but he says the wounds do not correspond with the knife found in Nitchie's possession."

"Did either of you see Nitchie carrying anything else?" Parker asks. "Anything at all?"

Both men shake their heads.

"Did they ask Nitchie about it or search him again?" Parker inquires.

Augie hesitates a moment, then reluctantly replies, "Now for the worse news."

"Oh, shit," Parker mutters.

"Nitchie's gone, sir," Augie says bluntly, "and the story from the MPs does not make a whole lot of sense. One of them claims that Nitchie somehow . . . made himself 'look' exactly like his partner and he basically walked right out the door."

There is a long pause as Parker shakes his head in disbelief.

"The haymakers just keep coming, don't they boys?"

*   *   *

Kaley and Dawson initially believed they landed at some type of military base, but as they moved about, they quickly wondered if the base had long been abandoned. They did not see any other military personnel and in fact, there did not appear to be another living soul walking the grounds. There is an eerie and unnerving quiet permeating the entire place, making them feel marooned in the middle of nowhere. When Fizer and Ruethorn realized Kaley had escaped, they anticipated the base becoming awash in bright lights, accompanied by the sound of blaring alarms and roving groups of soldiers scouring the base searching for them. Fortunately for them, this has yet to occur, causing them to question whether this truly is a military base and the all-too-obvious question if it is:

Where is everybody?

After Kaley and Dawson fled, they remained in the shadows, maintaining a close watch on the plane and anxiously waiting for their captors' reaction after they discovered their missing prisoner. A couple minutes passed and then Ruethorn emerged from the same exit Kaley and Dawson escaped thru a short time before. Ruethorn ventured several steps in a semi-circle around the back of the plane, peering into the darkness to determine if he could catch a glimpse of Kaley scurrying away. His search was brief, however, as Fizer hastily exited the plane, conducted a short discussion with Ruethorn as both men scanned the surrounding shadows, and finally, they seemed to decide they had more immediate concerns.

When Fizer and Ruethorn hurried to the opposite end of the base, Kaley and Dawson followed them to an isolated hangar. The hangar is located in an area of the base that is darker and more inconspicuous compared to the rest of the base, an element that worked to Kaley and Dawson's advantage as they tailed Fizer and Ruethorn. The two men entered the hangar while Kaley and Dawson decided to err on the side of caution and remain outside.

As they waited outside the hangar, Kaley and Dawson noticed a parade of other small-engine planes approaching the base, their lights small and barely perceptible even against the night sky. Subsequently, they heard the whine of a plane engine as each one passed overhead, followed by a familiar screech as the pilot applied the brakes upon landing. The planes seemed to be arriving on or around the same runway where Kaley and Dawson's plane landed only a few minutes ago.

Shortly after each plane arrived, they observed the intermittent appearance of small clusters of men and women entering the same hangar as Fizer and Ruethorn. These people silently emerged from the shadows, as if they were mere apparitions suddenly conjured up from the darkness. Oftentimes Kaley and Dawson heard the sound of their shoes echoing off the concrete before they actually saw them, but this was the only sound they made. They noticed that none of the people within each group spoke to one another or engaged in any conversation that might provide Kaley and Dawson a clue to what is happening here. Finally, their curiosity overcame them and they decided to move closer for a better look.

On the far side of the building, Kaley and Dawson find several small windows that allow them to peer into the hangar. When they peek inside, they encounter a rather unusual sight.

The hangar is filled with grave-looking men and women, the men outfitted in fine-cut suits while the women appear dressed for an important business meeting. Kaley and Dawson immediately notice a collective look of anxiety and nervousness that seems to pervade the group. There is minimal conversation and uncertain sideways glances.

"Looks like everyone is going to a wake," Dawson remarks.

"Yeah," Kaley agrees, "they're definitely dressed in their Sunday best."

Dawson spots Fizer and points him out, "There's our boy."

Kaley follows Dawson's finger and sees Fizer standing next to Ruethorn as they speak to a small group of men near them.

"Have they forgotten about us?" Dawson wonders.

"Doubt it," Kaley replies. "But it is strange no one seems to be looking for us."

As soon as Kaley says this, they both glance behind them to confirm that no one in fact is looking for them. They find no one sneaking up on them and there are no searchlights combing the grounds. They look at each other and smirk, recognizing that their paranoia is mutually shared.

After observing the scene inside the hangar for several more minutes, Dawson notes, "They look like they're waiting for something."

"Yeah," Kaley nods, "or someone."

As if on cue, the small door to the hangar suddenly swings open and a striking man in a jet-black suit enters, a group of men following closely in his wake. Kaley and Dawson immediately notice what little conversation there is instantly comes to a halt as all eyes look to the man who has just entered. The man walks briskly yet confidently. He scans the faces of the assembled group, his gaze seemingly taking in everyone around him, as if he is sizing them up.

The man walks towards a miniature platform located at one end of the hangar, which he quickly scales. The man pauses, looks out upon the group and patiently waits, in seemingly no hurry to speak. Unlike nearly everyone else in the hangar, the man appears calm and collected, as if he is out for a stroll in the park with nary a care in the world. After what seems like an eternity, but in reality is probably less than a minute, the man addresses the assembled group.

Kaley and Dawson cannot discern what the man is saying, but only hear muffled words here and there. Words like "foundation," "duty," "privilege," and "enemies" can be heard when the man's voice rises in pitch, but for the most part the man speaks in an even tone throughout. Shortly after beginning his speech, Kaley and Dawson become aware of something strange – the countenance of the people within the hangar starts to change. The anxiousness and apprehensiveness gradually fades and is replaced by faces that radiate confidence, self-assurance, and pride.

"Is this guy a motivational speaker or something?" Dawson asks.

"My sentiments, too," Kaley concurs.

The man does not gesture wildly or act overly demonstrative, but when he hits his high notes, he has full command of the room. Indeed, the audience is enraptured by the man and completely engrossed in his speech. They nod their heads and their looks of fear soon vanish entirely. The audience is his now and the man seems to expect nothing less.

At last, the man punctuates his speech by slapping one hand into the other and saying something about how strong they are and how their enemies will continue to fear them for years to come. At the end, the people do not applaud or shout testimonials, but rather all of them exchange a look of satisfaction, perhaps even arrogance.

The man steps down from the platform and the rest of the group starts filing out of the hangar. The man walks toward Fizer and Ruethorn, whisking them aside for a private discussion. Kaley and Dawson obviously have no idea what Fizer and Ruethorn may be telling him, but judging from the look on the man's face, a strong possibility is Kaley's escape. The man's façade never changes, but they can discern in his features a sudden, smoldering intensity, as if he is preparing to lash out at them. Instead, he nods his head and motions Fizer to follow him, while Ruethorn accompanies the rest of the throng outside.

The man and Fizer walk towards the opposite end of the hangar away from the group.

"Where are they going?" Dawson whispers.

They exit through a door around the corner from where Kaley and Dawson are standing.

"Let's find out," Kaley suggests, motioning for Dawson to follow him.

Kaley and Dawson slink towards the corner of the hangar. When they arrive there, Kaley cautiously peeks around the corner and then quickly pulls his head back.

"Shit!" he whispers. "They're walking right towards us."

Dawson looks at him in alarm as Kaley crouches low against the side of the hangar and motions for her to do the same. Dawson follows suit and they bunch against one another to appear as small as possible in the event the two men turn the corner. They hear a muffled conversation growing louder as the men move closer to their position. They both realize that there is not enough time to run and hide, as one way will entail dashing headlong into the group filing from the hangar and the other way will force them to flee across a vast, open space.

As their heartbeats pound in their ears and their breath seems frozen in their lungs, Dawson grips her knife tightly while Kaley wonders how much fight he has left in him. With Colonel Fizer playing the role of the adversary, however, neither of them likely needs any extra incentive in the event of a confrontation. Kaley considers whether they should simply jump the two men as soon as they round the corner.

He is about to propose this very idea when Dawson suddenly yields to her curiosity, leaning across Kaley's body and peering around the corner to determine their location. She sees Fizer only a few yards away, the other man slightly behind him. Dawson maintains her gaze an instant too long when Fizer suddenly looks straight ahead and spots her.

A look of shock crosses his face and he immediately turns to alert the man behind him. Before he can utter a word, however, they hear the *thwack* of a discharged weapon, the muted sound indicative of a gun equipped with a silencer.

Dawson sees Fizer's head practically explode, sending blood and brain matter splattering against the side of the hangar. She instinctively cries out in alarm before Kaley covers her mouth with his hand and pulls her back around the side of the building next to him. They hear the sound of Fizer's body striking the concrete with a dull thud. This is followed a moment later by a consecutive *thwack, thwack* as the killer appears to pump two more rounds into the colonel.

Kaley and Dawson again hold their breath as they nervously wait to see if the killer walks around the corner.

Well, two versus one now, Kaley thinks.

After several nerve-racking seconds elapse, they finally hear the man walk away from them, the sound of his footsteps fading.

Dawson pushes Kaley's hand away from her mouth and they wait another minute. They finally peek around the corner to find the killer gone, while the motionless body of the colonel remains. They cautiously move towards him, their morbid curiosity easily satiated as they stare at the wound to Fizer's head. It appears like someone took a sledgehammer to the colonel's skull as a large pool of blood has already formed underneath his upper body.

For Dawson, the shock of seeing someone murdered directly in front of her, let alone someone she knows, is numbing. For Kaley, this is not the first dead body who met a violent end he has seen and likely will not be the last.

"Come on," Kaley murmurs, glancing around, "somebody might come back to take care of the body."

Dawson continues to stare at the colonel, unable to take her eyes off him. She does not know what to feel for the man she relentlessly pursued and held such animosity towards in the last hours of his life. On the one hand, the colonel ignored her, deceived her, shot at a vehicle he believed she occupied, and in general seemed to be an arrogant prick who likely got what he deserved. On the other hand, he wore the same uniform as her and served his country for several decades, something she admires and respects. She does not believe anyone should have to die in the cold, cruel manner that befell the colonel, his back turned with no idea his life was about to come to a sudden end.

"Dawson . . "

She looks at Kaley.

"Let's go," he urges, "we're going to the wake."

Dawson nods and reaches down to retrieve Fizer's gun from his holster. She takes one last look at the colonel and then hurries after Kaley.

SIXTEEN

Spokane Plains Battlefield State Park

Inside the boundaries of Spokane Plains Battlefield State Park, nine miles west of Spokane and just west of the entrance to Fairchild Air Force Base, the helicopter gently touches down in a small clearing surrounded by a thicket of trees. The blades of the chopper gradually come to a stop as Rosenstein concludes telling Sean about the dual visits he received after Pattie's funeral.

Sean motions toward the front of the helicopter, "I asked Ms. Sloan about Sebastian, but I got the standard evasive response. He is actually . . one of them?"

"Yes," Rosenstein confirms. "He approached me not long after Pattie became sick and said he knew many things about me. He knew about the research Abraham and I conducted for the Foundation over a half-century ago, how they planned on eliminating me because they believed I would go public regarding the experiments, the fact that I was only alive because of Frank Parker, and the horrible things they had done to Pattie so long ago.

"He claimed he knew all these things because he had infiltrated the Foundation for some time, that they believed him to be an actual member. I was obviously instantly suspicious of him, thinking it was some kind of a trick and the Foundation was trying to set me up. I didn't think it was possible for *anyone* to infiltrate the group, but his . . .'demonstration' convinced me otherwise."

"Demonstration?" Sean repeats.

"That's when he *showed* me," Rosenstein states cryptically.

"*Showed* you?"

"That he is an extraterrestrial," Rosenstein explains.

"How?"

"He shifted right before my eyes," Rosenstein says evenly.

"You're shitting me," Sean responds incredulously.

Rosenstein shakes his head and remarks, "It was like looking into a mirror."

Sean considers this for a moment and then suddenly realizes what Rosenstein means.

"He shifted into . . you?" Sean asks.

Rosenstein nods.

"Jesus," Sean utters.

"After that," Rosenstein continues, "he laid out all the intricate details behind my research and everything else only a person on the inside could know. I drilled him with question after question and he knew everything the group had been doing right down to the letter, like he had actually been there from the beginning. Sebastian is the source of nearly everything Ms. Sloan has told you here tonight, and it is the exact same story he first shared with me."

"But why you?" Sean wonders.

"I thought the same thing, too," Rosenstein acknowledges. "Why did he choose *me* to share this information with? And I posed this very question to him. He responded that in all his years around the Foundation, no one had ever possessed the courage to challenge the group and threaten to expose them and their misdeeds to the public. I think that because of this, he believed he could trust me."

Rosenstein shakes his head and smirks. "It's amazing really . . . he seems so innocent, so naïve about humanity. He believes the human race as a whole to be quite extraordinary, and he is rather enamored by our inquisitive and exploratory nature, saying we always seem to be striving towards a better future for ourselves and our planet.

"At first, I wanted to laugh and tell him he probably had not read a newspaper or watched the news lately. There are wars raging throughout the world, people commit unspeakable acts of cruelty to one another, drugs and violence rule our large cities, hundreds of thousands of people die every day from starvation, and probably most telling, we are rapidly cooking our planet, the only place we can call home, to the point it could be uninhabitable within the next century. But I did not say any of that. I looked at him and realized he was truly sincere in what he believed.

"But it was clear to him that the Foundation is a cancer, a group capable of destroying everyone on this planet because they cannot harness and control their own power, let alone their massive egos and brazen arrogance. He knows we share a mutual hatred for them and he proposed a partnership. If I would agree to help him, we could bring about both the Foundation's and Jericho's downfall."

"Why do you think you can trust him?" Sean inquires. "I mean, what makes you think he isn't lying to you?"

Rosenstein considers the questions for a few moments before finally answering, "I probably couldn't even tell you, Sean, but I saw the earnestness in his face and . . I don't know, I just knew I could trust him. He seemed to want to help us."

By that, Sean assumes Rosenstein is referring to the human race, but it could also have more self-serving connotations.

"As I'm sure Ms. Sloan explained to you earlier," Rosenstein continues, "Sebastian claimed years ago to be a human abducted on nearly a hundred occasions by aliens. He suddenly appeared with classified documents in hand and forced the Foundation to deal with it."

"What do you mean?"

"They conducted numerous mole hunts and did not discover one extraterrestrial in their extensive searches – do you know how that was possible?"

"Not the slightest clue," Sean concedes.

"The Foundation did not actually *catch* any extraterrestrials, but that was because Sebastian forced them all to abandon their posts."

"You're losing me, Al," Sean admits.

With the patience of a saint, Rosenstein explains, "Sebastian became aware that Jericho and his comrades had infiltrated our society and were working in positions of power and influence in the government and defense and weapon industries. Sebastian somehow pilfered his classified and highly confidential documents from areas where he knew members of Jericho's group had established themselves. This was purposely done with the intent to raise suspicion in that particular area, compelling the Foundation to start whacking the weeds in an effort to uncover those they believed were responsible for supplying these documents to Sebastian.

"When Jericho learned of the mole hunts, he was forced to recall all of his 'colleagues' from their positions in order to avoid being discovered. And the Foundation learned, to their utter shock and dismay, how effective Jericho's group had been at infiltrating our society, as there was suddenly a mass exodus of various prominent individuals from notable posts in the industries I mentioned."

"Sounds like a mass disappearance to me," Sean remarks.

"It was," Rosenstein concurs. "These 'people' were never heard from again, like they had all fallen off the face of the earth. Colleagues and friends of these missing individuals were baffled, especially when they became aware of others in the same network who suddenly and mysteriously disappeared at the same time. Rumors and stories were of course rampant, from the belief that all of these individuals were foreign spies who were about to be exposed, to the theory that they were a secret branch of the CIA and NSA intent on bringing about radical change in American policies from the inside, to the speculation that they were part of a mind-control experiment run amok and they had been mass assassinated by the government.

"The fact is the Foundation would not even dip their toes in this water, as they quickly realized there would be no legitimate or even feasible story that could explain the mass disappearance of all these people. In essence, they chose to note it and then ignore it."

"So Sebastian sabotaged Jericho and his cohorts," Sean notes, "which ultimately benefited the Foundation."

"Yes," Rosenstein nods, "but in Sebastian's mind, he was acting on behalf of the human race. He was not ignorant of the correlation between Jericho's group and the Foundation given their adversarial position – harming one group would likely result in a benefit to the other group – and he viewed it from the perspective that the damage inflicted would outweigh the advantage gained.

"After that, Sebastian disappeared for a while because he was terrified Jericho would come after him for his . . betrayal."

"And so the first time you met Sebastian was after Pattie got sick?"

"Yes," Rosenstein confirms, "he visited me several times during Pattie's long battle. He was actually a great comfort, providing me hope for justice during what was a bleak and depressing time. He continually assured me that we will make the world a better place without the Foundation and Jericho in it, insisting that our time will come, and when it does, they won't know what hit them."

Of all the things Sean has seen Rosenstein passionate about over the years, he has never seen him like this. The rage, the anger, and the thirst for revenge seem all consuming, and for a moment, Sean is frightened that the man before him is no longer the man he thinks he knows.

*   *   *

Kaley and Dawson remain in the shadows as they watch the group migrate through a section of the base's outer fence that has been removed. In their eyes, it appears that the people are plunging into a deep chasm as the darkness of the surrounding area seemingly swallows them whole. When the last of the group disappears through the fence, Kaley turns to Dawson and says, "Let's follow them."

"Kaley, we have no idea what's out there or where they're going," Dawson argues. "Let's just find someone, report Fizer's murder, and let them straighten it out."

"Alright," Kaley says, as he starts limping towards the fence, "you find someone and report it, and I'll see what the hell is going on."

"Kaley-"

"At least let me have the gun," Kaley requests, motioning to Dawson's sidearm.

"No," she shakes her head, "I'm coming too."

Kaley looks at her and smirks, "Didn't really have to twist your arm, did I, Lieutenant?"

Dawson glares back at him, "Bag it, Kaley."

They hurry after the group and when they reach the fence, they both pause, hesitant to step off the cliff. They look at one another and Dawson shrugs her shoulders and moves forward, leading the way. Kaley follows her into the darkness and not surprisingly, they do not find a deep chasm or sheer drop to the bottom of a cliff. Instead, they discover several rather ordinary, run-of-the-mill, undulating hills in front of them.

They do not spot any members of the group they were following, so they decide to start climbing. As they traverse the hills, the stillness of the night air is punctuated by a stiff breeze that begins to blow. The moon is barely more than a sliver and while it does provide a scant amount of illumination, a patch of clouds roll in with the breeze, obscuring any light the moon produces. Gradually the breeze turns into a gust, and there is a sudden charge in the air. They both can feel it – an impending storm is approaching.

Nearly halfway up a particularly steep hill, Kaley and Dawson spy a dull light emanating from the other side of the crest. They scramble their way to the top, Kaley moving slower because of his injuries. Dawson is the first to reach the summit of the hill with Kaley following closely behind. They both stare in awe into the deep valley below, their eyes riveted by the sight before them.

In a voice barely above a whisper, Dawson asks a question Kaley clearly has no answer for.

"What is *that?*"

* * *

When Rosenstein contacted Moriah and agreed to assist the group in their pursuit at deciphering the extraterrestrials' code, he named his lone stipulation: Abraham must be a subject in the group's current serum experiments. Moriah was clearly taken aback at the request, let alone the fact that Rosenstein was aware the group had been testing the serum again. Rosenstein knows that Moriah has likely been driven to the brink of madness trying to determine his source, but Rosenstein maintains the utmost confidence his mole would never be unearthed.

Moriah did not feign surprise, though he claimed the serum is not an idea the group is realistically considering, deeming it a "last option." Rosenstein stated that nevertheless, he knows they will eventually test the latest version of the serum on human subjects and he wants Abraham involved. Moriah replied that Abraham is a sick, old man and his time on Earth is nearly over, to which Rosenstein shot back, "So is mine."

Moriah eventually relented and agreed that Abraham would be a subject in the serum experiments. When Rosenstein questioned how both parties could ensure the sincerity and good intentions of the other, Moriah made it abundantly clear that there would have to be a significant level of trust between them, an element that neither party would be willing to grant the other.

After nearly two months passed, as instructed by Sebastian, Rosenstein informed Moriah that he had deciphered the code. Rosenstein confirmed the intricate details of a coordinated global invasion and an unequivocal directive: no prisoners are to be taken or quartered. Rosenstein also identified a multitude of locations around the world where the extraterrestrials will gather prior to the attack. Rosenstein translated latitudinal and longitudinal coordinates at various locations and he informed Moriah that he would provide half of the locations to Moriah as a "good faith" gesture, but the other half would not be disclosed until he witnessed Abraham issued the serum.

Again, Moriah attempted to persuade Rosenstein to see the futility in forcing them to involve Abraham, insisting that the man's health was failing him and he would be dead soon. Moriah appealed to Rosenstein's conscience to ignore his selfish desire for vengeance and instead think of his obligation to his country and to the people of the planet. Rosenstein was not buying it, however, knowing

Moriah was simply trying to obtain what he wants without giving up anything in return.

"Around two weeks ago," Rosenstein continues his narrative, "I received a call I had been dreading for over four decades."

Rosenstein can barely make eye contact with Sean, his eyes focused on the floor of the helicopter.

"Moriah informed me," Rosenstein says somberly, "that he knows about my 'secret' family – about you and Isabella and Conor. That he has known about it for some time. My heart just . . dropped, I started to panic. I immediately thought he might try and come after you and your family and I . . I . ."

"You what, Al?" Sean asks.

"I was right," he states dejectedly. "Moriah claimed the initial locations I provided him made no strategic sense. He said my judgment was 'clouded with thoughts of revenge' and I could not be trusted. If that was not the most ironic thing I've heard in my life, then I haven't heard it yet. He indicated that he knew how to guarantee my 'compliance,' as he put it."

Rosenstein pauses a moment, clearly reluctant to continue, but he does.

"He informed me that he had discovered a way to ensure the locations I provide him are legitimate."

Sean glares at Rosenstein, knowing the direction this is going.

"The beach?"

Rosenstein nods shamefully. He starts to explain, falters, and at last is able to continue.

"The Foundation decided to perform the serum experiment on a sample of ordinary citizens rather than abductees. They likely wanted to see the effects of the serum on an 'untainted' group in the event they distribute it to the general public. The group found the perfect sample size in a suitably remote location – the small cottage town of Tamawaca, coincidentally a place where both your family and Abraham own summer homes. The sample group was retrieved using Jericho's old ship, the propulsion system having recently been engineered, and the experiment itself was conducted utilizing the extraterrestrials' own technology.

"Moriah warned me that if I attempted to contact you or warn your family in any way, you would all be . . 'fair game.'"

Rosenstein shakes his head morosely and repeats, "Fair game. I could only imagine the terrifying possibilities that term entailed. I argued that I would refuse to hand over the remaining locations, but Moriah countered that it would not prevent you and your family from being involved in the experiment. And that's when I knew."

"Knew what?" Sean asks warily.

"Moriah was planning on finishing his father's business all along. He had no intention of physically harming me, but rather something much worse than that – hurting my family, *your family*, the one thing I care about, the *only* thing I care about now that Pattie is gone. He knew that hurting you and your family would be worse than any physical pain he could inflict on me."

"And because of *you*," Sean sneers angrily, "my family is involved and directly in harm's way. Because of *you*, I might never see them ag-"

"Sean, even if I did not agree to help the group in the first place," Rosenstein interjects, "I'm sure that Moriah would have used your family as a means to coerce me into helping them."

"You should have come to me right away, Al," Sean seethes.

"I offered to give him all the locations, Sean," Rosenstein argues, "if you and your family were simply left alone, but he said it was too late for that. The only way he could guarantee I am acting 'on the level' is if he is holding something over my head, something I could not bear to see harmed. His one concession was that the serum would not be issued to you and your family if the locations are legitimate, a promise I had no faith in.

"I knew then that I had to warn you regardless of the consequences. I got a message to Professor Murdoch and instructed him what to do – wait until the last minute in case anyone is watching, but you and your family must be out of Tamawaca by July third. I asked him to direct you to my house and find a particular book."

"*Government Conspiracies and Cover-Ups*?" Sean recalls the name of the book on Rosenstein's shelf directly below the numbers and letters etched on his wall.

"Yes," Rosenstein confirms.

"Which led me to the treatise written by you and Abraham," Sean notes.

"And which subsequently directed you to Spokane," Rosenstein indicates. "But your family was supposed to be safely hidden hundreds of miles away from here."

"Which explains the note you left me," Sean concludes. "So what happened to Murdoch?"

"I don't know, Sean," Rosenstein sullenly replies, "but I would imagine the worst."

Sean does not need Rosenstein to spell it out for him as he silently curses another innocent casualty.

"How did you know I was not taken?"

"My inside source," Rosenstein reveals, "Sebastian."

"He was there?"

Rosenstein nods.

Sean recalls the running feet he thought he heard when he regained consciousness.

"So it was just blind luck that I happened to leave the beach when I did?" Sean asks incredulously.

Rosenstein nods again.

After a moment of silence, Rosenstein laments, "What gnaws at me is the fact that my intention was for you and your family to be safely tucked away at Tamawaca in the event the invasion began."

"What *should* gnaw at you even more is the fact that you were too preoccupied with revenge to be concerned about anything else, and now my family is paying the price," Sean harshly replies.

"But don't you see, Sean?" Rosenstein argues. "From the beginning Alex Moriah had every intention of involving your family no matter what. The elder Moriah never forgot about me and Frank Parker, and to his dying day he was resentful that we had 'escaped' the group's wrath. Alex saw a way to exact revenge on me and obtain closure for something his father was never able to do."

Sean does not know what to believe. Perhaps Rosenstein is right in assuming it was inevitable his family would somehow be involved, first as a possible means to coerce Rosenstein into assisting the group and now as a "motivator" to ensure he is acting in good faith. Regardless, Sean despises Rosenstein for affiliating himself with the Foundation after everything the group had put him and Pattie through. Sean and his family's relationship to Rosenstein could potentially cost them their lives, a prospect that does not seem fair to Isabella and Conor, innocent bystanders in all of this, along with everyone else who was on that beach.

"Listen, Sean," Rosenstein says, reading his thoughts, "they're going to be fine. We're going to get them out of here."

"We?"

Rosenstein motions towards Sloan, "Ms. Sloan will help you. Take this."

Rosenstein takes one of Sean's hands and firmly places a small object in it.

Sean stares at the object, which looks like an over-size key. Besides its unusual shape, Sean is enthralled by its luster, enhanced by a color somewhere between silver and gold, but with a much shinier hue than anything Sean has ever seen. It is simply. . . *stunning*. Like a priceless ruby or emerald, Sean is transfixed by the richness of its color and the inherent worth the object seems to radiate. He slowly raises the object to eye-level and studies it.

"Courtesy of Sebastian," Rosenstein notes.

He glances over his shoulder distractedly and urgently says, "I have to go now."

"Where are you going?" Sean asks.

"I need to deliver the other half of the locations to Moriah," Rosenstein responds. "I'm holding up my end of the deal."

Rosenstein turns to Sloan and looks at her with a fierceness in his eyes and intently states, "You have to get them out of here, okay? Do not fuck around, just *get them out.*"

"We will, Al," Sloan responds confidently.

Rosenstein stares at Sloan and at last nods his head. He looks between them, searching for the right words.

"If anything should happen to me," he starts, "I want you both to know that . ."

"Nothing's going to happen to you, Al," Sloan reassures him.

"Yeah," Sean agrees, "don't start getting weepy on us."

Rosenstein allows himself a small smirk before nodding his head.

"Alright, I'll save the tearjerker speech," he says, glancing at his watch. "We'll meet back here in . . thirty minutes?"

Sloan nods in agreement and sets a timer on her watch.

Rosenstein opens the door on his side of the helicopter and motions outside to Sean, "Now get moving."

Sloan slings a bag over her shoulder and exits out the pilot's door while Sean shuffles out the side door. He turns around and faces Rosenstein.

Despite all the secrets, the constant deception, and the conflicting emotions inside him, Sean cannot truly hate the man before him, *his father.* Sean knows how much the old man loves Sean and his family, and that he would never intentionally place them in harm's way. He also knows how much Rosenstein is tearing himself up inside for their involvement here tonight, and that he clearly wants to make amends for ensnaring them in his past. When this is all over, Sean hopes they can be a real family with no more secrets and no more lies. And hopefully, after tonight, no more enemies.

Now it is Sean's turn to fumble for the right words.

Rosenstein pats him on the shoulder, "I know, kid. Get rolling."

Sean hesitates, nods, and then finally turns and follows Sloan as they hurry away from him.

Rosenstein looks after them for a few moments with a heavy heart, his eyes growing misty. Finally, he turns around and reaches inside the chopper. He wraps his sweat-laden hand around a gun, checks the cartridge, noting it is fully loaded, and places the clip back.

He closes the helicopter door and hurries the opposite way, carrying the fate of the world heavy upon his shoulders.

SEVENTEEN

Spokane Plains Battlefield State Park is the site of the last major Indian battle of the Inland Empire, a term that refers to the town of Spokane and the surrounding Columbia River basin. This "Empire" extended into present-day northern Idaho, northeastern Oregon, and northwestern Montana. In September of 1858, the United States Army defeated three allied Indian tribes that consisted of the Spokane, Palouse, and Coeur d'Alene people. The U.S. Army was led that day by Colonel George Wright, whose force was outnumbered nearly two to one. However, with the army's infantry employing long-range rifles, four companies of artillery, and a battery of howitzer guns, the Indians were routed by the superior weaponry of the Americans, with casualties that included the Spokane chief's own brother and brother-in-law. The Americans suffered no injuries with the exception of a wounded horse.

While the current players may not be familiar with the history of the state park, a similar storyline may be playing itself out tonight. The group with superior numbers does not always emerge victorious, tending to be trumped by more advanced technology, especially in the realm of warfare. Which side has the advantage at this point is a question that remains to be answered.

Sean closely follows Sloan as she maneuvers their way through the darkness of the park. In the distance Sean can discern a dimly visible line of large, pine-covered mountains. A nervous, anticipatory feeling consumes Sean as he can hardly contain his excitement over *finally* discovering that his family is alive. Yet he tries to temper his excitement and expectations in preparing himself for the condition he may find them in. He avoids thinking about the trauma they have already endured and the lasting repercussions of this horrendous experience. First and foremost, he needs to find them and shepherd them out of here alive and well. If they survive this ordeal, they can handle anything that arrives in the aftermath.

Sean and Sloan arrive at the bottom of a steep hill and begin climbing. The wind has intensified and is swirling all around them, rendering each step an adventure as the steepness of the hill sharpens. Both of them feel a heaviness in the air, the elements foreshadowing a coming storm. At last they reach the summit, Sean's breathing somewhat labored from the effort while Sloan seemed to scale the hill with ease.

Sean follows Sloan's steely gaze into the valley below them and he gasps.

A large, circular, luminescent object, roughly half the size of a football field, sits in the valley, a battery of floodlights surrounding it. Dull, flashing lights cover the whole of the object, as if it has been adorned with holiday lights.

It appears that the object is on display, like some kind of bizarre art exhibit or museum piece. Sloan and Sean notice a large group of people filing into the other end of the valley, their attire formal and reserved.

"Come on, we have to hurry," Sloan indicates, and she starts half-running, half-sliding down the hill.

Sean follows her as he continues to maintain a watchful eye on the people at the other end of the valley. Sean can only speculate, but he would be willing to wager that these individuals are the members of the Foundation, and the object before them is the alien craft that whisked Sean's family and the other residents of Tamawaca away from their peaceful and serene vacation.

As Sean peers down at the craft, he realizes he could be mere minutes away from seeing his family for the first time in what seems like an eternity. Behind the doors of that craft they are held captive, and Sean wonders if they have any idea where they are or what happened to them. He also wonders if they are thinking about him or if they have abandoned hope that they will ever be rescued. Sean knows, however, one indisputable fact: he is coming for them and he will die trying to get them out of here.

With a surge of adrenaline and the prospect at last of finding his family, Sean recklessly charges down the hill. On several occasions he nearly loses his footing and tumbles down the hill, but somehow manages to remain upright. He overtakes Sloan and reaches the bottom of the valley before her.

The craft is even more impressive when viewing it in close proximity. It possesses a similar luster and richness of color as the key that Rosenstein supplied him. The radiance of the craft is dazzling and captivating. Even after residing at the bottom of a lake for sixty years, Sean notices there is no water damage or rusting on the exterior of the ship. The ship could have recently rolled off the assembly line, its shiny surface untarnished by the eroding forces of the water. At first glance, Sean does not see any windows for visibility or doors indicating an entry point. He also does not see any armament attached, but Sean would be the first one to admit that he is not sure what to look for.

What truly captures Sean's attention, however, are the lights that blanket the craft. Everything else around him seems to melt away as he suddenly feels a deep connection with the craft, a kinship even. It is almost like the craft is alive and has instantly formed a bond with him. Sean can only rationalize that the reason for this is the fact that the craft harbors the two people he loves the most in the world, but that still does not explain-

"They're hypnotizing, aren't they?" Sloan whispers behind him.

Sean shakes his head and immediately seems to emerge from a brief trance. For a moment, he nearly forgot where he was and who he was with.

"Yeah," he agrees, "they're . . mesmerizing."

Sloan nods, "There's a reason for that, Professor."

Sean looks at her curiously and she motions toward the lights.

"They're living organisms," Sloan explains. "The extraterrestrials use them to abduct their victims."

"How?"

"The lights use a pattern the human brain recognizes and is instantly suggestive to, luring their victims in voluntarily."

Sean considers this a moment and then responds, "You're telling me that-"

"Everyone on that beach walked into the ship of their own accord, Sean, including your family," Sloan finishes his sentence.

"My God," he mutters.

"A concussive wave is first discharged at the intended targets," Sloan explains, as Sean recalls being tossed from his cottage's front porch, "and this essentially clears the mind of all thoughts, creating a blank slate that assists in 'hypnotizing' their victims."

"I thought . . well, like there was some kind of . ."

"Beam?" Sloan smirks.

"Yeah, something like that," he sheepishly admits.

Sloan shakes her head and motions toward the flood-lights, "They're interacting with the illumination from the floodlights. Sebastian also indicated that these 'organ-isms' act together as a shield to incoming enemy fire."

"That's amazing," Sean says in disbelief.

Sean continues to stare at the blinking lights when he again feels himself slipping into a semi-trance. The lure is powerful and he shakes his head to snap himself out of it.

"Alright, I'm finished with the tour. Let's get my family out of here."

*   *   *

As they stare in awe into the valley, Kaley and Dawson abruptly turn their attention away from the object to watch as the group they were following begin stream-ing into the valley. Suddenly, Dawson points toward a man and a woman almost directly across from their position, scurrying down the hill. Though he has nearly two swollen eyes as a result of the beating he received from Ruethorn, something about the man looks familiar to Kaley, something he recognizes. Initially, Kaley thinks the man looks like his friend Sean O'Connell, but then he quickly dismisses the thought upon realizing how absurd that sounds.

What the hell would Sean be doing here?

Then he considers how this all started in the town where his friend's family owns a cottage, the town where an alleged terrorist attack occurred.

Are Sean and his family somehow involved? Are they in danger? Is this whole affair starting to come full circle?

The questions pile up in Kaley's head as he continues to study the man on the opposite side of the valley from them. When you know someone as long as the two of them have known each other, you are typically able to recognize one another from a distance because of a certain trait, such as their frame or gait. Kaley recognizes both of the aforementioned characteristics in the man across the valley from them, and his gut instinct is telling him with nearly absolute certainty, despite his mind's insistence that it seems utterly ridiculous and frankly too coincidental, that it is his friend.

"I'm almost positive that's Sean," Kaley insists, after explaining to Dawson about his friend's cottage in Tamawaca.

"Kaley, how can you be so sure?" Dawson skeptically asks. "You can hardly see with those lumps on your face."

"I know it is, Dawson," Kaley asserts, turning to her, "I just know."

Dawson looks unconvinced and then turns to watch the pair approach the bottom of the hill.

"And the woman?" Dawson asks.

Kaley shakes his head, "I don't think I know her."

After a few moments, Kaley starts hobbling down the hill and into the valley, "I'm going in for a closer look."

"Come on, Kaley," Dawson replies in exasperation. "Are you serious? We have no idea what's going on here."

"So let's find out," Kaley suggests.

Without waiting for a response, Kaley continues his descent, crouching low as he scampers down the hill, maintaining an eye on the group. Dawson looks around, unsure what to do, but also not wanting to miss any action. She decides to follow Kaley . . . again.

*　　*　　*

Sean follows Sloan as she leads him to what appears to be an entry point in the craft. She kneels down and rummages through her sack. She removes a pair of Glock pistols with silencers attached, handing one of them to Sean.

"Fully loaded and ready to go," Sloan indicates.

"I thought these are useless against the extraterrestrials," Sean notes.

"They're not for them," Sloan responds. "I'm not sure how many soldiers are guarding your family and the rest of them, but we might as well be prepared."

Sean nods and accepts the weapon, and then quickly checks the cartridge.

Sloan reaches into the sack and also removes a set of four throwing knives, handing a pair to Sean.

Sean places the knives in his waistband while Sloan slings the sack back over her shoulder. Sean does not like the idea of harming any more American soldiers, but whatever obstacles stand in the way of finding his family do not have a chance at this point. Besides, as far as he is concerned, they are as culpable as the members of the Foundation for their treacherous acts against their own people.

"Can I have the key?" she requests.

Sean hands her the key and she approaches the craft. She inserts the key into a slot Sean would not have been able to find in a hundred years of scouring the exterior of the craft, but Sloan locates it with ease.

Sloan removes the key as a few seconds pass.

Did it not work?

Sean cannot bear the thought of being so close and then being denied, his family only a short distance away.

Sean and Sloan exchange a worried glance when the door suddenly opens, accompanied by a sharp *whooshing*, what sounds like the emission of steam. Indeed, a small cloud of vapor escapes the craft and they smell something their olfactory senses have never encountered before. It is difficult to describe, but the aroma is partly sweet and partly pungent, not entirely offensive but not exactly enticing either.

They take a curious step forward and gaze through the doorway into a nearly pitch-dark corridor, the only illumination coming from a dim light on either side. Again, they exchange an uncertain glance and then look back into the corridor.

Sloan shrugs, "All I know is where the key goes, Professor."

Sean starts moving forward, fully prepared to lead the way to find his family.

Suddenly, from behind them, they hear someone call out, but it was too soft to discern what was said.

Sean and Sloan turn their heads and peer through the darkness and vapor to see someone stumbling towards them. They simultaneously raise their weapons at the approaching figure.

Sean aims and begins to squeeze the trigger when the figure exclaims, "Sean!"

Sean recognizes the voice, but his mind first needs to rationalize how it could possibly be the person he thinks it is. He eases up on the trigger and finally the man comes into view.

"Kaley!" Sean gasps.

Sean immediately notices that his friend appears to be in pretty rough shape. His face is bruised and bloody, and there is a large purple welt on the side of his neck. One of his hands has been hastily bandaged and he is walking with a pronounced limp.

As Kaley stumbles up to them, Sean places his hand on Sloan's arm, who continues to point her weapon at his friend.

"It's alright," Sean reassures her, causing Sloan to slowly lower the gun.

"Sean," Kaley huffs, in between large gulps of air.

Kaley nearly collapses into Sean, who holds up his injured friend from falling to the ground.

"Christ, are you okay?" Sean asks with concern. "What the *hell* are you doing here?"

"I might ask you the same thing," Kaley replies.

"When did you get so out of shape?"

"Screw you, pokey," Kaley retorts, referring to his friend's tendency to always be late wherever he goes.

"You look like shit," Sean remarks, studying his face. "What the hell happened? How'd you get here?"

"It's a long story," Kaley sighs. "You?"

"I'm sure it's an even longer story," Sean answers.

"Who's this?" Kaley asks, motioning towards Sloan.

"This is Ms. Sloan," Sean introduces her. "Ms. Sloan, my less than mint condition friend, Sergeant Jon Kaley."

Behind Kaley, a figure comes barreling down the hill and advances towards them.

Sloan instantly trains her weapon on the figure as Kaley glances behind him.

"She's with me," Kaley indicates.

He turns back around and says, "Sean, Ms. Sloan, meet Dawson, Second Lieutenant Dawson."

Dawson is doubled over at the waist with her hands on her knees as she manages to spit out a greeting between large intakes of air.

"You're dragging this poor girl into this?" Sean asks.

Kaley nods, "Yeah, it's my way of saying thanks. I owe her one."

"More than one, Kaley," Dawson corrects him again.

"Nice touch with the marker by the way," Sean says to Kaley.

"You found the lucky charm then?" Kaley asks. "It was a total shot in the dark if you came looking for me. I didn't even think you'd remember even if you did find it."

Sean's mood instantly changes as he apprehensively asks, "You saw what happened on that beach?"

"A part of it," Kaley confirms. "But the evidence I had . . . it's gone, I lost it in-"

"I'm sorry to break up the reunion," Sloan interrupts, "but we're working under a slight time crunch here."

Sean motions towards the craft. "It's got my family, Jon," he says darkly.

"What the hell is *it*?" Kaley asks.

"You wouldn't believe me even if I told you," Sean replies.

"Try me," Kaley challenges him.

Before Sean can respond, Sloan explains, "It's an alien spacecraft that is part of a conspiracy involving some of the most powerful people in the world. Sean's family has been abducted, along with nearly a hundred other innocent civilians, and all hell could break loose at any minute, so we need to go *now*!"

Kaley and Dawson stare at Sloan like she has lost her mind. Kaley glances at Sean to see if he should start laughing, but instead Sean states, "That about sums it up, and I can explain the rest later."

Sean nods towards Dawson.

"Lieutenant Dawson, are you packing?"

"Yeah," she confirms, and removes Fizer's gun from her waistband to show them.

"Good," Sean replies, "you're going to stand watch out here and shoot anybody who tries to get in. Jon, you come with-"

"Sean, I'll stay here and watch your backs," Kaley proposes, glancing nervously at Dawson. "Take Dawson with you."

"I can handle it, Kaley," Dawson says indignantly.

"It's not that," Kaley argues. "I'm not very mobile and wouldn't be much help in there. It would be better for me to stay in one place. I'll come give a holler if the shit starts to hit the fan out here."

"But we only have the one gun between us," Dawson points out.

"Here," Sloan says, as she tosses her Glock to Kaley. "I've got my knives."

"Problem solved," Kaley notes as he checks the ammunition clip.

"Alright, the clock is ticking," Sean says urgently, motioning for them to move.

Dawson looks anxiously at Kaley. She tries to settle her jittery nerves while at the same time she is concerned about leaving him alone in the condition he is in. She has performed exceptionally well under pressure so far and Kaley has faith she can pull through now. He nods at her and she tentatively returns the gesture.

Well, I wanted a chance at some action and it looks like I got it, she thinks, proving once again to always be careful what you wish for.

At the threshold of the entrance, Sean turns around, "No hero shit, Jon. You come get us if there are any problems. Don't go mixing it up out there."

Kaley assumes his friend is referring to the action on the other side of the valley.

"Get back here soon and I won't have to," Kaley replies.

Sean nods and enters the ship, followed closely behind by Sloan and Dawson. Kaley watches them as they descend down a darkened corridor and then they are gone, disappearing into the bowels of the craft.

EIGHTEEN

As Moriah and the rest of the Foundation members file into the valley, an air of confidence and self-assurance permeates the group. They have placed their fate in Moriah's capable hands and they hope and some of them pray that their trust is well-founded. At the moment, after his inspiring and moving speech, they believe it is.

Many of the Foundation members present tonight never believed it was possible to replace a leader like Joshua Moriah. When he passed away, there was a tremendous amount of infighting and bickering within the group over who would succeed him. The group was divided practically in half: one side was in the younger Moriah's camp, recognizing the same leadership qualities in him as his father and thinking it only natural that he replace him, while the other side argued that he was too young, too inexperienced, and lacked maturity to lead the group. Ultimately, all that was needed was one speech, a sermon the younger Moriah delivered to the group shortly after his father's funeral that convinced the skeptics he was the right man for the job. It was a speech not unlike the one he delivered in the airplane hangar only minutes ago, a speech that enraptured his followers and alleviated their anxieties, providing assurances of the group's continued dominance in the country's national and international affairs for years to come.

Now as they wait for the events of tonight to unfold, with the destiny of the entire planet weighing in the balance, they appear preternaturally calm and business-like, reflecting their leader's own demeanor. Considering the circumstances, their collective deportment is startling. Before them sits a craft from another world, while they prepare for a meeting they believe may decide the fate of this world. They are about to confront a creature considered to be one of the most dangerous on the planet, and they seem as composed and relaxed as can be.

Rosenstein suddenly hurries into the valley and approaches Moriah. The other members of the group peer at Rosenstein with utter disdain and thinly veiled hostility, their eyes narrowing on the man as he approaches. Despite the fact Rosenstein is assisting in this "endeavor," there is nothing he can do to compensate for his betrayal of the group so many years ago. The members view a traitor within the group as the most severe offense, punishable by death. A traitor from within is an extreme threat to the preservation of the entire group. Each of them knows a turncoat has the potential to bring about the downfall of the entire Foundation. They are also aware that he is the only person who has betrayed the group and lived to talk about it. Their hatred for him is absolute and irrevocable.

"Glad to see you could make it, Doctor," Moriah sniffs.

"I have the remaining locations," Rosenstein notes, patting one of the pockets of his coat.

"I was beginning to wonder if you care about that little family of yours," Moriah says.

Easy, Rosenstein thinks, *do not lose your head.*

"What happened to your son?" Moriah asks pointedly, his eyes piercing Rosenstein's.

Rosenstein panics for a moment, wondering if they have managed to capture Sean and Sloan already. He calms himself, however, and tries to maintain a poker face, feigning ignorance.

"What do you mean?"

Moriah motions towards the craft, "He's not aboard with the rest of them."

"I have no idea, Alex," Rosenstein responds.

"You haven't been helping him?" Moriah asks suspiciously.

Again, Rosenstein's heart starts racing and he contemplates whether Moriah knows something. Rosenstein probes the man's face for clues, but none are forthcoming.

"I haven't seen my son in weeks, Alex," Rosenstein responds evenly.

Moriah casts a dubious eye on Rosenstein for several long, heart-pounding seconds. Finally, he motions with his hand, "The coordinates, Doctor."

Rosenstein hastily reaches into his coat pocket. Instantly, several members of the Foundation surrounding Moriah suddenly have guns pointed directly at Rosenstein.

"Nice and slow, Dr. Rosenstein," Moriah advises. "The boys here have itchy trigger fingers."

Rosenstein glances at Moriah's "bodyguards" and slowly reaches into his pocket. He removes a small slip of paper and hands it to Moriah.

Moriah does not even bother to look at the slip of paper before handing it to a man behind him, who immediately disappears with it. Moriah, still staring daggers at Rosenstein, raises his arm, exposing a communication device attached to his wrist.

He presses a button on it and orders, "Bring them out."

*　　*　　*

The interior of the craft is bathed in near darkness as the three of them make their way through the Byzantine corridors. There are dim lights dispersed throughout the craft, but they provide scant illumination as the three of them feel as if they are trapped in some kind of carnival fun house, only there is little fun to be had. The walls of the interior are smooth and feel like rubber to the touch, but consist of an even tougher and grittier material. They notice a surprising lack of buttons, switches, or other items on the walls that might contribute to the functionality of the craft. As they move deeper into the ship, an almost suffocating heat starts to take hold, and after only a few minutes they are blanketed in perspiration. Besides a low humming noise, the interior is quiet with no other sounds except their own steady breathing.

As they advance through the ship, they notice at intervals darkened corridors that branch off from their current path, all of which seem to lead to *more* darkened corridors. Sean is tempted to explore these different avenues, but he prefers instead to remain in the same corridor through which they entered the craft, making it easier for them to find their way out, assuming their current path leads to his family. He does not want to start veering down corridors and taking multiple turns that may cause them to become lost, confused, or disoriented in this complex labyrinth.

The surrealness of the situation when they first entered the craft, the fact they are actually *standing* and *walking* in an extraterrestrial mode of transportation, soon fades as they realize they do not seem to be making any progress.

"Are we going around in circles?" Dawson whispers from the rear.

Sean turns around and wipes the sweat from his forehead.

"I was thinking the same thing," he indicates.

He nods to Sloan, "Any ideas?"

"I think we have to hurry if we want to get your family safely out of here," Sloan replies, as she anxiously glances at her watch.

Suddenly, they hear a burst of static.

The noise appeared to originate from somewhere behind them. Sean leads the way as they backtrack down the corridor, hoping the sound repeats itself. As they slowly pass a corridor on their right, they hear what sounds like voices in the distance, *human voices*. The three of them stop in their tracks and hold their breath. They listen intently, waiting for the voices to speak again.

After a few moments, they finally do.

Sean jerks his head in that direction and starts moving quickly down the corridor, with Sloan and Dawson simply trying to keep up. Sloan grabs his arm.

"Sean, take it easy," she warns. "We don't know how many of them there are."

Sloan intended the statement to not only be a note of caution, but also an opportunity to calm him down. She can clearly see Sean is keyed up and desperate to find his family, and she does not want him to do anything reckless that could get them all killed.

Sean nods his understanding and slows his pace down the corridor. After several steps, they hear a protracted mechanical noise, like the sound a garbage truck makes when it crushes its contents. Then the noise stops and suddenly, they feel a cool breeze wash over them.

Sean quickens his pace again as the corridor winds around to the right. Suddenly, Sean stops, causing Sloan and Dawson to run nearly headlong into him. He holds up a hand and creeps forward, the three of them holding their breath in anticipation. They spot a light ahead and notice the breeze has intensified.

"Come on, people, *move!*" a man abruptly shouts ahead, causing the three of them to simultaneously flinch.

Sean takes another couple steps and peers around the corner to his left. What he sees shocks him nearly senseless.

It is a cavernous and dimly lit room, although substantial light spills in from outside the craft through an opening not far from their location. There are rows upon rows of vertical tables, each the approximate size of a human adult. The rows stretch the entire length of the vast room, and located on either side of each table is a strange type of mechanism. The mechanisms resemble the robotic, automated arms one might find in a factory.

Sean immediately recognizes several people from Tamawaca – *they are alive!*

His heart sinks and chills rattle up his spine, however, when he studies their expressions. There is a blank, vacant stare on each of their faces, as if they have been heavily drugged. They all appear to be in a catatonic state, with no indication they know where they are or even who they are.

There are a number of soldiers with automatic weapons directing them down what appears to be a ramp leading out of the craft, which is where the light pours in. The captives shuffle their way past the soldiers, looking through them, but the soldiers continue barking orders at them to move faster and to keep walking, as if they are toddlers in need of guidance. Sean notices several people still remain attached to the vertical tables, their faces passive and indifferent. The sight is terrifying and wrenching to behold, and Sean is nearly inclined to start shooting and ask questions later, but he restrains himself.

He desperately searches the faces, looking for Isabella and Conor, trying to find his *innocent* family that should not even be here. His heart is pounding and he can feel his blood starting to boil, his face flushing hot with anger. Sean notices a pair of civilians in white coats who appear to administer some type of injection to each person before they are released from their respective "confinement."

Sloan peers around the corner with Sean and a small gasp escapes her lips as she absorbs the scene. There is not enough room for Dawson to look, so she asks in a whisper, "What's going on?"

Sloan turns around, her face draped in shock. She shakes her head and murmurs, "You don't want to know."

Sloan returns her gaze to the room and spots the men administering injections to the people still attached to the vertical tables.

Sean and Sloan harbor no doubts the content of those injections . . . *the serum*.

"These people may look completely out of it now," Sloan whispers to Sean, "but in a few minutes they may be stark raving mad."

Sean trembles with rage and grits his teeth. He turns to Sloan and speculates, "They're going to use them here tonight . . *to fight*."

Although Sloan believes the captives may be used as some kind of a diversion, she offers a less direct answer, "Possibly."

Sean continues to scan the faces of the people, his eyes darting left and right so rapidly that he is almost unable to focus.

Where the hell is my family?

He looks towards the back of the room and then at last, he sees Isabella and Conor.

YES! They are alive!

The instant relief at finding them, however, is strongly tempered by the state they appear in. They are as dazed as the rest of the captives and still attached to the vertical tables. They look haggard and listless. Sean's heart breaks as the guilt for failing to protect them or reach them sooner starts to rage inside him. Sean curses all of these monsters who could be so callous to do this to innocent people, particularly children. His eyes well with tears and his hands are balled so tightly into fists that his knuckles are stark white. His anger is uncontrollable. Vengeance is the sole occupant in his mind. He is a volcano ready to explode.

Sean watches in terror as the two men in civilian clothes approach his family and administer the same injection to them as they did to the others. Sean cannot stand it any longer and he starts to move forward, but again Sloan grabs his arm to stop him.

"Sean, no, you can't," she pleads. "Rosenstein gave me something to help them . . please look at me."

Sean looks back and sees the imploring look on Sloan's face, begging him not to do anything rash. He pauses and takes a deep breath.

"Listen for a minute," she indicates, as she pulls the bag off her shoulder.

She crouches down, reaches into the bag and removes two capped syringes, holding them up.

"Rosenstein gave me these," she explains. "He said what's in here could possibly neutralize the serum, but they pack a nasty punch. It's going to knock them out, so they'll be dead weight when we try and get them out of here, but it's a better alternative than . ."

Sloan lets the words hang in the air, finding it unnecessary to say anything more.

She peers around the corner and then turns back around.

"Look, your family is going to be nearly the last ones out. We wait until they pass us, take out the guards, administer the shot," – she holds up the syringes – "and hightail it out of here. Okay?"

Sean peers at her. "What about everyone else?"

Sloan opens her mouth, but then pauses. She knows Sean is not going to like the answer.

"Sean, I don't think we can . . ."

Sean looks away, clearly conflicted. He wants to rescue all of the captives and not leave one of them behind, but he knows they do not have time or manpower on their side.

He nods reluctantly.

"Faster, people, faster!" one of the soldiers shout.

Sean glances around the corner and then back at Sloan. He hands her the Glock.

"Here, you take this. I want your knives."

Sloan glances at Dawson, who at this point looks like a deer in headlights. Sloan does not argue but rather hands Sean her knives and accepts the gun, clearly able to recognize bloodlust when she sees it. Sean places the two knives in the small of his back while he holds the other two in his hands.

Those soldiers do not stand a chance, Sloan thinks.

The only one who has not seen what is awaiting them around the corner, Dawson finally sneaks a peek.

After a moment of observing the scene before her, she whispers, "Oh . . my . . God."

She looks back at them and her face is ashen.

Sean grabs her arm and asks forcefully, "Dawson, you okay? You've got to let me know cause we're going to need a third set of hands to get out of here."

It takes her a few moments, but she finally nods.

"Yeah, I'm fine, I'm ready," she states rather unconvincingly.

"Okay, we're counting on you," Sean says, as he continues eyeballing her. "Just remember – no hesitation. You shoot to kill, got it?"

Dawson nods her understanding.

Sean peers around the corner and notices that over half the captives have already been "escorted" out of the craft. Isabella and Conor are no longer restrained and they are slowly walking towards the exit. They are, indeed, bringing up the rear, a lucky break to be sure. Sean figures he is probably owed one at this point.

Sean counts six guards still in the craft, four of whom corral the remaining captives while the other two are stationed near the ramp that leads outside.

Pure adrenaline begins to pump through Sean's veins as he readies himself for battle. He knows it is not only foolish, but also reckless to fight when your only emotion is rage because it is uncontrollable and unpredictable. He needs to filter his anger and turn it into something useful. He must move quickly and without thought, trusting his training from so long ago and instincts that have dulled over the preceding years. Yet, he surprisingly realizes, he does not doubt either one of them for a second.

"Let's go!" a soldier shouts, as he shoves one of the captives forward who apparently is moving too slowly.

That one is mine, Sean thinks.

A majority of the captives have exited the craft, and Sean can clearly see his family now. Isabella and Conor both stare vacantly ahead as they shuffle forward, Isabella's hand draped on Conor's shoulder. Though she does not look particularly maternal, some internal protective instinct must be manifesting itself, as she seems intent on sheltering her son from any more harm.

Sean's jaw hardens as he sees them approaching.

Come on, Baby, just a little farther and I'll take care of the rest.

The two soldiers near the ramp exit, with one of them speaking into a radio that they are bringing out the last of the captives. Now there are only four soldiers remaining in the craft. There are two soldiers in the rear of the procession and the other two are in the middle, with captives scattered between them. Sean counts nine captives still in the craft, including his family. He will wait until the last of the soldiers pass their position.

Sean turns around, "I'll handle the rear guards, you two take the forward ones, alright?"

Sloan and Dawson both nod.

Sean looks around the corner and notices his family is nearly upon them. He is moments away from touching them himself, from confirming that they truly are alive. He can hardly contain himself. All he wants is to have them both back in his arms, sheltered away from these monsters.

He slows his breathing so his heartrate will hopefully follow.

Control . . control . . control.

Then, suddenly, inexplicably, Isabella stops.

Control . .

She turns her head in Sean's direction, as if she senses he is near.

Oh, shit, what are you doing, Baby? Keep moving.

She stares at the wall he is hiding behind.

Control . .

One of the rear soldiers pushes her forward with his automatic weapon.

"Come on, honey, time's a wasting," he says.

Fuck control.

Sean leaps from behind the corner and in one swift motion plunges a knife into the nearest soldier's chest, penetrating his heart and killing him instantly. The soldier barely has time to grunt as his eyes quickly glaze over.

Sean wheels behind the dead man as he starts to fall and, using his other hand, drags this knife across the other soldier's throat, slicing his jugular. The man makes a gurgling noise as he urgently places his hands to his throat, hopelessly trying to stem the flow of blood. The man's legs buckle, causing him to drop to his knees for a moment before he tumbles over on his side.

As the second soldier receives his comeuppance, the two forward soldiers turn in alarm.

One of them is instantly greeted by a bullet to the head from Sloan, dropping him in a heap. Dawson raises her gun to fire at the other man, but before she can squeeze the trigger, she hears a rapid, sharp whistle through the air. A knife enters the man's throat and becomes lodged there, the sharp end barely protruding out the other side. The man collapses to the floor, his legs twitching as blood pours from his body.

Dawson looks at Sean, who appears like a pitcher who has just delivered the ball to home plate, his arm forward and his aim true.

Who the hell is this guy? Dawson thinks.

Sean grabs his son and then his wife and squeezes them tightly, although they do not return the embrace. They continue to stare straight ahead, as if they had not witnessed four men killed within seconds directly in front of their eyes. The remaining captives stop and look around blankly, seemingly waiting to be told where to go or what to do.

Sean clutches Isabella and looks deeply into her eyes.

"Baby, it's me. Can you understand me? Do you hear me?"

There is no recognition in her eyes as Sean gently shakes her, praying to God that the damage inflicted by the serum and the experiment is not irreversible.

Sean tries again, "Baby, it's Sean, do you know who I am?"

His heart aches as he realizes she does not know who he is, and possibly does not even know who she is.

"Izzy girl," Sean cries out, a mix of anger and sadness in his voice. "It's me, it's Sean . . please just show me something, Baby . . ."

Sean glances at Conor and sees Conor studying him, like he is working on one of the puzzles he loves so much and cannot seem to figure out his next move. Sean's eyes well with tears again as he silently begs for his son to recognize him.

Sean looks back at Isabella and desperately pleads, "Come on, Baby, show me something, show me *anything!*"

After a few moments pass and Sean is ready to give up, Isabella suddenly blinks. A solitary tear runs down her cheek, and then another tear emerges from the other eye. She runs her hands across his face, as if she is attempting to familiarize herself with the contours and ridges she should be intimately familiar with by now.

After several seconds, she whispers, "Sean . ."

Sean nearly collapses in relief as he sees a look of recognition register on her face.

"Yeah, Baby, it's me," he confirms.

"Seanie," Isabella cries, and she wraps her arms around his neck.

Sean does not want to stop holding her, but unfortunately they do not have time for an extended family reunion.

"Sean," Sloan says urgently, "we need to give them the injections and get out of here."

Sean takes Isabella's arms in his, kisses her forehead, and nods at Sloan. Within seconds, Sloan is next to Isabella injecting the syringe into her arm.

Isabella cries out in alarm and grimaces. She stares at Sloan with evil eyes.

"I'm sorry," Sloan offers.

Isabella looks at Sean, and then her eyes flutter and roll back in her head. Her legs become rubbery and she starts to fall before Sean catches her and gently lays her down.

He holds his hand out towards Sloan, "Give me the other syringe."

Dawson leans over one of the dead soldiers and spies a patch on his upper right arm. The patch contains a skeleton brandishing a knife with a peach impaled on the top, and in the background there is a lightning bolt. Across the top of the patch read the words, "To the Attack, Never Retreat," and at the bottom of the patch, "Death Stalkers."

"These guys are Special Forces," Dawson murmurs to herself.

Suddenly, a crackle of static erupts from a radio on one of the dead soldiers. Then they hear, "What's the holdup? Where's the rest of 'em?"

"We need to go *right now*," Sloan insists.

Sean squats down in front of Conor with the syringe behind his back. He gently takes Conor's arm, who tries to pull away from him. Sean holds tight and tenderly inserts the needle into his son's arm.

"Sorry, buddy, it'll make you feel better," Sean whispers.

Conor whimpers when the needle enters his arm, but within a few seconds he loses consciousness. Sean catches him as he begins to fall and picks him up.

Dawson motions towards the other captives. "Are we just going to leave them here, Sean?"

A majority of them remain in the same spot they were when Sean and company ambushed the soldiers. A couple of them have wandered near the ramp, while one of them stares directly at Sean.

Sean looks at the man and recognizes Bobby Timmons, a neighbor from a few doors down. He is unsure whether Bobby recognizes him or he is simply curious what they are doing. Regardless, Sean knows they cannot take him or any of the other captives with them.

Instead, Sean exclaims, "Run, Bobby! Get out of here! All of you!"

Sean motions at the captives to move, but they continue to gaze back at him with impassive stares, none of them sensing the urgency of the situation.

"Bobby, you've got to get the hell-"

"Hey!"

A soldier has re-entered the craft and sees his fallen comrades.

Sloan reacts first, firing several rounds at the soldier while Dawson does the same. The shots miss their mark, but have the intended consequence of forcing the man to dive for cover.

"Take him!" Sean shouts, handing Conor to Sloan, who cradles him in one arm.

"Here!" Sloan exclaims as she tosses her gun to Dawson. "Cover our backs."

Dawson possesses both guns now and she fires several rounds at the soldier to keep him pinned down. She looks awkward trying to fire two guns simultaneously and it is borne out in the results. The bullets do not come close to the target, but the soldier still ducks for cover.

Sloan and Sean each take an automatic weapon from the dead soldiers and wrap it around their backs.

Sean scoops up Isabella and places her in a fireman's carry, while Sloan uses both arms now to carry Conor. She hurries back down the corridor through which they arrived.

Sean steals a last glimpse at poor Bobby Timmons. To Sean, it seems that Bobby's vacant stare has turned into a look of sadness, a crushing expression of lost hope. Sean curses himself for being unable to help, for turning his back on Bobby and everyone else, all these innocent people whose fate should not be decided by men and women who only see them as expendable, as a means to an end, a necessary sacrifice for the greater good.

"I'm sorry," Sean murmurs to Bobby, knowing how hollow and meaningless the words sound.

Sean turns and his focus shifts to shepherding his family to safety. He follows Sloan down the corridor, with Dawson bringing up the rear.

NINETEEN

"We got four soldiers down!" the voice shouts in Moriah's earpiece.

"Three armed intruders, two captives gone!" the voice continues. "We are in pursuit!"

Moriah curses under his breath and glares menacingly at Rosenstein. Moriah knows exactly which captives have been rescued.

"You bastard," he sneers at Rosenstein.

Rosenstein no longer attempts to feign ignorance, but rather a small smile escapes his lips. He cannot help it.

"Something wrong, Alex?" Rosenstein smirks.

"Your family is as good as dead," Moriah promises.

Rosenstein subtly reaches into his coat pocket, "You first, Moriah."

Rosenstein removes the gun from his pocket.

"Gun!" someone shouts.

As Rosenstein raises the weapon, one of Moriah's lieutenants smashes the butt of his gun against Rosenstein's temple, dropping him to the ground in a heap.

Moriah snatches the gun from his lieutenant and points it at the unconscious Rosenstein.

"Happy trails, Doctor."

Before he can pull the trigger, however, Moriah and the rest of the Foundation members become aware of an approaching sound, a rumble that seems to course through their bodies and rattle their bones. The ground starts to tremble as the sound grows louder and intensifies. The group looks towards the edge of the valley.

One of Moriah's lieutenants dreadfully utters, "Here he comes."

Moriah spots a figure at the edge of the valley walking towards them. There are several figures behind him and then more and more figures continue to approach, their numbers rapidly increasing. They seem to be multiplying as they emerge over the crest of the hill that leads into the valley.

Moriah does not even have to see the face of the figure at the head of the throng to know who it is, aware he can wear any face at any time. Moriah knows exactly who it is. It is finally, at last, the one they have been waiting for: *Jericho.*

* * *

Kaley's curiosity leads him to wander away from the entrance to the craft. He looks towards the other end of the valley, watching the mass of people gather and mill about. They appear to be waiting for something or someone, but he quickly grows restless when nothing seems to be happening. He glances back towards the entrance of the craft and wonders what is taking the rest of his party so long.

A few minutes later, Kaley watches several soldiers with automatic weapons lead a group of people dressed in civilian clothes from the craft. Kaley immediately notices something strange in the gait of the civilians – they seem to be shuffling aimlessly and without purpose.

Like zombies, he thinks.

After several more minutes, there is a commotion near the craft. A pair of soldiers suddenly sprint towards the ship. Something unexpected has happened and Kaley would guess that his companions have made their presence felt.

Kaley hurries back towards the entrance of the craft when he suddenly stops and listens. He hears a low rumble that seems to reverberate across the valley. The ground feels like it is shaking underneath his feet. Kaley glances towards the other end of the valley and sees several figures approaching over the ridge, followed by more figures and still more figures. Their numbers seem to exponentially increase with each new wave that follows. Kaley suddenly has an unsettling feeling that it is time to leave.

NOW!

He hustles towards the entrance and peers down the corridor, hoping to see them approaching, but there is no one.

Where are they?!

He quickly considers his options – either play the waiting game here or venture into the craft in search of them. There do not appear to be any immediate threats at this end of the valley and he has never been keen on waiting around for something to happen, thus rendering it an easy decision for him.

Kaley enters the craft.

After his third step, he suddenly hears the sound of gunshots ring out ahead, causing him to jump.

A figure emerges into view moving quickly towards him down the corridor. The dimness of the corridor creates a bizarre outline of the figure, startling Kaley and forcing him to take a step backward.

Is it an alien? Am I about to encounter a being from another world?

Kaley grips his gun tightly and then raises it at the approaching figure. He does not know where to specifically aim, so he decides to point the gun at what he concludes is the figure's "head."

Kaley breathes deeply and starts to pull back on the trigger.

Suddenly, Sean's face comes into view. Kaley releases the trigger and lowers the weapon.

Sean is holding Isabella on his shoulders in a fireman's carry, and Kaley immediately runs forward to help. Several more gunshots echo down the corridor, and then Sloan emerges into view, lugging Conor in her arms as she sprints towards them. When Kaley does not see Dawson following Sloan, he starts to panic.

Where is she? Did something happen to her? Did they have to leave her behind?

Although it was Dawson who essentially rescued Kaley, he still feels responsible for her in a strange way. She did choose to follow Fizer onto that plane, but if she had not done so, Kaley shudders to think what may have become of him. He knows that he likely owes her his life, and he does not plan on failing to repay that debt. He also recalls the nervous look on her face when they separated, and he surmises that she has probably never seen combat action in her life. The fact that she is acting as a liaison to General Parker, an administrative duty to be sure, seems to confirm Kaley's thinking.

Kaley reaches for Isabella, but Sean waves him off.

"No," Sean says, "cover Sloan and Dawson."

"Where *is* Dawson?" Kaley asks in alarm.

"She's coming," Sean replies, and he continues towards what is now the exit of the craft for them.

A moment later, Sloan sprints past Kaley and says, "Dawson's got a pair on her tail."

Kaley moves deeper into the craft and a suffocating heat abruptly takes hold of him. He again hears several gunshots ahead, their echo rattling around the corridor. Kaley can *feel* someone fast approaching, their footfalls vibrating under his own feet.

Come on, Dawson, come on.

Kaley shifts into a crouching position and aims his gun down the corridor, hoping he can keep the weapon steady. At last, he sees Dawson round a bend and continue sprinting towards him.

A moment later, he spots two figures rapidly closing in on her from behind.

"Down!" Kaley shouts.

She is about to dive for cover, but it is too late. A bullet strikes her from behind, sending her sprawling to the ground, sliding to a stop after several feet.

Kaley fires his weapon and drops both of her pursuers with four shots.

"Dawson!" Kaley exclaims, as he stands up from his crouching position and hurries toward her.

Kaley turns Dawson over and immediately notices she is conscious and she is bleeding, *a lot*. It appears the round penetrated her upper shoulder and passed straight through. She is shocked and dazed, but then she glances at the wound and shakes her head.

"It's not bad," she grimaces.

"It went right through," Kaley notes, as he examines the wound. "That's good."

Dawson nods, "Yeah."

"First time?"

"Yeah," she nods again.

"Doesn't hurt that much, right?" Kaley smirks.

"No," she grimaces again.

"Can you keep moving?"

As soon as the words leave Kaley's mouth, he senses a presence behind him, an uneasy feeling that is quickly confirmed.

"Don't fucking move," a man orders, his gun trained on Kaley's back.

Stupid, stupid, stupid.

Kaley scolds himself for failing to initially determine if Dawson's pursuers were dead and ensuring with absolute certainty that the immediate threat had been neutralized.

Kaley stares at Dawson and notices something strange – there is no look of panic or alarm in her eyes. She is completely calm and cool. Her eyes meet his and she glances down. Kaley follows her glance and sees that Dawson still clutches a gun in her hand, which is obstructed from the man's view by Kaley's body. Kaley looks at her and grins.

"Drop the gun and stand up," the man orders, "very, very slowly. Keep your hands where I can see them."

"You son-of-a-bitch," Kaley cries, "you killed her."

Kaley tosses the gun and leans over Dawson, his head bowed in mourning.

The man sees Kaley drop the gun and approaches, lowering his weapon slightly.

"She got what she-"

The man does not finish the sentence as Dawson wraps the gun around the side of Kaley's body and fires several rounds from a supine position, all of which strike the man in the upper torso. Blood spurts from several holes in the man's body as he squeezes off a couple of rounds from his automatic that travel harmlessly into the floor of the craft. A look of complete surprise blankets his face as he topples backward.

Kaley looks behind him and then turns back around, "Nice shooting."

"Just remember me in your Oscar speech," she responds.

"I will," he grins.

Kaley stands up and hurries over to the soldier. He checks the man's pulse for safety's sake, then takes his weapon and slings it around his back. He returns to Dawson and places her good arm around his shoulders and hoists her up. She grimaces and exhales sharply, then stares at the soldier she killed.

"Deserved?" she angrily asks of the dead man. "Is that what you were going to say?"

"Your first?" Kaley asks.

She nods.

"Hopefully your last, too," Kaley remarks. "Now let's get the hell out of here."

TWENTY

As Moriah and the rest of the Foundation members watch Jericho and his cohorts approach, Moriah orders the soldiers in pursuit of the intruders to abandon their chase and report back. There are seemingly bigger fish to fry now.

At his back, Moriah feels a restlessness and uneasiness among the Foundation members. A slight, hushed murmur spreads throughout the group as they all realize the scope and magnitude of the impending meeting. All of their planning and all of their preparation comes down to this moment, this point in time when humanity's fate will be decided and the timeline for the human race will be determined.

Will it continue uninterrupted as humanity progresses forward into a limitless future? Or will the timeline abruptly end here, tonight?

The residents of Tamawaca have been herded to the side of the valley, closer to Jericho and his approaching comrades than to the Foundation. The captives stand there silently, staring straight ahead or looking curiously around at their surroundings. Moriah briefly locks eyes with one captive who stands in the middle of the pack before he turns away and returns his gaze to the gathering horde.

Jericho walks toward them with a kind of cowboy swagger, a confident stride that is equal parts intimidating and forceful. It is the walk of someone who possesses a remarkable amount of power and is emboldened by it. His cohorts possess the same swagger as they follow closely behind him. The Foundation observes the full scale of Jericho's army as they swell across the valley. Moriah estimates that Jericho and his cohorts number approximately 250 to 300 strong. There are precisely 92 Foundation members present, but they are not alone here tonight.

Nevertheless, it is a daunting sight to behold as Jericho and his army stream down the walls of the valley towards the Foundation members, the ground trembling as they approach. The darkness of the surrounding area causes the figures to appear all the more menacing and sinister.

The wind is no longer gusting and whipping about as a sudden stillness pervades the night air, an eeriness that encapsulates the entire valley. A rumble of thunder can be heard in the distance as the storm moves ever closer. The moon is now completely shrouded by clouds, leaving the floodlights surrounding Jericho's craft as the primary source of illumination in the valley.

Moriah whispers to Bellini behind him, "If Jericho does not go for it, give the signal to commence targeting."

Bellini nods compliantly.

Jericho is nearly upon them now. His army has constricted behind him and now they appear as a compact, formidable group, their impassive and emotionless faces gazing at the Foundation members. The members of the Foundation have also banded together behind Moriah, the group returning their adversaries' piercing stares.

Jericho and his army abruptly stop thirty feet away from Moriah and the rest of the Foundation members. Jericho and his comrades appear as humans, but there is a striking animalistic quality to their faces, something indescribably barbaric and savage. There are a few moments of silence as the two groups warily eye each other. Finally, Jericho speaks.

"You stole something of mine," he indicates.

Moriah assumes Jericho is referring to his ship, but he does not respond, allowing Jericho to fill the growing silence.

"What purpose could it possibly serve you since you cannot decipher our code?" Jericho asks.

Moriah fails to grasp the direct correlation between Jericho's craft and the extraterrestrials' code, but he does not allow his confusion to show. Instead, he sees an opportunity to unload his first bombshell on Jericho.

"That is where you are wrong," Moriah replies confidently. "Dr. Rosenstein has deciphered your code, Jericho. We're becoming fluent in your language."

"Dr. Rosenstein," Jericho murmurs, his eyes narrowing into tiny slits.

Jericho glances at the Tamawaca residents and asks, "And Dr. Abraham?"

It is certainly a loaded question, and Moriah must be careful how he responds. He knows with nearly absolute certainty Jericho was on that beach, disguised as Abraham's nurse. Assuming Jericho was present, he must surely know Abraham was part of the experiment and should therefore be with the other residents who were abducted.

"He is dead," Moriah states succinctly. "He died en route."

Jericho studies Moriah for a long time. He motions toward the craft at the far end of the valley.

"You have determined the propulsion system," Jericho remarks, which sounds more like a statement of fact than a question.

Moriah nods smugly, "Yes."

"And you have brought my ship back to me?"

Moriah hesitates a moment, then replies, "It is yours if you want it."

Jericho gestures toward the captives, "And these are my sample abductees?"

Again Moriah tries not to let his confusion show.

Jericho knows these people are not alien abductees, but rather ordinary citizens, Moriah thinks. *Is this some sort of a trick? Why the clueless act?*

Doubt begins to creep into Moriah's mind, uncertainty as to whether he knows all the facts. He quickly pushes the doubt aside, trusting his assumptions and believing that Jericho is simply trying to rattle him.

"You know who they are, Jericho," Moriah asserts, "so here's what I propose. We know what is to occur tonight, and that you have no intention of allowing any of us to leave here alive. That is something we would like to convince you of otherwise."

Suddenly, the ground trembles again as the first few raindrops from the heavens begin to fall. Lightning flashes across the horizon as thunder periodically rumbles, but this is not the sound Jericho and his cohorts concern themselves with. There is a muffled roar that seems to be growing louder.

Jericho and his army look behind them and encounter their own daunting sight. They see at the top of the valley the silhouettes of hundreds of figures suddenly emerge, their shadowy forms visible only because of the diminutive amount of light emanating from the valley floor. The faces of these mysterious figures are not discernible, but rather they appear like hundreds of black phantoms standing watch over them. Each figure holds a weapon pointed in the direction of Jericho and his army.

"You are aware now that we have matched your technology," – Moriah motions towards Jericho's craft – "and we are fully equipped to repel an invasion. We have developed weapons capable of destroying you and your comrades anywhere in the world, and we have discovered an efficient and effective way to kill your race in close quarters."

Moriah nods toward the top of the valley, "You're outnumbered, Jericho, with each one of those soldiers carrying a weapon that contains sixteen rounds. I'm certain I do not have to explain what that round consists of.

"Here is what I suggest. Take your ship and the people we have tested our serum on and leave, call off your attack. A war would be catastrophic for both sides."

Moriah's jaw hardens and his eyes bore into Jericho with a blistering intensity. "But if it comes to that, we are more than prepared, and ready to fight to the end."

Jericho maintains his steely gaze on Moriah, not giving anything away.

"And if we refuse?" Jericho questions.

Moriah does not respond, but rather glances toward their reinforcements at the top of the valley, the implication clear enough.

Jericho slowly walks toward the captives and stands in front of them. He briefly surveys them, then turns around to face Moriah.

"So you would be willing to sacrifice all their lives if we simply walked away from here?"

"They're yours to study as you see fit," Moriah confirms. "But if you are committed to starting a war, *we are ready.*"

Jericho smirks and glances back at the captives, who are growing restless and more alert, their manner more agitated. All eyes are on Jericho as he considers Moriah's proposal. His army waits patiently for their leader to choose a course of action, while the Foundation members collectively hold their breath for Jericho's decision.

Jericho turns, locks eyes with Moriah, and dreadfully intones, "If it is a war you think you are prepared for, Moriah, a war is what you will get."

A flash of lightning courses through the area and the valley is illuminated as bright as day. The figures at the top of the valley are revealed to be wearing camouflage, their expressionless faces smeared in black, weapons at the ready. The figures do not hold standard automatic weapons, but something much more advanced.

The members of the Foundation never possessed a desire for war, clinging to a faint glimmer of hope that Jericho would see their show of force and agree to halt the invasion. The group held no illusions regarding the likelihood of this scenario playing out though, forcing them to revisit the serum they had explored so long ago. None of the members, however, believe the serum to be a viable or even practical form of resistance against the invaders. Elevating a normal person's aggression level against a vastly superior foe may be beneficial in hand-to-hand combat, but this would be a war ultimately decided by highly technological weapons. The simple logistics of distributing the serum to the general public in the event of a full-scale invasion are so challenging and intricate that to even consider it would be a precious waste of resources and a complete departure from logic.

The serum experiment is simply a cover, a disguise for one of their own.

Another flash of lightning reveals what appears to be a set of razor sharp, ten-inch claws protruding from one of Jericho's hands. He holds in his other hand a weapon that casts an ominous green glow on his face, the same weapon the Foundation has dubbed "the baton." Jericho emits a loud, screeching noise that echoes across the valley, a battle cry that clearly signals he has arrived at his decision. His army takes their cue and releases their own jarring cries, priming themselves for battle as each of them holds their own weapon and bares the same menacing claws as Jericho.

Upon seeing this, Moriah and each of the Foundation members take out their own weapons, similar to the ones the soldiers at the top of the valley train on Jericho's army. They now know that this is the point of no return, that Jericho has indicated his intention to fight here tonight, with an inevitable invasion to follow. If humanity is to survive, this date will be marked in history as the day when the entire world realized the existence of extraterrestrials, *hostile extraterrestrials*, with designs to conquer planet Earth and eradicate the human race. It now rests on the shoulders of the Foundation to defend humanity from these invaders, to save the human race from the abyss of extinction.

Moriah has one final card to play.

As Jericho moves forward to begin the attack, he suddenly stops, and a strange look crosses his face. His army notices it, too, for their screeching and wailing comes to an abrupt end. There is an extended silence as all eyes are once again on Jericho, who slowly turns his head to look behind him. It is at that moment everyone in the valley notices a man standing directly behind Jericho, an old man with scraggly gray hair who has emerged from the pack of captives.

It is R. Jonas Abraham and he is very much alive.

A sinister half-smile occupies his face as he stares directly at Jericho. Abraham is holding an object in his hand, the same weapon the members of the Foundation now hold. The rumble of thunder drowned out the sound of Abraham firing a round from the weapon squarely into Jericho's back.

Jericho immediately realizes what has happened, but more importantly he realizes there is nothing he can do to counteract the lethal blow.

Jericho's army looks on in horror as his body suddenly starts to shudder and his face twists into an expression that can only be construed as agony. Jericho begins violently seizing and a phosphorescent liquid pours out of his mouth and nose. There is a transparency to Jericho's skin, the creature's technologically-advanced endoskeleton clearly visible. The endoskeleton flashes several times through his skin, like a police siren, and there is a distinct blue tint to it.

Jericho manages to take a halting step or two towards Moriah before he falls to his knees, a look of total shock registering on his face. His body is being ravaged from the inside and after several moments, the life seems to drain from his eyes. He swipes his claws through the air in a feeble gesture of hopelessness and finally, he pitches forward, landing face down on the ground.

There are a few moments of silence as everyone in the valley stares at the fallen Jericho, perhaps in disbelief that he could be killed with such relative ease. Jericho has become an elusive and dangerous figure in the eyes of the Foundation, a creature equally feared and respected, spoken about with such reverence and awe that for him to be cut down so swiftly seems anti-climactic.

And this was exactly the Foundation's intention.

The group envisioned that Jericho's sudden death would have a disheartening and demoralizing effect on his army, immediately taking the wind out of their sails. It is also the Foundation's final chance to avoid engaging in a war against what they know is a vastly superior foe, notwithstanding Moriah's proclamations that they are prepared for an invasion.

As Jericho lies motionless on the ground, the realization of his demise finally sinks in. Jericho's army now looks uncertain and confused, having witnessed their leader suddenly and mercilessly vanquished. Moriah and the other Foundation members aim their weapons at Jericho's army, practically daring them to attack. The soldiers at the top of the valley remain still, seemingly waiting for Jericho's army to make their next move.

One of Jericho's lieutenants screeches and suddenly Jericho's army looks prepared to fight again despite the loss of their leader.

Moriah turns to Bellini and orders, "Launch the attack."

Bellini relays the order into a device attached to his wrist, which unleashes a two-pronged attack. The first prong is globally, as an operator for their space-based laser system begins targeting the locations received from Rosenstein. The second prong occurs "locally," as the soldiers suddenly charge down the sides of the valley towards Jericho's army. The soldiers shout a piercing battle cry as they gather speed down the steep slope and begin firing, arcs of blue light radiating from their weapons.

The scene is Armageddon-like: the ground violently shakes as if an earthquake has struck the valley, while there are rumbles of thunder, flashes of lightning, and the rain starts to arrive in droves. One can imagine the earth being torn asunder and everyone within the valley plunging into a yawning chasm below.

Suddenly, a woman captive dashes from the pack and tries to attack a member of Jericho's army, an attempt that quickly fails. The woman is obliterated in the blink of an eye by the extraterrestrial's weapon. The other captives do not react or even seem to notice, but it is clear their level of agitation is rising, their restlessness growing with each passing second.

Jericho's army looks hesitant and rudderless, collectively trying to discern who to attack and in which direction the most immediate threats lie. On one side are the captives, the group that initially appeared the least hostile but now are acting more aggressively and even worse, unpredictably. Directly in front of Jericho's army awaits Moriah and the Foundation members, their weapons drawn and at the ready. Behind them is a massive contingent of soldiers bearing down on them at full speed. They are literally surrounded by enemies.

Jericho's lieutenants look towards Moriah and appear to decide that if they are to die here tonight, they will take their most hated and recognizable enemy with them. They move forward and then suddenly, inexplicably, they stop, startled expressions on their faces.

Moriah's mind races as to what Jericho's army could possibly be waiting for, their hesitation unsettling. Moriah is about to instruct his group to open fire when the hairs on the back of his neck start tingling.

Something is wrong here, a hitch in the plan, he thinks.

Moriah and his lieutenants suddenly hear a loud, screeching noise behind them, a noise not unlike the battle cry Jericho's army produced only moments before. Yet the noise is different somehow, perhaps in pitch or volume, but different nonetheless. They turn to look and see something they never suspect or believe could be possible – over half of the Foundation members no longer appear human!

The Foundation has been infiltrated!

As Moriah and his lieutenants take stock of their group, they quickly realize this is not mere infiltration, but something much more insidious.

This is complete and total infestation!

Over half the members of the Foundation wail like banshees and gesture wildly, their own claws exposed by flashes of lightning. They seem to menace not only Moriah and the rest of the "human" element of the Foundation, but also Jericho's army as well.

The area is once again illuminated, a multi-pronged lightning bolt striking dangerously close to the valley. It is at that moment Moriah and the remaining members of the Foundation realize it is they who are now caught in the middle, encircled by enemies.

It is Moriah and his lieutenants' turn to look uncertain, alternately glancing between Jericho's force and the extraterrestrials that have infiltrated the Foundation. A number of captives suddenly sprint from the pack towards their nearest targets, which happen to be members of Jericho's army. Simultaneously, the soldiers from above clash with the rear column of Jericho's force, the sound of weapons discharged nearly deafening.

Jericho's army suddenly looks fierce again and primed for battle, their hesitancy evaporating when they quickly realize they are under siege from all sides. The extraterrestrials who have infiltrated the Foundation do not move, their patience startling as they wait for Jericho's army to make the first move.

And they do.

Jericho's army surges forward as Moriah and the rest of his lieutenants greet them with a wave of lethal fire.

*   *   *

Sean manages to carry his wife nearly three-quarters of the way up the slope when his legs scream for a brief respite. Added to the challenge of carrying his wife up a steep incline through the wind and rain, the slick grass requires extra effort and additional steps to maintain his balance, taxing his legs to the breaking point. He gently places her down on the ground, cradling her head as he does so. He glances behind him to find Sloan lugging Conor up the slope only a few feet below him, while Kaley and Dawson bring up the rear.

Sean notices Dawson holding her hand to a bloody shoulder while Kaley backpedals and covers them with an automatic weapon lifted from one of the dead soldiers, although no one appears to be following them. Sloan reaches Sean and places Conor next to Isabella on the ground for a much-needed breather.

Sean, in between large intakes of air, nods toward the valley, "Looks like they've forgotten about us."

"They've got more important things on their mind," Sloan responds.

At the other end of the valley, they silently watch as a large group, presumably Jericho and his army, assemble in front of the Foundation members, outnumbering them by approximately three to one.

A few moments later, however, they hear a low rumble that cannot be attributed to the thunder. A massive force suddenly emerges at the top of the valley and surrounds Jericho and his army. Instantly, the odds appear to tilt in the Foundation's favor.

"Who the hell are *these guys*?" Sean asks.

"I would guess they're the soldiers stationed at Fairchild," Sloan speculates.

"Good guess," Kaley says, as he and Dawson reach them and stop, grateful for the chance to rest. "The base is almost completely deserted."

Kaley examines Dawson's wound again.

"You okay?" Sean asks.

"Yeah," she replies, "it's just a scratch."

"Meeting of the minds?" Kaley remarks, gesturing toward the valley.

"Something like that," Sean responds.

"Who are all these people?" Dawson asks breathlessly.

"How much time do you have?" Sloan rhetorically asks.

"Those aren't just people down there, Ms. Dawson," Sean indicates.

Dawson appears momentarily confused before grasping Sean's meaning.

They are completely engrossed in observing the captivating scene before them when suddenly they hear the menacing wail and screeching of Jericho's army clear across the valley. It appears that negotiations are starting to falter.

Sean motions toward the figure at the head of the extraterrestrial army.

"Is that . . ."

"Yes," Sloan confirms, "that's Jericho."

"Who's Jericho?" Kaley asks.

The question goes unanswered when suddenly they watch in shock as Jericho's body violently shudders and convulses. From their vantage point they see a phosphorescent liquid gush from his mouth and nose, and his body seems to glow and flash a strange blue tint.

"Jesus," Dawson utters.

Jericho manages a few steps towards the Foundation members before he crumples to the ground. Sean looks behind Jericho and immediately recognizes Jericho's killer as none other than R. Jonas Abraham, who holds some type of weapon in his outstretched hand.

"Abraham," Sean whispers through clenched teeth.

"In the flesh," Sloan concurs.

There is a long pause as the valley becomes shrouded in silence, everyone seemingly contemplating this turn of events. After a few moments, Jericho's army suddenly resumes their screeching. Almost immediately, the group at the top of the valley starts streaming down the slope towards them, firing their weapons as they go and inflicting heavy losses on Jericho's army. Each of the extraterrestrials on the receiving end of these projectiles displays the same painful reaction as Jericho, their bodies violently trembling and quaking before quickly breaking down.

They watch as a woman from Tamawaca attempts to attack a member of Jericho's army, only to be promptly obliterated in a heartbeat, her body disintegrating in a cloud of blood.

Just like my men in the jungle, Sean thinks.

"Holy shit," Kaley gasps.

Sean reaches down for Isabella and exclaims, "We need to go right now!"

He pauses, however, when he hears more screeching from the valley, although it sounds different from the shrieking and wailing they heard before.

"Sean . . ."

Sean glances at Sloan and sees a look of disbelief on her face. She points toward the Foundation members.

". . . look."

Sean stares at the group of Foundation members, but it takes several seconds to register in his mind. Finally, he sees what Sloan sees and immediately understands her disbelief – *the Foundation has been overrun!*

Seemingly over half of the group is comprised of extra-terrestrials. In an instant, Moriah and his top lieutenants are suddenly trapped in the middle of this chaos.

When all of these disparate groups converge at the bottom of the valley, the battle cries are replaced by the sound of weapons. The sound emanating from the weapons used by the Foundation members and the soldiers is nothing like the sound of a conventional weapon – quieter and more abbreviated. In contrast, the extraterrestrials' weapon emits a high-pitched whine prior to being fired, a sound Sean is all too familiar with and which continues to haunt his memories. An echo carries these sounds back and forth across the valley, creating a cacophony of noise. Accompanying the discharge of these weapons are tracers of blue and green lights that suddenly appear and abruptly disappear just as quickly.

Absent the lightning, the effect of the frenetic lights on the valley floor is striking. It is akin to watching something out of a science fiction movie. The sight would have been actually quite dazzling if the scene was not punctuated with the intermittent screams and cries of the combatants meeting their demise.

The rain pours down in sheets and the lightning is drawing nearer, while visibility to the other end of the valley is becoming worse. Sean and company seem to simultaneously realize the longer they continue to observe this extraordinary scene, their chances of survival will conversely plummet. It is not worth risking their lives any more than they already have in order to satisfy their curiosity.

Kaley and Dawson have begun creeping up the slope while Sloan picks up Conor.

"Come on, Sean," Sloan says.

Sean continues to gaze into the valley, scouring the scene below.

"Can you see Rosenstein anywhere?" Sean asks, fully cognizant of the answer.

"No, Sean," Sloan responds, "maybe he made it back to the chopper already."

Sean knows Sloan is being hopelessly optimistic for his sake, but he can clearly see for himself the likelihood of surviving the deadly battle below seems slim. Given Rosenstein's age and fighting experience, it would appear his particular chances of survival are considerably worse.

Sean steals one final glimpse of the valley floor before turning away. He scoops up Isabella and places her across his shoulders again.

They scale the remainder of the valley slope and reach the summit. As soon as they arrive on the other side of the valley, they establish a slow jog and within a few minutes, they reach the chopper. There is no sign of Rosenstein. They place Isabella and Conor in the last row of seats, checking to ensure they have a steady pulse and are breathing normally, which they are, if a bit shallow.

The helicopter is not far from the valley and they continue to hear the sounds of battle and see the blue and green lights from the combatants' weapons filling the night sky. The lightning has lessened directly overhead, but it continues to flash throughout the horizon. The rain has also slightly subsided, but it is still a fairly steady flow.

Kaley fashions a tourniquet for Dawson's shoulder while Sean again checks on his family. He glances in the direction of the valley every few seconds in the hope of seeing Rosenstein returning to the chopper, but each time his hope is dashed when he spots no sign of him. There is only so long they can wait, but Sean simply cannot leave Rosenstein twisting in the wind. While he is certainly bitter about not being told the truth for so many years, he owes it to his mentor, his friend, and *his father*, to wait.

After several excruciatingly long minutes, Sean's anxiety exponentially increasing with each passing second, the sounds from the valley begin to lessen until only an eerie silence remains. The light produced from the discharge of weapons has abated, and now there are only sporadic flashes of lightning throughout the park.

Sloan has managed to hold her tongue during this unbearable wait, but now she finally addresses Sean.

"Sean," Sloan says gently, as she taps her watch, "it's been over an hour. He might not be coming back-"

She stops in mid-sentence, and it clearly pains her to continue.

"I'm sorry, Sean . . . but we have to leave."

Sean glances towards the valley again, but still there is no sign of Rosenstein.

"Sean," Sloan pleads, "we need to *go*. We can't stay here and Rosenstein would not have wanted us to wait for him."

Sean wants to argue with her. He wants to ask how she knows what Rosenstein would have wanted, but then he looks at Kaley's spent body and Dawson's bullet wound and realizes they have risked everything, just like Sloan, to rescue his family and remove them from harm's way. He will likely never be able to repay them for their bravery and courage, and he knows he cannot ask them to risk anything more in the remote chance Rosenstein returns to their rendezvous point.

Sean has not thought about it until now, but he also realizes how agonizing this must be for Sloan as well. Beyond the student-teacher relationship, Sloan and Rosenstein seem to clearly share a bond more intimate than that, a bond not unlike the one Sean has with Rosenstein. It must be devastating for her to be forced to leave him behind, too, but Sean knows that to risk six lives for one is foolish and illogical. None of them need to say anything, for Sean can see it in their faces – it is time to go.

But first, they need to conduct a final fly-by.

Sean turns to Sloan, "Alright, Ms. Sloan, fire it up. If Rosenstein's alive though, we're making room for one more."

TWENTY-ONE

Pure chaos ruled supreme.

After Jericho was killed, the valley erupted into a war where one could hardly discern friend from foe. Bodies were dropping left and right or were completely obliterated altogether as screams of pain and agony pierced the night. One of the more disconcerting noises was what sounded like metal meeting flesh as the alien combatants plunged their razor sharp claws into their human adversaries. The storm, with its driving rain, swirling wind, and relentless lightning, simply added to the confusion, transforming a chaotic scene into one of utter bedlam.

Rosenstein's eyes flutter open and he immediately feels a tingling on the side of his head. The sensation is not particularly painful, but rather more numb than anything, only a dull ache at this point. He places his hand to his head and feels a small wound, roughly the size of a quarter and not very deep. He does not seem to be bleeding profusely, but cannot be certain because the rain may be washing the blood away.

As he regains his senses, he notices something strange – the only sound he hears is the steady beat of raindrops. He hears nothing else.

Rosenstein places his hands on the ground and slowly pushes himself up until he is in a kneeling position. His head is swimming as he gazes, dumbfounded, around the valley.

The ground around him is littered with bodies practically stacked on top of one another, their limbs contorted into awkward angles. The bodies that lie face up display eyes that have glazed over and mouths that hang open, an expression of shock written on their faces. Of the human bodies Rosenstein sees, a majority of them have been badly mutilated, their torsos torn open to reveal their internal organs and their faces so disfigured that they have been rendered virtually unrecognizable. He spots several decapitated bodies and one body has been completely severed in half. The dead bodies of the extraterrestrials are nearly transparent, a clear outline of their endoskeleton visible. Pools of a phosphorescent liquid intermix with a river of blood, forming an unusual stew on the valley floor.

Rosenstein suddenly feels like he is being watched and he turns to look behind him. Several feet away amidst all of the carnage stands a lone figure who appears to be staring directly at him. Rosenstein squints through the rain.

"Who are you?" Rosenstein calls out.

A flash of lightning reveals the figure's face.

While it is a face Rosenstein recognizes, he no longer sees the soft and gentle features that define it. The face has hardened and become frightening and . . . *unfriendly*.

"Sebastian," Rosenstein gasps.

Rosenstein struggles to his feet and takes a few wobbly steps towards Sebastian, but then abruptly stops.

Sebastian has not moved, let alone acknowledged Rosenstein.

"Is that you, Sebastian?" Rosenstein cautiously asks.

"It is me, Doctor," Sebastian finally responds.

Rosenstein gazes at him curiously and then glances around at the bodies.

"Did you see what happened here tonight?"

"We more than saw what happened," Sebastian indicates.

"*We*?" Rosenstein asks.

"We *fought* here tonight," Sebastian remarks cryptically.

"Who fought?"

"*We* did," Sebastian motions towards the other end of the valley.

Rosenstein looks behind him and sees Jericho's craft. The floodlights surrounding it have toppled over and are no longer on. The lights that blanket the craft are now dim. When his eyes finally adjust, Rosenstein is startled to see the outlines of probably four or five dozen figures encircling the craft. They stand there motionless, like they are waiting for something.

"Who are they?" Rosenstein questions.

"They are *mine*, Dr. Rosenstein, they are *my soldiers*," Sebastian states forcefully.

Rosenstein looks back at the figures and then turns to Sebastian.

"They are yours? I don't think I understand."

"We have left something for you," Sebastian indicates, and he beckons Rosenstein to come towards him.

Rosenstein peers suspiciously at Sebastian for a few seconds, his hesitancy obvious. Nevertheless, he starts walking towards him, his feet sloshing in the muddy, sodden ground.

Sebastian steps in between several bodies before he finds the one he is searching for. He hovers over the body and motions toward it.

Rosenstein looks at the body, which is twisted on its side, obscuring the face from Rosenstein's view. A flash of lightning only reveals the person is not moving and appears to be dead. Sebastian uses his foot to turn the body over and Rosenstein exhales sharply, a stunned gasp escaping his lips.

Moriah!

His right arm below the elbow has been completely severed, and he has several deep wounds to his lower abdomen, his shorn intestines forming a revolting pile at his midsection. Contrasting with the surrounding darkness is the ghostly pallor of his face, which is white as a bedsheet. Splatters of blood cover the lower half of his face and neck. Surprisingly, he does not appear to be in shock, but his eyes are dead, the life slowly draining from his body.

"And your other . . friend," Sebastian motions a few feet away from Moriah.

Rosenstein instantly recognizes the body of Jonas Abraham from the stringy gray hair. If not for that, Rosenstein might not have recognized him at all. The man's face is covered in blood, a substantial portion of his skull missing. The man's legs are bent at extremely grotesque angles and he also has a deep wound on the side of his torso. His mouth is moving, seemingly pleading for help, mercy, or likely both, but no words can be heard as he stares directly at Rosenstein.

"Here," Sebastian says, tossing a gun to Rosenstein. "Revenge is all yours now, Dr. Rosenstein."

Rosenstein stares at the gun and then at Sebastian, who gazes at him in anticipation. Rosenstein reluctantly glances at Moriah and Abraham, their bodies battered and broken, their lives without hope of survival. Despite all of his anger and hatred for these two men, Rosenstein cannot help but feel a pang of sympathy for them, too. They will die in a field surrounded by hundreds of other bodies, a lonely death without their families by their sides. Rosenstein imagines that they will die wondering whether all of the harm they inflicted on the people of this planet along the way was worth it, whether it will ultimately save humanity from its demise.

The Foundation was a group initially formed and committed to the dominance of the United States as the lone global superpower. Tonight, however, the group has placed the entire world on their shoulders, determined to guide humanity through what could potentially be its most catastrophic crisis. The irony lies in the fact that despite the group's evil and cunning ways, their steadfast belief that sacrifices by a few to preserve the integrity of the whole is not only necessary but essential in such a world, is that they actually might be right. The landscape of today is plagued by both enemies seen and unseen, and they may arrive in the form of a self-righteous terrorist or the next-door neighbor who may in fact be an extraterrestrial. No matter the threat, however, from its inception the

Foundation has always recognized that there are typically an unfortunate few who will pay the ultimate price for the greater good. Finally, at last, it is the Foundation itself that has committed the decisive sacrifice, albeit unintentionally and unwillingly, which was something the group's victims understood all too well when their own fate was unilaterally decided.

The Foundation has always viewed its intentions as just and rational, but it was their means to an end that typically resulted in collateral damage they were continually willing to accept, primarily because it did not adversely affect them. Their unwavering belief that they consistently hold the best interests of the nation, and in this case the world, in their hands, and their rigid adherence to the conviction that their decisions are invariably the correct ones blinds them to any alternatives. Thus, while the group may champion the idea that they always maintain the interests of society as a whole at their core, at the same time they can be its worst enemy as well.

They have not been elected by the people to represent them, yet their all-consuming ideology that society needs them to set its course is what motivates them. They believe that they are needed to conduct the dirty work, to make decisions policymakers, presidents, and others in positions of power are too afraid to make on their own. With this responsibility comes great power, and as is more common than not with great power, the potential for being corrupted by it is sometimes irresistible. All of the old adages and clichés regarding the abuse of power ring true with the two men before Rosenstein, and one only has to glimpse at their shattered bodies to see that.

Rosenstein has no doubt the pain and suffering these two men are experiencing is assuredly worse than death. In fact, death is their only savior now and for them it cannot arrive soon enough. If Rosenstein wishes to exact revenge, if he wants true retribution, the one thing he *should not* do is end their lives with a bullet, for that would grant them an easy way out.

He is a doctor of medicine, however, and to prolong their agony is against everything he stands for, not only as a doctor but as a person, too.

He wordlessly raises the gun, points it at Moriah, and then fires two bullets into his head. He does not move from where he stands and shifts his aim towards Abraham. Abraham's mouth continues to move, but this abruptly stops when Rosenstein pumps two rounds into his head. The echo from the gunshots reverberates around the valley before dispersing into the night. The valley becomes eerily silent again except for the slowing beat of the raindrops.

All of the pleasure and satisfaction he imagined if this moment was to ever arrive is missing, the feeling more of closure than of revenge finally fulfilled.

Rosenstein drops the gun at his feet, leans down, and checks Moriah's pulse. He reaches for something on the ground and subtly places it in his pocket before standing back up.

"Well, Dr. Rosenstein," Sebastian says, "our plan worked, we have destroyed our enemies and obtained our revenge. We have made this world a better place."

"But not a safer place," Rosenstein counters. "Not yet."

Sebastian looks at him expectantly.

"You have eliminated any chance of resistance to your own invasion, isn't that right, Sebastian?"

A momentary look of surprise crosses Sebastian's face before he slyly smiles.

"How did you know?" Sebastian asks.

"I know a wolf in sheep's clothing when I see one," Rosenstein remarks. "Your role of the benign alien here to help the human race is a tired and worn cliché.

"Your claim to be a multiple abductee who was provided confidential documents by extraterrestrials in positions of power within the government and at various defense and technology firms was a rather clever ruse, and it forced the Foundation to clean up the ranks, which they did. Jericho's 'associates' were driven from their posts, which explained the mass exodus the Foundation witnessed when they conducted their mole hunts as a direct result of your allegations."

"Jericho was foolish for believing that he and his comrades could immerse themselves in society with absolutely no past to speak of and continue to go undetected," Sebastian replies. "The Foundation would have eventually discovered them."

"You cooked up a ridiculous story about using human slaves to dig to the core of the earth," Rosenstein continues, "that there would be survivors in the event of an invasion, which I suspect was a lie."

Sebastian nods, "You're absolutely right, Doctor."

"When you claimed that all alien abductees had undergone a 'procedure' that resulted in a loss of defiance and an increased passiveness, and who were suddenly predisposed to being controlled and manipulated, all of which were true, this caused the Foundation to consider developing something that could possibly counteract this, such as a serum. You knew the folly of such a venture and sure enough, the project was a disaster from the start. The serum would be impossible to distribute to the general public, even harder to control, and an enormous waste of time and resources."

"Time better spent attempting to replicate our weapons, our biotechnology, or our propulsion system," Sebastian suggests.

"You disappeared after the mole hunts not because you were afraid of retribution from Jericho, but because you needed to begin coordinating the operations of your own soldiers who were planning to assume the identities of various influential and powerful human beings.

"It is *your* group, your army Moriah referred to when he paid me a visit after Pattie's funeral," Rosenstein indicates. "You are the 'devourers' he mentioned."

"A crude term," Sebastian replies, "but somewhat accurate. And certainly a more effective way to infiltrate an enemy than Jericho's method."

Rosenstein motions toward the figures surrounding Jericho's craft, "So you and your comrades infiltrated the Foundation and I'm guessing you approached me after the group became aware of the excessive amount of communication Jericho was transmitting between the satellites. He was trying to convince the Foundation something big was on the horizon, something like a global invasion?"

"I certainly underestimated you, Doctor," Sebastian concedes.

"You knew the group would soon ask for my help in deciphering the code because you were at these meetings. The group was up shit creek and would do anything necessary to determine Jericho's strategy, including asking for help from a bitter, disillusioned former 'employee.'"

"In fact, Doctor," Sebastian clarifies, "*I suggested* we approach you regarding the code, and my cohorts within the Foundation helped sell the idea to the rest of the group."

"Clever," Rosenstein remarks. "I imagine it was not a coincidence you happened to approach me soon after my wife became sick. You chose a time when I was angry and resentful, but more importantly vulnerable and more willing to agree to any plans that called for revenge on them."

Rosenstein motions toward the bodies of Moriah and Abraham.

"But Jericho was not planning an invasion, was he?" Rosenstein asks. "You said it yourself at my house that night."

"Jericho used the ruse of an invasion to lure the Foundation members here so he could kill them once and for all. You see, Doctor, Jericho is – or should I say was? – nearing the end of his life cycle, and he did not know if he would have another chance to destroy the Foundation before his own time was up."

"So you saw an opportunity to take out two birds with one stone," Rosenstein deduces. "The Foundation and Jericho's army would destroy each other here tonight, leaving you and your army to benefit."

"Well said, Dr. Rosenstein," Sebastian smirks.

"That speech about Jericho being corrupted by humanity was nothing more than bullshit, wasn't it? Revenge had nothing to do with him being a 'disgrace.' This whole thing was about eliminating the competition."

Sebastian smiles knowingly, "That's true, Doctor, but I've always had one other motive."

"Which is . . . ?"

The smile on Sebastian's face suddenly vanishes and his expression turns grim.

"It was Jericho's fault *my brother* was mercilessly executed by the Foundation years ago," he says angrily.

Rosenstein ponders this for a moment before putting the pieces together.

"Gabriel?" Rosenstein guesses.

Sebastian nods. "Jericho and Gabriel were chosen as our representatives. While hundreds of us were simultaneously dispatched to Earth, they were hand-picked to learn more about your people, to explore your weaknesses, and to ultimately determine whether your world could be conquered."

"They 'crashed' on purpose, didn't they?" Rosenstein asks. "They wanted to be captured."

"Yes," Sebastian acknowledges. "And after Jericho believed he had learned everything he would need to know about the human race, he escaped."

"Leaving Gabriel holding the bag," Rosenstein concludes.

Sebastian wordlessly nods his head, a look of hatred simmering just below the surface.

There is a long pause between them as the rain slows to a light drizzle. Rosenstein's sweat-soaked hand fingers the object in his pocket, knowing he may have to use it if his primary plan falls through.

I need to keep him talking, Rosenstein thinks.

"So the first set of coordinates you gave me were the gathering locations for the rest of Jericho's army,"

Rosenstein indicates, "but how were you able to flush them out of hiding and coerce them to these locations?"

Sebastian holds up a tiny silver object approximately two inches long and rounded at both ends. Sebastian hits a switch on the object and both ends extend several inches, revealing a black, circular tube in between with a flashing light inside.

"Jericho's 'phone,' what he used to transmit information to the rest of his group," Sebastian explains. "Each device contains a unique set of symbols specific to that individual – think of it like a caller ID. Jericho's army believed that my instructions, *my orders*, were coming directly from him. They believed that he was finally planning to launch an invasion."

"And that's why the first set of coordinates I provided Moriah did not make any strategic sense. All of the locations were in vast, open spaces, perfect for . . say . . a laser to destroy them?"

"You're exactly right, Doctor," Sebastian confirms.

"And the second set of coordinates . . ?"

"Eight research facilities and bases around this country, as well as five similar installations in Russia, three in China, and one in Japan, all of which have replicated or nearly replicated our technology and house crafts similar to our own. Some of these places contained detailed files on us, files that are nothing more than dust now. The crafts have also been destroyed, along with many of the pilots who have learned the technology. All thanks to the Foundation's latest and greatest weapon."

Sebastian gestures toward the sky.

"So now we're back at square one?"

Sebastian nods sympathetically. "An unfortunate position to be in with our coming invasion."

Rosenstein pauses a moment and then asks, "No loose strings?"

"Glad you asked, Doctor," Sebastian responds almost cheerfully. "Over the coming weeks, all of the Foundation's associates and cohorts will be rounded up by General Theodore Parker. I have pointed him to a cache of evidence that will expose them all for crimes against this country and its citizens, as well as beyond its borders. That should take care of the few remaining individuals not killed here tonight who could possibly have knowledge of my race and its capabilities."

"So Jericho's army and the Foundation have been completely annihilated, and all the evidence and files with respect to your race, not to mention any of your technology humanity was able to replicate, has been wiped out," Rosenstein summarizes.

"And the majority of humans with knowledge of our race and an expertise in our technology are now dead, leaving only you, Dr. Rosenstein," Sebastian concludes with an ominous grin.

"I'm impressed, Sebastian, but I do have one last question for you," Rosenstein indicates.

Sebastian nods accommodatingly.

"What if the second set of coordinates I gave to Moriah were not the ones you gave to me?" he asks.

Sebastian pauses a moment, actually considering the question when he realizes what Rosenstein is implying.

He looks at Rosenstein, who gladly takes his turn with a sly grin.

"You may have destroyed Jericho's army and removed

the Foundation and all of their associates from power, but none of *our* technology – meaning mankind's – has been lost. Our ships are still intact and all of the technology, research, and files are still secure."

Rosenstein shakes his head in disapproval. "I still have friends in high places, Sebastian. I knew all along what those second set of coordinates contained."

Rosenstein pauses a moment to allow this to sink in.

"But there is one location I gave them within the second set of coordinates that is correct, Sebastian," Rosenstein notes.

Sebastian's breathing has become more intense as he glares spitefully at Rosenstein, his rage naked and terrifying.

Suddenly, a helicopter flies over the ridge of the valley and . . .

*　*　*

. . . the spotlight on the helicopter combs the valley to reveal the macabre sight below. Bodies are strewn across the valley floor and they notice Jericho's craft is still there, but now the floodlights surrounding it are no longer illuminated. The craft is surrounded by a few dozen figures who stand as still as statues.

Sloan pulls up and the helicopter glides to a stop, hovering above the valley. Sean shines the spotlight on the valley floor, trying to find any sign of Rosenstein or any sign of life for that matter. With the exception of the figures encircling Jericho's craft, there is nothing but dead bodies as far as the eye can see. Finally, the spotlight reveals two figures standing amid the corpses.

Sean spots Rosenstein, but he does not recognize the figure standing several feet away from him.

Suddenly, a bright light from the heavens above illuminates the entire valley.

Sean, Sloan, Kaley, and Dawson stare up at the beacon of light, enthralled by it but unable to determine the source.

The same thoughts course through each of their heads.

Is it an alien ship?

Have they come to collect their comrades?

Are they here to destroy us all?

Is this the beginning of the end?

Sloan quickly realizes this is no alien ship, but something else, something very much man-made. And she also realizes they probably have only a few seconds.

Sean stares at Rosenstein, who glances up towards the helicopter and sees Sean gazing down on him. He sees the fear on his son's face and knows there is only one thing a father can do at this point – reassure his son.

Rosenstein smiles sadly and waves "goodbye" to him. Sean has never been a lip reader, but he clearly discerns Rosenstein's last words as he mouths, "Love you, kid."

It is at that moment Sean realizes the same thing Sloan does.

The valley is being targeted! The laser!

"No, Al, no," Sean whispers.

"Sean, we need to go!" Sloan exclaims.

She urgently thrusts the helicopter up and away from the valley, causing Kaley and Dawson to topple nearly on top of each other.

Sean holds steady to the side of the open doorway as he watches Rosenstein the entire time, his eyes never leaving him, both of them aware it is the last look they will share on this Earth.

Rosenstein does not take his eyes off Sean either, even when the mysterious figure darts with lightning-quick speed towards him. Rosenstein raises something in his hand and suddenly, a beam pierces through the night sky into the center of the valley.

"NOOOOOOOO!" Sean screams at the top of his lungs.

Both Rosenstein and the figure disappear in the blinding glare of the light.

A moment of silence envelops the entire park, as if the world has suddenly stopped spinning and time has suspended itself.

A deafening explosion levels the valley as a vaporous cloud charges across it in all directions. The explosion lights up the night sky and the sound can be heard for miles around the park.

They feel a cold gust pass over them as the shock waves from the explosion batter the helicopter, sending it twisting and shuddering as Sloan fights for control of the craft. The helicopter pitches back and forth as Sloan attempts to steady it, with little success. The helicopter is suddenly barreling straight towards the ridge of the valley, a collision nearly unavoidable.

"Pull up!" Kaley shouts from the back, stating the obvious.

They are twenty feet away from impact, fifteen, ten . . .

Sloan pulls back and the helicopter suddenly lurches upward. The nose of the craft barely clears the ridge of the valley, but the tail rotor catches it, again sending the helicopter careening unsteadily through the air. Finally, after several more stomach-churning seconds, Sloan is able to steady the chopper and bring it under control.

Everyone breathes a sigh of relief as they stare back at the valley, which is a smoking ruin.

The enormity and magnitude of what they have witnessed is difficult to understand, and they cannot possibly be expected to readily digest the events of the past few days at that moment. Kaley, however, is not even thinking about that right now. He knows his friend is hurting, so he places a comforting hand on Sean's shoulder.

The helicopter turns slightly and heads due east, leaving the valley and everything in it behind as a son looks back and quietly weeps for his father.

*   *   *

As they approached Fairchild Air Force Base, Parker, Augie, and Anderson gazed out the windows of the plane to try and peer through the darkness below. They could not see anything from their vantage point, but that did not discourage them from trying. Their patience would soon be rewarded.

As the plane circled Fairchild, a sudden beam of light punctured the clouds, illuminating what appeared to be a deep valley slightly west of the base.

A moment later, a massive explosion rocked the valley. The sound echoed across the horizon and the night sky was as bright as a sun-drenched day. The shock waves from the explosion shook the plane and caused some jarring turbulence, but the pilot was able to maintain control of the aircraft.

Parker and Augie both agreed that they saw the clear outline of a helicopter flying away from the valley in the seconds after the explosion, although neither of them spotted any markings on it.

Immediately, Parker instructed the pilot to land the plane at Fairchild in order to investigate the scene below.

The eerie quiet of the base was more than unsettling, with not a soul to be found. When they arrived at the valley, however, they were stunned beyond words.

As they stand there now on a hill overlooking the devastated valley in Spokane Plains Battlefield State Park, all they see is a charred hole with smoke blanketing the ground. The ground has turned a charcoal gray color and the smell is overpowering, like a massive barbecue pit occupies the valley floor.

Parker stares at the valley below and wonders what happened here tonight. He can smell the fresh stench of death in the air, and he knows that whatever occurred here tonight, the underworld is preparing to receive a large group of arrivals.

TWENTY-TWO

One Month Later

General Parker labored for countless sleepless nights attempting to formulate a report for the President that made at least some semblance of sense. He endlessly contemplated the extraterrestrial radiation found in Tamawaca, but he remains unsure how its discovery fits into the overall scheme of things. He detailed in the report his suspicions of what occurred in Tamawaca, or actually what *had not* occurred, wholeheartedly believing with every fiber of his being that it was not a terrorist attack, but he is at a loss to offer an alternative explanation.

General Parker believed it vital to detail the inconsistencies and anomalies Dr. Nitchie revealed to Private Anderson concerning the scene in Tamawaca. Unfortunately, the mysterious doctor is still missing and obviously cannot substantiate his allegations. Stranger still, Bason and Stringer were actually telling the truth when they informed Parker, Augie, and Anderson just prior to their demise that no one from the forensic team had reported in sick. Therefore, Dr. Nitchie could not have replaced anyone, begging several questions:

Where had he come from? What was his motive and who was he working for? Who the hell was Dr. Nitchie?

After several inquiries, nobody within the scientific community had ever heard of Dr. Warren Nitchie. The man was a complete wild card, and Parker might have claimed he was an apparition if at least five people had not seen him with their own eyes.

As for the footage they possess of several helicopters depositing bombs across the surface of Tamawaca Beach, there was no sign of the residents in the recording and thus, it only created more questions rather than supplied any answers. Parker presented the footage to the President, along with several of his closest advisors, but they did not know what to make of it either. The bottom line, the President's advisors explained, is the residents of Tamawaca are presumed dead, and to start spouting conspiracy theories and government cover-ups would not only be reckless, but disrespectful to the victims' families. Parker and Augie thought it was all too convenient for them to hide behind the mourning of the victims' families as a justifiable and reasonable excuse for failing to uncover the truth of what happened in Tamawaca.

The President, however, pledged to General Parker that a thorough investigation of the events at Tamawaca would be conducted, albeit secretly and without public knowledge. Parker immediately volunteered to continue to lead the investigation, but he was rebuffed and informed that a "different perspective" was needed. They will likely seek someone who does not appear biased toward mysterious conspiracies and presumably, a person willing to toe the administration's line.

Parker was furious and insisted that he should be the one chosen to lead the investigation into not only the "attack" at Tamawaca, but also what occurred around the world approximately 30 hours later, believing unequivocally that the events were interrelated.

The American government, however, provided their own explanation to the Associated Press regarding these global events, failing to draw a connection between them and the terrorist attack in Tamawaca. News agencies around the world swallowed the story and subsequently printed it on the front page of their papers in bold headlines and meticulously dissected it on their newscasts. After all, the story thoroughly embarrassed the United States, and anything humiliating the most powerful country in the world will always be newsworthy.

Due to the Outer Space Treaty of 1967 and the Anti-Ballistic Missile Treaty, certain types of weapons, such as lasers, are strictly prohibited from being placed in space. The use of directed-energy weapons like lasers, along with high-power microwaves and charged particle beams, have been considered and researched extensively by the Defense Department. Numerous systems containing these types of weapons have been constructed and tested on the ground, but no systems have ever been tested in orbit.

Until now.

The government claimed that a rogue group of American military officers, which included various generals, admirals, and colonels, along with a number of high-ranking officials in the defense and weapons industries, covertly established a space-based laser system without anyone's knowledge, a story that certainly tested the boundaries of the imagination. It was noted that a space-based laser system has the potential to be the preeminent weapon in the next generation of warfare. Possessing a weapon in space allows an army to own the ultimate high ground, a distinct advantage over every other sovereign nation on the planet.

Treaty be damned, the group attempted to test the effectiveness and viability of the laser at several points on the surface of the earth, but a disastrous "malfunction" occurred. The weapon discharged at multiple locations around the world, in 16 different countries, none of whom were pleased to be a testing ground for the United States' next great weapon.

Fortunately and rather miraculously, there were few *human* casualties at the various points of impact on the ground. The only casualties occurred in the United States, at the exact location where the rogue group had gathered to test the weapon. It was believed that they were displaying the weapon's target illumination capabilities, using the specific location of the conspirators, when the laser inadvertently fired, vaporizing them all within a heartbeat.

Cries of protest and alarm were rampant across the globe as people demanded to know how such a group could have the funding and the capability to construct their own space-based laser system behind the back of the American government. It was suggested, and not subtly, that the rogue group was testing the weapon as a precursor to retaliating against those responsible for carrying out the terrorist attack in Tamawaca.

The U.S. government was roasted and vilified in the press for their incompetence, willingly taking it on the chin in order to avoid the tougher questions that would inevitably come if the discrepancies and inconsistencies of the story were explored further. Underground publications and the Internet were abuzz with unbridled references to strange and unusual "things" that had been found at these sites around the world, with multiple people claiming that these "things" did not have an address here on Earth. The mainstream media, however, virtually ignored this angle, focusing instead on the far more tantalizing story that the entire American government was apparently asleep at the wheel.

The government focused on assuring the world and the American people that a full investigation into this rogue group would be conducted, and that strict measures are already being implemented to ensure nothing like this could ever occur again. A special task force has been commissioned by the President to thoroughly investigate what happened. The task force would likely issue their report in a year or two when a much more newsworthy story is on the front page, and everyone except the families of those who lost their lives has nearly forgotten about these few terrifying days.

As for General Parker, at the direction of Dr. Nitchie, he had paid a visit to the Lincoln Memorial in Washington D.C. in the early morning hours and indeed discovered a key in Honest Abe's lap. The key was in a small container encased in cement that blended in with the rest of the monument. The key opened storage locker #5035 on Arlington Road to reveal a mountain of evidence that included documents, video and audio recordings, photographs, and other assorted materials implicating members of the Foundation and their multitude of associates around the world in various illegal and unlawful acts that occurred in this country and beyond its borders. In some instances, the evidence appeared to suggest the acts could be construed as crimes against humanity and war crimes. Some of the evidence stretched as far back as sixty years ago, while other evidence was as recent as several months ago.

With each passing day as Parker and Augie combed through the materials, they discovered more and more evidence implicating the Foundation in monumental events that occurred in the twentieth and twenty-first centuries. They found evidence relating to the Holocaust, the Korean War, the space and arms races with the Soviets, the Bay of Pigs, the assassination of the Kennedy brothers and Martin Luther King, Jr., the Vietnam War, Watergate, AIDS, the assassination attempt on Ronald Reagan, Iran-Contra, the crack epidemic, both Gulf Wars, the technology boom of the 1990s, 9/11, and an assortment of allegations involving vote rigging in presidential elections dating back to JFK. Not to mention various operations and actions initiated by the group in the affairs of other sovereign countries. The shock factor increased with each new piece of evidence unearthed.

Parker also came upon a huge cache of documents relating to some experiments conducted around 50 years ago outside of Spokane, Washington, that, if he read correctly, employed *human subjects* for their tests. There was mention of a serum and even notations implying that a group of subjects had not survived a battery of tests. The evidence was horrifying and ghastly, and Parker and

Augie did not believe it was a coincidence these experiments occurred not far from Fairchild Air Force Base and the site of that massive explosion.

They gathered the mountain of evidence and presented it to the Attorney General of the United States, who listened to them with tepid interest at best. When they concluded summarizing what they had discovered, he promptly informed them to leave it alone and that they do not need to "dig up ghosts" from the past. Parker asked the AG to simply review the evidence for himself before arriving at a decision. The AG promised he would evaluate the evidence and contact the general at some point to discuss it. Parker continues to wait for a phone call that will likely never come.

Thus, it has come to this: General Parker has decided to retire. All the years of dealing with politicians, bureaucrats, and special interests have taken their toll. He cannot forgive nor tolerate apathy, especially when it comes to the truth. Parker believes that oftentimes the American public simply needs to hear the truth, and they are sensible and intelligent enough to make their own judgments and form their own conclusions. It always seems to be that damage control or looking good for one's constituents is the order of the day, a fact he has accepted but never endured.

Besides, Parker had succeeded at what he had always promised himself he would do in the world of Washington, D.C. He was a fighter, a rabble-rouser, someone who did not roll over even in the face of stiff opposition. He battled entrenched authority and closed mindsets, challenged long-held beliefs and the manipulative ways he felt this country was sometimes governed. Parker had outlasted the "rogue" group, i.e. the Foundation, and now he would outlive them. A change, he believes, is potentially in the air, but when the truth still remains buried, he realized it is time for someone else to take up the fight.

"Good luck to you, Augie," Parker says, as they firmly shake hands.

"You're going to get bored, sir," Augie warns.

"If I do, I'll just come around and bother you," Parker replies.

Augie smiles and says, "You'd be welcome anytime."

They stand outside the Pentagon, the ink still fresh on Parker's letter of resignation.

"You keep giving them hell around here, you understand," Parker says forcefully, his intent all too clear to his protégé.

"Of course, sir," Augie affirms.

"Don't be a stranger," Parker indicates, "if you get in a jam, give me a call day or night."

"Will do, sir," Augie responds.

They stand there awkwardly for a moment or two, not knowing what else to say when they have said so much to each other over several decades of friendship. Nothing seems capable of capturing the emotions they feel.

Finally, Parker says, "Augie, in case I've never told you this, and I know I haven't, you are the finest soldier I have ever known and it was a privilege to work with you."

The general's sudden and unexpected outpouring of praise momentarily catches Augie off guard.

"Sir, I don't know what . . to say . ."

"There is nothing else to say, Lieutenant Colonel Hermann," Parker replies.

Augie stands rigid and crisply salutes the general, knowing it is the last time.

"It was an honor, sir," Augie says.

Parker leans in close and whispers, "Mine," and he gently taps Augie's prosthetic hand.

With that, the general turns and walks down the street into the bright sunshine of a beautiful August day in Washington. Augie watches him for a few moments and then turns and walks back towards the Pentagon. Two men for the first time walking in opposite directions, one satisfied with what he has accomplished in life while the other is intent on continuing his mentor's legacy.

*   *   *

The sun sits low on the horizon as it continues its steady descent to close out the day, the other side of the world in need of its services. It is hot and muggy, but with the setting sun and a steady breeze suddenly emerging, much-needed relief from the heat has finally arrived.

Sean and Isabella stand in front of the graves of Patricia and Albert Rosenstein with their heads bowed and their hearts still heavy with pain. Sean has visited every few days since Al's private burial, with Isabella usually accompanying him, but these visits have not assisted in the healing process or been as therapeutic as Sean had hoped. He expected with each visit, the pain might diminish, but instead he has found that the sadness and heartache have no intention of waning. The previous month has seemed like an eternity as their emotions have traveled a rollercoaster of extremes. When Sean is not focusing on his family, he frequently laments how cruel and unfair it was to discover his true connection to Rosenstein, only for the man to be taken away from him in the next instant.

In the immediate aftermath, Sean wanted to approach the media and disclose the truth of what occurred in Tamawaca, as well as everything he had learned from Sloan and Rosenstein that night. The problem is two-fold. First, he lacks evidence to support his story, and second, his focus and attention have been completely devoted to the health and well-being of his family.

After Spokane, his wife was unconscious for over 36 hours while Conor laid in a coma for nearly three days. After they initially regained consciousness, everything seemed fine, although both of them were, unsurprisingly, extremely tired and lethargic. They appeared to possess the same personality and disposition, and were seemingly unaltered by their ordeal. Sean considered it a blessing, but soon realized that for both of them to emerge unscathed from their shared nightmare, it would not only be wishful thinking but a miracle in and of itself.

Both Isabella and Conor have been prone to unprovoked, erratic bursts of anger and aggression lasting anywhere from a few seconds to a few minutes. This hostility was first directed at doctors and nurses, but after they were released from the hospital, people on the street, store clerks, and finally, Sean himself received the brunt of this vitriol. Isabella has improved each day as she gradually learns to control it, but Conor is not mentally strong enough to resist it and he typically succumbs to these bouts of rage. Conor has started taking medication not unlike what children with extreme hyperactivity receive, only his doses are much higher and the pills a hundred times stronger.

Sean and Isabella have cried themselves to sleep some nights as they curse the monsters responsible for their suffering. The fact that all of the culpable parties are now dead does not stop Sean and Isabella from continuing to feel an intense hatred for those responsible, thinking they got off easy compared to what their son will have to endure for the rest of his life. They have taken small comfort knowing that they were fortunate enough to even survive the ordeal, unlike their neighbors in Tamawaca.

They have yet to return to the small cottage town and chances are they never will again. It deeply saddens them that a place with such beautiful and previously lasting memories now conjures up such horrible thoughts and images. Isabella breaks into a cold sweat and nearly has a panic attack at the very mention of the town. She and Conor oftentimes wake up in the middle of the night screaming hysterically as a result of their still-vivid nightmares.

After a couple of weeks, Sean discussed what happened with Isabella, and he related everything to her that Sloan and Rosenstein had revealed to him. Needless to say, she was amazed by the story and completely stunned to learn that Rosenstein was actually Sean's father. She instantly saw how desperately Sean wanted to share this information with the world, how much it pained him to keep the truth locked inside him. Isabella, however, could not hide the emotions she felt, the anxiety and trepidation at the prospect of Sean revealing this story to the world. She, of course, assured him that she would stand beside him and support him if he decides to go public with the knowledge he possesses, and Sean harbors no doubt that she would support him, but he also realizes that revealing the truth may exact a heavy toll. He would be placing her and his son under an unbearable amount of scrutiny and a constant barrage of questions. Furthermore, without proof, he would be leaving himself and his family open to scorn and ridicule, and risk being branded liars and crackpots.

Sean, having trouble simply letting go and allowing the truth to remain hidden, turned to Kaley and Dawson. While Kaley could at least corroborate some of what occurred in Tamawaca and both of them could substantiate the subsequent events in Spokane, they were also hesitant as a result of the lack of evidence to support them. Kaley informed Sean about his deep-sea dive at the coordinates of the mysterious signal and the strange lights on the sea floor. He also told Sean about his uncle, Mike Eisley, whose life was lost at sea. Another innocent casualty in all of this, along with the evidence Kaley had obtained the night of the "attack."

Similar to his wife, Sean recognized Kaley and Dawson's apprehension at the thought of sharing their story with the public. Sean began to accept the fact that everyone involved simply wanted to move on, to not necessarily try and forget about the whole affair because it will be something they will remember every day for the rest of their lives. Rather, they would prefer not to relive the ordeal through the bright glare of the spotlight, which would be harsh and relentless: congressional testimony and proceedings, constant requests for interviews, an endless series of questions wherever you go, and worst yet, a full onslaught on the quality of your character and integrity.

Perhaps everyone believes the "bad guys" received their just desserts and there is nothing that can be gained by revealing what they know to the public. While Sean adamantly disagrees with this notion, he knows he does not possess the fortitude to place his family through anything that could inflict further undue pain or stress.

Ultimately, their collective fear lies in the fact of a complete lack of evidence to support their story. All of them could claim that they are only interested in letting the truth be known, but without any proof to corroborate it, their version of the "truth" could fall apart under a withering barrage of media questions and a skeptical public.

As far as the detailed history of extraterrestrials on this planet that Sean learned from Sloan, the woman seemingly vanished into thin air after the night in Spokane. She is the only person alive who knows what Sean knows, and probably a lot more. Unfortunately, since she was his primary source of information, her disappearance is a further deterrent to him revealing what he knows to the world.

So here they are, nearly a month after those dreadful nights, the truth still secreted away from the public and in jeopardy of never being revealed. Sean has considered writing a book detailing the entire experience, but he suspects this is only a fanciful thought. He still does not know what to do, but feels he cannot possibly conceal this extraordinary secret the rest of his life, and he does not know how everyone else can do the same.

They stand in the cemetery in silence, Isabella's head resting gently on Sean's shoulder. With his wife beside him, Sean feels lucky she and Conor are even alive, and he thinks perhaps he should try to move on, too. A part of him, however, insists the truth should be known, that the world has a right to know what happened.

After a few minutes, Sean takes Isabella's hand in his and motions for them to go. She nods silently and follows him as they walk down the cemetery hill that leads from the Rosensteins' graves. Sean briefly glances back as he continues walking.

Isabella motions in front of them, "Sean."

Sean looks ahead and sees Kaley, who walks hand-in-hand with Julianna Dawson. Both are wearing civilian clothes as Sean notices Dawson holding a bouquet of flowers.

"Would you look at that?" Sean whispers, thinking how love can be found in the strangest of places.

Isabella allows herself a small smile of happiness for them as she clearly sees the shared affection between Kaley and Dawson.

"Hey, Jon boy," Sean says.

"Seanie lad," Kaley replies, and they briefly embrace.

Sean kisses Dawson on the cheek and says, "Thanks for coming."

"Sure," Dawson responds.

Isabella gives both Dawson and Kaley a warm embrace.

"I heard Conor and I probably wouldn't be here if it wasn't for the two of you," she says gratefully. "Thank you both for what you did. There's really no words . . ."

"All in the line of duty, Izzy," Kaley gallantly responds.

Dawson glances at him in mock disapproval and turns to Isabella.

"How are you feeling?" Dawson asks.

"Better," Isabella nods, "every day I seem to feel better."

"And Conor?" Dawson asks hopefully.

Isabella hesitates, so Sean answers, "He's . . fighting, you know, hanging in there. He's with Izzy's parents right now. They probably have him locked in a cage by-"

Sean cuts himself off, realizing he may be closer to the truth than he cares to be. Isabella, desperately wanting to change the subject, addresses Dawson.

"The shoulder is feeling better?"

Dawson nods, "Yeah, it gets stiff from time to time, but it's-"

"Aw," Kaley interrupts, "she's fishing for sympathy, Izzy, don't let her pull you in."

For the first time in a long while Sean and Isabella laugh.

"What about you last week?" Dawson counters.

She turns to Sean and Isabella, "He was *still* trying to milk his injuries for all their worth. Asking me to make him a sandwich, get him a beer, run errands for him."

"Hey, I'm still recuperating," Kaley argues.

"And becoming a civilian I hear," Isabella remarks.

"That's right," Kaley confirms. "I've had enough of the military, it's time to move on."

"So what's it going to be?" Sean asks. "Private security? Protecting corporate bigwigs?"

"Who knows?" Kaley defers. "Time will tell. I'm going to sit on it for a while."

"Not too long, I hope," Dawson remarks.

They all chuckle, which is followed by a long, awkward silence.

"Listen," Sean says, "why don't we grab a bite to eat, a few drinks . . we need to unwind a bit. You guys interested?"

Kaley and Dawson glance at one another and nod.

"Sounds good to us," Kaley agrees.

He motions towards Rosenstein's grave, "We're going to pay our respects first."

"Sure," Sean nods. "We'll wait for you guys in the parking lot."

"Be there in a few minutes," Kaley replies.

As Sean and Isabella walk towards their car, Sean feels a strange sensation that they are being watched. Sean glances around the cemetery and sees a woman with dark sunglasses standing under a tree in the distance, staring their way. Sean instantly recognizes her.

Sloan.

"Baby, I'll meet you at the car," Sean indicates.

Isabella follows his gaze across the cemetery and also spots the woman.

"Who is it?"

"The elusive Ms. Sloan," Sean replies.

"That's her?"

Sean nods, "I'm going to say a quick hello."

"Sean, will you let her know how much . ."

Isabella's voice trails off.

"I will, Baby," Sean assures her.

A minute later, Sean approaches Sloan, who has not moved from her spot underneath the tree, like she is afraid to move.

"Ms. Sloan," Sean greets her warmly.

"Professor," she nods in return. Her expression is strained, almost nervous.

Her mind seems preoccupied as she looks beyond Sean towards Rosenstein's grave.

"I haven't had the courage to . . come visit," Sloan says haltingly in a near whisper.

"It's understandable," Sean replies.

Sean glances behind him at the Rosensteins' graves and sees Kaley and Dawson huddled together in front of them.

Sloan motions towards them, "They're both okay?"

"Yeah," Sean nods, "they're both fine."

"That's good."

Sean motions over his shoulder, "You going to have a talk with him?"

Sloan shakes her head, "No . . I just . . I can't."

And that seems to be the end of it. She will mourn him from a distance.

"How are you doing?" Sean asks with concern. "You disappeared after that night, I wasn't sure-"

"Yeah," she says as she looks down at the ground, "I had some thinking to do."

Sean nods.

After a few moments of silence, Sean decides that even though he is afraid to hear the answer, he has to know. He has to know for his own peace of mind.

"Have you thought about revealing what we know?" he warily asks. "About the Foundation? About . . . everything? The knowledge we have-"

"Is dangerous, Sean," Sloan interrupts. "The Foundation is gone, Sean, Al is . . gone. What good would it really do now?"

"People have a right to know the truth, Ms. Sloan," Sean responds, his voice rising. "They should know about a secret organization whose almost limitless power helped them practically dictate the course of this country for the better part of the last century. They should know so something like this can never happen again. They should know about the existence of extraterrestrials on this planet, and they should know how close we came to a catastrophic war with these creatures."

At this point, Sean is exasperated. Excluding the health of his family, he has wanted nothing more since that night than to reveal the truth, but he has not received support from the people he depends on the most. Sloan is his final hope, but it is obvious she is not ready to face all the scrutiny and questions either.

"Sometimes, Sean," Sloan contends, "it's best the whole world doesn't know certain things. It helps people sleep at night."

"That's not what Rosenstein would have wanted," Sean counters. "His life's work was about the pursuit of justice and truth, and not allowing the privileged and powerful few make decisions for the rest of us. He found and revealed conspiracies that otherwise would have gone unnoticed because he believed the constant questioning of authority leads to a more open society, a society that gives people the freedom to do and say as they please, to always be skeptical, to always possess doubt of what they are being told. He didn't want anyone to get away-"

"Get away with what?" Sloan interjects. "The Foundation has been destroyed, Sean, there is no one the truth would help at this point, there is no one to be brought to justice."

"Ms. Sloan, you were a student of his, how can-"

"I was not a student in the traditional sense," Sloan interrupts.

Sean appears puzzled for a moment.

"What do you mean?"

"I mean," Sloan explains, "that Rosenstein taught me things, but he never taught me anything in a classroom."

"Then how did he teach you?" Sean asks.

Sloan takes a deep breath and looks directly at Sean. She removes her sunglasses and Sean sees her bleary and bloodshot eyes, like she has been crying for days.

"I was a misfit, Sean, a delinquent," Sloan continues. "Al rescued me from that. He was the first person to talk to me, to tell me I could do things with my life, that I could make a difference."

"But how did you meet?"

"I was barely a month old when my dad answered an ad in the local newspaper that was seeking people for what they claimed was 'cutting-edge research.' At the time, my parents were struggling . . financially, and they were desperate for money."

Oh my God, Sean thinks. *The experiments.*

"My mother and I never saw him again," Sloan says softly.

"He was one of the . . human subjects?" Sean asks incredulously.

Sloan nods silently and grimaces, the pain still evident.

"After that, it was such a struggle for my mom and me," Sloan continues. "We lived in so many places, we were always on the move, trying to avoid creditors and landlords. After she sold our car, we stayed in church basements and homeless shelters, and sometimes . . . on the street."

Sloan falters a moment, but quickly gathers herself.

"Eventually, my mom couldn't take care of me," Sloan explains in a near whisper, "and I lived in foster homes and orphanages on and off for years. When I became a teenager, I started a life of petty crime that led to a half-dozen arrests and a future that was completely hopeless.

"One day I got busted for grand larceny. This time, they were going to charge me as an adult when a man on the other side of the country read about my arrest and spoke to the judge and the district attorney on my behalf. It was Dr. Rosenstein and incredibly, he had recognized my last name and knew who my father was and what happened to him. He . . . he saved me, Sean. He saved me from a worthless life.

"He and Pattie took care of me for a while and eventually he told me about the Foundation, about the group behind the experiments and responsible for my dad's death. At that moment, my mission in life became clear: the Foundation was going to pay for what they did."

"And so you had as much motive for revenge as Rosenstein, if not more," Sean notes.

Sloan nods, "And more patience than I ever thought possible. I've waited for their time to come for so long, I don't even know what to do now that it's over."

"You worked for them," Sean indicates. "You worked from the inside the whole time, waiting for your chance, and then it finally came."

"Yes," she confirms, "and now all I want to do is move on. I do not want to think about revenge or the Foundation anymore. I do not want to be at the center of what we know would be a firestorm if we decided to reveal the truth. It's over, Sean. The group has been wiped out and now it's time for us to move on."

There is a finality to Sloan's words that seems to close the matter without question or regret. Perhaps Sean can accept that maybe the truth will never be known, that history may not record this episode of humanity potentially on the brink of annihilation. Soon, all of this will be forgotten and the human race will continue its march forward into a bright and prosperous future. Humanity will advance blissfully unaware of enemies from another world who have threatened its existence and been vanquished, the human race spared its destruction.

"Maybe you're right, Ms. Sloan," Sean concedes.

He glances at the Rosensteins' graves, and then at his wife, who stands by their car looking over at him. He smiles and she returns the gesture. He turns back towards Sloan.

"Maybe it is time to move on," Sean says without reservation.

"Starting now," Sloan says, as she offers her hand.

Sean shakes her hand, "Thank you, Ms. Sloan."

"Good luck, Professor," she replies.

"Tell me," Sean wonders, "you're almost fifty years old and you don't look a day over thirty . . what's your secret?"

She smiles slyly and responds, "It's all attitude, Sean. You're as old as you feel."

With that, she turns and walks away, leaving Sean to marvel at the remarkable and extraordinary woman that is Ms. Sloan.

Sean walks towards his car when a feeling of relief suddenly washes over him. He finally receives a sense of closure to the matter and it feels . . *liberating*. He and his family can move on and allow this nightmare to slowly fade in their memories with each passing day, leaving it to melt into the past.

Still, he is glad he bought that land in the Arctic Circle. Just in case, of course.

*   *   *

The government employee responsible for monitoring this area of space was advised in no uncertain terms that there should never be any communication originating from one particular area within his purview. In a grave and foreboding tone, his superiors impressed upon him that if he is to ever hear any transmissions from this area, he must alert them immediately and without hesitation.

Well, he hears something. Though it sounds like gibberish to him, there is no doubt it is some type of communication. He reaches for the phone, but at the time he cannot possibly realize the magnitude of what this means or what is to come.

*   *   *

In the dark recesses of the cave, the device emits a soft beep, confirming the message has been transmitted. It has been sent and soon will be received by hundreds of thousands. They will quickly begin to gather, and then they will consolidate. Not long after they will march across the globe, their one enemy clear and without doubt: mankind.

Humanity will not continue to progress into a bright and prosperous future. Soon humanity will confront an enemy most of them never knew existed, but who they will quickly learn is far superior. The timeline for the human race has just become threatened, the future uncertain. It will be the greatest challenge humanity has ever faced.

The device is held up in the darkness of the surrounding cave and the glow illuminates the figure's face. Sloan smirks ominously and whispers to herself, "It has begun."